Re-discover a gentler kind of humour

Praise for the early works of Victor Canning:

'Quite delightful ... with an atmosphere of quiet contentment and humour that **cannot fail to charm**.'
Daily Telegraph

'There is **such a gentle humour** in the book.'
Daily Sketch

'What counts for most in the story ...
is his **mounting pleasure in vagabondage
and the English scene**.'
The Times

'A paean to the beauties of the English countryside
and **the lovable oddities of the English character**.'
New York Times

'His delight at the beauties of the countryside
and **his mild astonishment at the strange
ways of men are infectious**.'
Daily Telegraph

'A swift-moving novel, **joyous, happy
and incurably optimistic**.'
Evening Standard

'His gift of story-telling is obviously innate. **Rarely
does one come on so satisfying** an amalgam of
plot, characterisation and good writing.'
Punch

FLY AWAY PAUL

Victor Canning

This edition published in 2019 by Farrago,
an imprint of Prelude Books Ltd
13 Carrington Road, Richmond, TW10 5AA, United Kingdom

www.farragobooks.com

By arrangement with the Beneficiaries of the
Literary Estate of Victor Canning

First published by Hodder and Stoughton in 1936

Ebook ISBN: 978-1-78842-173-7
Print ISBN: 978-1-78842-177-5

With grateful acknowledgment to John Higgins

Have you read them all?

Treat yourself again to the first Victor Canning novels –

Mr Finchley Discovers His England
A middle-aged solicitor's clerk takes a holiday for the first time and meets unexpected adventure.

Polycarp's Progress
Just turned 21, an office worker spreads his wings – an exuberant, life-affirming novel of taking your chances.

Fly Away Paul
How far could you go living in another's shoes? – an action-packed comic caper and love story.

Turn to the end of this book for a full list of Victor Canning's humorous works, plus – on the last page – the chance to receive **further background material.**

To my wife

Contents

Two little dicky birds sat upon a wall
One called Peter, the other called Paul.
Fly away Peter, fly away Paul!
Come back Peter, come back Paul!

I
Good-bye to New York

When Paul Linney Morison left New York on the S.S. *Pandaric* for England his natural optimism lent him a certain indifference to the circumstances surrounding his sailing. By the time the ship was two days out, he had surrendered most of his indifference and was relying, almost desperately, for consolation on what was left of his optimism.

It is not easy for any man to be indifferent or optimistic when he is put into the bowels of a liner to take the place of a sick kitchen-hand and is faced with the prospect of a substantial term of imprisonment on reaching Southampton for stowing away.

Paul was not afraid; he was apprehensive, which is a more uncomfortable emotion than fear.

He leaned over the rail of the lower deck, where he was allowed to go for exercise, and watched the slight phosphorescence rippling away from the bottom of the black cliff side that stretched in a gentle, almost imperceptible curve to the liner's bows. It was a clear night, with Orion's sword swinging in the darkness. A cold, freshening wind, sweeping along the decks, brought to Paul the faint suggestion of land, land not more than two days away.

He lit a cigarette, tried to follow the dying red tip of the match as it fell into the creamy wave-streaked ripple, and then wondered how he could have been such a fool as to have involved himself in this tangle for the sake of what appeared to be, now he looked at it sanely and dispassionately, no more than a ridiculous foible. He blew a cloud of smoke and, while his ears fed part of his mind with the tune of a waltz coming from the ship's band in a distant ballroom, he tried to review and collect his reasons for stowing away, hoping that the analysis might discover him some justifying motive, but scarcely believing that it possibly could.

Paul Linney Morison was an American, born in New York in the year 1906 of an American father and an English mother. Although Paul had only been fifteen when his mother died, he had never been able to rid himself of the impression that his mother regarded her marriage to an American railroad engineer as a mistake of enthusiastic youth. It was no folly for an English girl to fall in love with a young American engineer on vacation in England, but to accept his proposal of marriage was a very different matter. Paul's mother had thought marriage to be no more than the extension into the future of the happiness surrounding love. It was only after her marriage, when wearied by a long succession of small town hotels and engineering camps, where her husband moved from one State to another supervising railroad cuttings, bridge construction and the dynamiting of mountain-sides, that she wondered if she had not made a mistake in leaving her mother country.

What she finally decided no one ever knew. Only Paul, as he grew up, half guessed what went on in her mind as she told him tales of her English home and relations. She had come from Wisbech, a small river port near the Wash, and as her nostalgia grew so her stories and descriptions of the town and surrounding country took shape and life, were painted in bold lines and rich hues by her willing imagination, and started little Paul's heart and mind rioting in a colourful haze that inspired the young boy into ineffectual revolt at the grey sidewalks of New York and the draughty weather-boarding of country hotels. As Paul grew up, England to him meant Wisbech and, although he had inherited most of his father's common sense, he had acquired from his mother a restlessness which occasionally filled him with a daring that paid no heed to the warnings of his intelligence.

Not long after the death of his mother, Paul went to an engineering college and his father—a large, morose man, whose idea of perfection was a railroad terminus with a façade like Notre Dame—saw little of him for four years. When they did meet after this period they discovered that they had drifted so far apart that they might have been strangers, and because they represented the extremes of the same type, they found it difficult to achieve any confidences. They were both uncommunicative, Paul because he possessed a natural shyness which a college life had strengthened rather than sapped; the father because his reticence came from years of isolation with men who were more used to deeds than dialectics. They both had an almost old-fashioned respect and courtesy for women. In Paul this courtesy and chivalry had been part of his shyness and had prevented him from making many contacts with women. In nothing else was he old-fashioned, unless it were in his keenness for study and his application to his job. At times they were both capable of great determination and greater obstinacy, Paul when he felt that it was for his own good and his father when he thought it was for the good of the people.

When they were together they made one another feel uncomfortable and, although they never could have said so, they knew that the only things which they really shared were the memory of a dead woman and a love of engineering. Paul's father, when the time came, obtained for him a position with an engineering firm on the eastern seaboard and then, with the width of the continent between them, their letters grew almost filial and paternal.

Paul worked steadily at his profession and, as he was a good engineer, promotion came to him until he saw his past and his future as an engineer spread before him like a graph, jagged with the inevitable steps of advancement; a future that was as clear as a genealogical table. Only once in this period did the errant restlessness acquired from his mother trouble him. He suddenly wanted to become an air mail pilot. Why, he never knew; but the desire was there and with obstinate patience he invested part of his savings with a firm which guaranteed the excellency of its tuition and the certainty of a job as a pilot. He learned to fly in his spare hours, but by the time he had listened to the various excuses of the firm to explain its failure to fulfil the second part of the contract, he had lost all desire to be a pilot.

Shortly after this he obtained a good post in New York. For two years he immersed himself in his work and, at the end of that time, was rewarded by the offer of an important position on a vast irrigation scheme to be carried out in Mexico by his firm. He accepted and his firm had magnanimously advised him to take a few weeks vacation before he started for three years in Mexico.

It was on the day before his vacation that Paul realised just how hard he had worked during the past two years. The reaction was very sudden and powerful. He sat in a restaurant with a few friends celebrating his good fortune and it was then, with the blaze of jazz music in his ears, his forehead hot with the atmosphere of the crowded room and his mind confused by the chink of cutlery and the wine he had taken, that he remembered an article he had read in an English magazine on the reclamation of the Wash from the sea. With a vividness that ten years had in no way dulled, there came back to him his mother's stories of Wisbech and the England which she had left only to mourn in secret. He let his fancy riot with the idea of Wisbech; he saw it as his spiritual home and, although he called himself a loyal American, he drew an immense satisfaction from the feeling that he was connected with that little town on the lip of the Wash, that he had part of his origin in England.

Under the growing and unaccustomed influence of wine he began to tell his friends about Wisbech. They chaffed him, but he persisted and disregarded their laughter. England, he said with a loquacity from which he would have shrunk normally, was the land of romance, of colour and adventure. There was antiquity and tradition, beauty and history, and he wanted to see it, especially Wisbech, before he went to Mexico. If he could see England first, then he could face the aridness of deserts with higher courage.

When a friend suggested that he should book a passage and go over on his vacation, Paul was swept away by the longing which he had always cherished for Wisbech. He would go. And then, another friend, marking his advancing state of exhilaration, scorned the prosaic idea of booking a passage. If England meant to him all he had said, and he had the blood of English seafarers and adventurers in his veins, why didn't he act accordingly and stow away?

In a gale of laughter they dared him and, when Paul hesitated, someone called him a coward and offered to bet him a hundred dollars that he wouldn't stow away. Paul, flushed with his own success and the noise of the celebration, accepted the challenge. He was no coward. For the second time in his life he gave way without thought to the impulsiveness that he had inherited from his mother. With noisy enthusiasm the terms of the bet were settled. He was to win one hundred dollars if he got to England without paying his passage money or subsequently serving a term in jail. He was to take only enough money with him to cable for cash when he was safely ashore. Had Paul stopped to think, he might have realised that he was accepting a joust with the impossible. But he was in no mood for thinking.

The next morning, although he was partly regretting his boast, he forced himself to carry out his word. The affair became serious. To draw back would make him the laughing stock of his friends—though most of them fully expected him to give up the bet.

He had committed himself and there was no turning back. He was not the kind to play false to his word, though it had been given under the aegis of wine, for he did not care to admit, even to himself, that at any time he had other than perfect control over his actions and thoughts.

The matter was arranged and he found himself on board the S.S. *Pandaric* with a steamship clerk, ostensibly on business, and left there to wander around in his light grey flannel suit and soft hat, dodging officers and deck hands, and longing for a square meal until the ship was too far out to have him sent back to New York. He played the passenger for fifteen hours and then was discovered. As he was taken to the captain he recalled a parting remark of one of his friends:

"Within twenty-four hours they'll have you and you'll be glad to cable for money to have your name put on the passengers' list."

Some perverse streak in his character prompted him to thwart what might have been a correct prophecy. The captain was not unduly annoyed. He had found during his career that stowaways were usually more interesting company than passengers. He explained the consequences to Paul, gave him an opportunity to recount his life story and cable for his passage money if he wished, and on his refusal to do either, sent him to help in the kitchens, imposing certain restrictions on his movements, and expressed the hope that Paul now realised just what sort of a damned young fool he was.

Paul did realise and he was glad that he had retained sufficient presence of mind not to give the captain his correct name. He had been apprehended, but he still clung to the possibility that he might evade any sentence and so win his bet.

As he leaned over the rail and watched the night filling the sky with stars and muffling the angles and deck vistas of the ship with soft shadows, he knew himself for a fool, and he knew also that he must see the affair through.

His insistence upon thoroughness, which had made him successful in engineering, forced him to face his position bravely. It was with more surprise than regret that he viewed his relapse from common sense and foresight. Here he was, twenty-six years old, an age when most young men were settling down to the respectability of married life, no more than a stowaway under the name of John Denver, with the prospect of a term of imprisonment before him, an important post which must not be jeopardised in America, and his only glimpse of England to be, not Wisbech, but the inside of a jail before he was shipped back to America, unless he agreed to pay his passage money and lose his bet. Although there was this solution to his difficulties, he found it gave him very little consolation and he decided that he would have to be hard pressed before he accepted it.

He lit himself another cigarette and wished that he had inherited even more of his father's shrewd good sense and less of his mother's romantic impetuousness. Perhaps, he mused, he ought to make a complete confession to the captain and end the farce immediately.

As he cupped his match and the light caught at the side of his face, a man passed and Paul noticed that his steps faltered perceptibly as the gleam of light rose and then died. A few seconds later, he heard the man's footsteps halt. Paul knew instinctively that he was probably going to return and address him. The man came back and coughed gently behind him.

Paul partly turned from the rail and nodded affably. In the bloom he could see a white shirt front shining between the half buttoned front of a thick travelling coat.

"Excuse me," the man spoke to him. "Would you let me have a match? I've left mine in the cabin."

"Certainly." Paul handed him his box and watched while he filled a pipe. He looked like the valet or secretary, so Paul thought, of one of the first-class passengers. The man cowled the bowl of his pipe with his hands and sucked at the stem. The light from his hands was reflected into Paul's face. He struck three matches before the pipe was well alight, and Paul had the odd impression that the man was watching him closely all the time. When he struck the third match he saw that the flame scarcely touched the pipe and that the man's eyes were watching his face and not the flame.

"Thank you."

The man handed him the box and walked slowly down the deck as Paul nodded. He disappeared into the dark shadow behind a ventilator and Paul forgot him as his mind went back to his own perturbing position. The distant band broke into a swinging foxtrot. Paul left the rail and with an effort set his face into a smile. As he undressed he was whistling the dance tune and had made up his mind that worrying would not help him. That night he slept as healthily and soundly as any man or woman on board.

The next day, as usual, his duties in the kitchen kept him so busy that he had little opportunity to muse over his predicament or come to any decision and, when the other hands at meal-times tried to draw him into conversation, he answered them politely but without detail as he had persisted in doing since he had turned scullion. While he was working, a party of passengers, under the guidance of one of the ship's officers, came into the kitchens on a sightseeing tour of the ship and—though Paul had forgotten him until then—he noticed among them the man who had asked him for a light on the previous evening. From a covert pride and dislike of having his condition publicised, Paul kept his head turned from the party. The news of the stowaway had travelled round and he felt that attention was upon him, and once he caught the man staring at him with an earnestness which he could only ascribe to an interest in his sudden notoriety.

That evening, with only another day to go before the S.S. *Pandaric* berthed at Southampton, Paul went on to the lower deck for his evening respite after the heat of the kitchens. The day was dying slowly into the soft dusk of a June evening and the sky in the west was filled with a wreath of twisted, smoky-hued clouds that muffled the vermilion splendour of the sun. The ship was hastening from the beauty of the west into the encroaching darkness before it. Five yards from the rail a black-headed gull kept pace with the ship and, as it swooped occasionally to the water, uttered a plaintive cry that served as an appropriate comment to Paul's mood.

He was so occupied with his thoughts, watching the delicate wing movements of the gull as it rose, breasting the wind and rolling with slight body movements as it feathered the air through its firm pinions, that it was a few moments before he was aware of someone standing by his side.

"Excuse me," a voice said. He turned and found himself facing the man who had asked him for a match.

"Hallo! Want another match?" Paul smiled and eyed the man. He was dressed in a dinner jacket.

"No—not this time," he replied, catching at the rail with his knuckly hands and swaying his lean body backwards. "Am I right in assuming that you are the young man who stowed away?"

"That's me—but I don't care to be reminded of it now."

"I understand your feelings. Still, you might have done a lot worse ... Mr ... Mr ...?"

"John Denver's the name." Paul's tone was not encouraging.

The man half turned with a sudden determination. "Excuse my curiosity and abrupt manner, Mr. Denver, But I think that there is more than a possibility that I may be able to help you—"

"Help me? What do you mean?" Paul immediately became suspicious. He was not sure that he liked this man who had the body and appearance of one well past his prime and yet showed in his movements and the timbre of his voice an energy and alacrity more usual in a younger man.

"Well, not me, perhaps. But my boss might be able to help you."

"Your boss?"

"Yes. I'm the secretary of Mr. Peter Angel. You've heard of him, of course?"

Paul smiled in spite of himself. "I've heard of and heard him. You say, you're his secretary?"

"Yes, my name's Simpkins. You don't seem very convinced?"

"Convinced—I don't mean to be rude, but, if you don't mind my saying so, I reckon there's about as much chance of Mussolini coming to my help at the moment as there is of Peter Angel." Paul shrugged his shoulders and dismissed the fantasy.

The man laughed at Paul's incredulity and took him by the arm. "Come with me and you'll soon admit that I'm not telling you any fairy story."

"Come where?"

"To Mr. Angel's state-room, of course," Simpkins paused.

"But I'm not allowed in that part of the ship. This is my place until they land me safely in jail unless I decide to pay the passage money."

The secretary shook his head vigorously and his dark eyes caught the reflection of the stars. "That'll be all right! Mr. Angel will put things straight with the captain if anything is said. I give you my word."

Without waiting for Paul to reply he led him along the deck towards that sacrosanct quarter reserved for the first-class passengers. Paul followed him, wondering, and consoling himself with the thought that, if nothing else happened and the man were telling the truth, he might at least have a glimpse of a man whose name was a household word in every American home.

II
Paul meets a crooner

Peter Angel threw away his half-smoked cigarette, carelessly poured himself a glass of whisky and then, sinking back into the uncomfortable embrace of a small armchair which did its best to accommodate his long body, forgot to drink his liquor. He stared meditatively at the electric light and rubbed a forefinger over his lower lip reflectively.

There was nothing unusual in any of these gestures or movements, nothing about his pose or thought-wrinkled face which was not common to thousands of other men at that moment. Every day men and women are throwing away half-smoked cigarettes, forgetting to take their liquor, and staring reflectively at the electric light in their rooms, offices or cabins. But while the majority of men and women may act thus in private and be sure that the world has not the slightest interest in their actions, there are some few whose nervous movements at such moments would interest millions and for the content of whose thoughts these millions are willing to pay. To have such an overwhelming curiosity evinced in one's private life a man or woman must become famous either as a film star, an international politician, or as a criminal of prolific or original homicidal tendencies. And Peter Angel was a man who combined most of the spectacular habits and a great share of the talents common to these three classes, and—so some said—richly deserved the fate which ultimately claims the homicide.

Peter Angel was a crooner. What he had been three years before this moment in the state-room of the S.S. *Pandaric* few people apart from himself knew, and he was reluctant to discuss it. He had appeared from a blue fog of nonentities and, within a very short while, had climbed the mount of public approbation until now radio companies fought to secure his services, love-stricken girls found solace from the rigours of unrequited passion as they listened to his mellifluous voice announcing the sonorous sentiments of his famous song, *I'm the Man in your Romance*, and young men with nicotine-stained fingers languished to the lilt of his amatory caution of *Don't Play Around with Fire*. Peter Angel was a crooner. He was a force in America. His voice could make wives forget their husbands and the dinner in the cooker, his songs purring from radios cheered naval ratings in the Pacific, accompanied poker games on transcontinental trains, and filled the occupants of the cheap seats at cinemas with a yearning that found its expression in ecstatic phrases. And, where no radios existed, his soft cadences worked their way on gramophone discs to Eskimos north of the Great Bear Lake, to Patagonians shivering in the last whip of a Cape Horn hurricane, to lonely African farmsteads and, somewhat cracked and roughened, to plantation outposts where his muted syllables competed nightly with the nittering of mosquitoes.

Now he was on his way to complete his vocal conquests and force Europe to march with Milwaukee in his triumphal procession. And his actions in his state-room would have thrilled millions and given reporters enough speculative material to fill columns. If the reporters could have had a glimpse at the telegrams that littered the small table by his side they would have had evidence for any story they might wish to concoct, since the messages were all incoherent or esoteric enough to justify any interpretation. The sanest message simply said—*It looks as though the baby will soon begin to cry*. That alone, as Peter Angel was understood to be single, was sufficient for a definite announcement of secret marriage, engagement, bigamy charge, or handsome donation to an orphanage.

But Peter would not have minded even if the telegrams had been made public. He had very quickly accustomed himself to accept publicity as a profitable evil, and his countless admirers and fans were regarded by him with good-humoured toleration. It was easy for him to be tolerant because he was so different from them. He was clever, whereas he was sure they were mostly admiring morons; and he was wealthy, whereas most of them were two payments behind with their hire-purchase instalments.

He stopped staring at the electric light, collected the telegrams and pushed them into a drawer. Then he drank his liquor and was placing the glass on the table when there came a knock on the door and Simpkins, his secretary, entered, ushering in Paul.

None of the men spoke for a moment. Peter looked across the room at Paul, his eye taking in every detail of his appearance and carriage. Then he shifted his gaze to Simpkins who was softly closing the door. Peter nodded with the glimmer of a pleasant smile playing round his mouth.

Simpkins came forward between the two.

"This is the gentleman." He turned to Paul. "Mr. John Denver—meet Peter Angel, *the* Peter Angel!"

"Pleased to know you," said Paul.

"And I am pleased to meet you, Mr. Denver, very pleased indeed. In fact, you cannot appreciate just how pleased I am," said Peter.

Paul was getting a little impatient of the mystery and his cautious nature was being irked by the atmosphere of tension that Simpkins had managed to weave around the situation.

"What do you want me for? What's the game—or is it a joke?"

Simpkins laughed and Peter smiled.

"No joke, Mr. Denver, I assure you. I want to help you—and I fancy you will be glad to help me in return. You know who I am, and all about me?"

"Sure, but—"

Peter stopped him by taking his arm and, as he moved across the carpet, he addressed Paul familiarly.

"Now, Mr. Denver, don't think me rude if I ask you a few questions. Believe me—" he went on hastily, "—I ask them from no sense of idle curiosity but because I fancy we are going to be of material advantage to one another."

Paul waited. He had learned from the press and other sources of the Angel charm and personality, and now he was experiencing it himself. There was something about this man, who seemed to be of his own age, which attracted and amused him. He forgot for a moment that he was a stowaway. He decided that it would be foolish not to hear what he might say.

"Fire ahead and I'll try and give you the whole truth."

"Good! Now—why did you stow away?"

Paul hesitated. He decided not to tell the man about the bet. If nothing came of the interview, the story might get back to the captain. There might, however, be a possibility that the crooner would really help him.

"I reckon I must have been slightly crazy for a while and I did it without thinking much," he said.

"Then why did you pick a boat going to England? Why not, say, have gone to South America—craziness wouldn't be quite so much out of place there as it would be in England?"

Paul took a cigarette from the case which Peter held out and answered: "As a matter of fact, I wanted to get to England particularly—"

"Particularly?"

"Yes ... I suppose it sounds rather sentimental. You see, I'm really half English. My mother was an Englishwoman. She's dead now; but she used to tell me stories of England and of her home town—place called Wisbech in East Anglia—and I decided that I'd stow away and try to get to Wisbech. I've one or two relations there who might be glad to see me."

Peter screwed his eyes and chuckled, and Simpkins shook his head, saying, "Sounds like Don Juan ... or Quixote to me."

Paul laughed. "No matter which you decide it is, I don't suppose I shall get there now."

"Don't say that—" put in Peter quickly. "You are going to see Wisbech, and you're not going to jail. Not if Peter Angel can manage it."

"But I don't understand you?".

"Listen, Mr. Denver. I'm going to make a proposition to you. You want to go to Wisbech, but at the moment you're heading for a possible mix-up with the police and jail. Very well. Now I'm going to England to open a big show at the Regina Theatre in a week's time—at least the rehearsals begin in a week's time."

"Well?"

"Not at all well for me. The moment I set foot on shore at Southampton I shall be deluged by fans and publicised up and down the country and unable to move without a cohort of cameras and pressmen about me. That's one of the disadvantages of being famous. I've been living in that kind of atmosphere for three years and it's getting me down. Simpkins will substantiate that—"

"That's right, Mr. Denver. It's playing hell with him."

"I still don't see where I come in."

"Right here. For the week before the rehearsals begin I want to have a quiet time looking round England. You know, without anyone knowing who I am, then I can go back to the theatre a new man. But I can't do that unless you help me."

"I'd like to help you very much, Mr. Angel," Paul declared politely, "but I don't quite see how I can?"

"You've gone too fast for him, boss. Sing it!"

Peter disregarded this irrelevant remark and led Paul to the mirror, a tall strip of glass let into the front of a wardrobe door.

"There!" he said with a flourish." Now do you see how we can help one another!" He went on enthusiastically. "Don't you see what stupendous luck this is for us! We're homomorphous!"

"We're what?" Paul looked at him.

"Sing it," echoed Simpkins, rubbing his thin hands together.

Peter made an expression of impatience and pointed into the mirror. "An apple cleft in two," he said, as Paul stared at their reflections in the mirror for the first time with any degree of comprehension; "is not more twin than these two creatures."

Simpkins, catching some of his master's excitement, came up. "And you both talk in almost the same way, sorta English. Can't you see—" He pointed. "See, Mr. Denver, you might be twin brothers!"

And it was so. Paul looked into the mirror, saw first his own tall, broad-shouldered body and a face fashioned in bold masses yet retaining in the straight nose and lips a hint of delicacy and waywardness which offset the ruggedness of his chin and the firmness of his forehead, and then he looked at the reflection of Peter Angel and he might have been looking at a wax replica of himself; an image, more expensively dressed, with its black hair suborned into regular waves with tongs. There was, as they stared into the mirror, something fantastic and uncanny in the almost perfect resemblance between them, as though nature had mixed her supply of moulds and used the same one twice.

Paul was amazed. "What a fool I was not to have realised it the moment I saw you! And I do talk something like you—that's the influence of my mother."

"I found it hard to believe myself when Simpkins told me and suggested this scheme. But it is true. Nature has forged an almost perfect counterpart."

"No one could tell the difference. At least, not when I've waved your hair and set you up in a swell suit," said Simpkins.

The remark brought Paul back to earth." I don't know about that."

"What don't you know?" Peter shot forward eagerly and there was a hint of anxiety in his dark brown eyes.

"It's so simple. You take my place tomorrow morning just before we land and I'll disappear—"

"Disappear? Where? And how will you get off the ship?"

He laughed lightly. "Don't bother about that. Money can still work miracles. What happens? I slide away unseen and have my week of joy, you go ashore and take all the publicity with Simpkins to help you and the stowaway is written off as having jumped overboard. When the week is up I come quietly back, and make you a present of, say, a hundred pounds and then you go off to this mudhole, Wisbech"

"That town isn't any mudhole! It's one of the finest—"

"I'm sorry, Mr. Denver. just a loose expression for which I ask your pardon. What do you say to that arrangement?"

Paul turned the idea over in his mind. With grave deliberation he considered all its aspects. If a man of Peter Angel's prominence was willing to take the risk of the subterfuge there would be little doubt that he thought it would be successful, and if it were—then he was released from the rather lame solution to his difficulties which he had almost come to accept as inevitable. He need not make a confession to the captain. He would have a chance after all of seeing Wisbech and he would also win his bet and turn the laugh on to his friends. It was the ideal solution. The more he thought of it, the more providential for him it seemed. With an effort he controlled his eagerness and forced himself to consider the suggestion carefully.

"What about people in England that know you—I can't bluff them. I may talk and look like you, but I can't sing for nuts."

Peter Angel poured himself a drink." You don't have to worry about any of those things. I don't know anyone in England—this is my first official visit. And you won't be required to sing—it's part of my contract that I don't make any public performance until the show opens, and you can always refuse at a private party if you get asked. Simpkins will watch over you. If you want more than a hundred …"

Paul waved aside the suggestion. With the thoroughness which was so firm a part of his real character he went over each point of the scheme, searching and probing for the weaknesses, and he found none. If Peter Angel could successfully get ashore there was nothing which could unmask the subterfuge. The two men watched him as he frowned and puffed at his cigarette, and Simpkins eyed Angel as the crooner fidgeted once or twice.

"You're taking a long time to make up your mind, Mr. Denver. Anyone else in your shoes would jump at the offer! To play the part of Peter Angel for a week and to enjoy the hospitality of London! Why, the possibilities are unlimited for a man with imagination. And if that side of the question doesn't appeal to you, see it from my angle. I've got to have peace for a while; I've got to escape from the noise and shattering publicity, otherwise I shall go mad, or even worse lose my voice! Music is one of the great benefactions the world has, and if you do this for me—and for yourself—you'll have the unspoken gratitude of millions to console you for any inconvenience it may mean. What do you say?"

"Well—" Paul bit his lip and considered this altruistic appeal to his intelligence. It sounded attractive, but he was cautious.

"What do you say? Have a drink and enrich your confidence in yourself by stimulating your mind with alcohol."

Paul took the proffered whisky. "I don't like the idea much. You see— it may sound strange to you—but I'm funny that way. Stowing away wasn't so bad. I had a reason, but this sounds more crooked. You know, deceitful. But, I guess if you say it's all right ..."

"Of course, it is—isn't it, Simpkins?" Peter turned to his secretary.

"Sure it's all right."

Against their combined assurances Paul capitulated.

"I'll do it then. And," Paul raised his glass, "here's hoping you have a restful time during your week of freedom!" After he had given his word he felt more at ease. Peter and Simpkins filled their glasses and drank.

"And let's hope you find playing the part of Peter Angel more enjoyable than I do. I should think a week is about the right length to extract all that is best without encountering a great deal of what is not so pleasant. Here's to Mr. John Denver, stowaway, alias Mr. Peter Angel, crooner!"

It was arranged that Paul should slip up to the state-room when the ship was a few hours from Southampton so that Simpkins, who also acted as valet, could wave his hair and dress him for the part of Peter Angel. As Paul had not been put on strict parole or confined to his cabin by the captain it would be easy for him to do this.

It was two hours later that he left the state-room, glad to get into the fresh air and leaving behind him a confusion of tobacco smoke and empty glasses. Through the half-open doorway he could hear Angel's pleasant voice mouthing dolorously

With wanton heed and giddy cunning
The melting voice through mazes running,
Untwisting all the chains that tie
The hidden soul of harmony.

For a crooner, whose prophet should have been Irving Berlin, Peter Angel broke all rules by adhering to Shakespeare when he was sober and transferring his affections to Milton's *L'Allegro* when the liquor began to make music in his mind.

As Paul walked back to his cabin, through the almost deserted decks where dark port-holes stared like blind eyes from the dull white of wood and metal, he began to recapture some of the enthusiasm which had started him on his venture to Wisbech. Now the possibility of seeing his mother's birthplace was with him again, and he thought, with a love that distance and imagination strengthened, of the quiet river that wandered through miles of rich fen country before it debouched into the Wash, of the narrow streets his mother had described, the stately Georgian houses with doorways that were the apotheosis of proportion, of leagues of orchards, white with apple and pear blossom, of fields of yellow and scarlet tulips bending unwillingly before the gentle breeze from the sea ... of men who dropped lines from the town bridge for eels ... of the quiet churchyard with its finely worked eighteenth-century grave-stones ... When he slept his head was the centre of a whirling dream wherein were mixed voluble shadows that merged to laughing Angels, rows of blossomed trees, rivers, dark-pantiled houses, cobbled streets, horses and traps, and the oval, dark-haired memory of his mother's face drifting like a tender moon above the confusion of his dreams.

The S.S. *Pandaric* moved gently through a calm sea, throbbing with its own mechanical life. On the port the Scilly Isles dropped into the star-studded bowl of sea and sky, the timid flicker of the Eddystone light beckoned regularly for a while until the dawn began to haze the darkness in the east ... and Paul slept on, dreaming of Wisbech, his mecca.

III

So this is England

The S.S. *Pandaric* berthed at Southampton at ten o'clock in the morning of the next day, which was a Thursday. Paul had, with some difficulty, managed to slip away from his duties, and in Peter Angel's cabin he submitted himself to the expert hands of Simpkins. With the aid of shampoo and hair tongs, Simpkins soon had Paul's hair dressed and waved into a convincing imitation of Peter Angel's.

"How's that?" he said, when he had finished. Paul stood up and surveyed himself in the glass, and Peter Angel came and inspected him.

"Fine, Simpkins! I can see that the whole business is going to go without a hitch."

"I hope so, anyway," said Paul, and then, at Simpkins's request, he entered Peter Angel's bedroom and began to dress himself in one of the crooner's lounge suits.

When he returned to the state-room Peter Angel was waiting for him, but a different Peter Angel. He had altered his face with makeup, adopted a short tarbrush moustache, and was wearing a comfortable old tweed suit.

"Well," he greeted Paul with a smile, "here we both are. There you are, Peter Angel for a few days; and here am I—going off to have the happiest vacation of my life. You are going to step right off this boat into the limelight and publicity of a famous character, and I, with the help of a seaman, am going to slip away into the unknown to rest and rusticate. I think we'll drink to it."

They did drink, but while Paul toasted the crooner, he could not entirely disencumber his mind from a strong element of apprehension.

Peter Angel might talk lightly and confidently of the scheme for changing places, but it was far from being void of danger. There were moments when he wished that he could be safely back in New York. Simpkins appeared to be the least impressed or excited of the three. Against Paul's almost taciturn acceptance of the inevitable and Peter Angel's enthusiastic, high-spirited delight at the prospect of anonymous freedom, the orthodox demeanour and steady imperturbability of the secretary were comforting, reassuring elements. Paul felt that if any difficulty arose, he would be able to rely on Simpkins; the gnome-like secretary seemed to exude an atmosphere of efficiency and discretion.

Paul did not know what Peter Angel's arrangements were, but when the disguised crooner stepped, whistling one of his own songs, from the state-room, he completed the first stage in Paul's metamorphosis, and the tall, dark, wavy-haired young man who was left behind became Peter Angel, crooner, idol of millions, a glorious, dolorous, animated voice with a wonderful power to evoke sentimentality and assuage or inflame erotic emotions. Simpkins immediately began to address Paul as "boss" and "Mr. Angel" to show that, with him, Peter Angel was an abstraction to be served, and that it mattered not what cipher carried the sartorial trappings of that familiar personality.

If the stowaway, John Denver, was missed before the S.S. *Pandaric* berthed, Paul did not at the time know, for he kept within his state-room until the last moment in order not to run any risk. His first glimpse of England, then, was not the long line of green-topped cliffs and grey beach which he had expected, but the grey roofs of custom sheds, and a stippling of faces that congregated around the bottom of the gangway leading down to the quayside.

"I've got a car waiting," said Simpkins, "but if the camera men pester you, just smile and nod and let 'em take their pictures. And maybe it wouldn't be a bad idea to say a few words to the Movietone fellows. They expect it, and regard it as a right which they can exercise upon the great."

"Very well," agreed Paul with some apprehension, and with a smile on his face he left the S.S. *Pandaric* to face England as Peter Angel, and there waiting for him were the envoys of the public; pressmen, cameramen, special reporters and newsreel men. They waited for him, ready to pounce and probe and to flatter and photograph, so that the millions who expected sensation and news at their breakfast table each morning might not be disappointed.

The first man to speak to Paul was a reporter from the *Daily Globe*, a short, fat individual, in a bowler hat and raincoat, whose breath was odorous with the whisky which he had taken to while away the time before the S.S. *Pandaric* berthed.

"Glad to greet you, Mr. Angel," he said. "Welcome to England!"

Paul nodded. "Thank you. That surely is very kind of you."

As he spoke, the crowd moved closer to him and he was pressed hard against Simpkins. The fat reporter seemed to have made himself chief spokesman.

"Have you got any message to the people of this country, Mr. Angel? You know the sort of thing …"

"Any message?" Paul frowned and hesitated, wondering whether he had been mistaken for an evangelist, but Simpkins was at his side. He whispered, "Go on, tell 'em something. Looking forward to a good time, anything like that."

"What shall we tell the public, Mr. Angel?" asked the reporter.

"Perhaps Mr. Angel would like to sing it!" came a voice from the back of the press. There was a laugh, during which Paul pulled himself together.

"No, I won't sing it," he said." You see my contract bars me from street-singing. But I can tell you that I've been looking forward to this visit for a long time. It means a lot to me and, although I'm over here to work, I also mean to have a good look at this wonderful country of yours."

"Good work," Simpkins breathed into his ear.

"Did you have a good crossing, Mr. Angel?"

"Yes, though once or twice I wasn't so comfortable as I should like to have been."

"And are you prepared to consider our policemen wonderful, Mr. Angel?" came the same voice from the rear of the crowd.

Paul laughed and, with a glance at Simpkins, said," I'll answer that question when I've made their acquaintance."

Simpkins pushed forward and waved an arm. "That's enough, fellows. Mr. Angel's given you a break. Come and see us in London, and maybe we'll do something else for you."

But the crowd would not let them go until Paul had spoken a few words into the microphone for the newsreel men and, even then, they were followed to the car which waited for them in the sheds.

"I'm beginning to understand why Peter Angel was tired of this life," said Paul, as he sat back in the car with Simpkins.

"You're only just touching the edge of it? You wait!"

And Paul was only just beginning to realise, for outside the docks was an even larger crowd, composed mostly of girls and women who had heard that Peter Angel was landing. It took Paul some seconds to appreciate that the crowd was a friendly one. Women pressed around, shouting and screaming, a few optimistically waving autograph books. They jumped on to the running board, clung to the door handles, thumped on the windscreen and windows, tried to climb in with the chauffeur, disregarded the few policemen who attempted to control them and, those who were not near enough to the car to attract his attention by shouting or thumping, blew kisses to him over the agitated heads of the others and sang the chorus of *I'm the Man in Your Romance*. To Paul, who had cherished the tradition that the English were an unemotional, aloof nation, the incident was a revelation. Young girls, spinsters, typists, shopgirls, nursemaids, housewives, barmaids … a whole horde of femininity moved in a shouting, arm-waving flux about the car for a few minutes, laying before his fame the enthusiastic offering of their charm and loyalty; and he—at Simpkins's bidding—smiled and waved in return, until the car had extricated itself from the crush and reached the noisy security of Southampton's main thoroughfares. It was not until an hour later, when they were having their lunch in the quietness of a roadside hotel, where they were unknown, that Paul entirely recovered from the novelty and distraction of the landing.

It took him some time to accustom himself to any new set of factors and this sudden rise into prominence had upset him for a while, but now his mind and body were gradually adjusting themselves to a new life. Ever since Peter Angel had suggested the change, Paul had been worried by its unpleasant possibilities, and this anxiety had been spoiling for him what enjoyment there might be in his new position. He had been timorous, apprehensive and reluctant. As he reflected, after a good meal, he saw that the man who had been so far playing Peter Angel was not the man compounded of the solidness and substantial virtues which marked him as an engineer. If he continued to play his part in his present mood he realised that he would obtain very little pleasure from the deception. And, because he possessed quite a definite control of his will, it was not difficult for him, now that the first step of the deception was taken, to make himself accept the new life in a lightened and more joyous spirit.

He began to take an interest in himself and in Simpkins, and, for the first time since landing, acutely appreciated that he was actually in England, England where he had always longed to be, and so far he had been too worried even to look about him.

As they drove to London, he started to repair the neglect which had characterised the first part of his journey. Paul never forgot that car ride, for it was his first glimpse of England, and although what he saw was overshadowed by his conception of the country peculiar to Wisbech, he revelled in the charm which spread out before him as the car sped on its way to London.

They passed through quiet little villages, where the early June sun struck fire from swinging inn-signs and filled open doorways with dark angles of shadow and dust-moted triangles of light. Paul eyed everything with a mild wonder; the scene was different from anything that America could ever give to him. There were cottage gardens filled with the riotous profusion of lavender and dropping roses, roses with scollop-shell petals of cream and ivory and great pink and red blooms that filled the air with richness and wrapped the gardens in sweet scent. Against a whitewashed wall, and reaching towards the sparrow- and mouse-infested labyrinth of thatch above, tall spikes of hollyhock hung tilting cups of colour to reflect the sunshine and a little girl swinging on a creaking gate waved her hand happily to the car as it passed.

Afterwards, when Paul tried to marshal his impressions of that drive, he found the task hopeless. His mind revealed to him only a lovely chaos of glimpses and bright moments. There were village ponds with noisy armadas of ducks rooting at the weeds, and lapping the muddy water through their yellow mandibles until it dripped from them in silver dribbles. Under a thick-shadowed chestnut tree, three old men sat on a circular seat and slept, while the bees hummed in the tall candle flowers above them and butterflies hovered about the foliage as though they were moths attracted by the flame of the blossom. The woodwork of the car grew hot with the drowsy heat, and Paul and Simpkins sighed at the pleasant coolness which greeted them, as they plunged into dark woods where the noise of their progress fretted against the thin vista of fir trunks. Over the crests of the firs, wood-pigeons rose in a smoky cloud of wings. And once they climbed from the twist of a little valley, where a small stone bridge crossed a stream that was dark and swift with the hint of trout, and bubbled in frothy humour over the moss-draped boulders in its bed, to the bare shoulder of a down, and Paul watched the soft-winged peewits flap, wailing and distracted, into a sky that was a thin blue with heat and worn in places to white shreds of cloud. Beyond the downs were fields of corn that waved tall stalks over dry furrows which sheltered the bright eyes of speedwell and pimpernel. Sometimes they passed through small towns; a clutter of traffic; vans, buses, private cars, a policeman at the fourways, white road signs and traffic-lights blinking, and then they were away from the grey huddle of houses and buildings into the country again.

From behind clumps of elm and across long stretches of parkland, mansion houses and halls showed themselves with Tudor stubbornness or Palladian grace and at drive gates weather-beaten griffins sneered over their shields and went on sneering after they had passed. Once they overtook a gipsy caravan, fresh with yellow and green paint, and hauled by a small brown pony with a branch of elder thrust through its halter to keep off the flies. Behind the caravan slouched a liver-coloured whippet and, as the car passed, Paul turned in time to notice a dusky face eyeing them from the curtained window, and saw a sleepy driver dozing with the reins in his hand.

Then the country began to fall away and deteriorate into straight, ugly mainroad, lined with building estates and gaudy with petrol filling-stations which skilfully advertised themselves by pretending to conceal their function. Huge placards, straddling across the roadway, invited one to become a tenant on the Happydays Estate and begin to live. *Why Pay Rent? The difference between a happy man and an unhappy man is the difference between owning and renting a house. Ten Pounds down and fifteen shillings a week for fifty years secures you a house;* and Paul, who knew something of architecture, wondered just how many of the houses on the Happydays Estate would be standing or habitable within fifty years. He saw in the twenty miles before they finally drew up at the Waldersen Hotel in the Strand an overwhelming conglomeration of styles; stucco that fathered top floors of oak beams and Welsh slate, bay-windowed horrors that sought vainly for beauty in the application of bathroom tiles along their façades, monotonous rows of council houses, and Tudor and romanesque abortions which were obviously built to a plan insisted upon by the owners; creations of such fantastic conformations that a child with a box of building bricks might have constructed them. And the names on the paint-blistered gateways of these houses ranged from the inanity of *The Cedars* to the vulgarity of *Osokosy*. Paul guessed that this efflorescence around the world's largest capital was only part of a general architectural inflammation that had affected the whole of the city's purlieus, and he was glad that he had not come to England with any romantic idealisms concerning London, for they would in that ride have suffered very greatly. This much was the same as many American cities; but he had come to see not the towns, not the industrial and suburban eyesores, but Wisbech, a quiet sleepy little port somewhere north of all this. He lay back in the car and forgot the streets through which they passed as he thought of Wisbech and his mother's stories. Some day, very soon now, he was going there to satisfy a strong desire, a desire strong enough to fill him with the impulse to leave America and finally impersonate a famous crooner. To Simpkins's surprise, he actually fell asleep and stayed asleep until the car pulled up quietly outside the Waldersen Hotel.

The news of his arrival had preceded him and a small crowd surrounded the car, cameras clicked and girls shouted and waved. He hurried into the security of the hotel and left Simpkins to concern himself with all the details of luggage.

He and Simpkins dined alone in their suite and Paul enjoyed a meal such as he had never before had in his life. He leaned back at the end contented and happy and nodded at the smiling Simpkins.

"Guess you feel as though you're walking on air?"

Paul nodded. "I've never been used to such luxury, but it certainly is one of the compensations for all the publicity Mr. Angel has to put up with. And such a life, I guess, needs some compensations."

"It does, but you don't have to worry. In fact," Simpkins passed one hand over his bald head, "you don't have to worry about anything while you're here. I'll fix up everything that is to be done. I'll see people, open all the mail, take all the phone calls, do everything … You understand that?"

"That suits me, if you want it that way."

"That's how it must be. You just play around and I'll see you aren't troubled by anyone much. You're doing very well so far. Though I shall be anxious about you for a while."

"You can depend on me. You shan't have cause to complain."

And for the rest of that day Paul did his best not to cause Simpkins anxiety. They went to a picture show, and after that to supper at a night club where the band, as a compliment, played *I'm the Man in Your Romance*, and Paul had to go on the dais to make a little speech, which, as he had taken a few glasses of wine, was not so difficult as he had imagined it might be, though it suffered somewhat from a slight incoherency; and, despite the clamour for a song from him, he refused politely but firmly and went back to his table where Simpkins, looking like a spruce Rip Van Winkle in his evening dress, smiled at him benignly as a schoolmaster does to a pupil of promise. Later, when a certain informality of conduct began to manifest itself among the diners, Simpkins piloted Paul back to the Waldersen where they found the rotund reporter from the *Daily Globe* waiting for them.

"Hope you don't mind me coming in and waiting for you," he apologised." My name's Cableton, Dick Cableton, and I've been told to keep an eye on you while you're over here by my paper. I thought I'd pop round and discover your reactions after your first night in town."

"That's very good of you, Mr. Cableton," answered Paul. "Very good, but if you want my reaction it's simply this—I feel like a long sleep and I'm going to have one."

"Very sensible, too, Mr. Angel."

"Perhaps you'd like a drink, Mr. Cableton?" asked Simpkins.

Cableton's red face glistened as he turned and nodded. Paul was too tired to bother with a drink, and he left the reporter and Simpkins to entertain one another while he went off to bed. How long the two stayed talking and drinking he did not know, for he had not been in bed many minutes before he was sleeping soundly.

IV
And this London

It was Thursday evening when Paul arrived at the Waldersen, and, by the following Sunday evening, he was thoroughly tired of London and playing the part of Peter Angel. He felt that he was no more than a well-dressed dummy in a huge shop-window, and denied even the insentient unconcern of shop dummies. Whatever he did, said, and sometimes whatever he did not do or did not say, was broadcast by means of newspaper and camera until the already familiar face of Peter Angel became one of the lasting impressions that made up the mental picture gallery of notabilities which is common to all people.

The main doorway of the Waldersen attracted a permanent cluster of eager spectators, and whenever Paul appeared he was greeted with ecstatic and amatory remarks by girls who, from their fleeting glimpse of him, gathered to themselves enough material for talk and gossip to last them for months, and who somehow imagined that their having seen him in the flesh, gave them an immeasurable superiority over those poor, unfortunate beings who knew him only from the films and newspapers or by the sound of his soft, caressing voice.

Although he was too wise to object, Paul knew that most of the publicity was deliberately planned by Simpkins and Cableton. Simpkins, because he could assess the commercial advantage of publicity to himself and his master, and Cableton because publicity was his job and also because friendship with Simpkins gave him access to the apparently unlimited supplies of whisky and drink which were always at hand in the suite and without which he appeared to be incapable of movement. Paul had composed his mind to the acceptance of a certain amount of publicity, but three days of Simpkins's intensive barrage found him seething with rebellious irritation. Simpkins never let him out of his sight. He was photographed feeding the pigeons in Trafalgar Square, looking at the tower of Big Ben, asking a policeman the way to Hyde Park, distributing copies of his famous song in a Charing Cross Road music store, smoking in a luxurious chair at his Waldersen suite, and it was only with extreme difficulty that he prevented the enthusiastic Cableton from having him photographed in his rose pink silk pyjamas. His refusal sent the reporter back to the siphon murmuring sadly "What a pity, what a pity … a picture like that would have sent the world mad."

He went to the cinema and saw the newsreel of himself landing from the S.S. *Pandaric* and heard himself speaking a few trite sentences of welcome, and he had to confess to himself that he really did look like Peter Angel. He could scarcely repress a satisfying feeling of pride as he watched himself, a tall, athletic, broad-shouldered figure dressed in a smart lounge suit, coat half open, with a soft hat of unmistakable American cut on his head, come striding down the gangway. That was one of the few moments in a three days' whirl of publicity which gave him some satisfaction. For the rest he was soon tired of the crowds around his car, sick of the eternal click of the cameras, and the insistent banter of reporters. He was tired of being stared at as though he were as stupendous as the Pyramids and as rare as the missing link; he was tired of the eager faces of girls and women, and he was filled with joy when a cabby cursed him fluently for stepping carelessly off a kerb almost under the taxi wheels. For a moment he was a human being again—and then the whole thing lost its sanity as Cableton seized on the incident and made a story from it. He was Peter Angel, a glorified voice, he had lost all essential individuality. Paul Morison had vanished entirely and the only trace of him was a small paragraph in the daily newspapers:

Two hours before the S.S. Pandaric from New York berthed at Southampton on Thursday, a stowaway, John Denver, an American who had been put to work in the kitchens, disappeared. It is thought that he jumped overboard and has been drowned or has managed to get ashore in some way. The police have been instructed to keep a watch for him.

Paul had smiled when Simpkins had pointed the paragraph out to him. No one, he thought, was ever likely to connect Paul Morison with John Denver the stowaway.

Generally, he had little time for reflection, for Simpkins had every hour of his days mapped out for him. Simpkins had been in England before and knew London well, and for three days Paul was whirled around with him and very soon forgot most of the places they visited. At the end of three days his impression of London was centred closely about the Waldersen, for to him the hotel was the one stable thing in a world of continual movement. He consoled himself for his hurried life with the thought that soon he would be free and have money in his pocket to take him to Wisbech, but until then he had to play the part of Peter Angel, and, as he was fundamentally an honest man with a very strong sense of rectitude where he had placed himself under obligations, Paul did everything that was required of him. Only his natural shyness made the continual publicity a delicate form of agony.

On Friday he gave interviews to reporters, made a sight-seeing tour of the city, signed copies of his song—a request made so unexpectedly that Paul had to perpetrate the fraud and hope that it would pass undetected—and went to a theatre show in the evening. On Saturday there was more sight-seeing and more interviews and then a call in the evening at Broadcasting House, where he went on the air in the *In Town Tonight* programme. The furtive and upholstered silences of Broadcasting House tended to overawe him, and the ensuing dialogue between himself and an announcer consisted mostly of inane questions from the announcer, such as "Are you enjoying yourself in England?" "What's the name of your new show?" "Do you get many letters from people?" and monosyllabic replies of "Yes" and "No" from Paul. As his contract barred him from singing, a gramophone record of his song was played and the millions of listeners-in were perfectly satisfied, felt themselves somehow in touch with the great, and then settled down to ten minutes of street-cleaning as a London County Council roadsweeper, who followed Paul in the programme, gave a résumé of a day from his life. Sunday saw Paul, for form's sake as Simpkins explained, attending a service at St. Paul's, then luncheon with a London theatre owner who was anxious to make his acquaintance, a drive to Henley to have tea with a society hostess who was toying with the idea of taking him up—an idea which Paul with his diffidence and inconsequential mode of conversation completely destroyed, and then an attendance at a Sunday theatre to see the presentation of a new Russian play—this, as Simpkins explained, to put themselves right with the highbrows.

When he dropped into bed on Sunday evening Paul was tired and nauseated and ready to revolt. The next morning when Simpkins showed him the programme for the day he did revolt, swiftly and effectively. With a cunning that had its origin in desperation, he lured the secretary into the bathroom, locked him there, put on a brown tweed cap, raincoat and grey plus-fours, gave instructions to an amused page-boy to unlock Simpkins half an hour after he had left by the side entrance, and so escaped to find himself with a whole day of freedom before him.

When Simpkins, resigned but annoyed, was released from the hygienic confines of the bathroom he found a note for him on the table

"Sorry to do this, Simpkins, but I guess I've earned a day of freedom. I shall be back about eight to take up the harness again, but until then I'm a free man. Don't worry, I'm still Peter Angel."

* * * * *

And Simpkins, with a wisdom born of long years of secretaryship and management of temperamental celebrities, decided that he could do nothing. He sent out for a batch of illustrated American magazines, stretched himself along a settee with drink and smokes at hand and prepared to spend a lovely June day in, what he considered, was the perfect manner.

And while Simpkins idled on the settee, Paul was sitting in the bows of a pleasure steamer enjoying a shilling trip down river from Westminster Bridge to Greenwich. His cap was pulled well down over his forehead to lessen the chance of recognition and his coat collar turned up against the buffets of waves that sent little showers of spray inboard to wet the passengers. There was a fresh east wind coming up the river and driving the water into regular series of waves through which the steamer cut with a pleasant slapping sound as though the river were patting it familiarly. There were about a dozen passengers aboard and standing in their midst was a man who described, in Cockney accents, the various objects of interest as they passed.

Paul watched the scene change as the boat sped downstream. Along the banks stood dirty cliffs of warehouses, great ridges of grey stone that were hotels and office buildings, and as they left the quick shadow of a bridge the dingy cupola of St. Paul's rose, at first timidly, over a stretch of walls and roofs. Grey lazy plumes of smoke hung low over the skyline, gasometers and factory buildings came down to the water and thrust wooden piers and algae-draped quays into the muddy flow. Over the detritus that formed in the tidal whirlpools knots of gulls hung and dipped, and led by a heavily respirating tug a string of coal barges, flat, broad-beamed and low in the water, came filing by on their journey upstream to power station and gasworks. On the sides of warehouses and buildings, long advertising legends hung in minatory colours and lettering, boasting the virtues of meat extracts and daily papers.

Paul revelled in the sense of liberty which was his. He listened half heedlessly to the Occidental dragoman. For him the site of the Globe Theatre meant a small boy sitting on a wharf-edge, a fishing line listless in his hands and his jaws working rhythmically round a sweet. He forgot the story of the Dutch eel boats that from the time of Charles II have been allowed to use the Pool without charge, as he watched a police patrol boat come curling away from Wapping Stairs and go upstream on the crest of a milky wave. Below the Tower Bridge the shipping was thicker; cargo boats with red and black funnelbands and Plimsoll marks well above water, grain boats with lines of washing domesticating their superstructure, tramps, dirty, rusted and with shag-chewing seamen lounging in their bows using coiled anchor chains as couches, and little boats sculled with an oar over the stern as men and boys collected floating wood and flotsam.

There was life in the Pool, a resting life, life that was pausing between labour. Here came cargo boats after the pounding of the Bay of Biscay and the long Atlantic washes. Against wharf-sides and in docks lay white Swedish boats whose rigging and deck plates had known the grip of ice and felt the sting of North Sea hail. Up the river came traffic from every quarter of the globe, ships whose timbers had scorched in South American ports of fantastic name, ships that bore the mark of collision and storm-fury, ships that carried death in strange diseases among their crew and often flew the quarantine flag, and with them came the ghosts of ships and crews that had vanished in the long spaces of the ocean or piled on the vicious rock-fangs of deserted coasts. Paul felt the romance and the tragedy, the splendour and the labour that were represented in the short stretch of water, and he wondered whether Wisbech would prove an epitome of this, a smaller but, in its way, just as noble a river town as London. When he landed at Greenwich he gave the guide sixpence and decided to return to London by tram. It took him an hour to find his way back to Westminster, and from there he walked happily up Whitehall, across Trafalgar Square and finally to the bottom of Tottenham Court Road where hunger discovered him and he entered a Lyons' Corner House to have lunch.

That lunch cost Paul one shilling and sixpence, not a twentieth of what he and Simpkins would normally have spent on a lunch, but to Paul it was like partaking of the food of the gods. He sat by himself at a table, glorying in his nonentity. Of the hundreds of people about him, not one guessed that he was Peter Angel.

The waiter, who with skilful movements across the crowded floor, brought him his plate of *crème fermière*, and was a Angel fan and had plastered his Cricklewood bedroom with magazine photographs of the crooner, never dreamt that he was handing soup to his almost mythical hero. The orchestra played *I'm the Man in Your Romance*, and hundreds of heads wagged to the rhythm and jaws worked in unison with its captivating beat. As the subtle exhilaration of the tune mingled with the steam of potatoes, the piquant odour of hors-d'oeuvres and the crisp smell of waffles, men and women laughed and talked and masticated within this marble palace, and in a far corner sat Paul, sat Peter Angel, who had given the song a prominence which rivalled that of the League of Nations.

Of all the expensive meals he had eaten and had been forced to eat in London, Paul remembered very little, but of that one shilling and sixpenny business man's lunch he never forgot one single detail. The *crème fermière* was hot, silky and well-flavoured, and he forgave it for being a potato masquerade; the fried fillet of cod with chipped potatoes and tomato sauce was fragrant with juices that excited and stimulated the palate; his enjoyment of the baroness pudding was heightened a hundredfold by the fact that he ate it as himself and not as the ghost of a celebrity, and the cigarette and coffee which soothed the meal into quiescent and comfortable disintegration completed a metamorphosis in Paul's mind. He was himself again.

He sat for a while admiring the walls of inlaid Italian marble, watching the deft movements of the waiters, and eyeing the polygenous crowd of dark-skinned Jews, fresh-shaved business clerks, brilliantined junior clerks, red-nailed typists, and inquiring provincials in London for the day; and around him rose a babel of voices, making shelter and cover for him, voices that spoke with the accents of Devon, Northumberland,

Wales and a hundred other districts, and sometimes the languages of the Teuton and the Oriental.

He left the sanctuary of the restaurant and then, to escape from the heat of the street and the reek of petrol fumes and sun-scorched dust, he entered the tube station opposite the restaurant. A notice caught his eye and half an hour later he found himself in the streets of Camden Town on his way to the Zoological Gardens.

Whether his visit to the Zoo was a subliminal tendency, a desire to emphasise his own freedom by pitying the captivity of the animals, is debatable. Paul himself was incapable of such subtleties. He fed buns to the polar bears, laughed at the absurd dignity of the penguins, was slightly disgusted by the fundamental effrontery of the baboons, perspired in the heat of the reptile house as he watched the pythons, exhausted his small change in feeding the insatiable sea-lions with fish and, when the heat became too much for him, retired into the cool, cavernous recesses of the aquarium. Here, in a universal green light, he moved peacefully on tired legs, watching the grim movements of a pair of pike imprisoned with swift-darting minnows, grew round-eyed at the wonder of starfish and sea-anemones, and breathed admiringly as brightly coloured tropical fish flashed in tiny shoals through waving bands of sea-grass.

He was like a schoolboy playing truant; everything, even well-known things, had a fresh wonder, a beauty and simplicity which radiated from his own sense of happiness. For eight hours Paul wandered and did what he wanted to and not one of the thousands of people about him suspected his true identity, and then when he was beginning to think of returning to the Waldersen and taking up the responsibilities of a public life, his luck which so far had favoured him with a perfect day, disappeared.

From the Zoo he had travelled back to have tea at a café in Hyde Park, and then as he was walking slowly down the left-hand side of Oxford Street he discovered that he was without cigarettes. He stopped outside a tobacconist's shop and was about to enter when he noticed a cigarette slot machine standing in the doorway. To save himself time and trouble, Paul put his shilling in the slot and pulled at the drawer to obtain his packet of cigarettes. The drawer stuck tight. He jerked hard, but still the drawer refused to open. He tapped the machine gently to loosen the coin should it have jammed anywhere, and then tugged at the drawer again. Still it remained fast closed.

"What a machine!" he muttered quietly, and then went inside the shop and complained to the assistant. "Stuck has it?" The assistant was a melancholy individual with a head that balanced itself on sloping shoulders without the visible support of a neck, like a ball on top of a gate post. "We'll soon see about that."

He came round the counter and followed Paul to the machine. But even the masterly, and apparently knowing, efforts of the assistant could not prevail. Between them they tapped it, shook it, thumped it, kicked it, pushed it, jerked it, jarred it and cursed it, but the machine refused to give up its prey and its glass eyes decorated with coloured cigarette cartons seemed to grin devilishly as the two men wrestled in the heat. Normally Paul would either have demanded another packet of cigarettes from the shop and left the assistant to cope with the machine, or the assistant would have had the courtesy to offer him a packet and so have dismissed the difficulty until expert knowledge could have been brought to bear on the problem; but the sweltering closeness of the day had enhanced the melancholy of the assistant until he had no room for courtesy, and Paul was fired into stubborn resistance at the obstinacy of the machine and refused to leave it. Here was a mechanical problem that appealed to his mind. So they continued their efforts to induce the machine to disgorge its unlawful prey, and as they stamped and panted in the narrow doorway a small crowd of interested spectators began to form.

After five minutes of struggling Paul straightened himself up and, taking off his cap, wiped his hot forehead. As he did so three girls who were passing, stopped, attracted by the crowd and then saw him. In a moment the mischief was done.

"Oh! It's Peter Angel!" The three gave tongue simultaneously. Their remark was like a fire tocsin. The melancholy assistant was no longer melancholy, the onlookers no longer merely interested but avid, and the three girls rushed forward struggling at their handbags for autograph books, and with them came a growing crowd attracted in the same mysterious way as vultures discover carrion. Paul found himself besieged.

"Give us a song, Angel!"

"Sign my autograph book, please ..."

"Isn't he lovely. Look at those eyes!"

"Sing us a song."

"Isn't he divine? I wish he were the man in my romance ..."

Paul staggered back against the shop-front and held up his hands. "Please, ladies and gentlemen, please ..." But his protestations were swept aside and lost. He was a public figure and—the logic was unanswerable—public property, and if he had not acted quickly he would have been torn

42

to pieces there and then and divided amongst the thickening mob. In a few seconds, the busy efflux of pedestrians up and down Oxford Street had ceased and each one was concentrated on that few yards of pavement outside the tobacconist's shop. The crowd swelled and overflowing into the road, stopped the line of buses and cars, causing a traffic block that had its repercussions two miles away at the bottom of Ludgate Hill, and brought half a dozen policemen angrily to the scene, and in the midst of the frenzy Paul sought to protect himself.

He did not know what to do. His feelings vacillated between despair and panic. He tried to speak to the crowd and ask them to drop away, but they ignored him, and if those in front had wished to comply with his demands the press of those behind would have prevented them. For a few awful moments Paul stood hesitatingly and then, before a policeman could work his way into him, he decided. Peter Angel or no Peter Angel, public figure or no public figure, he was not going to be crushed, not even if the crushing were done with the best of intentions. He pushed the melancholy assistant into his shop, squared his shoulders and putting his head down charged into the crowd. Like a battering ram he headed along the pavement and with great thrusts of his arm he cleared a way for himself as Richard the First might have cut his way through menacing Saracens. The crowd at the sight of his shoulders and determined face parted before him and then closed behind him and followed. In a few seconds he was through the thick of the crowd and hurrying down Oxford Street as fast as he could go, and behind him came the undaunted pursuit, shouting his name and, occasionally, facetious remarks.

Paul was now genuinely alarmed at the confusion behind him. He felt his heart pounding with a silly fear and like a hunted animal he suddenly broke into a run to try and shake off pursuers. A joyful shout rose behind him and two hundred people, despite the weather, became converted to the new sport of crooner-hunting. They tore after him, bubbling with talk, laughing with good-humour, and calling to him playfully. Paul increased his pace, dodging pedestrians on the pavement before him and forced now and then to jump over the outstretched feet of mistaken citizens who imagined that he was a runaway thief or public nuisance. For twenty yards Paul tore down Oxford Street, hoping to shake off the crowd. The outcry behind him increased and he began to wonder what would happen when he was stopped by some philanthropic person or overtaken by the crowd. He decided that it would be folly to continue running down the busy Oxford Street, and turned up a side street. Part of the crowd followed him. There were far fewer people in the side street, but he knew, as he panted forward, that at any moment someone might trip him up or attempt to hold him back. As this thought was beginning to assume disquieting proportions in his contemplation of the immediate future, he was conscious of a motor horn hooting in the roadway by his side and he glanced across to see a long green limousine moving abreast with him. As he looked, the door of the car opened and a hand beckoned unmistakably towards him.

Paul glanced round, was appalled by the herd of humanity behind him and then, as the hand beckoned again, jumped into the roadway and, at the expense of a ripped trouser leg, scrambled into the moving car. The door slammed behind him, the engine accelerated, the car shot away down the street, was fortunately treated by traffic lights and then, with the crowd fading well in the distance of road-crossings and long stretch of pavement, turned aside into a maze of narrow thoroughfares. The car sped in and out for a while, the driver saying no word, and then gliding swiftly into Soho Square, drew up in a quiet corner, as though the driver were certain that there was now no danger of pursuit.

Paul recovered from the undignified position which his hurried jump into the car had dictated, and as he sat upright the young lady who was at the wheel smiled at him and put her hands round his neck. Then:

"My poor darling—did they nearly massacre you?" she cried softly, and kissed him on the lips and pulled his nose. Paul was left staring at her with wide eyes.

V

Gone to Earth

Margaret Sinclair was a modern young woman. She had read Marx's *Das Kapital*, and H. G. Wells's *Outline of Science*, and she thought she understood the Balkan situation. She could handle anything from a motorcycle to an aeroplane. She had once travelled especially to New York to see *Green Pastures* and was an inveterate *habituée* of the Old Vic. She preferred the summer to the winter, because cold weather turned her nose an unbecoming and tenacious blue colour that powder could not aesthetically conquer, and her love of music was catholic enough to enable her to enjoy both Gershwin and Bach. She had several familiar phrases that qualified her for the adjective modern, such as, "I think all charity is demoralising," "I loathe children," "The lower classes suffer as much from snobbery as the aristocracy," and "Twentieth century life is too complicated to give people time for happiness." When she said these things her forehead would pucker into three vertical little lines, somewhat like a very formal *fleur-de-lis*, as though she hated to have to admit these cold truths, and forgot that she seldom passed a street beggar without putting her hand into her bag, that children thought her the most interesting person in the world and pestered her for stories, that her sympathies were definitely democratic, and that she was as happy in the roar and clatter of London as she was in the quiet countryside about her father's Bedfordshire house.

Paul could not, of course, know these things as he stared at her. He saw a young woman of moderate height, dressed in a well-cut Donegal tweed coat and skirt and a blouse of fawn silk with a brown tie that toned with her shallow felt hat that carried a little green feather along its brim. Her hair was a light brown, bleached by the sun with wayward streaks of yellow. If her face had been oval she might have been almost beautiful; as it was, it was more nearly round, and while a few people thought she was pretty others thought they were closer to the truth in describing her as pleasant-looking. Her hat now was pushed to one side and her hair was a little ruffled where she had impetuously embraced Paul, and her grey eyes were still laughing at his obvious confusion.

"Peter, darling," she said, "this is me, Margaret! Don't stare at me as though I were a ghost! Look, I'm alive—pinch my arm and see."

She held out her arm but Paul did not accept her test of her material existence. Unaccustomed as he was to the ways of women he was prevented by the respect which he bore them from asking her what she meant by her unorthodox behaviour.

"I know you're no ghost," he answered, wondering who and what she was. "Ghosts ... don't kiss ... act like that."

"Did you like it? I'll give you another one. There's no one looking, unless it is the ghost of De Quincey who haunts this square."

"No, no, please—don't do that!" Paul drew back to his seat.

"Why, darling, you look positively scared of me That's hardly the way to respond to your gallant rescuer. Oh, Peter," her voice became sweet and tender, "I'm so glad to see you again. It's seemed like ages since we parted. You didn't expect to see me so soon, did you?"

"No ... no, I didn't," Paul answered truthfully.

"But what a piece of luck my coming along at that moment. Father and I only got back from the Continent today. He grew tired of losing money in the Casino, so we came back. I knew you'd be surprised to see me. I was on my way to the Waldersen when I met you."

As she was speaking Paul did some rapid thinking. From her remarks he understood that she was a friend of the real Peter Angel, and her return to England looked as though it might have disastrous effects for himself. He could only guess at the basis of her acquaintance with the crooner, and he could see that it was probably so intimate that it would require a great digression from his probity of conduct to allow him to masquerade before her as Peter Angel with any success.

"I say, that's fine. We ... I hadn't expected you yet, you know ..."

Margaret sighed. "Thank goodness you're coming out of your stupor at last. I'd begun to think that the shock of being chased by that man-eating crowd had upset your mind. I must say you didn't react very promptly or properly to the providential return of your beloved. Now come on, let's stage the greeting over again—and properly this time."

She leaned over from the wheel, and the horrified Paul had not the slightest doubt of her meaning. He—in some unaccountable way—was her fiancé, and he was required to act as such. He was too amazed to be amused at the incongruity of his position, but his amazement did not prevent him from realising that unless he gave this young lady the impression that he was Peter Angel things might become very awkward for him and various other people.

"Peter, darling, you do still love me, don't you?"

From this almost pathetic charge Paul could not escape.

"Of course, I do ... darling. Don't be absurd ... of course I do." And to reaffirm his love he put his arms round her shoulders and kissed her. It was a disturbing experience, and proved that there is in love a far greater mental than physical element. If Paul had even had a slight acquaintance with the girl her lips were soft and eager enough to make a kiss something to be remembered with delight, as it was he had to restrain himself from shuddering at the enormity of his crime.

He released her and she looked at him strangely.

"What's the matter with you, Peter? You might have been kissing the side of a battleship ... not a bit like you were in Chicago."

"I'm sorry ... darling."

"But—I guess it must be that chase. Yes."

Paul grasped at this excuse: "Yes, it was the chase. It upset me. I still don't know quite whether I'm on my head or my heels. You see ... running in the heat ... I feel quite dizzy."

As he spoke a bold scheme developed inside his head. He was going to get clear from this imbroglio as quickly as he could and let Simpkins take charge. "And ... I feel as though I might faint any moment." He pulled at the knot of his tie dramatically.

"Oh, my poor darling! What a brute I've been not to think of it! You must have a rest. I'll take you—"

Where Margaret was going to take him Paul never knew, for he chose that moment to go off into a faint. He even groaned slightly as he crumpled up in his seat and murmured, "Water, fetch me a glass of water!"

As Margaret looked at the slack figure, her face tautened with alarm. Then she opened the door and sprang out.

"Oh, dear, dear ..." Her hands flew up and down in distracted gestures. Her eye caught the sign of a restaurant and she flew across the square to fetch water. As she went Paul opened one eye cautiously, watched her well out of sight, and then as she entered the restaurant he slipped from the car and ran down Greek Street and to safety as fast as he could go. He never looked back. In Shaftesbury Avenue he jumped on a bus and ten minutes later entered the Waldersen by the back entrance to rouse the snoring Simpkins from his sleep on the settee.

"Eh? What? Why? Who is it ... Hallo, it's you." Simpkins came out of his coma. He looked up at Paul, saw his pale, worried face, and his eyes narrowed to thin slits.

"And now, what have you done?" Simpkins stood up. "I knew you'd make a mess of things—going out like that!"

Paul resented the man's attitude.

"I haven't made a mess of anything. It's you—you and that crooner Angel. I agreed to take his place in London—but," Paul worked himself up into a state of anger to relieve his feelings; "but I didn't damn well agree to play the part of fiancé for him—and what's more I don't intend to! Why, man—she kissed me and then made me kiss her! What do you think of that? And in a car right bang in one of London's well-known squares. I can't stand that. I shall go cuckoo." He walked up and down the room restlessly, glad to be able to speak without fear of involving himself in complications.

"Fiancé, girl, kissed you?" Simpkins wrinkled his bald forehead and stuck out his angular chin. "What are you talking about, Mr. Angel."

"Oh, forget the Mr. Angel part! I'm finished with that if I have to be mixed up with any women. You told me he hadn't any friends in London or England—a damned lie!"

Simpkins saw that he would have to humour Paul. "If you'll try to tell me, plainly and without the emphasis of damns, perhaps I can figure out what's happened," he suggested, lighting a cigarette.

"I'll tell you all right." And Paul did tell him, and when he had finished his story he felt calmer and, somehow, happier.

Simpkins's reaction to his story was direct and expressive. He whistled loudly, blew out his cheeks and then, as he threw his cigarette into the fireplace said, "Hell!"

"I'm glad you don't feel so happy about it. What are we to do? And, anyway, who and what is she?"

"You want to know?" Simpkins sat down and held his head between his hands. "Well, you're a decent sort of guy, so I'll tell you. Margaret Sinclair's her name. Her father's a big shipowner or something over here—pots of money. She's a sweet kid, and she's secretly engaged to Peter

Angel, though—and don't let this get any further—between ourselves she's far too good for him."

"And," Paul put in, "she was almost too much for me!"

Simpkins went on with his explanation. "She met Mr. Angel in Chicago last fall and they fell for each other all right. I couldn't understand that—she seemed such a sensible kid—"

"What's wrong with Mr. Angel, then?"

Simpkins waved a hand. "Oh, he's all right. Clever chap and all that, but he's not her type. That's it—not her type. Mind, I like him. He's been good to me, but that doesn't make it any different. They got engaged secretly and she came back to England with her father. That's one of the reasons why Mr. Angel decided to come over and appear in England, so he could see her, and they're going to break the news to her father. What his feelings will be I can't even guess—"

"And knowing all this you persuaded me to play his part in London!" Paul felt that he had good cause to be angry.

"No, no! Nothing of the kind. Miss Sinclair's been on vacation somewhere in the Mediterranean and Mr. Angel didn't expect her back for another week or so yet—she told you herself she had returned unexpectedly."

"Well, she's back—and from the little I've learned about her she'll probably be on her way here now. What are you going to do? Can you get in touch with Mr. Angel?"

Simpkins stared at the floor, and if Paul had not been so concerned with his own thoughts and apprehensions he might have noticed that the generally imperturbable secretary was showing a very worried face. "Yes, I can get into touch with him, but that won't help at the moment."

"Why not tell her the truth—if she's his fiancée she would understand and keep her mouth shut? It's a very simple explanation."

Simpkins brushed the suggestion aside at once. "Impossible! Peter Angel would be furious, and besides do you honestly think any woman can keep her mouth shut? No, sir—not these days."

Paul did not think that Simpkins's objections were very sound, but he shrugged his shoulders and decided that he would allow himself to be advised as the secretary wished so long as his impersonation was concerned with the professional and not with the amatory pursuits of Peter Angel.

"We've got to bluff her until Mr. Angel gets back. I'll wire for him right away, but until then she must be stalled." As Simpkins finished speaking the telephone bell rang.

"I'll bet that's her," said Paul as he watched Simpkins pick up the receiver.

It was. The conversation that followed was entirely to Simpkins's credit as a dissembler.

"Hallo," he answered. "Who! Why, Miss Sinclair, this is a pleasure, I had no idea you were back! Today. I hope you had a nice vacation? Worried? What about? You met him in Oxford Street? What? What? WHAT? Impossible! Why he's only this minute left the hotel. Yes—just a few minutes ago. He came rushing in, told me that he was going down to the country to spend the night with a friend. No, he didn't say where. Someone concerned with his new show I gathered. Yes, it did seem sudden. Am I worried about him? Well, to tell you the truth he has acted a little queerly lately. I believe he's heading for a nervous breakdown—all this publicity. Yes, perhaps that explains his queer conduct with you. What else could? What am I going to do? What's that? You're coming round ... But, Miss Sinclair, I assure you that ... What? Hullo! HULLO! What? No, this is not Hampstead 5736—" Simpkins slammed down the receiver and spun round.

"She's coming round!"

Paul laughed. Miss Margaret Sinclair was not a woman to be trifled with. "What do we do now?" he asked, his mind full of objections.

Simpkins was in no mood for humour. "We do a lot and we do it quickly before she gets here. I might lose my job if we make a mess of this, so you must help me."

"Anything you say—so long as I don't have to kiss her again!"

In quick sentences as he dashed about the suite packing a grip for Paul, Simpkins explained what was to be done. Paul was to go and book a room in one of the cheaper hotels near the British Museum and stop there the night. He was to send Simpkins his address in the morning and he would then be given further orders. Simpkins explained his plan as he scurried around throwing collars and shirts into a grip.

"But supposing someone recognised me?"

"We must risk that. Here better take this cash to keep you going. Now—for the love of Mike—beat it or I'm sunk!"

With a grip in one hand, nearly twenty pounds in notes in the other and a bewildered, half-amused, half-apprehensive look on his face Paul found himself thrust into a lift. His last impression of Simpkins was of a bald-headed, disturbed, worried gnome shooing him with waving palms and exhorting him for the love of various obscure deities to leave the hotel by any way but the main entrance for fear of meeting Miss Sinclair.

Half an hour later, Paul was lying on the uncomfortable bed of a Columbus Hotel bedroom, his hands behind his head, his eyes fixed on the fly-spotted ceiling, wondering what was going to happen next. And while he lay there, Simpkins was doing his best to mollify a distinctly suspicious Miss Sinclair, who had a very definite impression that the secretary was lying to her. It took him three-quarters of an hour to pacify her and to persuade her that all she could do was to leave the hotel and come back in the morning when there might be news from Peter Angel.

"Really, Miss Sinclair, there is nothing wrong with him. Just overstrain. He'll be back in the morning and will probably wonder what all the fuss is about—"

"I hope so," came the determined reply. "The way he treated me was nothing less than mean. After all I'm engaged to be married to him! If he treats me like that now, what will be his manner if I do marry him?"

Simpkins did not attempt to offer any postulate as to Peter Angel's marital habits, but returned from the lift and reached for the whisky decanter. His hand had scarcely closed round its neck when a page boy knocked on the door and in response to his call entered with a telegram.

Simpkins slit the envelope, and then in front of the boy swore with a nautical heartiness that captured the boy's admiration.

"All right—no answer!" He flung the boy a tip and then, as the door shut, collapsed into an armchair. The telegram fluttered slowly to the ground and remained there face upwards. It said, very simply

The baby has squealed, good and hard.

For perhaps half a minute Simpkins remained inert. Then he shot to his feet and repeated the performance, which he had recently given to Paul, of packing a grip. Twenty minutes later Simpkins left the Waldersen Hotel, grip in hand, but not one of the hotel employees who saw him go recognised in him the secretary of Peter Angel, the crooner. His bald head was covered with a realistic wig and soft cap, his long features were enriched by a short brown moustache, and a pair of pince-nez hid his dark eyes. On the third floor of the Waldersen Hotel the suite of Peter Angel was silent save for the echoes of street noises, and in the fireplace of one of the bedrooms a pile of burning papers turned, with crackling and minor subsidences, to light-coloured feathery ashes.

No one recognised Paul as he dined that evening. He sat in a shaded corner of the room, underneath a highly coloured and unpleasing painting of Columbus holding in his hand an exhausted pigeon while with the other he kept a firm grip on the wooden rail of the *Santa Maria*'s swaying poop. After dinner he went to the cinema and saw a boring story of a Red Cross nurse who had to choose between her English lover, her honour and a German firing squad. After the turbidity of the Red Cross epic, the absurdities of Mickey Mouse were like manna in the desert, and then he watched himself in the newsreel throwing sprats to the gulls and waterfowl on the Serpentine with Simpkins hovering, less audaciously than the gulls, in the background.

When he slept that night he had a curiously mixed dream in which he was showing Margaret Sinclair the sights of Wisbech, a dream which was rudely interrupted by the sound of a drunken commercial traveller staggering along the corridor to his room singing—*I Want to Go Down to the Sea Again*—to his own arrangement. After that he slept restlessly, roused by the bouts of traffic noise and the quick flashes of light that filtered through the window from the city.

And while Paul tossed on his bed, Simpkins bit his nails in the darkness and occasionally laughed sharply through the hanging frond of his moustache, and Margaret lay awake in bed trying to reconcile Peter Angel's astonishing actions of that day with those of the man she had met and loved in America, and finding the reconciliation very hard to achieve.

VI
Fly Away Paul

It was raining when Paul woke, raining in a soft, quiet drizzle that filled the morning with a gentle blend of murmurs and cloaked the rattle of traffic that floated into his bedroom from the streets around the hotel. He lay in bed for a while, in his favourite attitude, arms at the back of his neck and his eyes watching the ceiling as his mind roamed from one thought to another with inconsequential adroitness. Then, hearing a clock strike ten, he stirred himself and wrote a note to Simpkins at the Waldersen, asking him for instructions as to his procedure and also giving him his address and assumed name at the Columbus Hotel. He rang the bell, gave orders for the note to be taken immediately to the Waldersen, and ordered his breakfast to be brought to him in bed. He was determined not to run any unnecessary risk of identification by breakfasting in the hotel room.

"And let me have a morning paper," he added as the page boy left the room.

Long afterwards when Paul reflected on the subject, he saw that had it not been for that chance order to bring him a paper with his breakfast, the whole of his future might have pursued a very different course. In the folded pages of the *Daily Globe* as it lay before him on the tray while he ate his breakfast Nemesis was swaddled. Nemesis lay quietly in her cradle of divorce court proceedings, murders and cricket results until Paul had finished his cereal and drunk his coffee. Then he lit a cigarette, balanced a pillow comfortably behind his head, and drew his knees up into a hillock to make a rest for the paper. The moment he shook the creases of the *Daily Globe* into order, Nemesis gave a loud wail and startled Paul from his peaceful digestion of his breakfast and cigarette, for there in the centre of the first page was a large photograph of Peter Angel, and above the photograph ran two headlines in thick type and from the photograph two columns of matter hung like Chinese banners. For a moment Paul stared at the headlines and columns in amazement and then with his heart pounding he read:

FAMOUS CROONER DISAPPEARS
WANTED BY POLICE
CHARGE OF FRAUD AGAINST PETER ANGEL
MILLION DOLLAR SWINDLER—HAVE YOU SEEN HIM?

Peter Angel, crooner, world-famous radio singer and filmstar, is wanted by the American authorities on a charge of fraud amounting to nearly one million dollars. Three men have been arrested in New York, and the English police are looking for handsome, debonair Peter Angel in connection with a gigantic radio fraud. Peter Angel, who landed in this country a few days ago and who has been staying at the Waldersen Hotel, has disappeared.

HOME FOR AGED PEOPLE

A year ago Peter Angel lent his services to a nation-wide appeal for subscriptions to found a chain of Homes for Aged People in the United States of America. The appeal, which resulted in a response of over two million dollars, has now been discovered to be a gigantic swindle. Half of the subscription money has been appropriated by the four men, of whom Peter Angel was one, who instigated the appeal and so far only one home has been built and this has not yet been opened.

SOMEWHERE IN ENGLAND

All ports are being watched and it is certain that Peter Angel is in hiding somewhere in England with his valet-secretary. He speaks with an almost perfect English accent, but his well-known features should make detection only a question of time.

Paul read on. The newspaper gave further details of the swindle and a short history of Peter Angel, from which it became clear that the crooner had been born in England and had lived the life of an adventurer ever since a boy. Under various names he had a criminal record whose chief characteristic was audacity. On the centre page was an editorial:

> ... *Readers will have seen the account of the disappearance of Peter Angel who is wanted on a charge of fraud in America. That such a public character is guilty of so heinous a crime many people will find difficult to believe, and we still hope that it may prove to be a ghastly mistake.*
>
> *It is almost too fantastic to credit that Peter Angel whose songs have cheered millions in times of depression, whose films have been permeated by the spirit of purity, and whose private life had appeared a model of rectitude, is guilty of such an offence against humanity. But if he is guilty—then humanity will have been dealt a blow so strong that no one could be ostracised for expressing doubts as to the intrinsic goodness of human nature, and Peter Angel will richly deserve the fullest punishment which the law can inflict for his culpability, and we, in company with others, will only be able to murmur sadly ...* Stat magni nominis umbra ...

Paul read everything there was to read and when he had finished he threw the paper aside and bit his lips.

"I'm damned! I can't believe it!" That was his vocal reaction. He stared at the end of the bed, his thoughts too chaotic and confused to give him any comfort or guidance. Then his hand gradually stopped shaking, his heart quietened from its trembling fear and he was able to think clearly and logically. His first thought was that he was no longer afraid. He had done nothing. He was not Peter Angel. Very slowly and deliberately he went back over the whole chain of events, and he saw that his presence on the S.S. *Pandaric* had been a godsend for the crooner. The subterfuge had not been planned in order to relieve the crooner of the strain of his abnormal publicity, but to enable him to have three or four days to get away and cover his tracks. He must have known, mused Paul, that the radio fraud was soon to be unmasked, and he had used him. And in using him he had given him an opportunity to land in England and see Wisbech.

Paul lit a cigarette. He tried to be fair-minded. The crooner had obviously taken part in the swindle. Paul was not concerned with that. But he was concerned with the rest of his actions. He could not blame Peter Angel for using him. Any man would have done the same, and in a roundabout way Paul sympathised with the crooner. He was faced with a very difficult problem—the problem of his subsequent action. What was he to do? One thing was very clear, he had to become Paul Morison again; to say that was easy, but to become himself again was far from a simple matter. If he went to the police and told them the whole story it would help them very little. He could not say where Peter Angel was, or even where Simpkins had gone. The two would still be at large, somewhere. And he would—he knew enough about the law to realise that it held no place for sentiment—be apprehended as a stowaway and there would be no Wisbech for him. There was even the possibility that a confession to the police of his position might involve him in long-winded affairs of court that would eventually prevent him from returning to America in time to take up his appointment. He had already taken one mad chance—he did not intend to risk his hard-won promotion again. And he still wanted to go to Wisbech, wanted to more fervently now that there was a possibility that he would be prevented, than he had ever done. Besides, he argued with himself, he had earned the right to visit Wisbech after these hot days in London.

For once the curious admixture of sensibility and nostalgia for Wisbech within Paul formed a complementary whole. He would go to Wisbech and enjoy himself for a while. He had enough money to last him for a time. He would cable for more when that was gone. By that time the real Peter Angel would be in the hands of the police. Then he would slip quietly out of the country and back to America. By doing that, he decided, he would be causing no trouble at all, and if the worst happened and he was caught as Peter Angel he could deny it with truth and reveal himself as John Denver, alias Paul Morison, stowaway. He had spent a whole day in London almost without being recognised as Peter Angel, it seemed to him very probable that he could travel to Wisbech and then leave the country without being troubled. Once he had made up his mind Paul obstinately refused to go back over his arguments. He was not going to be mixed up with the police, and he was going to see Wisbech—that was what he had left America for.

He dressed himself, washed his hair to take out the waves which Simpkins had assiduously kept in each morning with tongs, and while he was packing his grip sent the page-boy to find out the times of trains to Wisbech. The police he knew from the paper had given a description of him, but this did not specify the clothes he was wearing. The pageboy returned, telling him that there was a train in half an hour from King's

Cross Station, and a quicker one in an hour's time from Liverpool Street Station. Paul decided to go from King's Cross, and with the page boy carrying his grip he went down the lift, paid up his bill and left the hotel to get a taxi. He made no attempt to avert his face or avoid the looks of the hotel clerk and other people he saw, for he realised that the one way to incur suspicion was to attempt to avoid people or act nervously. He was Paul Morison—not Peter Angel.

As he drove in the taxi to the station, he saw the placards on the pavements before newsagents' shops and most of them were concerned with the crooner. Have You Seen Peter Angel? Famous Crooner Disappears. And one—Will He Sing in Sing-Sing? Paul smiled, and felt quite safe. He had no very high opinion of the English police.

At the station he found he had a quarter of an hour to wait. He bought his ticket and a copy of the *Strand* magazine, then he settled down on a seat to read until his train came in.

* * * * *

When Margaret Sinclair awoke that morning, the uneasiness which had accompanied her sleep all night had turned into definite doubt and suspicion. She was worried at Peter Angel's strange action and also slightly annoyed at his discourteous treatment of her. A perusal of her morning paper made her forget her annoyance and sent her, full of searching questions and fears, to the Waldersen as quickly as her car could take her. She ran into the hotel, took the lift to Peter Angel's suite and arrived outside the door at the same time as the messenger from Paul's hotel with the note for Simpkins.

The messenger smiled as she stood with her hand on the handle of what, had she but known it, was a locked door. "You going in, miss?"

Margaret nodded.

The messenger held out the note, apparently under the impression that Margaret was an occupant of the suite. Long afterwards Margaret wondered why she said "It's for Mr. Simpkins, is it?" and as the boy nodded she took the note, handing him a tip from her bag. Then she stood outside the door, musing, until the boy should have disappeared from the corridor, for she could now feel that the door of the suite was locked.

When the boy had gone she walked down the emergency stairway and read the note which Paul had sent. It read:

57

Simpkins,

Jonathan Leate at the Columbus Hotel will find me. Shall expect to hear from you today, but whatever you arrange I refuse to have any more to do with that woman.

For a moment Margaret could not believe what she saw written. Peter Angel, her Peter, was staying at another hotel under an assumed name and—which was the hardest to bear—wanted to have no more to do with her. She sat on a window ledge and tried to straighten things out in her mind. When she had read the newspaper account of the fraud, she had not believed it. There was a mistake somewhere. But now, the note in her hand proved that Peter Angel was guilty, otherwise he would not be hiding under an assumed name in a cheap hotel. And he didn't want her. Why not? Her mind could only supply one answer to that question. He still loved her, he must do, but because of this disgrace he refused to see her, wanted to cut her out from his life so that his shame might not touch her. The nobility of his action overshadowed the magnitude of his crime and she felt a great pity and sympathy for him. She screwed the note into a little ball and then hurried from the hotel. She would see Mr. Jonathan Leate of the Columbus Hotel. She would prove to Peter that her love was no mean thing.

But when she arrived at the hotel it was only to be told by the hotel clerk that Mr. Jonathan Leate had gone. What she would have done then is doubtful, had not a page boy offered the information with an outstretched palm, that Mr. Leate had gone to King's Cross to catch a train for Wisbech and if she hurried she might still catch up with him. Margaret did not stop to wonder why Peter should want to go to Wisbech. She felt that there was little point in wondering at the universal strangeness of action which was characterising her fiancé, until she could catch him and ask him directly all the questions which were burning within her mind.

She swung out of the side street into the crowded Euston Road, threading her way through the mountainous omnibuses, and fretting at the impartial insistence of traffic lights, finally reached King's Cross Station.

It took her three minutes to find Paul. He was still sitting on a seat reading his magazine. She walked up the number one platform scrutinising everybody. Paul's head was bent to his magazine, but as she drew level with him he looked up and their eyes met.

For a few seconds they both remained motionless, while around them locomotives screeched and passengers hurried up and down with cases and parcels. They were isolated units of immobility in a universe of commotion and movement.

"Peter!" Margaret came to life and moved towards him quickly. Her movement wakened Paul to the danger of his situation.

With a half-suppressed moan of despair he leapt to his feet, flung the magazine to the ground and bolted like a rabbit stung on the flank with a shot-gun pellet.

"Peter!" Margaret cried pleadingly, but Paul did not stop. He dodged up the platform through the crowd, swerved into the booking office hall and disappeared from her sight. As he ran he could feel his heart pounding with the quick fear of his narrow escape. Margaret Sinclair was the last person in the world whom he wanted to see at that moment. Outside in the road, he halted. He knew quite well that she would follow him, and with a wisdom born of his anxiety he ran down the roadway a few yards and then doubled back into the station through another entrance. Once on the crowded platform he felt safer, and walking quickly he moved to the main entrance and out into the roadway. On the pavement he paused for a moment and looked round. There was no sign of Margaret. He smiled at his own cleverness and walked slowly down the road from the station, wondering what he should do now. His reverie was rudely interrupted by a voice behind him.

"Peter!"

He looked round and there was Margaret, a little out of breath with running and her hat slightly awry where she had pushed quickly by people. Paul leaped round, gave one scared look at her and then, regardless of his life, dashed into the roadway to escape her. He swerved round the back of an omnibus, made a taxi-driver pull up dead with a screaming of brakes and an outburst of oaths, dodged under the outstretched neck of a brewer's horse and, with a jump worthy of an Olympic champion, gained the opposite pavement before a maliciously-minded errand-boy could trip him up with his front wheel. Faintly from across the traffic, he heard Margaret shout once more, and then running desperately he was away up a side street. His mind had place for only one thought. He had to evade her, had to get away before she put the whole of London on his heels … if he didn't then he would never see Wisbech, and perhaps endanger his New York appointment. A little way up the street a red neon light sign hung over the pavement. *Coaching Station*. Paul ran inside and in doing so almost knocked over a large man in a white driving coat and red cap.

"Hey! Hey! What's the bleedin' hurry, mate?" The man caught him by the shoulder in time to save him from falling to the ground. "What's bitten yer, mate?"

"Leave go—I'm in a hurry ..." panted Paul.

"In a hurry, are you?" The driver laughed." You shouldn't leave it so late another time. Which coach do you want?"

Paul, fretting at the delay, looked at him.

"I ... I ..." His hard breathing interfered with his articulation.

"Which? Is it the Leicester one? 'Cos if so you're almost too late. I'm just off!"

"Leicester ..." Paul looked at the man, and an idea began to grow in his mind.

"Yes, Leicester. Got yer ticket?" The driver turned towards a large motor-coach behind him.

"No, I ... I haven't had time to get a ticket," said Paul. "Is it necessary?"

The driver laughed. "Blimey, you did get out of the wrong side of the bed. Course you got to have a ticket. Here, if it's Leicester you want, 'op in and the conductor'll take your money. We 'aven't time to wait for you to go to the booking office."

"Yes, yes ... that's a good idea," agreed Paul. "Leicester."

"Good idea! Course it is." The driver laughed affably, and then swung open the compartment door of the coach and helped Paul into a seat. "There y'are, mister, and next time, as I said, get up a bit earlier or you'll miss the bus!"

The door slammed and as Paul subsided on to a well-padded seat the engine of the coach roared into a steady, throbbing life and the great black and green monster rolled from the coaching station into the street. Paul sank back in his seat and slowly regained his breath. He was still a little bemused with the swift onslaught of events. Three things, however, were clear. He was still safe, he had escaped from Margaret, and he was on his way to Leicester. Just where Leicester was Paul was very undecided. It was a town in England, he knew, but beyond that—nothing. He heaved a sigh of peace and pushed his hat back on to his forehead to cool himself, and as he did so a man sitting in a seat opposite him said, "You only just managed to do it, young man."

The coach swung into Euston Road and passed away into the traffic as Margaret Sinclair leant against a post-box for support after her running. She saw the coach go by and she saw Paul, and as she rested a very determined expression crept over her face, an expression which slowly gave way to a smile.

VII
Money will buy anything

Mr. Richard Partingale was educated at a time when the Education Acts were yet to be and the three R's represented the most that a dame school could impart, and he believed very firmly that the proper study of mankind is man. He had studied mankind from those early years when he had earned five shillings a week cleaning and repairing bicycles in a small shop behind Charing Cross Road during the day, and weakened his eyes by reading popular mechanical and engineering weeklies at night. He had discovered, too, that the study of mankind could be made very profitable, and at the age of fifty he could look back on a life which most men would have envied.

As a young man he had been poor—so poor that it was surprising that the experiences of his earlier days had not left him with a lasting bitterness—until he realised that mankind was willing to pay a good price for something which it wanted. At first he had given them bicycles to ride on their half-days; tall, ungainly, heavy machines with hard tyres. Then he had given them lighter, pleasanter machines, and, when the petrol combustion engine provided jokes for genteel magazines and subject for laughter on the streets, he risked his savings and those of a few other fanatics in a motor-car business. He had been successful. His business grew, he prospered and bought out his partners, so that at the age of fifty he was the millionaire owner of a concern that sent cars all over the world. There was not one portion of the globe where roads existed which had not at some time reverberated to the song of the engines which he loved so well, and there were some roads where the noise of his engines was so insistent that it was a nuisance.

To look at, he was extremely unlike the popular conception of a millionaire. His body was not bloated with good living, his digestion was sound, he wore neither fantastically expensive nor disgustingly shabby clothes and his only collection was a series of cigarette-card pictures of British Birds. He was a short, dark, energetic man, his face creased with deep lines where once he had frowned and now smiled too much, and he was a philanthropist, though he never used the word himself.

When Paul flopped into the seat of the motor-coach opposite him, he was amused at the young man's disarray and, because he liked the look of his frank, good-natured face, he decided that as soon as he had regained his breath he would talk to him. And he did.

"You only just managed to do it, young man," he said, smiling.

Paul looked across at him and nodded.

"Yes—it was a near thing. But I caught it—that's the great thing."

"Aye—a miss is as good as a mile!" A fat man in front rolled his great head round on its bearings of flabby flesh and jerked the remark from a ridiculously small mouth for so large a face. Then—taking the startled silence of the two for agreement—his head rolled back into its normal position, and Paul heard him rustling a paper bag as he began to feed himself with sandwiches against the rigours of the journey.

Paul looked at Mr. Partingale and smiled, and both felt that they had established between themselves a temporary intimacy; but it was not until they were well out of London that Paul really began to like Mr. Partingale, and by that time they were sitting together, smoking one another's cigarettes and talking like old friends. There was something about the short man which induced a reciprocal spirit of friendliness.

"Are you travelling on business?" Mr. Partingale asked as the coach rose over a hump-backed bridge and threw them all a little from their seats.

Paul smiled to himself and answered: "Well, not exactly. This is a sort of vacation for me."

"Oh, a holiday ..." Mr. Partingale nodded. "What are you going to do?"

Paul hesitated. "Well, it rather depends ... I'm sort of ... sort of at a loose end."

Mr. Partingale seemed to understand. "And a very good thing to be, young man." He rubbed his hand across his dark chin as he went on. "After a year's hard work, it's good to have a holiday and to feel that you are your own master at least for two weeks. Free, to go where you want to, to do what you want to ... that's a grand feeling."

"Yes, I suppose it must be," said Paul, without thought.

"Why, you talk as though you didn't know it was. Haven't you had a holiday before, then?"

Paul hesitated. He was conscious of having said the wrong thing. He was saved by the intervention of the fat man, who had been listening.

"Holidays! Bah!" The great neck creased like melting tar. "Never 'ad one in me life! Never want one in me life! Work all the time—that's my motto. Nothing like work!"

"Oh!" Mr. Partingale eyed Paul amusedly. "And what is your work?"

"Fish-and-chips—that's me!" The fat man underwent a convulsion which terminated by one arm shooting back over the seat and flourishing a card on which was inscribed

ALBERT ARTHUR CONNOR
FISH AND CHIP SALOON
18, WESTGATE ROAD, PIMLICO
EAT MORE FISH!

He withdrew the card and said, "And when I sell rock salmon, it is rock salmon and not dog fish."

"And you've never had a holiday," said Paul, glad to have attention taken off himself.

"Never! Worked all me life. Goin' to die workin'. Wouldn't be here now, but me brother died and I'm going to bury him."

"And you haven't any hobby or entertainment?" Mr. Partingale was interested. He was always interested in men with decided views.

"Entertainment! Huh! Lot o' slop they give you these days. The last play I saw was called *Thrown to the Lions*. There was a play. Some sense in that. But that was before the war. It 'ad meaning, but nowadays nothing but legs, legs and clever talk wot nobody understands. No, Sir, I've no time for hobby or entertainment!"

With this last remark he turned back to his seat, shook his paper into erratic folds and began to study the racing page.

"A most unusual man," said Mr. Partingale. "I could do without a holiday, I think, if I was interested in my work, but I should have to have occasional entertainment or a hobby. What are your hobbies?"

Paul, caught by the direct question, had no answer. He had had hobbies as a boy, but lately his work had demanded all his time. He guessed that if he began to explain about his work then this curious, but very friendly, man would want to know all about him and that might become embarrassing.

"Oh ... various things ... I ... Well, what are yours?" He felt the question to be rather rude, but it was a way out.

His expedient was successful. Mr. Partingale welcomed the question. His hobbies? He had two, he explained, bird-watching and engines. He loved birds and he loved speed. He did not say much about his love of engines but he talked for a time about birds. Paul listened, glad not to be questioned, and as he heard this man telling of long hours spent lying in damp grass, of cramped minutes waiting for a comcrake to show itself, and of peaceful moments in the balm of evening watching swifts screaming up to the eaves of thatched barns, he was filled with admiration for him. Here was a man who made ordinary things like sparrows and rooks seem exciting and interesting, a man whose eyes shone with sympathy as he told of a whitethroat building her nest for the third time in an attempt to bring off her brood before they suffered the fate of the earlier broods and were crushed by young pigs rooting in the nettles where the nest was hidden.

"They're beautiful things, birds," he said. "I wish people would realise that more and try to protect them ..." He went on talking for some time, and as he talked the coach had left the outskirts of London and was heading northwards. They passed along the great main road, little skirls of dust rising behind them, and on either side flashed the occasional sheen of canal or long black railway embankments that the tall elms and beeches did their best to hide; and by the roadside dusty stitchworts trembled in the breeze of their passing and young rabbits sat bolt upright, eyeing the strange monster with unfrightened eyes. Paul found it difficult to divide his attention between Mr. Partingale and the countryside. One moment his mind would be full of a bank, waist high with yellow nettles and canopied by great hanging blooms of wayfaring tree, and the next he would hear Mr. Partingale's voice describing the difference between the damage done to cherries by blackbirds and starlings respectively, and then he would forget everything as he remembered Margaret's face before he had dashed across the roadway. But for her he would be on his way to Wisbech. Now he was going to Leicester. Still, once there it would not be long before he was on his way again to his mother's home town.

Paul came out of his reverie in time to hear Mr. Partingale end a sentence with "... and that's what I would like most in the world."

Paul nodded as though he had been listening. Mr. Partingale smiled at him and then, because he often was in a position to give men what they had asked for when he put the question to them, he said to Paul:

"And what would you like most in the world at the moment?"

Paul rubbed the back of his head and chuckled. This little man was amusing. Once he got on to a subject nothing could shake him from it.

"I don't know that it's worth wasting time over that," replied Paul. "I'm not likely to get it."

Mr. Partingale refused to relinquish the topic. "You never know."

Paul shook his head. "Nobody could give me what I want. I've got to get it myself."

"Don't you believe it, young man. There's nothing in this world which couldn't be got for you—if you wanted it and someone else had the money to buy it."

"What do you mean?" Paul was startled somewhat by the intense note which had crept into Mr. Partingale's voice. The man was alive, and vibrant with the intenseness which comes from unshakeable conviction.

"I mean money'll buy anything these days ... anything."

Paul laughed and shook his head again. "Not anything. There are a lot of things it won't buy."

But Mr. Partingale would not accept this statement.

"Nonsense! You can't name a single thing which money couldn't buy. Happiness, comfort, health ... nothing. It can protect the unjust, oppress the innocent, feed the hungry, elevate the unworthy ... what is there it can't do?"

The fat Albert Arthur Connor swung round and fixed a lachrymose pair of eyes on Mr. Partingale. "Can't buy love," he declared and then turned his head as though overcome by this grave deficiency in the power of money.

"No," agreed Paul, "and it can't always buy freedom for a man." He wished as a matter of interest that he could put his present position before Mr. Partingale and then ask him to elucidate it by the aid of money.

"You're both wrong. Used rightly it could do both."

"I can't believe it," said Paul. Mr. Partingale refused to be shaken. He pulled at his crisp wiry hair with one hand and sliced the air with the other.

"But I know. Listen," he became confidential, "I know a man, a very wealthy man, more than a millionaire, who gives a lot of money to charity, but not in the ordinary way. He doesn't give thousands at a time to hospitals and organised charities. He doesn't believe in that kind of thing."

"What does he do then?" Albert Arthur Connor twisted back and forth sharply.

"He goes about giving his money away himself to the people he meets. He has a theory that the people who are most in need of charity are those who would ordinarily never get it or dream of asking for it. I remember when I was a young man that the one thing in the world I wanted was a pair of field glasses for bird-watching. If he had come to me then and given me five pounds to get them I should have been mad with joy. And that's how he gives his money away. Talks to people, to respectable workers, men and women who just manage to make both ends meet, and then when he knows what they want he helps them. Five pounds to a man who has never known what it is to have all that money to spend on what he likes means more than a square meal to a beggar who will soon be hungry again."

"Wish I could meet him!" Mr. Connor twisted again. "Want a set of blue and white tiles with scenes from history on 'em for the wall of my saloon. Always was fond of history."

"I don't agree with you." Paul was very determined. "Charity in that way is all wrong. You can give to hospitals and institutions, but not to individuals. If you'd worked hard and saved for your glasses from your wages, going without other things, you would have appreciated them much more. Make a man work for a thing and he values it."

"Not always, young man. Men appreciate generosity, and this man I'm talking about knows that. He likes to bring pleasure unexpectedly into the lives of ordinary folk ... "

"Still," Paul interrupted him, "this is rather getting away from the point that money can buy anything. Most things perhaps, but not everything."

"That's true." Mr. Connor winked at Paul, and then addressed Mr. Partingale. "You try and buy a fresh breeze in London on a hot day!" He laughed and turned away rumbling, so that the creases of his neck rose over his collar in pink, orderly, controlled and unbreaking waves.

Mr. Partingale made a gesture of annoyance. "Money could take you to a place where there was a fresh breeze."

Paul laughed, and as he did so he gathered the impression that Mr. Partingale resented his laughter. He was quick enough to perceive that, pleasant and affable as the man was, here was one pet theme upon which he felt strongly and about which he found it hard to bear any contradiction.

"Well, I won't fall out with you about it," he said, "but I can't agree with you."

"Listen," Mr. Partingale leaned forward and as he did so Paul glimpsed over his shoulder a splash of black and white where a magpie rose from the lee of a thorn hedge and flew, looping and dipping, over a green wheat field, then through the mumble of the coach noises he heard Mr. Partingale go on: "Listen, you tell me what you most want in the world. Just as a matter of interest—and I'll prove that it could be bought for you."

The man sat back, having delivered this challenge, and regarded Paul closely. Here was a stubborn young man who would not see the sense of his arguments. It was not the first time he had met his kind and never before had he failed to make his point; indeed, it had become a matter of honour with him to persuade people to accept his theory of the estimability of money as a cure-all.

Paul hesitated. He knew quite well what he wanted most in the world at this moment, but he had no intention of telling this insistent little man what it was. He had almost reconciled himself to the telling of a lie when the unsuppressible Mr. Connor came to his rescue. He rose in his seat and, turning, leaned over the back of his seat.

"Here," he nudged Mr. Partingale and said very loudly. "What about him? Now what could money do to help him?" As he spoke he thrust a folded paper under the man's nose, and one of his pudgy fingers underscored a thick headline.

Paul started so violently that he thought he must give himself away, but the two men did not notice his confusion. "What could money do to help him?" demanded Mr. Connor, and he jerked his finger at the photograph of Peter Angel which occupied the centre of the page. "He's got plenty but it won't help him now." He glowed and expanded with satisfaction at this master-stroke of refutation.

Mr. Partingale, who apparently had read the account of Peter Angel's fraud in his own paper, seemed to have no answer, and before he could make any evasion Mr. Connor went on determinedly, following up his triumph.

"The one thing he wants in the world, I reckon, is to be free, but not all his cash—or other people's—will help him!"

Mr. Partingale recovered himself. "Money would help him to evade the police ..."

Mr. Connor snorted. "Nonsense ... not the English police." He turned to Paul, as if for confirmation of the infallibility of the English police, and as he did so he stopped and stared hard. Paul felt his beady little eyes on his face, searching and wondering; then Mr. Connor broke into an exclamation.

"Strike us! Look at that!"

"Look at what?" Mr. Partingale questioned.

"That!" Mr. Connor, as he spoke, lifted the newspaper level with Paul's face. "Why—you're his double! Did you ever—" he turned to Mr. Partingale, "—see anything like that!"

Paul tried to be unconcerned, but he could see that Mr. Albert Connor's loud remarks had attracted the attention of the rest of the people in the coach.

"Why, so it is," agreed Mr. Partingale, and he put up a hand to turn Paul's face to the light so that he might better compare it with the photograph. From any other man Paul would have resented this familiarity. He accepted it meekly, seeing the wisdom of compliance.

Paul laughed, not very convincingly. "There is a certain resemblance, isn't there—"

"I should say there was!" exclaimed Mr. Connor and Paul noticed that a belligerent tone had crept into his voice. As he spoke he half rose in his seat and looked around to the other passengers.

"But … but, of course, I'm not Peter Angel," Paul went on truthfully enough. "Why," he tried to force a disarming laugh, "if you like I'll sing you a song, that'll be proof enough."

"Don't bother, young man," said Mr. Partingale dryly. The other passengers, however, did not seem to share Mr. Partingale's disinterest. Mr. Connor's words had set a train of thought working in their minds, and they were all wondering whether this obviously confused, rather handsome young man could be the Peter Angel whose photograph figured so prominently in their morning papers. They felt themselves to be perhaps on the edge of a sensation. For once they were close to a piece of real excitement, and—as their lives were mostly dull, humdrum, happy enough, routines of work, sleep and little pleasure—they were reluctant to let slip any opportunity which might bring them into the prominence and exalted glory of seeing their names in the immortal type of the daily papers.

"No, don't bother," agreed Mr. Connor with sudden gentleness. "We believe you, of course," and he laughed in a gurgling, unpleasant way that filled Paul with more alarm than his previous terseness.

But Mr. Connor did not believe Paul. He was by nature one of those men who are always willing to believe the worst of their fellow-creatures, on the principle that by believing the worst his pleasure was supreme when persons proved worthier than the low opinion he held of them. Though he said there was no need to bother, Mr. Connor was bothering, and the rest of the passengers were bothering. They turned again to their papers and rustled them menacingly, disturbingly, and in their minds was the one thought—"What if this should be Peter Angel?" The question titillated their imaginations.

Paul glanced about him. Apart from the driver and conductor and Mr. Partingale and Mr. Connor, there were four other persons in the coach; two women and two men. There was a thin-faced poultry-farmer, going north to visit relations and worried by the thought of his hens left in the care of an assistant who might easily lie in the sun all day reading *Quentin Durward* and forget to water or feed the hens. He itched with nervousness as he thought of hens lying parched and gasping in the shade of night arks as the hot sun beat down, and he blamed himself for taking this holiday. He saw his Wyandottes with outstretched wings, dying of heat stroke, his brain conceived pictures of fowls running giddily round in circles from vertigo ... heat-stroke, vent gleet, swollen crop ... There seemed to be no end to the complications which sun and lack of water could effect while his man sat in the shade of the walnut tree and sucked at an empty pipe over his Scott. He clutched his paper viciously and promised himself that if anything did happen while he was away then he would make his assistant pay. Peter Angel ... there was another waster, a good-for-nothing ... He'd like half an hour with him. The thought of finding Peter Angel, of bringing him to justice was like a balm to his distraught nerves and he turned to Paul, scrutinising him.

Paul saw the look and turned away, only to catch the eyes of Miss Elsie Rayner. She looked at him and in her mind there was no doubt as to his identity. He was Peter Angel. She had spent too many hours walking up and down the darkened aisles of a cinema, flashing her torch across the thick gloom, to be mistaken, and now he was sitting behind her while she rode away on holiday to forget such things. It was unfair that the ghost of an unpleasant occupation should chase her like this. Her firm lips, thin and taut and angry as a bramble scratch on white flesh, moved with an unvoiced protest against the indecency of mankind as she nodded across to the elderly lady on her right.

Her gesture was observed but evoked no corresponding emotions in the breast of Mrs. Grabhurst. Mrs. Grabhurst could have no sympathy or common feeling with such as Miss Rayner. She was a widow and rested now in that state, glad that death had taken from her a man who had never been faithful to her. She was happy now without the worry of her husband, but she still retained her contempt for girls of Miss Rayner's type; flighty, greedy, puffed-up and painted hussies who had no cares for a woman's feelings and no care for any man beyond the pleasure and presents they could elicit from him. As for Peter Angel, if the young man behind was Peter Angel, she had no sympathy for him. He had probably made some woman's heart ache; he was unfaithful, shiftless and as bad as most men, no doubt, and he deserved probably far more than he would ever get, and if she could do anything to put him in the hands of the police she would.

And in front of Mrs. Grabhurst sat a tall, bullet-headed man, with the hands of a labourer and the unmistakable stamp of an ex-soldier. He was Mr. William Freeman, known to the patrons of his public-house as Billy-Boy. When he had got into the coach he had looked round, assessed Miss Rayner as no worse than most barmaids, catalogued Mrs. Grabhurst from her acidulous features and overpowdered face as another widow on the look out for a man though unwilling to admit it even to herself, and the three men as beings entirely removed from himself except perhaps Mr. Connor, until he had heard the latter mention fish-and-chips. Mr. Freeman was a good sort, he loved his beer, his darts, his jokes, his wife, his public house, his Sunday papers and, above all, himself. His mind approached that mythical organism to which the editors of most dailies address their editorials. He loved other people to tell him what to think, unless they tried to do it in his own bar and then he could be virtuously obstinate in the face of the most exacting logic. He was an Englishman, he loved sport, loved the noisy enthusiasm of football crowds, the excitement of coursing and the risk of horse-racing. In the back chamber of his mind, not very far from the surface, crouched the lusting emotions of the tribesmen who had been his forerunners; and at the prospect of hunting a criminal his arteries swelled with the increased beat of his heart and the palms of his hands moistened a little with sweat. He was a hunter who hunted without care for aught but the joy of chasing, of holding and killing.

Paul was conscious of the open suspicion and subversive feeling that flowed about the coach from one passenger to another. They said nothing, they sat brooding with dark thoughts, but the emanation of their secret thoughts seemed to come back to him like a wave, a wide-spreading, sky-reaching wave that hung above him interminably, threatening to break and engulf him. He could partly guess at and appreciate their emotions, and he wished that he could rise to his feet and explain himself, explain that he was not Peter Angel, but that was an impossibility. He was sure that nothing could persuade them or shift them from their own convictions. He sat wondering whether any more would be said of him. Only from Mr. Partingale did he derive any support. The little man smiled across at him reassuringly, yet even beneath his mildness, Paul sensed that there was a certain asperity; Mr. Partingale had not forgotten he had criticised and deprecated his theory of the omnipotence of money.

The coach plunged through a small town whose streets were alive with men and women on bicycles pouring from a large factory and then, when it was well into the country again, it stopped outside a small hotel to give the passengers an opportunity to obtain refreshments and stretch their legs.

Paul got down with the other passengers, but he did not go inside with them. He sat on a bench in the front of the hotel and watched a gardener potting flowers. He was glad of the few moments' respite from the unpleasant tension of the coach. The rest of the passengers went inside and with them went the driver and conductor.

From his seat Paul could just catch the mumble of their voices but they were too far away for him to hear what they were saying. He guessed that they were probably talking about him. Had he been able to overhear distinctly what they were saying he would not have sat back so easily on his bench and smoked his pipe. He watched a robin fidgeting around the gardener in the hope of worms as he turned the soil.

"Going to be a nice day, after all," said Paul, longing to have someone to whom he could speak without awakening the fear of being recognised. The gardener, either because he was deaf or had no desire for conversation, made no reply. He just went on methodically planting out his flowers as though nothing else in the world mattered or could affect his occupation. Paul envied the man his placidity.

VIII
Music hath charms

After a little while the passengers came out and Paul climbed into the coach with them. As the coach moved off Paul gathered the impression that, whereas they had gone into the hotel a heterogeneous collection of individuals with no concern for one another, they were now banded together, and welded into a unit which for the moment had only one purpose. The atmosphere of suspicion seemed entirely absent, yet in its place was a smug, contented air of assurance, as though they had all come to a decision which was entirely to their liking. Paul wondered what had happened and whether he had been a fool to continue with the journey. He sat smoking in the back seat, his body lifting and falling with the rise of the coach until his pipe was spent. Then, as he knocked the dottle out and placed the pipe in his pocket, a strange thing happened. The coach was passing through a thick beech wood when slowly it slackened pace and finally came to a halt. Paul looked up, surprised, and as the driver got down from his seat and came round to the door of the coach to join the conductor, he had time to observe that he was the only person evincing surprise. The driver swung himself up the steps and standing just inside the door, looked first at Mr. Freeman and then at Paul, and Paul looked first at the passengers and then at the driver.

"What's the matter?" he asked the man. "Anything wrong with the engine?"

The driver, his lips seemingly glued together, nodded towards Mr. Freeman, and Paul looking in that gentleman's direction saw that he had risen from his seat and, coming a little way down the gangway, was pulling at his coat lapels like a tradesman councillor about to make a speech at a local flower-show.

"What is all the trouble?" asked Paul, though at heart he knew that this halt could only mean one thing.

"Just this," said Mr. Freeman quickly, as though he were glad of Paul's remark which gave him the opportunity to start his speech at a cogent point; "Me and the rest of the ladies and gentlemen in this coach—" he looked round and got the slight murmur of approval which was due from them, "—have 'ad a little discussion while we was 'aving lunch—"

"And what has that to do with me—if it has?" asked Paul, regaining his confidence now that the preliminaries were on their way.

"Just this, mister whatever your name is." Mr. Freeman looked round for approbation as he scored this point. "We've decided that as true British citizens what believe in keeping their King and Country first, we've got a duty to do. Mind you, we want to play fair. Fair play's a jewel. But there's something what 'as got to be faced and I'm not the man to shirk it."

"What are you talking about?" Paul stood up and at the movement everyone but the driver and Mr. Freeman started expectantly.

"About you, mister whatever your name is. We want to know who you are and what you are. That's a fair enough question and you know why we're asking it. If you can answer that satisfactorily then we'll say no more and the thing's over and done with and everyone concerned 'as acted like gentlemen."

"He won't tell the truth, though. Men never do!" Mrs. Grabhurst rose to her feet and shrilled the words at Paul,

"Now then, now then—" Mr. Connor turned on her. "We agreed that Mr. Freeman should be the speaker, didn't we? Well, you hold on then. Now, this is how it is," said Mr. Connor, addressing Paul. "We've got our suspicions of you, mister, from the photograph in the paper, and—"

"I'm doing this," said Mr. Freeman quickly, eager to retain his privilege of spokesman. "Listen, mister, we don't mean no offence and we 'ope you won't take none, and if you agree with us there's only one thing to be done."

"And what's that?" asked Paul.

"He's Peter Angel, all right," came Miss Rayner's voice in the pause which followed this question.

"Just this. We'll go along to the next town and stop for a few minutes at the police station and you can give your name and address to the sergeant and then the matter's finished."

"Yes—that's all." Mr. Connor was speaking and his rotund face was alive with excitement at this unusual incident which was happening in his life. For years he had done little more exciting than slice potatoes into chips, clean fish and listen to the sizzle of fat in the vats, but now he was on the brink of a tremendous happening which would focus upon him perhaps the limelight of publicity. Even as he spoke he was mentally assessing the advertisement value to his business of this adventure.

"If you're not Peter Angel, I'm sure we'll all apologise handsomely, and if you are—" He shrugged his large shoulders.

"Say what is this?" inquired Paul, with a little smile twisting his lips. "A lynching party? I thought England was a free country?"

"So it is, mister, so it is—and that's why we're bothering about you," said Mr. Freeman.

"Yes—we're suspicious!" shrilled Mrs. Grabhurst. "You won't deny that you're an American, will you?" Paul eyed this vociferous lady for a second and then replied politely: "My dear madam, of course, I wouldn't. But if you're going about the country holding up every innocent American on suspicion of being Peter Angel, then the American Embassy are going to be putting in overtime dealing with grievances from my countrymen."

"Then you are an American?" put in Mr. Partingale quietly.

"I certainly am!" declared Paul firmly, and added to himself, "and if you lot of English folk think that you can hold me up like this and get away with it you're mistaken." He had done nothing wrong and he was beginning to resent the interference of the passengers. If he told them the whole story it was extremely unlikely that they would believe it, and he certainly had no intention of being interviewed by the police, if he could possibly prevent it. Once the police got hold of him he did not know what might happen, and he decided to guard against such a contingency by avoiding it.

"There you are—I knew it, I knew it all the time! He's Peter Angel." Miss Rayner pointed an accusing finger at Paul, who took no notice of her eager condemnation.

"But I assure you, ladies and gentlemen, that I am not Peter Angel. Isn't that enough for you without pursuing this farce any further? If you take me to a police station and get my particulars then the story will probably get into the press and you'll look a fine lot for having made such a mistake. You'll be the laughing stock of the country." Paul played upon their cherished dignities in the hope of making them relinquish their idea. He had not the slightest intention of meekly following them to a police station, but before he took other action he decided to explore the possibility of turning them by ridicule from the plan which they had evolved over their lunch.

"We'll take that risk," said Mr. Freeman stoutly. "We've got to do that. It's our duty and we ain't going to shirk it. Live and let live's me motto, and you can't expect us to rightly believe that you ain't Peter Angel unless you go to the police with us. I don't say I don't believe you or not. That ain't the point. You're a gentleman, that's plain, and as a gentleman it shouldn't be hard for you to agree to what, as everyone else here is agreed, is the sensible thing to do. Now what do you say?"

Paul did not know whether to be flattered or annoyed at Mr. Freeman's liberal interpretation of his social standing. He was a gentleman and as such was required to put his head into the noose of the law. Even in the midst of his consternation he could afford a moment to chuckle at their grotesque seriousness and stubbornness. They were all so ludicrous in their cross-examination and intenseness. As he stood facing them the whole affair seemed like some bad parody of a film situation.

"You're all making a big mistake. I tell you I'm not Peter Angel. I'm an honest American, a hard-working American now having a holiday in England. I certainly didn't expect to be mistaken for a crooner when I left home. That gives me a laugh."

None of the others was amused. They continued to face him with hostile, suspicious and inquiring stares.

Miss Rayner broke the silence. "He's him all right!" she muttered.

"I wouldn't believe him, not if he said he was the Shah of Persia," Mrs. Grabhurst added; her capacity for doubting men was unlimited.

Then Mr. Partingale, who had been hardly more than an interested spectator of the entire proceedings, spoke.

"I think that this affair is tending towards unpleasantness," he remarked quietly, "and that is hardly fair to this gentleman, who, it is more than probable, is quite innocent of all you suspect. Let us try and act like rational human beings and not like schoolchildren—" He waved Mr. Connor's incipient protest into submission, and because he had been the least enthusiastic at their lunchtime conference and the most level-headed in his doubts of Paul's integrity, they listened to him with respect. "You want proof that this young man is not Peter Angel. He looks something like him we agree, but beyond that we have nothing, If you take him to the police they can verify his credentials and if he is innocent that may land you in some trouble. Already, I may say, he has told me in private conversation that he is an engineer, and I myself think it quite likely that you are all mistaken; but apart from what I think, I know that you are quite right to be anxious to do all you can to bring a wanted man to justice. It is the proper thing to do. Now, let us be sane about it all. There is one proof which we can try here in this coach which will finally settle the matter in a way which can reflect upon us no discredit or undue publicity."

"What's that?" The chicken-farmer jerked his small head forward, like a giraffe darting at a leaf.

"The police station's the only proof I'll accept," insisted Miss Rayner.

"Please, please … Let's hear what the gentleman has to say." Mr. Connor waved his flabby hands, caressing the air. "What other way is there?" he asked.

"This—" Mr. Partingale, as he spoke, was looking at Paul, and Paul guessed that this man, although he was trying to calm the others, had very definite ideas as to his identity. "If this gentleman is Peter Angel, he will be able to sing, if he is not then he won't be able to sing. I suggest that we ask him to give us a song. That'll be all the proof we need."

This suggestion caused a stir in the coach. Paul opened his mouth to protest and then shut it again. As an engineer he was acknowledged to be an expert, but as a singer, his abilities called forth no eulogies. At college be had been dubbed the Bullfrog and in the depth of a lusty male chorus his voice had that peculiar disturbing quality which put everyone off the right note. Even on the football field, his voice when raised to a shout, never failed to distract attention from the most thrilling moment.

"That's a good idea!" roared Mr. Freeman. "A darned good idea!"

"Yes—let him sing us a song and we shall soon know!" called Mr. Connor.

"But, I can't do … I …" Paul looked around helplessly. He would rather go to the police, he thought, than do this.

"Now then, young man," said Mr. Partingale kindly. "Let's have a song and finish this nonsense. We're wasting time."

"But is this necessary, I mean … my voice … It's …" He was going to say not at all good.

"Come on—give us a song and get it over," urged Mr. Connor.

"Either that or the police!" snapped the chicken-farmer.

For one moment Paul considered the police. Then he decided to make the supreme effort. It was a safer, if more exacting, way out.

He stood up firmly, his brain working quickly as he tried to think of a song. Of the hundreds of songs he had maltreated in his college days, not one could he remember. He gripped the back of the seat with one hand and with the other rubbed his throat as though he were anticipating the first stage of strangulation.

"As you like," he murmured weakly, and he drew a deep breath. He held the breath some time and then expelled it because he could think of no song.

He breathed again, and the sound of the intake whispered along the low vault of the coach like the rustle of mice behind a wainscoting.

"Come on!" grumbled Miss Rayner irritably. Paul looked at her gratefully and expelled his breath again.

"Just a second, please. I'm not used to this kind of thing ..." They made no reply but stared at him uncompromisingly as judges.

A flicker of relief enlivened Paul's features as he thought of a song and then, screwing up his eyes and releasing his hold on his throat, he began to sing. His head was thrown back with the extravagant gesture of a town-crier, his whole body vibrated with the energy behind his words, and he was in an agony of self-consciousness, but he forced himself to go on.

The coach party started. Mr. Connor, who had once been a choirboy, sat down heavily. The chicken-farmer shut his eyes so that he might not have to see as well as hear the wonder, and Mrs. Grabhurst, who had a bad voice and knew it, secretly congratulated herself.

The noise which Paul was making was terrible. Had he been asked to imitate the rattle of two trains passing in a tunnel and blowing their whistles at the same time, no one would have questioned his virtuosity. Mr. Partingale regarded him with genuine alarm. It did not seem possible that a human voice could combine the intense shriek of a file being drawn across metal with the barbaric snarls that accompany jungle films. Yet it was possible. Paul outshrieked the largest file and would have put to shame a chorus of baboons.

Fortunately, Paul kept his eyes shut and did not appreciate the effect of his song on the company. He stood, like a first mate in the midst of a Cape Horn snorter, bawling his words and determined that all should hear. Audibility, Paul knew, was one of the chief points in singing.

Mr. Partingale, who was well-travelled, and the most cultured man in the coach, recognised, after a while, what Paul was trying to sing.

"It's the *Star-Spangled Banner*," he whispered to Mr. Connor. But that gentleman was leaning forward on his seat, his face wrinkled in pain and his hands clapped over his ears.

Mrs. Grabhurst heard, however, and the whisper passed round the coach.

"*O'er the land of the free and the home of the brave ...*" The last line jangled on the air for a few seconds and then died. Paul opened his eyes, let his body adopt a natural stance and gazed round the coach with a satisfied air. He was innocent of the havoc he had made. He was sure though that he had convinced them he was not Peter Angel.

"Well," he said. "What do you think now?"

Mr. Partingale looked at him sadly and shook his head.

"I'm afraid," he said gently, "it'll be some time before I've recovered enough to think."

"I don't know what you mean?"

"I mean," went on Mr. Partingale, "that we should probably have been wiser to have taken your word that you weren't Peter Angel."

"So you're sure now?" Paul looked from one to another and found himself regarding faces that portrayed horror, wonder and consternation.

"That's a voice, you've got, mister!" breathed Mr. Freeman admiringly. "I thought I only had to say 'Time, gentlemen, please' to clear my bar, but if I had you working for me, you could clear every bar in the district at one go." He laughed easily, and Paul taking the joke in good part, smiled indulgently.

It is doubtful whether they would have further questioned Paul. But from the top of the coach came Mrs. Grabhurst's voice.

"Ha! Very clever, I don't think. Very clever! But anyone can pretend not to be able to sing. That's easy!"

This outburst provoked some support and weakened the feeling which was growing that Paul could not be Peter Angel.

"Yes, and not only that—what did you have to sing the American National Anthem for?" Miss Rayner resented Paul's choice of a song. It was, now that the possibility of his being the man she thought him was slipping away, the one thing with which she could find fault. "What's wrong with *God Save the King*? He's Peter Angel all right, otherwise he wouldn't have chosen that song. Just like his cheek."

"Please, please ..." Mr. Partingale attempted to sooth the angry woman.

"Aye, there's something in that," Mr. Freeman agreed, rather laboriously. "It ain't 'ardly decent to sing the *Star Bangled Banner* over here. We don't want no American stuff. It's an insult to the King!"

Paul realised too late how unfortunate his choice of song had been. It was just like these stubborn, insular people to take umbrage at such a thing. They seemed to forget that his sole point had been to disprove the contention that he was Peter Angel.

"Oh, come, come," Mr. Partingale interposed; "this gentleman has given us enough proof now that he isn't Peter Angel. We must drop this matter and apologise to him."

"Apologise—drop the matter! Not us!" Mr. Connor, seeing the way the others were inclined, came to their aid with a loud outburst. "We'll see this through. It's a duty! I'm not taking that as proof—not me!" The more he thought of it the more certain he was that such a horrible noise could only have been a false exhibition. No ordinary voice was like that.

"All right," agreed Paul, trying to be patient in the face of their supreme illogicalness. "If you don't like that song, I'll sing *God Save the King*." Without waiting for their approval he stood up bravely preparing to sing again. Mr. Freeman, revolting at the suggestion of his travestying the English National Anthem, waved him down quickly.

"No more singing, no more singing—that don't mean a thing. It's better for you to come along to the police station."

Paul drew a deep breath and plunged his hands into his jacket pockets with a gesture of exasperation. He was reaching the limit of his control. It was hopeless to tell these people the truth, and he certainly had no intention of being taken to a police station. He had hoped by singing to have made the identification of himself quite clear. Now, however, in a pig-headed fashion these people refused to accept this final proof. He felt that he had sufficient justification for losing his temper.

"And what if I refuse to go with you to the police station? I consider I've given you enough proof. Can't you believe now that I'm not Peter Angel?" Under the stuff of his suit Paul's shoulders and body stiffened with anger. He'd show these small-minded, slow-witted islanders that they couldn't trifle with him.

Mr. Freeman paused before he replied. He fidgeted with his lapels, smoothed the backs of his hands and his small eyes roved in their sockets like those of a pike that lurks in the weeds waiting for minnows. He felt, did this publican, that he had the honour of the English police force and the well-being of the nation with him, and he had to make an important decision. He glanced round for moral support before replying. He caught Mrs. Grabhurst's steely eyes, Miss Rayner's sneering lips; he saw Mr. Connor, fat, solid, indignant and suspicious; he passed quickly by Mr. Partingale's mild eyes and half-humorous smile to the worried, anxious chicken-farmer, and then to the broad, unintelligent faces of the driver and the conductor. The driver was holding in his oily hand a spanner which he had been concealing behind his back. The appearance of the spanner gave Mr. Freeman more moral support than the sight of his fellows, it enriched his self-confidence and lent to him a sensation of power and domination.

"I'm sorry, mister," he said at last; "but—without offence—we can't take your word or singing as a proof. You must come along to the police station." Having delivered this ultimatum Mr. Freeman wiped the back of his hand across his mouth and watched Paul closely.

As the man finished speaking there flared up in Paul an immense anger and indignation at the perversity of these people. The whole affair had been undignified and childish. He was in no mood for rational thought. He was conscious only of his intense annoyance at their stupid insistence. Logically, perhaps, the wisest thing would have been to submit gracefully to their proposals; emotionally there was only one course and that was to defy them. And Paul at that moment was more full of angry emotion than cold logic. He felt himself filled with a wild fire that ran through his body and gave him a rashness and boldness which ordinarily were foreign to him. His hand in his pocket closed over the bowl of his pipe and at the contact he was filled with an impish joy. He held the pipe in a tight grip.

"You won't believe me, eh?" He jerked the words out and there was about them an incisiveness which for the first time induced a tense, dramatic note into the situation. Before it had been a ludicrous, seriocomic imbroglio, but now that had all passed and he knew that his only resort was in action, quick, striking action. "Well, that's too bad, too bad. You think you're pretty good as policemen, don't you? Why, a child could kid you and get away with it. Now, listen, if you don't believe me, you don't; but that's as far as it goes. But I'm not coming to the station with you. Steady—" he cried as Mr. Freeman and the driver made a move for him. "You'd better not move because I mean business!" As he spoke he pushed the stem of his pipe against his jacket so that it pointed straight at the driver. Paul was as surprised as the passengers by the harsh tone of his utterances. He was discovering a new personality within himself. It was a few seconds before the significance of this movement penetrated the wakened perceptions of the group. Then Miss Rayner saw the protuberant pocket and screamed.

"Cut the noise!" commanded Paul, and he motioned the driver to move into the coach. The man obeyed, dropping his spanner, at a movement from Paul's pocket. "Now stay there and try to behave sensibly. You wouldn't believe me before, but I guess the gun will settle all your doubts."

It took them some time to habilitate themselves to this new turn of events. Mrs. Grabhurst clutched at her handbag anxiously and Mr. Freeman licked his lips nervously.

"I'm sorry to have to frighten you like this," said Paul to the ladies, lifting his grip with his free hand; "yet as an American citizen, I resent this treatment and I feel justified in taking the law into my own hands. Once more, I assure you all that I am not Peter Angel. And now, goodbye!"

Still keeping his pipe directed towards the group he backed from the coach. His movement towards freedom had a very definite effect. It convinced them all that he was Peter Angel and it showed that they were letting slip by them an opportunity to reap the reward of fame. The driver, who was regretting his lost spanner, looked at the menacing pocket as Paul backed and into his brain came a slow idea. It was possible that this man was only bluffing. As he turned the suggestion around in his mind he became enamoured with the possibility and suddenly found himself imbued with a strange courage. For years he had driven coaches and nothing had happened to him more exciting than running over hares and chickens, but now he was face to face with a crook, and with a shock he realised that once his first fear had gone he was full of daring.

"Garn!" He looked around quickly. "He's bluffing us. I'll bet he's not got a gun. Come on, don't let him get away."

No one came to his support but, undeterred, he took a step forward. Paul, realising that his bluff was slipping, jerked his pocket forward. The driver, left to himself, threw all caution from him and jumped forward. Everyone waited for the sharp crack of Paul's revolver and everyone but the driver was surprised to hear only Paul's light laugh as he withdrew his hand from his pocket and, leaping down the coach steps, started to run.

"I said so!" cried the driver exultantly. "Come on!"

His cry rallied the others. Released from the threat of a revolver they found their courage and as Paul dashed across the road they poured from the coach in pursuit.

"After him!" yelled Mr. Connor.

"Don't let him get away!" shouted Mr. Freeman.

"He's our man!" screamed the chicken-farmer.

"We'll show him," panted Mrs. Grabhurst.

"I said so—he's Peter Angel!" affirmed Miss Rayner. And together they bundled from the coach and took up the chase. Only the conductor, who suffered from rheumatism, and Mr. Partingale, who was now pretty sure that Paul was Peter Angel, appreciated the absurdity of trying to catch a healthy young man who was running to save his freedom.

They retained their seats in the coach to wait until the others should return, and Mr. Partingale took out his notebook to make a memorandum of Mr. Connor's address so that he might send him a set of blue and white tiles for his saloon.

IX
Out of the frying-pan

Paul crossed the road in three strides, vaulted a gate and was running as hard as he could down a beech drove before the first of his pursuers had reached the gate. He had no doubt that he would be able to outdistance the coach party. He decided to take no chances with them. Holding his grip firmly in his hand, he stretched his legs and ran down the drove which faced the gateway at top speed. His feet made a crisp, rustling noise on the dead leaves that lingered in the grass and he trod heedlessly on the frail anemone leaves that still showed their fresh green, though their flowers had long ago withered and died. High in the branches of a beech a jay heralded the cavalcade as it straggled over the gateway and panted into the drove. The driver led the way, his faced red with courage and exertion and his arms jerking rhythmically at his sides like one of his coach's connecting rods. Behind him came Mr. Freeman, his great body moving up and down over the uneven ground like a four-master making heavy weather round the Cape; and after Mr. Freeman bunched Mr. Connor and the chicken-farmer, both panting and blowing but filled with a lusty desire to catch Paul and so accomplish their duty towards the rest of the country. And in their wake came the two women—Mrs. Grabhurst holding her umbrella at the ready like a lancer, and Miss Rayner keeping her small straw hat in place with one hand in a manner that greatly impeded her speed.

Through the wood they went in hot pursuit and as they went all the creatures of the wood knew that they were there. The noise of their plunging and shouting echoed through the silences of the trees and woke the birds and beasts to awareness. A green woodpecker stopped its tapping and remained a broken branch until they had passed. In the bushy bole of a beech a robin squatted low on her eggs and wondered at the strange interruption of the wood's serenity, and a hare lying in its form of downtrodden grasses got up at their noise and flashed between the smooth trunks, leaping the rising woodsage and fallen branches.

It seemed to Paul as though the wood would never end. He passed clumps of elder that hung white flower bunches against the grey background of beech trunks, struggled through narrow openings in young hazel pallisades, and always behind him he could hear the crash of feet over the dead leaves and the leafy protest of low-lying boughs where Mr. Freeman and the driver drove a way for their fellows. And as he ran a quick elation began to conquer Paul. He knew that he should have been worried, but his mind refused to take anything seriously. Even if he were caught it would have been no more than a glorious game; yet in the minds of his followers there was no humour. To them the chase was serious. Life was a grim, exacting business and they were no actors in a wild burlesque, but serious individuals with a purpose and a plan.

Mrs. Grabhurst flourished her umbrella as she staggered and felt her breath going from her. For two hundred yards she had run with all her strength and then, like a car running short of petrol, she gave two or three sharp coughs and came to a standstill, her umbrella point lowered in defeat and her body quivering with the force of her violent breathing. She watched Miss Rayner trail away in the wake of the men and then was nearly scared from her wits by the sudden flapping chatter of a magpie that flew away from a thorn bush by the side of the path.

Another hundred yards saw the end of Miss Rayner. A patch of wet, decaying leaves which the sun never struck caused her downfall. She felt her legs skid, knew her body was toppling and then, in a wild flurry of mud and leaves, slid sideways to the earth with her hand still triumphantly holding her straw hat in place while the other probed with unwilling fingers into the soft, treacly mud and leaves.

The men still panted in the rear of Paul, losing ground at every step, for Paul ran with legs that derived additional energy and life from the spirits which rose high within him.

The wood cleared before him and he was coming out into an open space occupied by a small artificial lake. The water lay very still and black under the clouded sky. Its surface reflected the grey pallor of the clouds and stared solemnly upwards as though mourning for the death of the leaves that fell each autumn in great drifts into its depths. Around the edges tall reeds and sedges grew, and yellow points of colour showed irises. As Paul neared the lake a coot rose quickly from the surface and with trailing legs disappeared into the safety of the woods. Across the lake, which was no more than fifty feet wide, ran a low ornamental wooden bridge built of small timbers and green with moss. On to the bridge Paul thundered, his echoing footsteps frightening the carp and dace that loved to lie in the shade of the bridge. And, two minutes after Paul had crossed, the driver appeared and was after him. And close behind the driver came Mr. Freeman. His face was redder and his panting heavier as he breasted the slight slope to the bridge. His first step on to its boards was his last, for his rubber soles got no grip from the soft coating of moss that decorated the rotting boards. His foot shot up, his body lurched backwards and with a quick gravity that was somehow in keeping with the ponderousness of his whole personality, he sat down and stayed down, too exhausted to rise; and there, as he sat, came Mr. Connor and the chicken-farmer to join him. The moss betrayed Mr. Connor as it had betrayed Mr. Freeman and he, too, fell ungracefully to the ground. With his progress blocked and his speed too great to allow him to reduce it in time to avoid them, the chicken-farmer had no alternative but to fall upon them. He fell, and in falling struck Mr. Freeman a sharp blow on the back of the head and thumped Mr. Connor in the rear with a sound like the half-hearted explosion of a paper bag.

"Eh!" The exclamation came from Mr. Freeman and Mr. Connor simultaneously. "Mind yourself!" But their warning was too late. Rebounding from them with the impetus of his own speed the chicken-farmer rolled slowly down the bank, grasping at the dock-leaves and spikes of wild parsnip for support and came gravely to rest in a sitting position in the shallow water, his hair tangled with the tenacious embrace of goose-weed.

For four seconds the chicken-farmer was too stupefied to move, and then with an unpleasant sensation about his trousers which had been unknown to him since he was an infant, he struggled out of the shallows.

"We'd better give it up," said Mr. Connor, rising and rubbing himself.

"He's too fast for me," said Mr. Freeman. And then, with a satisfied glance at the chicken-farmer's discomfort, he felt the back of his head and muttered something about clumsiness which went unheard, for at that moment the bridge began to vibrate with footsteps and the coach-driver appeared, panting and swinging his peaked cap in one hand.

"He's got away all right," he said in reply to their unspoken question. "Too fast. He can run."

"What do we do now, then?" asked the chicken-farmer, squelching up the bank and freeing his hair from goose-grass.

"Go back to the coach and get on with the journey. I've wasted too much time already. I've got my job to think of."

"That's about the only thing to do. We can notify the police at the next town. We shall have done our duty," Mr. Freeman advised. "'Tain't safe for fellows like that to be loose. Danger to society."

Saddened by their failure, but not despondent since they could still inform the police, the party slowly made its way back through the woods. And as they went Paul lay nearly a mile away in a field resting after his run. Above him in the grey sea of the sky a choir of larks was filling the world with sound, and about him in the fescue and meadow grasses small insects and flies filled their own little world with song and strife. A small brown butterfly perched on top of a mallow and signalled to him with stiff wings and, unknown to him, a grass snake slithered silently away to find security and peace beneath a rotting log in the lee of the hedge. From the crest of a field beyond the wood he had seen the driver turn back and he knew that he was free from pursuit for a while.

When he had rested Paul picked up his grip and followed the field path until it brought him to a road. It did not look like a main road to him, with the image of American main roads in his mind, yet it was, and only two minutes before he reached it the coach from which he had escaped had passed by, for the chase had taken him round in a semicircle. He walked along the road, unconscious of his danger, until he came to a village.

The village was built about the three sides of a triangle. On one side was an inn with a sign that swung out from a cluster of clematis vines, on the other stood a grey-stoned church with tilting tombstones and an ivy-covered tower, round which a pair of jackdaws were flying, and on the third dozed a row of cottages fenced with rotten wood palisades, swaying at crazy angles and supported in places by a luxuriant growth of periwinkle and white convolvulus. Between the church and the cottages was a small wicket gate leading away to fields, and in the distance the country rose to a small roll of hills crested with clumps of elm and beech.

Paul pushed his hat back for comfort and, because he had not yet decided what he should do, he strolled to the middle of the triangle to inspect the ornate fountain which disgraced the simplicity of the buildings of the village. Four cherubim, in a permanent state of inflation, puffed water through their lips at a contorted dolphin in whose open mouth two tiny ferns had taken root, bathing their fresh green fronds in the spray. In the pool around this statuary floated an unhealthy collection of frayed cigarette ends, waterlogged matchboxes and ears of corn where horses had shaken their food bags, and in the water, lonely like a galleon from an armada that finds itself stranded in some dirty backwater, wandered a goldfish, its eyes glassy with the fading memory of happier days and its mouth working rhythmically. Paul felt sorry for the fish. Somehow its plight seemed a parallel to his own. They were both in strange surroundings, both used to different lives, and both committed to an existence whose chief element so far was a perpetual limitation of freedom. Full of sympathy he picked up a breadcrust which lay on the cobbles and, breaking it, dropped the crumbs into the water for the fish. As he did so he heard a car enter the square behind him and draw up. Without looking round he went on dropping the crumbs, but the fish, used to an enforced diet of cigarette ends and the slimy weed which coated the sides of the fountain, waved a lazy tail and disregarded the manna that drifted slowly down through the brown water.

Paul dropped the last crumb, mentally classed the fish as one of those stubborn fools who do not know what is good for them, and then straightened up. A shadow fell across him and he observed in one swift glance two things: a long green car which was vaguely familiar, and a woman, whose brown hair and straight figure were definitely familiar.

He could not believe the evidence of his eyes, and then as though to confirm what he saw was no illusion, the woman spoke.

"Peter! Peter—why do you keep running away from me?" Margaret Sinclair moved forward quickly to grasp him by his coat lapels and her action woke Paul to life. Here she was again! He ducked to avoid her grasp and, as he doubled and made for the wicket-gate by the church, he caught from the corner of his eye a vision of Margaret stumbling on the edge of the fountain as she tried to save herself from falling under the impetus of her forward movement. Paul did not stop to see more. He reached the gate in twelve strides, was through it and away across the fields as fast as he could run. And from behind him he heard a shout as Margaret, undaunted, took up the chase.

Paul was a good runner and he was confident that he could soon shake her off. He sped across the field, which was a yellow and green enamel with kingcups, over a stile in the hedge and then up the slope of the hills riddled with rabbit burrows. And behind him, losing a little, but still fresh, came Margaret, and there was a firm twist to her mouth and an angry glint in her eyes. This time she would catch him and settle matters. She ran doggedly behind, determined not to give up the chase, and as she ran her right foot squelched noisily where she had been obliged to put it into the fountain to save herself from a total immersion. And the sun, as though it had saved all its splendour for that moment, chased away the lofty cloud masses and bathed the whole scene in strong light.

The birds from their hedge-perches, watched and sang; a chaffinch bobbed from one whitethorn branch to another and encouraged Paul with a melody; a lark rose from under Margaret's feet and swore beautifully as it soared, and the grasses shook their feathery plumes in the wind of their passing and whispered rude comments to the trembling trefoils and the wide-eyed speedwells. Overhead a couple of rooks tumbled and cawed, wondering at the actions of the two, and young rabbits sat on the edge of their holes and held their paws up in devotional attitudes until the thud of feet sent them scampering into the dark recesses of the hill-side.

But neither of them had eyes for the things about them. Paul saw the clumps of beech as something he had to reach and pass. He had no time to admire the smooth glory of their trunks or watch the grey squirrels moving in arched leaps along the outstretched branches, and Margaret had no time for the trailing dog-roses and scented wild briar except to mutter an impatient word as they reached for her dress and drew sibilant fingers across its material.

Whether Paul would have escaped from Margaret in a straight flight, or how long Margaret could have endured the pace, are matters which will always remain unsettled. Paul could perhaps have overcome and worn down Margaret's physical abilities. He was no match, however, for the geographical formation of the country over which he ran. He crested the hilltop and in long strides tore down the other slope, and half-way down he was aware that before him lay a river. Not a wide river, but too wide to be jumped. It flowed, very deep and very dark, beneath low banks that were fringed with stiff willow rods and decorated by bosses of celandine that admired their reflection in the cool waters and sometimes washed their leaves in the swift spates that followed summer thunder showers. Paul saw the river and hesitated. For a second he thought of swimming, but as quickly rejected the idea. Then away to the right, behind an island of alders and birch, he caught the grey glint of a bridge. Like a hare doubling before a greyhound he swerved away to the right along the river bank. It was this action which gave him to Margaret. She reached the hilltop and saw him running along the river's edge, saw that he was making for the bridge, and saw that by taking the hypotenuse of the triangle she could, if she sprinted, reach it at the same time as he did. Why she never broke her ankle in a pot-hole, or how she negotiated the two hedges in her way, Margaret never quite understood. She ran as she had never run before and when she reached the bridge her whole inside was dull with exhaustion and, as she clung to Paul's ankle as he was about to climb the parapet of the bridge on to the roadway, she wondered whether her breathing could ever become normal again.

Paul, realising that he was caught sat, half on the bridge and half in the air, waiting for Margaret to speak. He felt very foolish with a young woman clinging to his ankle in such a way that his trouser was ruffled up and exposed two inches of hairy leg and a purple suspender clasp. Margaret, before speaking, tightened her grasp on his leg, placed her foot in a niche of the parapet and hoisted herself inelegantly alongside of him.

"Now, Peter Angel!" she said breathlessly, "will you please explain this foolishness before I finally lose my temper with you and call the police!"

"I ... I ... I ..." Paul did not know what to say. He was so confused that he could not think logically for a time. "You shouldn't follow me," he said at last.

Margaret looked at him curiously. "What ever do you mean? Shouldn't follow you? But aren't you my fiancé? Haven't I a perfect right to see you? Whatever is the matter with you—acting in this perfectly absurd manner?"

Paul heaved a deep breath. What was he to do with such a girl?

"Surely you've read the newspapers?" He gained time for himself with an evasive question.

"I have," she replied, "and what about them?"

"But you know what I've done. At least ..."

"I don't care what you've done. You know I love you, Peter, and that's enough for me. You must have had some good reason for doing it. And anyway, if people were stupid enough to be taken in by it—then they deserve to lose their money."

Paul was aghast at this attitude. "But you can't mean that?"

"I do," said Margaret firmly, and, although Paul did not notice it, a light had come into her grey eyes which had not been there when she had stepped into the fountain. "I know father and other people would think it shocking, but that's one of my theories. If people persist in being foolish then they've only themselves to blame when someone clever like yourself comes along and exploits their foolishness."

"But ... but ... oh, what am I to do? Why did I get into this mess?" Paul could contain himself no longer. He wished he were safely back in New York, or quietly idling in Wisbech, anywhere but with this girl and the confusion which she had created.

"Do!" Margaret laughed and then laid her hand tenderly on his shoulder. "Peter, dear, you do love me, don't you?"

Paul looked at her. At that moment he was far from loving anyone, and for her he felt a positive dislike which—had society been such that he was at liberty to carry his emotions into action—he might have characterised by pushing her backwards from the bridge into the river.

"Say you do, Peter ..." Her hair was blown over her forehead and her face, flushed with running, was very pretty. Paul hesitated. He was, with her, still Peter Angel and a peculiar loyalty to the real Peter Angel told him that he had no authority to tell the girl that he didn't love her. The real Peter Angel still did love her and perhaps was trying to get into touch with her.

The position was very puzzling. He knew very little of this young woman, certainly not enough, he considered, to justify his taking her into his confidence. She might go at once to the police, she might even refuse to believe him. If he wanted to preserve his precious liberty he would have to act with the greatest circumspection. It would not be long before he could slip away from her, perhaps only a matter of a few hours—until then, he decided, the best thing to do was to pretend to be Peter Angel. Then, once he had left her, the difficulty would be solved, for she would not trouble him again.

"Well ..." Paul muttered nervously, "you're making it very difficult for me, Margaret, in my position." It was the first time he had used her name, and as he spoke he saw that she was watching him with a new expression on her face.

"But you haven't answered my question, Peter." As Margaret spoke there was a humorous hint in her voice which, had Paul not been so occupied with his own anxieties, might have been apparent to him and aroused his curiosity. "Peter, say you love me ..."

Paul ran his fingers through his hair with a gesture of capitulation. It was entirely against his principles to assume the love which belonged to another man, but necessity forced him to it. "All right—if that's what you want. You know I love you."

"Peter, darling," she drew closer to him on the wall and, while the water made little runnels of sound as it swept by the grey arches and drew forth long streamers of green where it caressed the waving flannel weeds, she took his arm and laid her head on his shoulder. "And I love you."

Paul would have enjoyed her gesture had he been able to free his mind of the thought that he was usurping another's privilege. As it was he sternly repressed a desire to put his arm round her, and shifted awkwardly. He might have been less, or even more uncomfortable could he have read Margaret's thoughts.

"But—" Paul woke to an urgent realisation of the awkwardness of his position. "—we can't sit here for ever. You must leave me and not see me any more until this trouble has blown over. If I were caught and it was known that you had been aware of my whereabouts—why!" he waved his free arm to express the immensity of trouble which would descend upon her.

Margaret sat up and her face had assumed a serious cast. Only the sunlight playing about the tips of her lashes and gilding the faint down on her cheek seemed to belie the concern of her eyes. "But, Peter, darling, I'm not going to leave you. My place is with you. You are an outcast because you have proved too clever for society, and I shall stay with you, to help you and to give you my sympathy and encouragement in times of trial. Oh, I shall love being with you and fearing every policeman. Look at me—look, I've almost got a haunted look in my eyes already!" She laughed and squeezed his arm tightly.

"But ... but ..." Paul was helpless. Why couldn't she understand that he did not want her. "You can't do that, Margaret! It's—it's not right."

"Why not? I love you—isn't it natural that I should be with you at a time like this. No, you can't put me off, Peter."

"But ..." Paul disengaged his arm and slipped to the roadway," you can't do it! I ... I ... oh, can't you understand that I may have to go to all sorts of ends to escape detection and you'd be a hindrance, not a help."

"Oh, no, I wouldn't. No one would dream of looking for you with a woman. They think you're alone—and I don't mind what you do." There was a wide, ingenuous look on her face, "I'm quite prepared to sleep under hedges with you, to hide on moors and dodge policemen in back alleys! Oh, I shall love it and at the same time I shall be helping you!"

Paul shook his head, and said very firmly, "Much as I appreciate your offer, I forbid you to come with me."

And Margaret looked back at him and said with equal determination, "And I'm coming with you. You want someone to look after you. Why, you're only a baby! I'm sure I could handle a policeman much better than you ..." As she spoke she felt a great affection for this perturbed, somewhat awkward young man.

"But you can't come!"

"But I can!"

Their dialogue might have lengthened into a duet of determined affirmation and polite negation had it not, at that moment, been drowned and obliterated by a volume of sound that suddenly rose into the thin summer air and filled the void with incessant noise. Paul glanced round. Coming along the road was an open lorry loaded with empty milk churns that danced and rubbed tinny shoulders against one another to the pitching of the vehicle. They both stepped back to allow the lorry passage and as Paul moved an idea swept into his mind. The tail-board of the lorry was lowered. As it came abreast of him he ducked, grabbed his grip, and with one quick swing was scrambling on to the tailboard. He hoisted himself to security and then turned. Margaret was standing motionless by the bridge, staring after him. As the lorry turned a corner to lose the bridge, he waved one hand and blew her a kiss, at the same time thanking his fates that he had managed to shake her off.

He was filled with the conflict of two emotions: happiness at his early good fortune in disposing of Margaret, and regret for the rudeness and brusqueness of his manner of leaving her. He satisfied his chivalrous impulses with the consolation that he had taken the only course.

It was some seconds before Margaret fully appreciated what had happened. Then she leant back against the parapet and shook her head. He had eluded her again, but this time with a difference. Previously, she had imagined—though curious little things had already awakened her suspicions—that she had been chasing her lover, but now she knew that the young man on the lorry was no more Peter Angel than she was Jenny Lind. If her inspection of him had not entirely convinced her that their resemblance was only superficial, then his use of her Christian name had supplied her with the last proof. Peter Angel had always called her Retta.

"I wonder who he is and what it all means?" She asked the question of her reflection in the river as she used it to tidy her hair. And then, because there was something about Paul which excited her sympathy, she decided that he should not escape her so easily. He had to be looked after until she discovered more about him, and she would do it. With this fixed determination in her mind she walked slowly back to her car, and it was not until she reached it that she realised that she had not once thought of the real Peter Angel or wondered where he was or what he was doing. As she slipped her gears home she knew that she could not rest until she had found again this rather nice young man and, as she came to her decision, so Mr. Partingale walked into his Leicester hotel carrying a copy of the latest edition of the *Daily Globe* and he, too, had made up his mind that Peter Angel should be forced to acknowledge the potency of money as a cure-all. But, whereas his decision was derived from a desire to defend his convictions, Margaret's—so she was telling herself—came only from her natural curiosity.

And while this was happening Paul sat uncomfortably on the tail end of the lorry, his shoulders pressed for support against the grumbling milk churns and his feet swinging about the dust and exhaust gases that were spewed in the lorry's wake. He was unhappy for a moment, remembering Margaret and his own rudeness. He watched the country slide by him, river and fence and receding telegraph poles. A starling chittered and whistled to him from the top of a pylon, cows looked up from their grazing, horses stood in the shade of chestnuts.

He was being carried forward, somewhere, anywhere, he was seeing England, but wherever he went he knew that he would not be entirely satisfied until he came to that little town sleeping by the muddy Nene and dreaming of the long ago days when its wharves were abustle with Dutch and Nordic seamen and its warehouses bursting with grain from the prolific fenlands.

And over two hundred miles from Paul the real Peter Angel lay on a remote Cornish beach, his body slowly tanning under the sun, his chin itching with the growth of a beard and his eyes straying from the copy of *Vanity Fair*, which he had propped against two large pebbles, to watch the graceful flight of the gulls as they danced in the air above a shoal that rippled the jade waters with points of silver. All around him the coast slept in the grateful heat; the waves hissed up the beach and splashed the hot rocks, flies feasted round the blazing gorse blooms and somewhere, unseen, a lamb was bleating for its dam which had sought the deep shelter of the rising bracken to escape the bloodthirsty blowflies. In another week, he thought, Simpkins would have arranged things for him and then, hidden by his hairy camouflage, he could leave the country. His mind went back to his book and never once did he think of Paul or Margaret. He was the complete hedonist.

X
Paul goes native

As Mr. Edward Wimpole pushed open the door of the Hare and Grouse public hotel he felt his load of depression lift a little and life suddenly seemed a brighter, more wholesome affair. Yet he was still far from being happy or light-hearted. He moved up to the bar and ordered his half-can of ale. Then he moved to his accustomed seat beside the now empty fireplace and, crossing his legs carefully, placed the ale on the mantelshelf next to the advertisement for potato crisps. The hour which he spent in the bar, almost unfailingly, every night was an oasis in his otherwise aimless existence. For an hour he forgot the scolding of his wife, her constant nagging and reproaches, and he was a man's man—so he thought; though most of the other regular customers of the Hare and Grouse regarded him, with more exaggeration than truth, as a nuisance, a whimperer, a moaner, a miser and a dismal reminder of the degradation which can follow unbridled wifely tyranny.

To look at he was a thin, white-faced man, with a head that was too large for his body and eyes that were too large for his head. He somehow gave the impression of a pallid fungus peeping from the dark crack of a cave, timid, hesitant and exuding a ghostly, unhealthy atmosphere. His navy-blue serge suit was wrinkled about his knees from his crab-like walk, and the shoulders were sprinkled with a fine dandruff that came from the two moulting wings of greyish white hair which rose above his ears in an abortive attempt to cover the nobular ugliness of his bald crown. His hands were knuckly, and as he sat he cracked them absent-mindedly and sometimes sucked noisily through his teeth, as though he were a carter encouraging his horses.

It was very cheerful in the bar. Some commercial travellers were drinking whisky and retailing stories to the hurricane accompaniment of full-bellied laughter in one corner. The barmaid, a lofty creation of peroxide and black satin, was displaying the regularity of her new dentures to four pallid youths who tried to make up their lack of colour by the blatant display of their check coats and neckties. By the window a farmer was explaining to another group just what kind of Test cricket team he would have chosen, and implying from his tones that there must have been a grave delinquency somewhere that his opinion had not been asked. Elsewhere a schoolteacher with a racing edition under his arm was explaining to a friend his candid and colourful opinion of a certain parent who had come to the school and made audible objections to the fervency with which he had corrected a boy for throwing ink pellets. Mr. Wimpole half listened to him and then smiled to himself slightly as he heard the friend murmur that boys would be boys. It gave him a definite sense of satisfaction to think that possibly the boy had thrown and hit the teacher with a soggy ink pellet. That was the kind of thing he had always longed to do at school, yet had always lacked the courage to perform. Lack of courage had been the cause of his failure throughout life. He had dreamed his dreams and had been too timid to attempt to make them realities. He tried to remember his schooldays, but all that would come back with clarity was an impression of a pale, nervous boy in an eton collar that seemed to clamp him to the earth like a millstone, and the reverential smell of choir stalls where he had sung. Had he the courage now, he could shake off the yoke of a termagant wife and laugh with the men around him ... but it was too late—he knew that. No one wanted him, and his wife, he liked to imagine, only tolerated him because of the pension which had accompanied him on his retirement from the local government service after fifty years devoted to the management of public lavatories and town sanitation. And the pension was small enough, so small that he was slowly encumbering himself with debts due to the recklessness of his wife.

At seven o'clock, as Mr. Wimpole was slowly finishing his second half-can, Paul came and sat by him. The milk van had taken Paul into Leicester and he had dropped off, not very skilfully, at the entrance to the town and then taken a tram into the city. As it was getting late in the day he had decided that he must stop the night in the town and, disregarding the necessity for caution since he could do nothing to minimise the risk he ran, he booked a room at the Hare and Grouse and, after supper, drifted to the bar.

Paul nodded to Mr. Wimpole and sitting down lit himself a cigarette. Mr. Wimpole nodded in return and watched Paul. He compared the healthy, flushed face of the young man with his own paleness and envied the strong body which sprawled over a chair in direct contrast to his own spidery limbs and twitching hands. He cracked his joints and then, because he felt lonely, said, "Nice day after the rain this morning."

"Lovely," answered Paul, putting down his empty glass. "Lovely—England wants some beating in June."

Mr. Wimpole nodded. "Flaming June ... It's the best month of the year. It's a pity to have to live in a town at such a time ... but we can't have everything, can we?"

"No," Paul agreed, and then seeing that Mr. Wimpole's glass was empty, went on, "but we could have a drink together. What will you have?"

Mr. Wimpole was surprised. No one ever treated him, no one ever evinced the smallest interest in him, yet this young man had accepted him naturally and was offering him a drink. He was touched and felt happier. "Beer—that's kind of you."

"Not at all. I'm glad to have someone to talk with. I've been chasing about a lot today and it's good to be able to sit down at peace and know you're free from worry for a while."

The drinks were brought and after they had drunk one another's health, Mr. Wimpole sucked his teeth and ventured, "You've had a busy day?"

Paul waggled his head. He was feeling comfortable and happy now. After the excitements of the day, the swift onslaught of events and the nervous succession of escapes, the security of the pleasant bar was very gratifying. Mr. Wimpole seemed so harmless and innocuous after men like Mr. Freeman that Paul spoke freely, too freely.

"Yes, I've been very busy—too busy; but tomorrow will be better. I'm off to Wisbech—sort of vacation. Do you know Wisbech?"

"I can't say I do. I wish I were going somewhere tomorrow. You're lucky to have something to do, young man ... I didn't catch the name?"

Paul hesitated then gave him the name under which he had registered, Jonathan Leate.

"Leate ... Mine's Wimpole. I wish I had something to do with my time. I'm retired. Once a man's retired," he went on bitterly almost, "he's done for. No interest in life—just waiting for ... well, for the end."

Paul would not accept this fatalism. "Nonsense—there's always something to be done. Why, you look full of years yet," he lied encouragingly.

Mr. Wimpole shook his head. "Not me, I know better than you. You're lucky to be young and happy and free as the wind. You keep your freedom at any cost."

"My freedom—"

"Yes, you protect it at any cost. I lost mine and life hasn't been worth living since. It takes everything from you and makes you bitter. I wish I could have my days again—I'd act differently."

"I expect we all would," said Paul with feeling, and wondered what this little man full of self-pity would think if he knew the truth about him.

"Yes, we all make mistakes, even the best of us. Even the greatest. That gives me some consolation at times. Even the great Dr. Johnson made his mistakes. Do you read much?"

"Only technical stuff engineering, that's my job," Paul let the words slip before he knew it.

"Engineering, eh. Building things—lovely. If I'd only had a chance I could have done things, too …" The extra beer which Mr. Wimpole had taken broke down the reserve which was his usual protection against the world and, aided by the frankness and youthful sympathy which Paul offered to him, he began to tell Paul about himself. He outlined his life as a clerk, and his mistake in marrying the wrong woman. He eased himself of the worry of his debts by detailing them to Paul. For fifteen minutes he paraded all his small grievances and inhibitions until Paul began to feel uncomfortable and longed for Mr. Wimpole to finish his depressing story.

"Dr. Johnson was always in debt, and he made a mistake by marrying a woman much older than himself, though he would never admit it. You want to read Johnson and Boswell. I know them by heart and it's a great consolation to me to feel that many of my troubles were Dr. Johnson's troubles, too. He was a grand man, a wonderful man—there's none like him today. If I could only pay off my debts I should be happier and might get some happiness in my old age, but what hope is there …" He cracked his joints quickly so that they sounded like the sharp rattle of burning twigs and then looked at Paul.

Paul did not know what to say. He felt like telling the man to take a hold on himself and shake away his miserable depression and self-pity. What he did say was, "Well, we all have our troubles, don't we? Some small and some bigger."

"That's true," agreed Mr. Wimpole, "and mine have been mostly the bigger ones. Boy!" He lifted his hand as a newsboy pushed his ruffled head round the bar door. The boy came over with the paper and Mr. Wimpole spread it out, thus completing his nightly rite of a few drinks and an evening paper.

"Never anything interesting in it, but I like to have it," he explained to Paul.

"Is that so?" Paul put down his glass and glanced uncomfortably at the paper. Papers had suddenly assumed a different character. Previously they had meant news and entertainment; but now he knew them from the angle of the person who featured in the headlines and paragraphs, and he hated them. They were dangerous.

They had the evil power to unmask him to the world and set towns and villages on his trail, to make every citizen suspect him and every child fear him. He edged away slightly and pretended to be interested in the conversation of the barmaid, though he was watching Mr. Wimpole closely. As the man shook the paper preparatory to opening it, Paul could not endure the possibility of being recognised any longer. He stood up and addressed Mr. Wimpole lightly.

"What kind of entertainment is there in this town?" he asked. "I might as well do a show as yawn in the bar all the evening."

His ruse was, as he had hoped, successful. Mr. Wimpole forgot his paper.

"Entertainments—well, there's little else but pictures, these days."

"No theatre?" inquired Paul, glad to see that Mr. Wimpole had forgotten his paper.

"There's the repertory theatre. A very fine company at the moment. You might do worse than see that. I don't know what the play is—some romantic, South Sea island story, I believe."

"We'll toss for it," said Paul jocularly. "Heads for the living drama and tails for the celluloid sob-stuff."

The coin fell, head upwards.

"The theatre it is—are you coming with me?" asked Paul affably.

Mr. Wimpole shook his head. He would have liked to have accompanied Paul; but he was too much a creature of habit. At eight o'clock his wife required him to come to his supper and he knew what would be entailed if he were more than five minutes late.

He left the public bar with Paul and outside, after giving Paul directions to the repertory theatre, he parted from him.

From the little he had seen of the town Paul decided that he liked Leicester. It had an air of strength and cleanliness, and the buildings grouped themselves together with a solid confidence that was expressive of the pride which the townsfolk took in their city. Everything had an air of civic pride; the shops were well filled and their windows brightly dressed; the policemen in their white cuffs and helmets had a prosperous, genial look, as though they found the ordering of this town a pleasant business that brought them more laughter than sorrow; the men and women were well dressed and even if some of them were unemployed they appeared to be bearing their burden with a cheerful fortitude, as though they knew that it was merely a matter of time before they found places in the hosiery and boot and shoe factories; and even the great moon which hung above the city, filling the sky with pale radiance and dimming the quick brilliance of the red and blue neon lights of the shops, watched over the city with a complacent, satisfied expression which might have meant that of all the towns over which it held dominion there were few that pleased it so much as Leicester and fewer still where the sharp beams of its light found a responsive clarity and freshness in the tangle of streets and pavements.

As Paul opened his programme, where he sat in the stalls of the theatre, so Mr. Wimpole sitting in the front of the tramcar on his way home opened his evening paper, the *Evening Saturn*, which was the offspring of the *Daily Globe*. The first thing which Mr. Wimpole saw in the paper was a photograph of the young man with whom he had been talking in the Hare and Grouse. It was some time before he really could bring himself to believe that the photograph was that of the man he had just left, and when the possibility of mistake had gone he found that he was trembling with nervous excitement, trembling so much that the leaves of the paper rustled unwillingly in his white fingers as he read the account beneath the photograph.

In twelve hours the press, of which the *Daily Globe* and the *Evening Saturn* formed so substantial a part, had passed from mild sorrow and wondering incredulity at Peter Angel's crime to righteous and strident indignation. The *Evening Saturn* editor was astonished, and he hinted that the *Daily Globe* editor and the editors of all the other papers were similarly astonished, that this man should have eluded the police even for twelve hours and, while gently castigating the police for their inefficiency, the *Evening Saturn* with a large oratorical gesture called upon its million readers to help in the search for this super-criminal, this audacious huckster, this renegade who thought that he could make England his refuge from justice; and, as an added inducement to its readers to keep an open eye for Peter Angel, the *Evening Saturn* announced that in conjunction with the *Daily Globe* and with the consent of Scotland Yard, a reward of one thousand pounds was offered for any tangible information which might lead to the arrest of Peter Angel.

"England has no place for this American who has forfeited his right to our renowned hospitality, and it is the duty of every British citizen to forget this man's sentimental appeal, to forget his position as a celebrity, and to do his or her best to bring him to justice. So confident are the *Daily Globe* and the *Evening Saturn* of the integrity and efficiency of our police and the vigilance of their readers that the apprehension of Peter Angel is confidently assumed within twenty-four hours ..."

There was also a small account of the escapade of a young man in a motor-coach travelling from London to Leicester who had been taken for Peter Angel, but the paper discounted this, although the young man had got away, as probably a false clue, for—it pointed out—already there had been half a dozen similar incidents that day concerning innocent people. The real Peter Angel would be in hiding, not risking capture in a public conveyance.

Mr. Wimpole did not believe this. He would not allow himself to believe it. The more he considered the facts the more convinced he became that the young man he had just left was Peter Angel, and at the contemplation of a possible reward of a thousand pounds he could feel his heart leap within his breast like a trout flinging itself at a lasher. There were, within his reach, one thousand pounds, and all he had to do was to find a policeman and persuade him to come to the Repertory Theatre with him to interrogate the young man.

Hardly able to control his excitement, his thin face flushed with a wash of colour for the first time in years, Mr. Wimpole got up and worked his way along the swaying tram. He had forgotten that he was due at his home for supper, all thought of his wife had flown from his head at the tremendous possibility of winning a thousand pounds. As he slipped off the tram and stood hesitantly on the pavement, there floated before him in a magical pattern the curling, tantalising pound sign and a brave, desirable procession of ciphers headed by an upright, martial figure one. With all that money the gates of earthly paradise would be open to him. No longer would he fear his wife, no longer would he walk in fear of her wrath and domineering temper—he would be free; a man with an army of pound notes before which his wife's sharp onslaught would fall away and weaken. And all he had to do was to find a policeman and take him to the theatre.

He looked around him eagerly and, as if in answer to his wishes, a tall, dark figure detached itself from the shadow of an acacia tree that whispered over a garden fence, and came towards him. Half babblingly, almost incoherent in his haste, Mr. Wimpole told his story to the policeman, and as he proceeded it was so obvious that he was convinced of his discovery that the policeman decided that it would be wise to investigate, though he half hoped that Mr. Wimpole would be proven wrong, since it seemed, somehow, a direct contravention of the rules of existence that a criminal should be detected and apprehended by an ordinary civilian and not by an officer of the law. Stifling his professional pride he fell into step beside Mr. Wimpole and they headed for the theatre.

At the theatre Paul was suffering from boredom. The play was entitled *Naked and Ashamed*. The programme informed him that it had been a great success in London and had set Mayfair and the smart world talking; whereas actually it had lasted four nights in London, its failure being due chiefly to the misleading title. It concerned the adventures of a young society girl who seemed unable to make up her mind which of three men she loved and, so Paul decided before the first act was done, was probably hampered by the congenital lack of a mind to make up. Finally she had to be shipwrecked on a South Sea island with her chauffeur to discover what a paragon of manly virtues had been sitting before her for years. Until they were alone, almost naked and not ashamed, on the island, she had regarded him as nothing more than four square inches of neck at which she shouted orders but, under the strong light of the limes and midst the creaking canvas scenery of the island, the chauffeur in a pair of tattered shorts was displaying his back and chest and a pair of attenuated hairy legs and demonstrating that for love he could work miracles and cook coconuts in seven different ways.

Paul watched the progress of the girl's love affair for two dreary acts. As the curtain came down for the interval, he expelled a great gust of breath and wondered whether he would skip the last act and return to his hotel. In the hope, characteristic of most people, that the last act might compensate for the paucity of the first two, Paul decided to remain in the theatre.

He sat listening to the buzz of conversation behind him and watching the faint smoke drifts that rose into the air, moving on a slow draught away from the auditorium towards the sweeping proscenium. For a while he read the advertisement notices on the drop curtain and then, feeling in his pocket for cigarettes, he found he had run out. He turned in his seat and summoned an attendant. A girl came to him, carrying a tray, and he bought a packet of cigarettes. As he paid her and was about to sit down his eye was arrested by a movement at the far end of the gangway. Paul remained half standing, half bent towards his seat, the cigarette carton clutched in his right hand like a talisman. Coming down the gangway towards him was a policeman and Mr. Wimpole. He recognised the little man at once and he saw, with alarm, that he held screwed into a baton in one hand an evening paper. Paul knew at once what had happened as he saw Mr. Wimpole come trotting like a worried starling down the gangway towards him. The thought of entering into explanations in the crowded theatre dismayed him. It was much simpler for him to slip away before they saw him. This time he was dealing with the police and he knew better than to stop and argue. He stood up, looked quickly about him, and seeing no other way of escape, he moved rapidly, but not giving the impression of undue haste, along the front row of the stalls and through a small doorway. As he ducked into the doorway the lights went out behind him in the auditorium and he fancied he heard Mr. Wimpole cry out.

When Margaret had been given the slip by Paul, she had stood for some moments on the bridge wondering what she should do, and then, because the afternoon was wearing on and she knew that it was useless to attempt to pursue the lorry, she had walked slowly back to her car and driven on to Leicester. She went to Leicester because it was the nearest town of any size and because she guessed that the milk-lorry was probably heading in that direction. And she, too, after her meal had reviewed the entertainments which Leicester offered and had decided in favour of the repertory company. Although neither of them knew it, she and Paul had been sitting within a few yards of one another for most of the evening; and when Paul had hurriedly vacated his seat at the sight of Mr. Wimpole and the policeman, Margaret had noticed the young man some rows before her rise and hurry along the front of the theatre. She paid little attention to him, for just then the lights went down and the curtain rose. Neither did she notice with any attention the hurried consultation which took place between Mr. Wimpole in the gangway with the policeman until there was an angry murmur of "Ssssh" from the audience around and then, wondering what trouble there was, she watched the two return to the back of the hall and fade into the darkness.

The curtain rose to reveal the desert island scene. In the foreground the girl lay on the yellow sands, beneath the shade of a palm tree that creaked as it swayed. Scattered over the sand were a few coconuts and various conch shells and the bleached proboscis of a swordfish. The chauffeur sat upon an upturned box listening to a spirited monologue from the girl, wbicn had contributed largely to the play's failure in London. She seemed unable to accommodate herself to the fact that they were alone on the island. Just us, alone, alone, was her cry, and the chauffeur seemed content to sit and listen to her. The audience listened to her with patient boredom.

But the kindly Fates decided against boredom and as the girl was about to finish her monologue, the palm tree stirred as if a breeze were blowing its branches and the island reverberated to the sound of heavy and hurried footsteps, and a young man suddenly dashed upon the stage, looking anxiously over his left shoulder as though pursued.

With rude unconcern for the solitude of the two, the young man dashed forward, hitched his foot in the proboscis, and fell full length into the girl's lap. The audience watched this comic turn in perplexed silence. They had not been expecting a knockabout farce. The girl pushed him roughly from her and he sprawled in the sand for a moment, then sitting up he faced the footlights. There was on his face a look of mild inquiry which changed slowly to one of wild consternation and his face flushed a deep scarlet colour which the lights enhanced.

A low cry came from his lips and like a deer which had strayed from a park on to a busy main road he leaped up and headed for the wings. But the chauffeur, incensed at. the intrusion, muttered some unintelligible protest and caught at his leg. The move was unfortunate, for Paul fell forward as though he were diving into the sea of the backcloth. His head struck the canvas and he rolled over, and as he rolled the chauffeur fell with him. A flying foot caught one of the struts supporting the palm tree and the graceful creation of canvas and wooden slats toppled and subsided gently upon the struggling pair, and as it fell the audience woke as though from a dream.

An indignant voice close to the footlights exclaimed with partisan fervour: "It ain't right, that's what it ain't …" And then was lost in a lusty roar of approval that had its birth in the gallery.

There was a silence after the roar and then a confused bickering of protest and commendation broke out all over the auditorium.

The island girl jumped to her feet and, with no apparent reason, grasped the proboscis like a double-edged sword. As she stood above the heaving palm tree a dishevelled figure broke loose from its shelter and shot across the stage like a rabbit.

With admirable feminine vigour and determination the girl swung the proboscis at Paul. The villainous weapon missed him by an inch, slipped from the grasp of the girl and whistled through the air with the sound of an angry wasp. It struck the canvas palm tree, tore through the painted struts and as Paul sprinted into the darkness of backstage he heard, merging with the rapturous roars of the crowd, a thin howl of pain penetrating like the whine of a high-explosive shell over a battlefield.

Behind him the lights went up and the curtain came down. Margaret, who had recognised Paul at once, found herself the only person in the audience who understood the true nature of the interruption. She sat in her seat, trying to make up her mind what to do while the theatre manager came to the front of the curtain to apologise for the incident.

As the lights went up Paul knew that if he wanted to escape he had to act quickly and without blundering any more. He was shaken and nervous from his experience. In the flash of illumination he saw a twisting angle of stairs and at the top a door. Without a thought for where the door might lead, he leapt up the stairs and throwing open the door was through and had it closed behind him before the stage hands and actors had recovered enough to look for the intruder.

Paul, closing the door behind him, was confronted by a young man of about his own age, with waved hair and mild, ingenuous eyes. He was dressed in a morning coat and top hat, and he was surprised when Paul kicked him in the stomach. Paul did it gently, but firmly. It was necessary.

As the door closed, the young man had stared at Paul, and then in a petulant tone had said, "Really! What do you mean, bursting into my dressing-room like this?"

Some intuitive process in Paul's mind had told him that here was a man with whom it was useless to argue or logically remonstrate. He had decided upon action. With careful deliberation he had steadied his back against the door and raising his right leg, given the man a push in the stomach which had sent him reeling across the room to subside, like a wind-snapped tulip, into a large wicker basket for dirty linen that rested against the opposite wall. He lay there, his legs sprawling over the side of the basket and his top hat masking one eye.

Paul interrupted the incipient protest with a curt movement of his hand towards his pocket and said, assuming a harsh tone, "You stay where you are, buddy, and keep quiet, or I'll fix you so well that the undertaker's man will refuse to handle you as an incomplete corpse. I'm desperate ..." Paul widened his eyelids and attempted to induce a wild look into his eyes to convey an impression of fierceness. Secretly, he was very pleased with his facile assumption of the air of a desperado.

"But ... but ... what does it all mean?" The man tried to rise.

"Listen—I told you to be quiet. Keep where you are," and to help the actor maintain his grotesque position Paul thrust at him with one hand and sent him deeper into the unpleasant bog of linen. "I've got to think."

He turned the key in the door lock, listened for a moment to the sounds outside of men and women running and talking. One set of footsteps stopped outside the door and someone knocked. At the knock the realisation of what he was involving himself in made him pause; then, with the thought that he might as well be hung for a sheep as a lamb he jumped to the wicker basket and caught the man by the throat.

"You do as I tell you," he muttered roughly.

"Hullo, Mr. Hammerton, is there anyone in there with you?" came a voice from outside the door.

"Say no," whispered Paul.

Mr. Hammerton gulped and then called in reply, "No, there's no one here but myself."

"O.K." came the voice, and the footsteps receded from the door.

"Good for you," said Paul, releasing the man. He looked round the room and the sight of an open cupboard gave him an idea. Inside the cupboard were various suits and theatrical costumes and a tall red fez hanging to a peg. The fez presented a way of escape to Paul. He went to the cupboard, eyed the suits and then choosing one which seemed to be about his size, he began to divest himself of his own grey suit.

Mr. Hammerton watched in silent amazement. With a resignation which was admirable, he sat uncomplainingly in the wicker basket, not daring to move, until Paul had changed his clothes. Paul faced himself in the glass. The suit, a blue one with a light red stripe in it, made him look different, but his face was still the same. If he wanted to escape from the theatre he knew that he would have to do something about altering his features.

"Here—you come here," he jerked the command at Mr. Hammerton, "and see that you do as I say quickly." Outside the noise had subsided and he could hear the sound of the players going on with the last act.

"What do you want?" Mr. Hammerton struggled from the basket, righted his top hat and stood by Paul.

"I want to be an Indian, fez and all!"

Mr. Hammerton, with some justification, decided that he undoubtedly was in the presence of a madman. "An Indian?" There was incredulity in his voice.

"Yes, an Indian, a regular silk-scarf and carpet-seller. You must have seen 'em about the towns. Come on—get on with it. I'm in a hurry."

Paul grew impatient and Mr. Hammerton had a ghastly vision of headlines detailing the disembowelling of a promising young actor in his dressing-room by an escaped lunatic. "I don't quite understand you," he admitted with some trepidation.

"You're dumb!" exclaimed Paul. "Make me up as an Indian and hurry, will you. Get hold of the greasepaint."

Then Mr. Hammerton understood. Inspired by a growing fear, he seized the greasepaint and began to make Paul's face into that of an Indian. Paul watched sideways in the mirror as his skin slowly became a dusky brown.

"That's pretty good—now for the fez!" Mr. Hammerton handed this to Paul and watched him perch it sedately on his head. The metamorphosis was complete and astonishing. Paul had entered the room a modern young man and now he stood a tall, dark-eyed, brown-skinned son of the East, his body erect under the red fez.

"What are you going to do now?" asked Mr. Hammerton, his curiosity conquering his fear.

Paul looked at him sternly and did not reply. Instead he moved across the room, took down a length of towelling from a hook and—without a word of protest from the quiescent actor—began to bind the man. He used five towels and a large coloured handkerchief before Mr. Hammerton was neatly trussed and stood in a corner with a gag in his mouth.

"Now," said Paul gently, "you stop there until someone finds you—and behave yourself. I'm sorry to have to do this, but necessity compels me. I can understand how you feel."

As he spoke he was moving round the room collecting silk scarves and neckties. When he had enough he stopped, and for the first time he was conscious of the extreme seriousness of his position. He was up against the whole of the theatre and it was more than likely that all the doors would be watched.

Paul was correct. The manager had been interviewed by the policeman and now while the policeman and Mr. Wimpole stationed themselves at the stage entrance, which was in one street, the manager and another policeman stood in the main entrance.

Paul moved out of the dressing-room, locked it and left the key in the lock and then, holding his silk spoils over one arm, he shuffled down the corridor. He had no sense of his direction. He just walked on, through twisting passages, down a few stairs and although one or two persons passed him they merely gazed curiously at the barbaric figure and then passed on. Behind him he could hear the murmur of voices from the stage as the play went on.

Paul turned a corner at the bottom of a corridor and before him was the stage door into the street, and standing at the door he recognised Mr. Wimpole and a policeman. Knowing that hesitation would be fatal, Paul walked straight up to them and, before either of them could speak, he was addressing them. He was imbued with a cold courage that filled him with a strange confidence.

Holding up a lovely length of silk evening scarf which had been the joy of Mr. Hammerton's heart, he chanted:

"Nice gen'lman buya da scarf? Velly good, velly cheap!" Paul, beneath his pigmentation, had time to congratulate himself upon his, so he thought, wonderful simulation of the Oriental speech.

"Scarf—we don't want no scarf!" retorted the policeman. "What've you been doing in there?"

"No wants da scarf? Velly good scarf. Come all way from Kashmir. I bring heem. Wanta da handkerchief?" Paul turned and thrust a red handkerchief with a paisley pattern into Mr. Wimpole's face. The little man backed away at the proximity of the huge brown face and the flourishing handkerchief.

"Oh, go away—I don't want anything from you." He turned to the policeman." Do you think he's given us the slip?"

"Not him! Not a chance. Here, cocky," the policeman turned to Paul. "You seen a tall young feller-me-lad in there with a grey suit and cap? American."

"You mean dark mans, like me?" asked Paul dully.

"No, no! American. A white man, you know."

"Yes, I knows!" nodded Paul vigorously. "Americano."

"Yes, that's right—an American."

"Yes, yes, Americano."

"Well, have you seen him?" inquired the policeman irritably.

"Who?"

"The Americano!" The policeman snapped his fingers angrily. "The American!" he bawled suddenly, as Paul looked blank. "Have you seen an American in there—tall feller?"

A gleam of understanding shot into Paul's eyes. He nodded his head excitedly.

"Tall fella—yes, I know him," he said brightly. "Solda da scarf to him just now. He lika da scarf. Say, come again next Friday he buya da more scarf. You buya da scarf also?"

The policeman screwed up his face at this display of intelligence and then, with a glance at Mr. Wimpole, took Paul by the shoulders and, with the air of a rebuking father, propelled him into the street.

"Here, sonny, you goa da homa and stoppa da homa for longa time. Hop it, will you, and don't waste my time with your scarves. Hop it!" He gave Paul a parting push and Paul, taking his advice, hopped it up the street and into the market, while the policeman and Mr. Wimpole continued their vigil.

Paul stood on the grey pavement and wiped his forehead. He was free. It seemed almost impossible that his childish disguise should have passed muster. A light breeze blew from the east and to him where he stood came the sound of trams lurching along their rails and above, round the cornices of a grey-stoned building, a trio of bats fluttered on dusky wings and added the flickering of their quick shadows to the bright play of sparks that lit the ambient sky at intervals where pulley-arms passed points on the overhead wires.

As Paul stood thinking, he decided that though he was for the moment safe, he could not long remain so. Very soon, if not already, Mr. Hammerton would be released, and then the chase would commence in earnest for a tall, dark man wearing a red fez, He had to rid himself of his disguise as soon as possible, and he could not go back to his hotel to do it.

XI
To Wisbech

A small boy was the first person to meet Paul after he had left the theatre. He was standing in a doorway opposite a row of cars parked by patrons of the theatre, and he was standing there in the hope that benevolent car owners might reward him with small tips for watching their cars, and even if he got no tips, as was sometimes so, there was always the cheerful possibility that he might cadge a cigarette card from them. He was a very small boy and should have been in bed, but his passion for knowledge kept him roaming the streets in search of cigarette cards. He had a collection which meant more to him than many a fabulous collection of ceramics gloated over by millionaires or long, echoing galleries of paintings locked away from the world by wealthy connoisseurs.

He saw Paul coming towards him, noticed without undue interest the dark skin and lofty fez and, as Paul came abreast of him, he stepped into the pathway.

"Got any fag-cards, mister?"

Paul shook his head and as he did so he noticed by the kerbstone a long green car, a car that evoked familiar memories in his mind. He stopped, forgot the boy and looked at the car, and he had no doubt that it was Margaret's. How it came to be there he did not question. He only knew that in his present difficulty it presented a very simple solution of his troubles. As he looked at it an idea germinated in his mind. For a while he was troubled by the suggestion. It meant acting unmannerly towards Margaret, and he had already been rude enough to her. Then his good sense conquered his good manners, and was aided by his American attitude towards cars as necessary incidentals to every full life. He swung open the door and threw his silk wares on to the back seat. Sitting in the driving seat he tore a leaf from his notebook and scribbled on it

So sorry—but I had to borrow your car in a hurry. You can guess why. If you still want to help me, please keep this to yourself and I'll wire you tomorrow at the Hare and Grouse to let you know where to pick up the car. With many apologies for this liberty.—P. G.

"Here, sonny—" he called to the boy, and held up the note. Then remembering his dusky identity he went on, "You wanta to earn a sheeling, no?"

The boy regarded him with disfavour and made no reply.

"You wanta to earn a little money to buy da sweets, no?"

Still the boy regarded him with an unintelligent stare.

"Here!" Paul gave up the attempt. "Give this note to the lady who will come along for this car directly, and here's a shilling for your trouble. You certainly look dumb, but you can manage that, can't you?"

The boy's face brightened with a smile and he nodded his head as he took the note and the money.

"Yes, sir," he answered, "I'll do that. You haven't got any fag-cards, have you?"

Paul shook his head as he started the engine and slipped in the gears. "Sorry, sonny, but if you'll let me have your address I'll send you all I get," he said absently.

"Will you?" the boy's voice rose exultantly above the beat of the engine." It's number fifteen, Royal ..." The rest of the address was lost as the car moved off and the boy was left alone with his money and note. He looked after the dwindling tail-light of the car for a moment and then spat ceremoniously and emphatically after it.

Paul knew that Margaret would not inform the police of the loss of her car. Something told him that if she had been so anxious to come with him and help him, she would not object to his taking her car for a while.

For the next hour Paul drove through the night and then, tired by the extreme excitements of the day, he found a small by-lane and, pulling off the road on to the green sward, he switched off his lights and within five minutes he was sleeping heavily, stretched along the back seat.

He slept all night without a break and about him in the darkness the bats wheeled and soft-winged owls floated up and down the fields searching for the movement of voles and mice. In the tall rye grass little pin-points of green phosphorescence marked the slow movement of glow-worms and signalled to the sabre-winged males which fluttered across the tops of the cat-tails on an errand of procreation. From the hills where the cattle moved, cropping in a world of shadows, came the breath of trodden marjoram and the sweet smell of crushed thyme. Velvety moths steered erratic courses through the air channels like blown leaves. Once there came the protracted whimper of a rabbit, stupefied before a stoat, and then the night swept on bearing its burden of night-flying victims and marauders. Its blackness covering the cruelty with a kindly cloak, it passed across the fields and hedges, through the woods, over rivers and down the steep valleys of the hills, and where it passed it left behind some of the sorrow which characterised its sombre garb, sorrow in little puffs of fur where a fox had torn and ravaged, sorrow in pathetic pellets of mixed bone and fur where an owl, crop gorged, had ejected what it could not digest of field mouse and beetle. Glow-worms worked through the tall grasses, shone in the lee of stately, hairy-calyxed poppies and illuminated the wonderful tangle of grasses and mosses that formed a universe as strange and complex, as cruel and kind and as harsh and relentless as the wider universe in which men and women lived. Somewhere in a clump of hazel boughs a thrush chirped and spread its wings wider over its fledgelings as a nightjar screeched close by, but Paul heard nothing. He slept on and his dreams took no substance from the night about him or the incidents of the past hours. He was dreaming of Wisbech and his mother.

Paul woke very early. There was a heavy barrage of clouds hanging over the distant roll of hills, and a protesting little wind drove through the thin spinneys of beech and along the edges of the spruce plantations that held their emerald green fingers to the glowering sky. A glance in his driving mirror reminded him of the orientalisation of his skin, and he drove carefully along the road until he found a stream. Here, with certain difficulty and handfuls of grass, he managed to clean the brown pigment from his face and hands, though traces of it still lingered under his nails and in the sharp valleys of his skin about his eyes and nose. He stopped at a village shop and purchased some food for breakfast and a cake of soap.

Like a hardy campaigner who knows that, although cleanliness may be next to godliness, a square meal is a more comforting and wiser preamble to a day which may be full of surprises than a wash, Paul ate first. His stomach comforted with rolls and breakfast sausage, he wandered down to the edge of a tiny river and, brushing the white-crested arrowheads away from the brink, washed himself thoroughly until there was no trace on his skin of the brown pigment and no sign in his movements of the night's stiffness which had crept over him in the car. The fez, in a moment of elation, he set drifting on the bosom of the stream and pelted it with stones until, battered and crumpled, it collapsed and sank towards the gravelly bottom of the stream to frighten caddis grubs and inquisitive minnows. As it capsized and disappeared below the surface Paul was reminded of a film he had seen of the wreck of an airship, and—without conscious homology—he resolved that he would send Mr. Hammerton two pounds at the theatre to compensate for the loss of his scarves and fez.

At the next village Paul purchased a map and directed his course towards Wisbech. He drove happily through this new land he had come into and his mind was almost at peace.

Paul, while he had an intelligent interest in the history of England, was not obsessed by the idea of seeing places where famous events had occurred. To him the history of England, the romance and chivalry and the meanness and dark crimes, formed a background against which he saw the country, a background against which Wisbech shone out fairer and more desirable than any other part of the country.

As he drove during the morning towards Wisbech, following the route from his map, he passed places that were rich in Norman tradition, passed battlefields where the destiny of kings had been fought out and castles where intrigue had made the summer air ring with the screams of young life dying, but he knew nothing of this and cared little for it if he could have known. He saw the countryside and the villages and towns as they were and his pleasure from them was such that for a while he forgot that he was Peter Angel with a whole country after him. The places he went through had curious names which he soon forgot; Billesdon, Allexton, Wansford, Castor ... he passed them all happily. The sky was filling with dark grey masses that swung aside from time to time to let the sunlight slip down to the earth, and the country was enveloped in a soft browny light that dulled the quick surface of the rivers, painted dark shadows under the lofty heads of trees and trembled across the fields of young corn and mowing grass in shimmering catspaws.

The car was very pleasant to drive, giving an exhilarating feeling of power and control, and he forgot everything but his own happiness at the prospect of soon reaching Wisbech. He swept round corners, the wind of his passage disturbing the trailing bryony and shaking the dust from the heavy-headed valerian. Daring finches and sparrows crouched on the road before him until the radiator was almost above them, and then went whirring into the air to fall away over hedges as though it were all part of a game they played, like silly children seeing how near to danger they could go. He stopped once where a gilded red and gold sign of a Rose and Crown hung from the beetling roof of an inn and had lunch by an open window around which purple clematis flowers hung to form a frame through which wafted the scent of roses and wallflowers. The road went up and down, across river and through cutting, by tall larch plantations and through narrow lanes where from opposite sides chestnuts and ash met to throw the road in shade.

He passed through Peterborough and knew from an information board that there was a cathedral, but he did not stop for the west front or decorated windows and painted ceilings, but went on over a new and brightly white bridge into a country that gradually grew flatter and greener than any he had passed before. He was entering the fenlands, the land of cultivation and slow muddy streams, where there was little but sugar-beet, corn and potatoes and where the trees gathered in isolated clumps, the remnant of a once picturesque and powerful army. In places the road ran along embankments, on one side the deep, straight channel of a river and on the other the steady sweep into the distance of fields. Above him gulls, from the not far distant sea, hung like dust motes in the air and on the rivers coot and duck worked their way among the reeds that fringed the banks, and once he caught sight of a grey and white heron standing stiffly by the water, its beak held to the thundery sky like a menacing sword.

After a while the road entered a small area where the fens for a space relented of their monotony. The river curved and threw off a small arm which broadened into a mere, about which a thick barrier of willows and ash ran in a semicircle. Rough pasture came down to the open fringe of the mere and in a hollow behind the willows a small stream gushed and sang a song to the bending briars and rank broadleaved garlic. As Paul came opposite this spot the engine coughed and spluttered and then ceased. He knew at once the trouble and acknowledged that he had only himself to blame. He glanced at the petrol gauge and saw that his tanks were empty. He wondered why he should have overlooked so obvious a requirement and could find no excuse for himself.

"Now that certainly is a nuisance!" He swung out of the driving seat and mouthed the words aloud. He leaned against the car and wondered how far it was to the nearest station or whether he could borrow a gallon from some passing car.

There was nothing in sight except a small cottage away on the horizon, and he knew from his own experience that few cars were on the road. He was about to take out his map when a drift of smoke and the fierce splutter of a fire taking flame attracted his attention. The smoke was coming from the hollow and Paul crossed the road to investigate. As he did so a head and shoulders appeared above the briars and he found himself looking at a middle-aged man, dressed in a khaki shirt and a pair of shorts.

Paul nodded to the man and then walked into the hollow. The man stood by the fire which he was refuelling and looked at Paul.

"I've run out of gas," said Paul. "Could you tell me the nearest place to get any?"

The man smiled and shook his head." You've got a walk of five miles before you if you're thinking of fetching any. I've got a little in the tank of my motor-cycle, but I can't get it out even if I could spare it. Got far to go?"

"I'm heading for Wisbech from Leicester."

"Mm ..." The man paused and fanned the fire with a piece of cardboard thoughtfully. Then he swung round on his hunkers and eyed Paul. "If you care to wait until I've had my tea and a bathe, I'll give you a lift to the nearest petrol station on my cycle and we can bring back a tin."

"I say," Paul was grateful, "that's certainly very nice of you."

"Don't be silly. Anyone would do as much for you. You'd better have some tea with me while you're here. Do you object to strawberry jam and cut cake?"

Paul laughed. "I seem to have struck oil."

He watched while the man put a tin kettle on the fire and then he went inside a small tent which occupied one side of the hollow and helped to cut the bread for the jam. While he was doing this he had an opportunity to study the man. He was short and very stocky, with the blunt, muscular frame of a rugby player. His hands were large, rough and thick from hard work and he explained that he was by trade a carpenter, though he was at that moment on holiday or, if Paul liked to know the truth, unemployed.

"And do you always live in a tent?" asked Paul.

"Not always. You see, I've worked pretty hard during my few years and now that I'm out of a job I thought I'd invest a little of my savings in a holiday before I begin to look for another job—"

"You don't seem particularly worried about your bad luck," remarked Paul, as they sat down inside the tent before a small table to have tea.

The man paused and Paul saw that his broad face was grown very stern; his sandy coloured eyebrows, that were islets isolated from the mass of short, stiff hair which covered his head, pressed down over his eyes until there showed no more than two glimmers of light, like the slits that come into a darkened room under an ill-fitting doorway. Paul, without evident reason, had the impression of a lecturer about to come to his main argument or his climax.

"No, I'm not worried!" exclaimed the man emphatically. "It's not in the nature of Bert Clements to worry about himself. That's my name," he explained. "You see," he went on, after taking a huge bite at a piece of bread and jam, "I've lived too long among the class which is constantly in and out of employment to let it worry me any longer. Worrying doesn't help, nothing seems to help except toleration of the awful facts. One week you are working and making money, and the next—phut!" He snapped his fingers and the gesture sent Paul's eyes to the doorway through which he could watch the passing shades on the water and see the green car on the roadway.

"Nothing can ever alter such conditions until we reorganise, and perhaps scrap, the existing social structure." He said this with his eyes shut as though it were a phrase, a thought, which had been with him so long that it now lacked sense or meaning.

"What do you mean?"

"Just this!" And now he spoke with added force and conviction. "So long as industry and commerce are controlled by private individuals with the sole idea of making a profit for themselves and their shareholders, so long as men are regarded merely as labourers and units in a vast, cruel machinery which must pay its five, ten, twenty and a hundred per cent. profit each year—then you will never get any humanitarian principles introduced into industry!"

"You sound as though you were a Socialist," said Paul, who to some extent sympathised with the man's views.

"Socialist!" Bert Clement's mouth snapped like a shark taking a fish. "Socialist, Conservative, Liberal—I'm none of them! I'm a working man who regrets that the principles which Christ laid down in His sermon on the Mount have never been intelligently or sincerely adhered to by humanity. Three million unemployed, thousands of half-empty churches, thousands of crammed public houses, warehouses full of rotting grain, fields of unpicked cotton, millions of hungry and ill-clothed men and women—there's a paradox for you! There's a fine thing for a man to point to two thousand years after the death of Christ! Doesn't it make you wince? It does me!"

"You certainly paint a dismal picture," said Paul, "but there is a bright side to it, you know."

"I know—but what good is it to give a man cake on Monday if he must starve for the rest of the week? No, the only thing to do is to make a clean sweep of everything and begin again."

"But that would be impossible." Paul's tidy mind was appalled by the thought.

"Nothing is impossible. It would be difficult, I'll admit, but not impossible. If humanity wants a thing bad enough then it'll get it. They could direct their whole lives towards one end during the Great War, and soon they'll be directing their whole lives towards a reconstruction of civilisation—it only needs a few more millions out of work and then you look out!"

Paul could not altogether agree with this. His politics, if they were vague, were at least tempered with prudence, and the idea of fashioning the world over again was too much for his orderly nature.

"No," he said decidedly, "I think the only way to wipe out the evils which exist is through a gradual change and the slow eradication of anomalies. And the world seems to be doing that now."

"Nonsense! The world is doing very little else but look after number one. It's the man who really feels the pinch who will eventually alter things, men like me, and then the revolution will come."

"Revolution?" Paul was worried by the term.

"Yes, revolution, the gateway to a new era of sanity on earth and a decent living for all men. And when it comes it may not be bloodless."

"I can't believe all you say. I'll admit the world is in a bad state, maybe, but I won't admit that it can't be altered sanely and without bloodshed. There's been enough of that already. Men are changing and I've enough faith in human nature to believe that very soon everyone will be working towards the same end as you have in mind. Men are decent at heart, you know, and trust one another!" For Paul this was a long statement and as he finished it he felt rather proud of himself. It sounded good and represented what he thought. But he was totally unprepared for Bert Clements's reception of his credo. He tilted his camp stool backwards and regarded Paul where he sat on the edge of a camp bed. He opened his mouth and broke into loud laughter. He rocked to and fro and occasionally, to punctuate his gusts of mirth, he smacked the small wooden table before him and made the tin cups and plates jump like a class of boys at drill.

Seeing Paul's astonishment he quietened down. Shaking his head in the last rumblings of his merriment, he rubbed his sandy coloured hair and said; "Well, well, some folk take the biscuit. I think that's a rich statement, coming from you! I should say you did know that men believe and trust one another. Where would you be if they didn't?"

Paul's brows wrinkled with puzzlement. "What the devil are you talking about?" he asked somewhat irritably.

"Talking about! Why, you, of course!" Bert smacked the table again and chuckled. "Who should I be talking about but you. You believe in the rest of men and they trust you! They did trust you too—didn't they, Mr. Peter Angel!"

XII
Mr. Wimpole takes the trail

Paul felt his whole body surge with momentary panic at the words, and he stared at Bert Clements as though that gentleman had struck him a blow in the face. The moment of amazement passed and he leapt to his feet, but before he could leave the tent Bert waved a conciliatory hand towards him.

"Sit down, mister, sit down. You're all right with me." Paul, realising that flight could help him very little, sat down.

"How on earth did you recognise me? And what are you going to do about it?" he asked anxiously.

Bert Clements leant back and picked a paper from the floor. "Just your bad luck, I suppose. I happened to be reading the article in the *Daily Globe* about you, describing how you might be somewhere in the Leicester district, only two minutes before you came along. When I saw you I recognised you almost at once, for your photograph was fresh in my mind. And remember, you said you'd come from Leicester. That clinched it. But to get back to our argument—"

He seemed to regard the fact that he had been taking tea with Peter Angel as of far less importance than the continuation of their argument. "How can you have the nerve to say what you had just said? Why, you lifted thousands from people who were mugs enough to trust you."

"Look here," Paul, exasperated, half rose to his feet. "I'm not standing that from—"

"Keep your hair on, Mr. Angel! I'm not blaming you or even criticising what you did, in fact I've got a certain admiration for you. I might have done the same myself. You knew what you wanted and you got it. Trouble is you're paying the price now. But I don't think you ought to speak as you did—it's not sincere and I can't stand insincerity."

Paul did not know what to say. He certainly was not going to tell this man that he was not Peter Angel; that would only add to his complications and sound like a very lame excuse. He wondered what he was going to do.

"Well," he admitted. "Perhaps it was wrong of me, though I can't quite see it. Anyway, now that you know who I am what are you going to do?"

Bert Clements was silent in thought for a while before he replied. "I don't know quite," he said at last. "When I first recognised you I made up my mind at once that I would get that reward. It's a lot of money, and it was a police station I was going to take you to, not a petrol station. But while we were having tea and talking I altered my mind. After all, what have you done? You've fleeced a few million people of some of their cash, they all gave voluntarily and probably didn't miss the money, and that makes you a social outcast. And how many men are there today who are doing far worse than you have done, and doing it under cover of the law. Thousands of employers are now robbing their employees not of some of their spare cash, but of the cash they need for food and clothing—and no one ever dreams of outlawing them, so why should you be?"

"I must admit," said Paul, grateful for the other's logic, "that yours is a very interesting theory, very interesting, but it doesn't settle what you intend to do." Paul was still worried about the outcome of this disclosure.

"What can I do?" asked Bert Clements. "I believe in sincerity. What you have done is as wrong as what others are still doing, yet they will never be punished. And do you expect me to take their side against you, to make you an example while they go scot-free? No, so long as this world is content to be run on competitive lines, each man against another, then I say victory to the strongest and I take no man's side. As far as I'm concerned you can walk out of this tent a free man and need have no fear from me. In fact, I'd be more willing to help you than to harm you. They can keep their thousand pounds. It would be blood money if I won it!" There was a fierceness in Bert Clements's eyes and voice as he made this vast renunciation. Paul could not help admiring the man's resolution.

"Say, you're rather unusual. Not many men would have done a thing like that. I'm very, very grateful to you, Mr. Clements."

"Don't thank me, Mr. Angel. Thank the economic conditions which exist at this moment. Under other circumstances I might gladly turn you in to the police."

"I don't know what to say," said Paul, a little shame-faced as he spoke, and wished that he might tell this man the whole truth about himself.

"Finish your tea and don't say anything," suggested Bert Clements wisely.

"And will you still give me a lift to get petrol?" Paul asked the question, rather like a schoolboy trying to ingratiate himself into the good graces of his master after a whipping by asking an unneessary question.

"Why not?" asked Bert." You still want some, don't you? But before we go for it, I'm going to have my bathe. What about it? Are you coming in, too?"

Paul found it difficult to reconcile this man's apparent unconcern towards his identity. The fact that he had a wanted man eating with him seemed of less importance than his daily bathe. For a moment Paul wondered if, under his Socratic calm, there lay a deeper subtlety, a wily scheming that had for its end his ultimate capture. He looked hard at the stout, hairy-kneed figure before him, and decided that he was not capable of such dissembling.

"I'd like to come … but I haven't a swimming suit—"

"Swimming suit! Blimey—this isn't Brighton. You don't have to be ashamed of your body out here in the fens, and you needn't be afraid of scaring the moorhens—they've watched my plump carcass too many times already to be shocked at anything. Come on, get your clothes off and I'll race you to the island."

Against Bert's infectious enthusiasm Paul was not proof, and in a few moments they were both disturbing the water of the mere with their swimming. It was very pleasant and warm in the water and Paul, as he swam slowly towards the island in the wake of his new friend, felt that the cool, companionable water was washing from him all the discomfort and dirt and frenzy of the past few days.

He watched Bert's shoulders rise and fall in the lapping water and the sight of their strength and firmness comforted him; they seemed to stand between him and the shouting, following world; and away beyond the horizon, not many miles away, lay Wisbech. Within a few hours he would be walking about the streets of the town, and all the alarms of the past days would be no more than riotous memory.

They hauled themselves from the mere and sat on a fallen willow log, their feet trailing in the water and the rough bark marking their skin with red patterns.

"Pity the sun ain't shining," said Bert. "But it's quite warm in— enjoying it?"

"I certainly am."

"What are you going to do with all that money—if you get away with it?" asked Bert, after a pause. "You'll be a rich man. Going to have a good time? I wouldn't blame you."

"I don't know rightly," said Paul, pretending to be composing his mind to the disposition of his mythical fortune.

"I know what I'd do," said Bert, picking a green speck of duckweed from his groin. "I know exactly."

"What would you do with it?" inquired Paul, glad to have the onus of wealth transferred to another's shoulders.

"Do—I'd take a course at Ruskin College and then I'd spend the rest of my life trying to wake up sleeping dogs and make folks understand things."

"It would be a great temptation to forgo all that and be selfish and have a good time," suggested Paul.

"Don't you believe it. Mind, I'm not a saint—no, sir! I like my beer and I like a bit of female company at times, but at heart I'm a true altruist. Live for other people—that's my motto, and it brings happiness and—"

What else altruism brought beside happiness Paul never learned or even speculated. At that moment, he caught Bert's arm in a tight grip.

"Would you believe it!"

"Believe what?" questioned Bert, and then his eye followed the direction of Paul's arm. He saw that away on the road a small car, somewhat battered and very dusty, had drawn up alongside the green splendour of the sports car.

"Looks like someone else out of petrol," he said as he watched a man step from the car. "I'd better start a business giving people lifts."

From Paul's heart there rose a quick thudding protest, for the man stepping from the car presented a familiar figure.

"That man ..." he confided stammeringly to Bert, "his name's Wimpole and he's following me ... probably after that reward. What the devil shall I do?"

Bert Clements appreciated the situation at once and he refused to be startled into confusion. He raised one arm and with a swift movement pushed Paul over the side of the log into a deep bed of flags.

"Stay there for a minute," he commanded. "He can't see you."

"But I can't stop here"

"Yes, you can. You keep in hiding on the island and I'll swim over and see what he wants."

120

"My clothes—they're in the tent and he'll see them and there's the car. Hell! Why did that little pest have to follow me!" Paul's temper was not improved by the cold caress of the mud which formed the foundation of the bed of flags. It was oozing slowly round his hindquarters and flanks.

"Leave all that to me, but if you want to save your bacon keep hidden." Saying this, Bert slipped quietly into the water and began to swim towards the shore. As he did so, Mr. Wimpole left his car and moved across to the tent.

Mr. Wimpole, as Paul guessed, was following him in the hope of gaining the reward. The hunting spirit was up in the little man. After Paul had evaded him at the theatre he had remembered the remark he had made about going to Wisbech and—after some trepidation and a quarrel with his wife—Mr. Wimpole had decided to invest the price of a car ride to Wisbech in the hope of spotting Paul. Trusting to signposts and without a map, he had—despite a boasted sense of topography and direction—very soon lost his way. As his wife had so often remarked to him, losing his way was the only thing he could be relied upon to do. Mr. Wimpole was no Herodotus; he possessed a small car, but it was seldom that he ventured farther than twenty miles from Leicester. Today he was feeling like an adventurer, and his boldness had infected his blood stream with a zest that made it difficult for him to keep still.

As he reached the tent, Bert came up from the water, his nakedness stencilled against the bright grass. He nodded affably to Mr. Wimpole.

"Excuse me a moment," he said. "Must get a towel." He dodged into the tent and put Paul's clothes and his cup and plate under the camp bed. Then he came to the tent opening and, rubbing his back hair with a towel, regarded Mr. Wimpole.

"Good afternoon. Looks like a thunder-shower."

"Yes," agreed Mr. Wimpole, though his thoughts were far from meteorological matters. He was obsessed by the possibility of winning a thousand pounds and being able to enter into a new phase of existence. "I seem to have strayed off my road a bit. Not very often I get lost. I wonder if you could put me right, or direct me to a signpost. Once I get to a signpost I shall be all right."

"Where are you heading?"

"Wisbech, but I'm pretty sure I'm off the main road."

"I don't know about the main road, but you're still on the right road. If you carry straight on you'll hit a signpost about five miles along which will give you your position."

While they had been talking the grey masses of clouds, which had been growing heavier and darker for the last hour, suddenly grumbled under their weight of moisture, and a sharp finger of lightning scored the gloomy sky. The piled clouds, like a herd of frightened cattle, seemed to break and waver at the thrust, their bellowing broke out anew and stronger and then, with a lusty roar, they rolled forward in a stampede. Their roaring shook the trees and earth and sharp lightning flashes were thrown from each crash of their hooves. Tossing and snorting before the fear of the wind that raced from the east and whipped them into a higher frenzy of fright, the clouds vented the rain upon the earth.

The rain was at first no more than a whisper in the distance. Then the sound grew and across the flat fields and muddy ditches and drains the foreguards of the rain army appeared, streaming down from the sky in long, steady regiments and battalions. Over the fields, bowing the thick-eared wheat, ravishing the grasses and flattening the feverfew, the rain came in splendid battle array, and the sound of its tramping and onrush grew from a tiny murmur to a tumultuous ululation; a fierce pagan song of battle, the full-throated song of rain, lusting and relentless like the hordes of Cyrus sweeping down upon the unready Croesus. In a minute the army had covered the visible earth and the spearpoints of wind-whipped rain flashed in the pallid light, flattening everything that refused to bow before it. The air was full of rain and thunder and the horizon shrank, as a snail contracts into its shell, as the atmosphere thickened.

Everywhere there was rain and noise; noise that crept into empty cattle sheds and rattled the rusty galvanised iron sheets and shook the wormy beams so that the dried dung and dust fell earthwards in thin, drifting whorls; noise that loosened the ladybirds from the underside of dockleaves and left them stranded, antenna waving and legs combing the air, as they lay on their backs until the rain floated them away on tiny runnels that swirled through the grass-root jungles and over the hard ground; rain that glistened on the dry blades of grass, painted the white of the campions a fresher hue and picked out the cinquefoils with startling brightness and rolled rioting to the ground. It went everywhere, pouring off flower and tree, drumming against the thin laths of the willow branches, pounding on the corky barks of the field maples and sliding down the clayey slopes into the ditches and rivers.

Mr. Wimpole and Bert Clements at the first lash of rain on their faces dived for the shelter of the tent, and as they took their seats on the camp bed the rattle of the storm on the taut canvas filled the tent with an incessant crepitation that effectively killed all conversation. Paul, alone on the island, crept closer to the trunk of a leaning willow where he had gone for shelter.

The willow proved poor shelter. The rain slashed through its leaves, rushed in erratic rivulets over the rough bark and dropped in gurgling, happy runnels upon Paul. He crouched with his bare back against the bark, his feet sinking deeper into the mire at the base of the tree and his right arm holding, in a pathetic gesture of defiance, a form of protest against the uncivilised behaviour of the storm, a large dock leaf over his head. As a gesture, as a protest, the dock leaf may have been symbolic, but as a protection from the storm its effect was negligible. The storm laughed at him and spouted mouthfuls of cold rain over him until his hair, like an Exmoor bog, grew heavy with its treasure of moisture and started small streams that trickled over his forehead, swirled about his nose and mouth and fell in cascades from the point of his chin. Down his neck and spinal column, rising into minute rapids at each slight vertebrate protrusion, flowed another river that called tributaries from his shoulders and ribs until the swollen stream, gorged as the Nile in a rainy season and swift as the Teign after a summer storm, divided just above his coccyx into two branches that debouched into different oceans. One went down his right leg into a muddy sea and the other down his left leg into a reedy Sargasso of bedstraw and bindweeds which were slowly being drowned by the rising waters. He might have been a fountain piece, crouched like a faun or bedraggled satyr, spouting water for the delectation of an artistic municipality from every projection of his body.

He looked around him for better shelter. The island was composed mainly of great tangles of osier and bramble, through which water-rats and voles had worked little paths. Around its fringes floated untidy blankets of water buttercups and lilies. Above the undergrowth rose banks of dog-roses, their petals now despoiled and twirling giddily on the lake's surface under the bombardment of the rain, and over the water a few elder trees hung their branches of white flowers, as though they were the faces of virgins averted from the masculine frankness of Paul's anatomy that gleamed, white and unnatural as a fungus, amidst the greenery. A moorhen, clucking angrily at the storm, passed by him along a small path and disappeared into a thicket of rushes, and a beetle coated with blue enamel and ferocious with red antenna began to crawl up the inside of his leg in the hope, since the lower regions denied it, of finding shelter in the higher.

The beetle decided Paul. He flicked it off with his finger. There was no shelter on the island, and he could not return to the tent. He walked, regardless of the rain, since he could not get any wetter, to the far edge of the island so that it formed a screen for him from the tent, and slid into the water. He swam with the rain hissing about him and forcing the water into miniature jets about his face with its violence, towards the far end of the lake where, in a field of turnips, stood a small shelter. And as Paul pulled himself out of the water with the aid of a tree stump, the noise of the storm abated enough to allow Bert Clements to talk comfortably to Mr. Wimpole.

"Seems to be blowing over," he said.

"I hope it does soon—I'm in a hurry," replied Mr. Wimpole, and he cracked his joints in puny defiance of the thunder crashes. Bert poked his head round the canvas and surveyed the sky. It was one vast plain of maroons and deep purples shot with long swathes of rain and illuminated at times by angry tails of lightning that gave to the country a green-blue radiance. He glanced towards the island. Amidst the rain and the vegetation he could not make out the form of Paul. He grinned to himself at the thought of the crooner waiting out there. It was, he thought, an appropriate justice that the elements should punish him. Then he withdrew his head.

"Wisbech—did you say?"

"Yes—that's where I'm going," said Mr. Wimpole. "Special errand I'm on—very important. And of course this rain has to hold me up. That's like life, isn't it?"

"It's like rain, damned like rain," said Bert. "But why worry?"

"I do worry—that's my nature. I can't help it."

Bert ignored this, and Mr. Wimpole went on, "You see, this is a special errand."

Bert smiled and wondered what Mr. Wimpole would say if he knew that he understood what his errand was. "What is it—a police job, or something? You sound as though you were a detective or something like that?"

Mr. Wimpole had not, until that moment, considered himself in the light of a detective. He was merely out for the reward, but at Bert's words he saw himself in a moment of heroic characterisation as an emissary, a free-lance of the police. He nodded in a way which suggested that he was, perhaps, a detective.

"Blimey—you aren't a 'tec, are you?"

At the admiration in Bert's voice Mr. Wimpole was pleased. It was seldom that such awe fell to his lot. "Something like that," he admitted with ill-assumed casualness.

"Well, now, that's very exciting, I'm sure. I ain't never spoken to a detective before."

"They don't usually let people know what they are," confided Mr. Wimpole magnanimously. "But it won't do any harm to tell you. Keep it to yourself, though."

"You bet I will!" Bert agreed eagerly. "Who are you after? I bet you have some exciting times, don't you?"

Mr. Wimpole considered this. Feeling that it would be inhuman of him to disappoint this man's wonder and attention, he nodded darkly.

"Sometimes. I've had some very nasty moments. But you have to take the rough with the smooth. It's all in the day's work, you know."

Bert, delighted at this turn of the conversation, gradually led Mr. Wimpole on to an account of his adventures, and Mr. Wimpole, discovering an entirely new character in himself, was surprised to hear himself describing manhunts and moments crowded with death and danger in the pursuit of criminals. He cracked his joints and detailed the most thrilling episodes in a tired, matter-of-fact voice, which he considered appropriate to one who has lived a life of excitement. He sucked his teeth and shook his head as he came to the end of a particularly apocryphal reminiscence.

"I get fed up sometimes, you know, and long for a quiet job in an office, but at heart I know there's nothing for me but this work. I've got to have danger or I'll stifle." His vivid exploits of imagination had heightened his colour and set his heart fluttering, but he kept a calm manner. He glanced out at the diminishing rain and, emboldened beyond normal by the new character he had found in himself, he nodded carelessly to Bert and, thanking him for his directions, walked jauntily out into the rain towards his car. Mr. Wimpole, who dreaded the least dampness for fear of rousing his sleeping neuralgia and rheumatism, had indeed suffered a rejuvenation of spirit to walk so heedlessly into the rain. He squelched through the puddles cheerfully and his hand lay snugly in one pocket coiled round the butt of an imaginary automatic.

Bert lay back on the camp bed and, as the sound of Mr. Wimpole's car whimpered across the susurration of the rain, he let out a bellow of laughter and rolled over on the blankets, his naked legs thrusting at the air like a fakir wriggling in ecstasy on a bed of nails. For some time he lay chuckling, and then, recovering himself, he sat up and decided that the joke was too rich to be communicated to anyone else. He must keep it for his own enjoyment for ever.

XIII
Margaret persists

Paul left the water and sprinted across the small patch of open ground to the shed. He plunged through an open doorway into the shadows. For a moment he could see nothing. Then, as his eyes accustomed themselves to the dim light, he saw that the shed was divided into two distinct parts by a wooden partition about five feet high. Each section of the shed was served by a separate door.

Standing by the partition, he stamped his bare feet on the hard trodden floor and ran his hands through his hair and over his body to wipe off the water. He shook his head and, through half-closed lips, blew a sigh of relief at finding shelter.

As he did so there was a faint stirring on the other side of the partition and a familiar voice said:

"My poor Peter! You are wet, aren't you. You'd better dry your hair before you get cold."

Paul leapt round as though he had been bitten, and over the top of the partition found himself staring at Margaret. She was sitting on an upturned feeding trough, her arms widespread and her hands grasping the sides to give her balance. From where she sat Paul realised that all she could see of him was his head.

For some seconds he eyed her strangely, like a madman who hears mocking fancies playing in his brain and sees fantastic visions floating before him. It was unbelievable. It was untrue, impossible—the water and coldness must have affected his brain. Yet what his mind told him was impossible, his eyes, with cold, sane justice, showed him to be true. It was Margaret, and a Margaret who looked very attractive. Her hat was off, and her brown hair, damped by the storm, clustered about her forehead and ears in close curls. Her face was flushed with colour and, although her nose was shiny, there was a beauty in the pose of her body and the thrust of her shoulders as she balanced, which Paul could not help but admire. He did not allow himself to admire her for long. His first reaction had been to run, but he had schooled this by reminding himself that he had nowhere to run and had to avoid Mr. Wimpole.

"What are you doing here?" he asked sternly.

Margaret was not put out by the tone of his question. She rose from her seat and started towards the partition. A wave of panic flooded through Paul. He thrust up an arm and shouted "Stop! Don't come any closer!"

Margaret stopped short and eyed him with wonder.

"Whatever is the matter with you?" she asked curiously.

"Please ..." He waved a worried hand over the top of the partition. "Please stay where you are. It's not safe ... It's ..."

Margaret frowned and half smiled.

"Anyone," she said, "would think you had the plague."

"It's worse than that," confessed Paul.

"Worse than the plague? My dear Peter—what are you talking about?"

Paul saw there was no gracious way out of the confusion. He swallowed nervously and said: "I've got nothing on."

Margaret looked at him, and a little *fleur-de-lis* of wrinkles decorated her forehead.

"You've what?"

"I've got nothing on!" repeated Paul. "I'm naked!"

"Naked?"

"Yes, naked. I haven't any clothes. I was caught in the storm."

"Haven't you even got a pair of trousers on?"

"Nothing. I tell you I was caught in the storm."

"But you don't usually go about in storms with nothing on, do you?" asked Margaret, and there was a wicked light dancing in her eyes.

"Of course not!" Paul said quickly, and he explained briefly what had happened to him. As he finished speaking Margaret began to chuckle.

"I don't see that it's anything to laugh at," said Paul. Margaret looked up at his face.

"Indeed it isn't. It's a very serious affair," she said sympathetically and continued to laugh. Then seeing the embarrassment on his face she stopped and smiled indulgently. "Never mind, dear, we'll see what we can do for you."

She slipped over to the trough and held up a sack. "This will help you for a while, anyway."

She came back to the partition and handed the sack up to Paul, who disappeared from her sight for a moment as he draped it about his middle. Then he appeared again.

"Thank you—I feel more comfortable now."

"And so do I." Margaret put her hands on the partition and looked up at him."

"And now," said Paul, trying to be stern once more, "perhaps you will tell me what you are doing here."

"The same as you," answered Margaret. "I'm taking shelter from the storm. It was a lovely storm, wasn't it? I watched it from the doorway for a long time, until I began to be a tiny bit frightened."

"Lovely is hardly the adjective I should use. How did you get here? I thought I told you that I didn't want you?" Paul found it hard to be severe and to cultivate a firm attitude while he was under the discomfort of holding the meagre sack about him. He was discovering that although clothes may not entirely make a man they lend him a valuable air of authority.

Margaret noticed his discomfort." That's what you said, but I didn't choose to obey you. Besides, I've as much right as you to be in this shed."

"I know that," said Paul, grabbing at the sack which began to slip." You haven't any right to follow me about, though. You know I asked you not to do it."

Margaret looked at him, at his dark hair, doubly black with the rain, and his shoulder muscles catching the light and playing with it as he shifted uneasily. He was rather a splendid young man, she thought, but he obviously needed someone to look after him.

That was certainly not Paul's conviction. He did not consider himself to be helpless, unless semi-nudity constitutes helplessness.

"And I don't care what you say," said Margaret firmly. "I've come and I'm stopping. You want someone to look after you. You nearly made a mess of things in the theatre at Leicester. Try this safety pin."

Margaret handed Paul a large safety pin to fix the sack. Paul accepted it without comment.

"What do you mean?"

"You know what I mean. I was in the theatre. And that reminds me— why did you take my car? That wasn't the right thing to do."

"I'm sorry about that, but it was the only thing to do—" countered Paul, "and I left a note for you."

"I never saw it—"

"Then how did you follow me?"

"Ha!" Margaret smiled. "Those who revere the gods, the gods will bless."

"What do you mean?"

"That I was lucky."

"I don't understand you."

"You will when I explain."

"Then perhaps you will kindly do so, without pushing any more quotations at me."

Margaret told him with a wealth of irrelevant detail that made Paul itch with impatience as he sensed that she was deliberately trying to make him uncomfortable.

As Paul had driven away from the theatre she had come out in time to see her own car pass her with a black man at the wheel. Natural curiosity had emboldened her to hail a passing cab and follow him until he had drawn up and settled down to sleep. Leaving the cab some hundred yards away she had crept up to his car, or her car, and seen that the black man was really Paul. At first she had been going to waken him and demand an explanation; but he had looked so tired and exhausted that she had decided to let him have his sleep. Satisfied that he would sleep for some time she had driven back to Leicester in the cab, hired a car from an all-night garage and driven out again to where he slept. She had intended to keep an all-night vigil, but sleep had overcome her noble resolution and she had awakened in time to hear Paul driving away. She had followed and had been filled with curiosity at the determination with which he made his way across the country. It was obvious that he was making for some definite goal and she had determined not to discover herself to him until she found out where he was going. She had kept fairly close to him until he had drawn up at Bert Clements's tent. She had passed while they were having tea, stopped a few miles down the road and, walking back to see what was happening, had been caught in the storm.

"Just think how comforting it would have been to you, Peter dear, last night, if you'd known that I was watching over you."

"Comforting is not the word I should use!" said Paul ungraciously." I wish you would realise that—much as I love you—I don't want you with me. It's dangerous for you."

"All the more reason for my being with you. My place is at your side. Oh, darling, can't you see I'm full of anxiety for you and want to help you? After all, remember I only knew you for a little while in America and it's natural that I should want as much of your company now as I can get, despite the awkward circumstances."

"But think of your position, Margaret. And your father—what would he say?"

"He's long ago given up saying things, dear. He's a wise parent and accepts the inevitable folly of children."

Paul began to walk up and down.

"I don't know what to do with you," he admitted.

He watched the trickle of water from his legs making dusty-surfaced puddles in the ground, and debated whether he should disillusion this young lady without further delay. For a moment he was tempted to do so, then his caution forbade him. If he told her, she might insist that he went to the police with her, and then would begin an endless series of complications, complications which he was anxious to avoid. He was sorry for her that the real Peter Angel should have so ruthlessly left her and flouted her love, yet he could not but admire her fidelity to the crooner, even though he himself happened to be the unfortunate recipient of her loyal demonstrations. And if he confessed his identity it would not be easy to explain the readiness with which he had accepted her favours in the past—at the thought of the first time he had kissed her and other incidents Paul blushed and quickly decided that the only decent way was to proceed with the masquerade and slip away from her at the earliest opportunity. An act which he did not anticipate would present any difficulty.

"Don't worry, darling, I'll look after you. Where are your clothes?"

Paul, acknowledging to himself that it was useless to keep anything from her since she shared so much of his secret, told her all that had happened since leaving Leicester.

"What a nice man this Mr. Clements must be," was her comment. "So unusual with Communists, too. They're generally so full of ideas that they haven't time for kindness and understanding."

She moved to the doorway and looked out. The rain had steadied into a thin drizzle.

"The small car's gone now," she informed Paul. "I'll fetch your clothes for you."

Paul started up in a protest, but she had gone. He sat down and then chuckled. If he had been Peter Angel he could have welcomed her bubbling optimism, for he was not immune from the charm of her manner and she was pleasant to look at.

Margaret did have a very definite charm when she set herself to be pleasant. She crossed the fields to the tent and, entering, introduced herself to Bert Clements as Peter Angel's fiancée. Disregarding the man's surprise, she explained the position very clearly to him and then, taking Paul's clothes and a towel, went back to the shed.

From that moment Margaret took control of the proceedings and Paul could do no more than accept her presence as inevitable. It was useless to try and shake her off at the moment, and it would alienate Bert's sympathies, since he was impressed by Margaret's efficiency.

Over a cup of tea, brewed to induce heat into Paul's shivering frame and to counteract the imminence of any cold, they discussed their plans, and it was decided that it was unsafe for Paul to go to Wisbech and that they should all sleep that night in the tent. Bert—tactfully—offered to walk down the road and drive Margaret's car back, leaving, as he thought, the lovers alone for a while.

While he was gone, Paul lay on the camp-bed reading a copy of *The Listener* and made polite returns to Margaret's questions, though she contented herself for the most part by listening to the soft murmur of the rain on the canvas and musing. Her thoughts might have surprised Paul could he have known their content. When Bert returned they whiled the evening away playing three-handed nap with a dogeared pack of cards with a picture of Tower Bridge on the back, and then they went to bed. Paul and Bert took a five minutes' walk in the rain while Margaret undressed and got into the camp-bed. As they walked along the road Paul debated and rejected an impulse to run away into the gathering mist. When they returned, Margaret discreetly buried her head in the clothes until they were lying, sharing two car rugs and a blanket between them, on a groundsheet alongside the camp-bed. Soon they were all asleep.

The miracle of speed and rapid travel happens so often today that it has lost, except in occasional moments of reflection, most of its wonder. As he stood outside a tea shop in Matlock, Paul was overcome with a sudden wave of wonder at the speed and unexpectedness with which he had travelled within the last few weeks. From America he had come to see Wisbech, but Wisbech had been denied him. Instead he had seen the south of England, London, Leicester, the Midlands and the bleakness of the fens. Now he stood on the fringe of the Peak District and marvelled at the calm acceptance with which he had met all these changes.

They had left Bert that morning. He had driven Margaret's hired car into Peterborough, left it at a garage to be collected, with enough money to meet the bill, while Margaret had driven Paul, unprotesting, away from Wisbech towards Matlock, to throw Mr. Wimpole and possibly the police off their scent. They had adopted this plan after some discussion. They were all agreed that it was wise to go as far from the Wisbech area as possible to avoid Mr. Wimpole. Matlock had been chosen in a purely arbitrary mood by Margaret and Bert. Paul had been content to accept their decision.

They had reached Matlock in the early afternoon and, after garaging the car, had gone to a tea shop. During the drive Paul had said very little, but Margaret had more than compensated for his paucity of conversation. During tea Margaret had still talked while Paul ate solidly of brown bread and honey. His first impression of Matlock was unfavourable. He did not like the winding gorge, the dark, leafy atmosphere of dampness and shadow, and he was unimpressed by the grey houses that climbed the hillside in little terraces.

"Well," said Margaret as Paul paid the bill and they stood outside; "what do we do now?"

Paul considered for a moment before replying. He had not lost sight of the fact that he had to give Margaret the slip. Here was his opportunity— an opportunity to do it gracefully and politely.

"I'm going to walk right out of this town and lose myself for a few days in this Peak country you've been telling me about. I should like to take you, of course, but you obviously can't come on such a rough trip in your clothes. You're not fitted for that kind of thing, either. I shall probably walk miles each day—"

"You will?"

"Yes. I'm glad you realise you can't come. I've appreciated your help, Margaret. You've been a wonder and I'm proud of you. Still, we must part now. I'll get in touch with you when this trouble's blown over. Meanwhile—" He laughed pleasantly at the ease with which his plan was working. "Meanwhile—Goodbye and thank you. Think of me sometimes—"

Margaret nodded her head sympathetically." A very good idea. I'll think of you often."

"That's kind of you, Margaret," said Paul gratefully. "Goodbye!" He held her hand for a moment and then turning away began to walk up a small hill that faced him. He had not gone three steps before she was at his side.

"I'll think of you often, darling, because I'm coming with you."

Paul stopped, then warned by her attitude he realised his impotence. He compressed his lips. He was far from complacently accepting her presence, but he knew that he was helpless to shake her off. He knew enough about her now to understand that when she had made up her mind there was little hope of her altering. He realised that silence was the best policy—this was not the time for a quarrel—and he swung up the hill, not abating the length of his stride for her, determined that at the first legitimate opportunity he would rid himself of her company. And Margaret followed, her breath coming quickly as she kept pace with him and a little wind ruffling the tendrils of her hair where they strayed from the sides of her hat.

So they went on, and as they toiled up the hill the sun, coming over the edge of a cloud, smiled at them, and a thrush, perched on top of a hazel branch, sang a mocking song.

Where they were going, they knew not. Paul had lost his grip in Leicester and still wore the actor's blue suit. He was hatless, and his only defence against the world was the money in his pocket. And Margaret, without a thought for her own convenience, was almost as destitute of toilet refinements as he. She had her handbag and a certain amount of money. The hill was long, and as she grew hotter she took off her short coat and walked with the wind ruffling the skirt of her frock and fretting at the small hat which she had pushed back upon her head for comfort.

Walking by his side, unable to pursue any conversation since she needed all her breath to keep pace with him up the hill, Margaret considered the ethics of her unladylike pursuit of this young man. He was not Peter Angel, that was now very obvious, though she saw no reason why she should inform him that she knew his secret. It amused her, and at the same time aroused her sympathy to watch the stubbornness with which he played his part. Why he did so she could only half guess. She knew that he must have some strong incentive to assume a love for her when it was so clear that he did not want her company. Her curiosity worked about the possibilities of his identity, and she decided that— whether he liked it or not—it was a good thing to keep with him in case he got into trouble, then she could come forward and prove his innocence, if necessary. She wondered who he was, this athletic, stern-faced young man who walked as though he were determined to reach the Irish Channel by sundown. She guessed that with anyone else he might have been cheerful and good company, but with her he was nervous and worried. Perhaps it was an excess of chivalry that made him worried for her safety. She knew that he was not a criminal. He was too nice for that and not clever enough, but just what he was she would never ascertain unless she kept with him and broke down his frigid reserve.

Paul was worried. He was worried by his enforced behaviour to Margaret. It was unlike what she was entitled to expect from a fiancé, and he knew that if he made himself too boorish he was imperilling his position by arousing in her the suspicion that he was not Peter Angel. It was difficult to play two parts simultaneously. He glanced at her as she walked by him and, his pity excited by her distress, he slowed up.

Margaret shot a grateful glance at him. "Thank you, Peter. I'm sorry if I've annoyed you, but if you'll only consider things sanely, this is the best thing for us to do. Don't be angry with me any more."

Against this overture with its hint of tears, Paul was not proof. He cherished romantic ideas of womanhood and to make a woman suffer was abhorrent to him. He decided that outwalking her was the wrong way to escape. That could come later, and until then it could not do any harm to be pleasant to her.

"I'm sorry, Margaret ... but my nerves have been all on edge lately and perhaps I've acted rather badly ..." Paul made the admission willingly, knowing that it was demanded of him. But Margaret would not accept it.

"Oh, no you haven't, Peter, dear. You've been wonderful and it's really all my fault. There's nothing to forgive."

"That's all right, then. We can start from scratch again, eh?"

"Oh, Peter, it is nice to know that you're not going to be angry. Peter, darling ..." Margaret came closer to him. "There's one thing which would show you mean what you say. You haven't done it for a long, long time—"

"What do you mean?" asked Paul, immediately suspicious.

"Kiss me . . ."

They stopped and Paul stared at her for a moment, then the appeal of her eyes was too much for him. He put his arms around her and did his best to feign an amatory enthusiasm, and—to his surprise—he discovered that the operation was not so unpleasant as it had been on the first occasion. They went on walking and Paul surreptitiously wiped the kiss from his lips. He was not entitled to it. Margaret saw the action and guessing its meaning was filled with a gust of admiration for him.

They reached the top of the hill and a wide plateau stretched before them, a plateau cut into odd geometrical shapes by long straggling stone walls on which clumps of yellow stone-crop reflected the light.

"Peter, darling," said Margaret after a while, "why were you going to Wisbech?"

Peter hesitated before he replied. He said, "I thought I might get a boat there and leave the country."

"I don't think you could have managed that," Margaret said. "The police would be watching the ports for a while. You'll be safer in these hills for a time with me."

"I wonder," reflected Paul.

"Anyway, why Wisbech? Why not Bristol or Liverpool where you'd have had more opportunity of getting a boat?"

"I ... I ... I thought that in a smaller port I would stand a better chance. It's the big ones that are watched."

"That's true," agreed Margaret. "But it will be better to wait for a few days until the police have relaxed their vigilance and then try."

"I reckon I could get by the police now," said Paul.

Margaret laughed. "This is England, remember, and it isn't often the police are after a man like yourself, so they won't be sleeping."

"Well, they haven't got me so far, have they?"

"No," admitted Margaret. "You have been lucky, darling. Still, from now you'll have me to help you."

"It looks," said Paul, smiling, "as though my luck's going then."

Margaret laughed and tossed her head back with a characteristic gesture. "Stupid old thing. I think it's all very exciting and unusual, and I'm sure that if my father knew about it he would be thoroughly annoyed with me. I like people to be annoyed with me. Either that or in love with me—"

"Well," said Paul quickly, "up to now I've been annoyed with you—" He stopped, realising the implication of his unfortunate words.

Margaret turned to him and smiled. "And now—" she prompted maliciously. "Go on, say it. And now you're—"

But Paul would not say it. Instead, he blushed. Then they looked at each other and laughed together. It was the first genuine laugh Paul had shared with anyone since reaching England.

For the rest of the afternoon there was a truce between them. They walked on, along the dusty road that wound over the undulating plateau, between the thick, crazy stone walls towards a distant ridge of hill which was crowned with a mist of trees. They talked about books and, when it was obvious that the discussion bored Paul, Margaret let him talk about engineering. Paul skilfully disguised the fact that he was an engineer, and as Peter Angel, pretended an interest in mechanics and hydraulics of which she had been unsuspecting. And when that subject was finished the talk wandered from one thing to another in a pleasant easy fashion that made the miles seem shorter and the hills less steep. Margaret was entertaining company. At times her opinions were dogmatic, but she had a spontaneous humour which attracted Paul and occasionally he found himself wishing that the situation was not such a morass of subterfuges so that he might meet her on open ground and enjoy her company without the handicap of his enforced deceit always above him.

The country they passed through was open and uninteresting. Sometimes a copse of trees would break the wide expanse of upland, or a low bank of thorn and elder. Mostly all that could be seen were lengths of wall and white roads that twisted away into the distance as though anxious to leave the sterile waste and reach the security of pleasanter country. On the walls wheatears flirted and sang their mating songs and coveys of rooks came sweeping low over the ground on their way back to their rookeries, and around the small artificial meres bands of peewits stepped daintily over the dried hoof marks left where cattle had come to drink. This was the prelude to the Peak district, that great sprawling mass of limestone and millstone grit which forms the southerly end of the curving range of the Pennines. From where Paul and Margaret stood it would have been possible to walk, obliquely crossing roads and rivers in the valley dips, along the whole length of the chain until the glitter of the Tweed signalled the approach to the Scottish border, along hundreds of miles of that great carboniferous uplift which occurred when the world was young, a great range which has now been denuded and whittled down to a mockery of its former grandeur, but is nevertheless a formidable mockery, for there are places on the hills where, in some years, the snow lingers after Midsummer Day and where the skeletons of sheep lie bleaching in the wind and rain with only the grouse to call their obsequies and the beetles to perform their last services. They were standing on the last wide vertebra of the backbone of England.

They followed the sun into the west and as it sank below the crest of the great tableland, filling the little valleys with mist and cool shadows and touching the tumuli and tree tops with pale shafts of crimson and purple wefts of light, they came to a small cottage set in the angle of two roads. In the garden gaudy marigolds made a golden border behind which flared great spikes of blue and pink lupins and banks of Royal Clarkia, while along the edge of the sanded path which led to the doorway trailed a line of fragile London Pride, their pinky white heads and ruddy stems trembling in a faint westerly breeze that was springing from the sea, disturbed by the setting of the sun. On the porch of the cottage there was a small white board with a notice painted on it in black letters of unequal dimensions.

BED AND BREAKFAST.
NEW LAID EGGS.
MINERALS, TOBACCO, ETC.

Neither of them was interested in new laid eggs, the product apparently of a few Light Sussex fowls and Wyandottes that scratched in a pen at the side of the cottage, or in the minerals and tobacco, and what was betokened by the "etc." they never inquired, but both of them felt that with the approach of night it was time they found a lodging.

Paul stopped as Margaret did and they looked at the sign. Then they looked at one another.

"Well?" said Margaret.

"I think," replied Paul, "we'd better halt our caravan here for the night."

"My legs tell me that that is more than a good idea." Margaret pushed open the gate and walked up to the porch. The air was fragrant with the scent of untidy syringa and heavy rambler roses. In the bleakness of the uplands the garden was like an isolated paradise, a detached Halicarnassus of loveliness.

Margaret knocked at the door, and a woman answered her knock. She was a woman built upon sound geometrical principles. Her face was a pleasant circle with her features wisely situated to give her a permanent expression of amusement, though one eye, the left, had a downward droop towards a wart that clung like a limpet to the side of her mouth, as though she were continually giving it a reproachful glance for its audacity in coming so close to the orifice through which she absorbed the sustenance which maintained the decapitated pyramid that was her body. The pyramid rested stoutly on two cylinders encased in coarse black woollen stockings and shoes with steel buckles, which had been in her family since one of her male ancestors had received his quietus in the Peterloo riots. She wore, since it was late afternoon and she had finished her hard work for the day, a dress of black *crêpe-dechine*, very tight round her bust and held tighter still round her neck by a Wedgwood brooch of some obscure female divinity. Only her hands, lined with scrubbing and housework and reddened by the country air, denied her prim elegance and showed her as a cottage wife.

"Could we," asked Margaret, smiling at the woman, "could we stop here for the night?"

"Come inside, would you please?" she requested and she pivoted her body round to give them room to pass her. She conducted them into a small living room and, before they had time to inspect their surroundings, she went on: "What would you be wanting? I've got a nice double bed that I'm sure you would be comfortable on and the sheets are well aired. I sleep in it myself twice a week to keep it from getting damp, but not only for that, of course. My husband's an unsteady sleeper and I like to give him a good night's rest at times, so we sleep one in each room. I'll take you up and show you."

While she was talking both Paul and Margaret were accommodating themselves to the startling revelation that they had been taken for man and wife. Paul, was the first to recover. He stepped forward and caught Margaret warningly by the arm. The feeling of his hand on her arm woke Margaret and a merry light sparkled in her eyes.

"Yes, we'd like the double bed. My husband, unlike yours, is a very sound sleeper so we shan't be uncomfortable."

"Aaaah. … Ugh …" Paul made incoherent noises in the back of his throat at this movement and Mrs. Asher, for that was the woman's name, turned to him sympathetically.

"You sound as though you've picked up a cold, sir. I'll see you have a hot drink before you go to bed. This way, please."

She stretched out a large arm and shepherded the two up a narrow wooden stairway into a large bedroom that overlooked the front garden. In it was a massive bedstead, covered with a pink and black eiderdown and shining with brass knobs and cast-iron excrescences. The wall was papered with a pattern that might have been inspired by the floral beauty outside in the garden, but missed by a long way the simplicity of the garden and achieved an overwhelming horror which was remarkable chiefly for the preponderance of an unknown flower, in form a hybrid between a marrow blossom and a begonia, which lavished itself over the room and was followed by a host of lesser floral atrocities. On the mantelshelf was a marble clock with one hand missing and hanging from the walls were two pictures of classical derivation and execrable execution, and a cross-stitched pin-cushion. The only objects of beauty in the room were a tall bow-fronted chest of drawers in rosewood and a Queen Anne sofa of delicate line which stood, aghast at the Victorian horror of the bedstead, on shapely cabriole legs.

"This is it!" said Mrs. Asher proudly. "It'll be seven-and-six the two for bed and breakfast. Happen that was too much, I could come down a little, though …?"

"Oh, that'll be quite all right. Thank you. It looks lovely," said Margaret, and as the woman left the room to fetch them hot water to wash with before their meal, she turned to Paul.

"Don't you think it's gorgeous?"

"What," said Paul the moment Mrs. Asher had disappeared, "do you mean by letting her think we're married? Haven't you got any moral sense at all? What has happened to you, Margaret?"

"Moral sense!" Margaret scoffed. "Don't talk rubbish, darling. It's horse sense. You see I know that, for all you've been very nice to me today, you still don't like the idea of my being with you, and if we had single rooms you'd more than likely try to give me the slip somehow. But here I can keep an eye on you all night!" She sat down on the bed and moved her body up and down, so that when Paul replied his words had an accompaniment of squeaks from the springs.

"If you think I'm going to sleep in that bed you're wrong."

"But you are going to sleep there."

"I'm not—you … you must be utterly depraved?"

"No, I'm not, but you're going to sleep there."

"And with you, I suppose," suggested Paul bitterly, sarcastically.

"Oh, no, I shall sleep on that lovely sofa. Doesn't it look lonely in this loathsome room."

Paul had no opportunity to reply, for at that moment Mrs. Asher came in with hot water.

"There you are, my dears! And the supper will be waiting for you as soon as you're ready." She went out.

Margaret poured the water into the basin and, to Paul's horror, slipped off her dress and began to wash.

"Don't pretend to be shocked, Peter Angel," she admonished him through a mass of soap bubbles. "You've seen me in a bathing dress, haven't you? This slip is much more decent."

Paul sat on the sofa and pretended to be interested in the picture of Hippomenes throwing golden fruit to Atalanta as they raced. Why any man should go to all that trouble to win a woman he could not, at that moment, understand. They were a curse, a nuisance, destroyers of peace and reputation, an encumbrance and a danger, and the particular woman in the room before him seemed to have inherited all the more revolting and annoying characteristics of her sex. She was shameless. He felt prompted to take her by the shoulders, push her into the clothes cupboard by the fireplace, lock her there and bolt from the house, but a heavy sense of weariness from walking and a knowledge of the ineffectualness of such a course killed this idea. He made a secret vow that if ever the day came when he could speak freely, when he could take the guard off his tongue and actions, he would tell her just what he thought of her and when she was suitably impressed by her wickedness, forget all romantic conventions and spank her until she admitted her deficiencies and apologised to him for her bad behaviour. He felt very stern as he frowned at the badly proportioned Hippomenes.

When Margaret had finished her toilet Paul washed. Then, refreshed from the fatigue of their walk, they went down to supper.

Mrs. Asher was a liberal woman and her meal was as prodigal as her body. They sat in the common-room of the cottage where a fire burned in the kitchen range and ate at a long table covered with a green cloth. There was cold ham and tongue, a fresh salad of lettuce, young onions, tomatoes and cold potato, and after this cold custard pie, mincemeat enfolded in thin slices of pastry and warm bread and jam, the bread not long baked in the oven. During the meal they were silent, both of them discovering their hunger, though now and then Margaret shot gleeful looks at Paul and chuckled to herself at his obvious embarrassment.

When the meal was over Margaret, before Paul could intervene, refused Mrs. Asher's offer to allow them to sit in the front parlour and asked to be allowed to sit in the common-room with her.

"My husband will be in soon," said Mrs. Asher. "If you don't mind you can stay here. I expect you're glad of a little company if you've been walking all day."

"Yes, we haven't seen many people. I should think you get rather lonely living out here, don't you?" inquired Margaret.

Mrs. Asher shook her head as she cleared the table.

"There's too much to be done to give me time to be lonely. I've been married fifteen years this last Easter and I've never been further than Buxton since then. Have you been married long, if I may be so forward?"

Paul twitched on his chair and eyed Margaret anxiously, but she was undaunted.

"Not very long, Mrs. Asher. As a matter of fact, this is our honeymoon!"

"You don't say!" Mrs. Asher was delighted at this information. "You're a lucky gentleman, sir," she addressed Paul; "and I wish both of 'ee many days of happiness together. You look like a nice couple. Ah, it's a lovely time, the honeymoon. Me and the husband went to Blackpool for a week. I shan't forget it in a hurry. I lost my new parasol in the picture house there and the sea brought me out in a rash so that I couldn't bear to lay down at nights, it was so sore. I had to sleep in a chair. But the husband didn't mind. I told you he was an unsteady sleeper and likes a bed to himself."

"Oh, we're not doing anything like that," went on Margaret. "We thought we'd like to go off together walking, going anywhere we liked and enjoying ourselves."

"Everyone to their taste, of course. I often get young couples stopping here, doing the same as you. But sometimes," as she spoke Mrs. Asher threw a reassuring glance at the ring on Margaret's finger, "I know they ain't married, yet what can you do? I don't hold with such things, unsanctified by holy matrimony, as don't no other decent person, but you can't be rude to folks, and we've got to make a living."

There was a decided stress on the word decent and Margaret was glad that she had had the wit to put the little ring she wore on to her marriage finger and turn the stone inwards, so that it showed a plain gold band. Paul got up, feeling too uncomfortable to stand this indelicate conversation sitting down, and pretended to examine the books on top of the shelf by the window.

He heard Mrs. Asher and Margaret settling down to a long talk on the immorality of young girls and the joys of marriage. He tried to forget them as he studied the titles of the books. But the books could not make him forgetful. He took down a book, *The Defence of Plevna, 1877*, and stared at the frontispiece which represented a bearded Turk, Mushir Ghazi Osman Muri Pasha. The aloof eyes of the hirsute Turk gave him no comfort. Underneath the picture was an Eastern proverb— "Though an enemy be as small as an ant, act as though he were an elephant." That might be all right with some things, but Paul wondered what the Turk would have done with Margaret. Perhaps he would not have been unduly worried. A man who had behind him a racial tradition of polygamy and the plenary delights of a harem would know how to deal with Margaret. He put Mushir Ghazi Osman Muri Pasha back on the shelf and forgot the defence of Plevna for the Stock Exchange Investment Handbook, but this did not hold him for long.

141

Mrs. Asher interrupted her talk to light an oil lamp, and soon the rose-coloured globe was spreading a soft glow over the room. Paul sat by the window between the lights and read the *Elements of Agriculture*. The precise, technical terms soothed him and struck a familiar note in his mind. He immersed himself in the rotation of crops, swine fever and the fodder values of hop trefoil and clover, and Margaret watched him as he sat, a darkly shadowed figure by the window, and felt a great wave of sympathy and pity for him come over her. He was so pathetic and so amusing in his indignations. If Mrs. Asher had not been in the room it would have been difficult for her to restrain herself from going over to him and kissing him, like a mother mollifying a sulking boy, on the cheek.

When the twilight was merging into night and the bats were circling above the cottage, Mr. Asher came in. He was introduced to the two visitors, and Paul, as he shook hands, could see that Mr. Asher had been paying a call at the local hostelry.

Mr. Asher was a poet. He had all the emotions and sensitiveness of a poet, but lacked the ability to express himself through the medium of words, and this longing for adequate expression to his fancies broke out in his unsteady gestures and extravagant body. Where Mrs. Asher was solidly and regularly geometric, Mr. Asher was wildly and fantastically irregular. His face was lop-sided, so that one eye almost looked down on the other, the corners of his mouth ran from one plane to another and his nose, eschewing the earth, pointed like his thoughts to the heavens. At first glance he might have been mistaken for an idiot, at a second one perceived beneath his fantasy a shrewd, capable personality that indicated itself in his strong arms and the neatness of his clothes that almost hid the angularities of his tall frame. Tonight, however, Mr. Asher had forgotten his mundane virtues, his capabilities and shrewdness, tonight he was a poet. He had been having his pint, he had taken more than his pint, and the beer had drowned the common man and floated the poet to the top, so that now, after walking home three miles, he felt within himself all the mounting thoughts and urges which he could not properly express. His first words, when he sat down after being introduced, astonished Paul and Margaret, but not Mrs. Asher, who in fifteen years had reconciled herself to her husband's oddities.

"I've seen a ghost," he said. "A white ghost riding on an old nag, holding a bloody sword in one hand and a Bible in the other."

"Nonsense, George," said his wife. "Them's your fancies again. He gets them at times," she explained to the two.

"I've seen a ghost, I tell you. It came down from the spinney, jumped the wall and stood in the road afore me, as might be you're before me now."

"What did you do?" questioned Paul, rather glad of this diversion.

"Do! 'Taint the first time it's happened—"

"That's true enough—" put in Mrs. Asher.

"Be quiet, old lady. It stood afore me, and then what?" He looked round the room to see that he had their interest and his eyes rolled in their sockets like planets slipping round the edge of a cloud.

"And then what? It begins to read from the book in its hand. Holding the sword up, like a pikestaff, it reads, and I can remember every word on it. It says aloud to me: '*Deliver me from the workers of iniquity and save me from bloody men!*'"

Paul felt an inclination to laugh, and then he forgot it, as he saw that Margaret was uncomfortable in the man's presence.

Mr. Asher went on. "That's what it read, and then it rode away down the road on the nag, muttering as it went, '*Deliver me from bloody men!*'" His manner changed suddenly, as though the stirring exultation of beer were ebbing, and he said in a matter-of-fact voice: "That's what it said, and before the night's out we shall have a thunderstorm. It always happens so. Well, good night, lady, and good night, sir. Time for me to go to bed." He rose and marched out and they heard him clump upstairs to his room.

Mrs. Asher chuckled good-naturedly. "He's a good man," she said half-excusingly. "'Tis true he gets a bit wild at times. But I don't try to hold him. A shrewd tongue won't change a man's nature, any more than a stick'll teach a cat not to steal milk. I wouldn't change him for anyone."

After this it was not long before she intimated that it was bedtime, and Paul found himself following Margaret up the stairs and holding a candle whose flame flickered and dipped in the draught.

The moment the door was shut Margaret came up to him.

"I'm so glad you're here, Peter, I shouldn't feel safe in the house with that man. He may be harmless, but he frightened me."

Her confidence in his presence covered Paul with a swift pride. He forgot for a while that he was plain Paul Morison or Peter Angel and was simply a man in whom a female had recognised a protector. He mastered his pleasure and said sternly, "Don't be foolish—he's quite harmless. Anyhow, I can manage him if necessary."

"Oh, Peter," murmured Margaret, now recovered from her fears, "you're so strong and wonderful."

Paul was puzzled by the note in her voice and had an uncomfortable suspicion that she was fooling him. His sternness increased.

"Well, Margaret, I don't know about you, but I'm more than ready for bed." He moved across to the far side of the sofa and without looking at Margaret began to undress. She watched him until he had reached the tie and shoe stage and then, realising that he intended to take possession of the sofa, she discreetly turned her head and surveyed one of the pictures until she heard the springs creak. When she turned she saw that Paul had wrapped himself in a blanket from the bed.

"You know, darling," she said softly, "I'd be quite willing to sleep on the sofa. I've done it often—"

"Don't be silly," mumbled Paul, wriggling into a semi-comfortable position. "I couldn't allow that."

"But I like sleeping on sofas. It's an art—"

"I can believe that," came the muffled answer. "How many years does it take to acquire?"

"Then won't you have another blanket?" Paul sat up and looked frowningly at Margaret.

"Listen, Margaret Sinclair," he said sternly, "if you don't hurry into that bed instead of standing there pretending you'd like to sleep here, I might take you at your word and change places—"

"Oh, Peter!" exclaimed Margaret, laughing, "how terrible that would be."

She undressed and, using her slip as a nightdress, climbed into the tall bed.

They lay awake in the darkness for a while, Paul trying to make himself feel annoyed with Margaret for imposing this discomfort on him, and Margaret grateful for the comfort of the bed and full of sympathy for Paul.

XIV
Enter Michael

It would have been beyond any man but Mr. Asher to say just how much truth and how much fancy there had been in his story of the ghostly rider, or what connection there could possibly be between psychic phenomena and atmospheric disturbances. Yet at half-past three that morning Margaret was awakened by a tremendous crash of thunder. Across the night and through the darkness of the room it blared like a fanfare of discordant trumpets and the earth was lit up by a vivid flash of lightning.

The rolling of the thunder reminded her of Mr. Asher and his ghost and as she lay, half awake on the bed, her mind began to play her tricks. Between the crashes she thought she heard the beat of hooves on the road and once she could have sworn she caught the sound of a wild voice calling. She lay, eyes open, staring round the room and between flashes her fancy painted morbid images in the dark corners and fashioned grotesque creatures from the massy substances of the furniture. She tried to control herself and felt her flesh creeping as the storm filled the night with wildness. She, alone, it seemed was awake in this house, and to her solely came the horror and terror of the storm. She lay, stiffening her limbs and telling herself not to be a fool, but another flash of lightning followed by a roll of thunder that seemed to indicate that the heavens were falling about the house made her jerk upright in bed. There was a pause, a tiny silence in which she caught the regular breathing of Paul, and then a curlew, disturbed by the storm, came flying close to the house, and as it passed the window it whistled, churling and eerie. The weird sound sent a quick spasm of uncontrollable fear spurting through

Margaret. She gave a scream, and rolling from the bed, swept a blanket about her and leapt for the warm, human safety of the sofa.

Paul woke with a start, his ears ringing with the echoes of her scream and his shoulders gripped by her hands.

"Eh? What? What's happened?" He sat up and discovered Margaret.

"Oh, Peter," she said, her voice weak and appealing, "I'm so frightened by the storm. Isn't … isn't it silly of me?"

"Storm?" Paul's question was answered by a peal of thunder and quick beat of rain on the window. "Oh—it'll blow over."

"I know, but I'm frightened. This dark room and that man, and …" Paul smiled in the darkness. It was gratifying to him to discover this weak side of Margaret. It gave him an advantage over her and compensated him for many things. He was filled with a generous condescension.

"You're all right," he said soothingly, and then, the slave of his chivalrous impulses, he slid from the sofa. "You'd better get into bed again—you're showing too much of your shoulders to be decent where you are. I'll sit on the end of the bed and talk to you." He stood for a moment, forgetful of his shirt, and then slipped a blanket about himself.

"Oh, Peter, darling, I can't let you do this. You're too kind."

"Perhaps I am," agreed Paul moving towards the sofa. "Anyway, you lie there and forget your fears. You don't have to worry. You can talk to me."

Margaret crept into the bed and Paul settled himself on the foot and started to talk.

After a time the storm began to abate and Margaret's drowsiness returned. The talk lapsed from conversation to a monologue as Paul went on describing his difficulties and experiences in learning to fly. From flying he went on to shooting and fishing in the Adirondacks, and from hunting to New York theatres and then, getting no response from Margaret to a question, Paul realised that with a feminine disregard for courtesy she had gone to sleep. He heard her breathing develop into a regular rhythm and returning to the sofa, tried to sleep also. He slept fitfully, and as soon as it was daybreak he washed and dressed himself. He sat on the edge of the sofa and read a Victorian moral story of a road-crossing sweeper until Margaret wakened and the house breathed again the reassuring sounds of life and preparations for another day. It never occurred to him in that hour while the house was still and Margaret slept, to creep away. Later, when he tried to analyse why, he could only satisfy himself by pretending that it was because he did not want to miss his breakfast.

By four o'clock that afternoon Paul had given Margaret the slip. The day proved hot and bright, the air was cleared by the thunderstorm and the country freshly washed by gouts of rain. They left the cottage and walked, still westwards, through a country that became hillier and wilder, across long moors and through twisting valleys where streams swept over mossy boulders that were the haunt of white-breasted dippers and hovering dragonflies.

Paul had enjoyed the day. There was a peace and stillness about the larch woods that filled the valleys and a fragrance in the thyme-covered slopes of the hills that entered his soul and made him forgetful of his vagrancy and the police behind him. Sometimes they passed white quarries, gashed in the sides of the hill, where dusty workmen leaned on their hammers by the side of the heaps of stone.

Their conversation sprang from the things around them and once, when a young rabbit got up at their feet from a clump of sorrel, they both raced away after it, laughing and panting until it disappeared into its bolt hole. And at midday they lay in the shade of a crab-apple tree and ate the sandwiches which Mrs. Asher had prepared for them. Before them the Peak country stretched in a lovely vista of rounded domes and huge molehills of land with here and there a sharp scar-face and cliffs. In tiny hollows the white sparkle of cottages showed and once on a distant ridge a lorry moved like an ant.

The heat of the afternoon, however, made them tired and when, very early, they came to a village sleeping where a stream, almost a river, curved between two hills they decided to stay for the night. It was a large village with two hotels. They entered the smaller, the Fleckington Arms. This time Paul ordered the rooms, two single rooms, and Margaret, lulled into a sense of security by the camaraderie of the day, made no protest. It was now that Paul decided to leave her. He knew that she had enough money to pay her bill and her fare back to London, if she chose. While she was in her room washing before tea, he wrote her a polite note, expressing his regret at the action he was taking and making what excuse he could. He found, to his surprise, that he was more sorry at the thought of losing her company than he had imagined.

Leaving the note with a servant for Margaret, he slipped out through the inn yard and was half a mile from the village before Margaret properly realised that he had gone.

For an hour Paul walked quickly, avoiding the roads and paths and making a line across country so that his trail would be difficult to follow.

The country into which he walked grew wilder and more desolate and, when he judged that he was safe from pursuit, he began to look for a path or roadway which would lead to a signpost to give him some indication of his whereabouts. His efforts to find a pathway were unsuccessful. The only paths he found were sheep-tracks that ended in patches of bright, green bog covered with feathery moss and gurgling deeply in the solitude of the hills, or rabbits' runs that scored faint brown lines across the heather and fescue grasses and finished in impenetrable brakes of bramble briars and uncoiling bracken fronds.

It was some time before Paul would acknowledge that he was lost. He was not worried. Just as the ostrich is reported to seek safety from its pursuers by hiding its head in the sand, so Paul consoled himself by assuming that the more completely lost he was, the less chance there was of any of his followers finding him.

He passed over a knife-edged ridge that confronted him, picking his way over the loose stone screes and watching the stone-chats that played among the rubble. The moor beyond the ridge gave him no help; it swept away in a long, bowl-like depression to a further ridge, nearly two miles away. And then, remembering that he had not slept very well during the night and had walked a long way, Paul sat down under a wind-deformed hawthorn which stood by the side of a small mere.

The sun was hot, the sighing of the upland breeze in the hawthorn pleasant to the ears, and the wing-noises of the insects' hovering above the growth round the mere lulling. Making himself comfortable in the shade, it was not long before Paul was asleep.

He slept for an hour and the only thing on the moor which was aware of his presence was a young bullock which, coming to the mere to drink, shied away over the smooth turf to stand in the meagre shade of a low wall, its tail swinging and its nostrils expelling great gusts of air. Paul had not seen the bullock. He slept on peacefully while the sun dipped and little cloud shadows chased one another over the grass.

At the end of the hour Paul was awakened by the bullock. It rushed by within two yards of him. The sound of its hooves rattled in his ears, and the shock of its passing made the ground tremble beneath him and shook the aphids from the tall grasses.

Paul sat up, unconscious of the real cause of his awakening. Then he saw the bullock. It was galloping away, heels tossing, head lowered to the ground and great grunting sounds bellowing from its mouth. As Paul watched it his eyes grew round with wonder, for perched upon its

148

back, like a mariner on a storm-tossed raft, was a man. The bullock was galloping in a great circle and as Paul stood up there came to him, borne on the wind, the disjointed, careless words of a song. At least, it was more a rhapsodic incantation than a song, though it sounded to have more tune than the monotonous rise and fall of a chant and its subject appeared far from canonical. The sense of the words was vague. The singer seemed to be calling upon all the elements to witness his triumphal ride and to each of the two verses which Paul heard came this chorus:

> *I'll go for a ride on the wild bull's back*
> *And add a new sign to the Zodiac.*
> *So up in the sky with the help of Cider*
> *Hoist now the sign of the Drunken Rider!*

Each verse, as though to compensate for its hesitant rhythm, was terminated by a lusty "Whoa!" that served only to frighten the bullock into more frantic tossings and swervings. The bullock in its galloping came back towards Paul again and he stepped into the shelter of the tree. It stampeded towards him, its hooves crushing over the grasses, knocking the purple from the thyme and bugle and spilling the glory of knapweed and tall sorrels, and as it passed within a yard of him Paul had an opportunity to observe its rider.

He was no older than Paul, and was dressed in a pair of flannel trousers and a grey sports shirt. About his middle was twisted a green tie and on his feet, as they clipped the sides of the bullock, Paul noticed open-work leather sandals. The most conspicuous feature, however, was his hair. Over a broad face there rose an unruly, flaming mass of red hair; not ginger, not yellow, but royal, shameless red. Paul had no time to observe any more, for the bullock had careered by and was away over the moor again.

As Paul watched the bullock making its second circuit, he was reminded of Mr. Asher, and wondered whether this had been the rider who had spoken to him the previous night, but the sudden memory of a bawdy line from the young man's song drove this idea from his mind. Amused and puzzled, Paul watched the bull. It was growing wilder and more annoyed each moment and its huge head was tossing and waving as it jerked, galloped, bucked and swerved to try and relieve itself of the noisy human. But the man kept his seat, one hand clutching the animal's neck and the other held aloft in triumph like a cowboy at a rodeo. Round came the bull again and this time as it neared the tree it adopted different

149

tactics to shake off the irritating burden. Five yards from the tree the bullock plunged all four feet firmly into the ground and with a great slither that raised dust and tore savage marks in the turf, it jerked to a standstill. The check to his impetus was too much for the rider. With a loud yell, partly alarm and partly wild exultation, he shot forward over the bullock's head, described an almost perfect parabola and then came heavily, but with a certain grace, to the ground two feet from Paul. He rolled over like a shot rabbit, his shoulders and legs wisely bunched together to take the fall and then came to rest by banging the back of his head against an old molehill. The effect of the blow was astonishing. The man grunted, his legs and shoulders relaxed their curled position and with a dignified motion his body stretched itself into a horizontal plane and he lay there, his eyes shut and his head resting against the molehill.

Paul was alarmed at his sudden stillness. He rushed forward and caught the man's shoulder and shook it. There was no response. The head waggled limply and from his lips issued a peculiar whistling. Paul looked up. The bullock was fast disappearing towards the distant ridge. He rose and dashed to the mere, filled his cupped hands and hurrying back flung the water into the man's face. The effect of the water was almost instantaneous. The man's eyes opened, his face flushed with colour and he sat up rubbing the back of his head. He looked at Paul without surprise, seeming to accept his presence as part of the natural order of things.

"The heavens be praised that I'm an Egyptian, not a Persian," he reflected as he stood upright, continuing the rubbing of his skull.

"It's the shock," said Paul sympathetically. "You'll be all right in a minute. I once fell from a girder when I was a boy and for an hour after I recovered consciousness I went about under the impression that I was the Statue of Liberty." He took the man by the arm and led him gently to the shade.

"I believe you think that the blow has interfered with my mind? Disabuse yourself, sir, of that thought. I was merely referring to an observation which has been made by several antique writers, chiefly of the Hellenic kind—"

"I know," agreed Paul; "and you get a kind of sick feeling in your tummy, like you do before an examination. You sit down there and I'll fetch you some more water."

He was about to hurry away when the young man began to laugh. He shook his head and his great mouth opened until it almost hid the snub nose that rested like a hillock below the two pools of his blue eyes.

150

"Listen, whoever you are—I'm quite all right, and I certainly don't want any more of that water. It's full of cyclops—the one-eyed crustacean, not the giant—and stinks! I was referring to the toughness of my skull and comparing it to the well-known durability of the Egyptian cranium as compared with the Persian. Your education has been neglected, young man. You want to read Smiles on Self-Help."

Paul realised that the man was not suffering from shock. "I'm sorry," he said. "You certainly had me worried for a moment. Do you mind telling me just what you were doing on that steer?"

"Not at all," replied the young man. "You see, I was trying to recapture some of the glories of my lost youth. I once did a spot of cow-punching in Arizona and today, seeing the bullock standing handy by the wall, I dropped on to it to see if three years of respectability and vegetation had dulled my skill."

"Well—and has it?"

"Not a bit, not a bit, but that ride has filled me with a nostalgia for those days—and raised a bump on the back of my head!" He laughed.

"You don't seem to have improved that molehill any, either."

"Never mind. Nature in her slow way will repair both damages. But what are you doing up here at this time of day?" He asked the question with a frankness that in anyone else might have been taken for rudeness. The smile on his freckled face showed Paul that his interest was of an impersonal kind.

"Well, to tell you the truth, I'm lost."

"That is a happy state to be in. I've been lost several times in my life and I rank them the happiest moments. Once in the Australian bush—I was trying to make a living shooting 'possums, once in Ceylon when I gave up tea planting and tried to do a circular tour of the island, and once in Limehouse when I was trying to find one of Thomas Burke's haunts. Don't you feel happy now at this moment to think that you are nowhere, not in the world, outside the skin of civilisation and thrown right back on your own resources? I'll bet you do."

"I hadn't thought about it much," confessed Paul. "You see," he admitted somewhat lamely, "I went to sleep when I found I was lost and since awaking to find you tearing round on that steer I haven't had much opportunity to contemplate my own condition."

"You're an American, aren't you?" The question came suddenly and Paul was at once on his guard.

"Yes, I am—" He got no further. The young man leaned forward and took his hand.

151

"I'm glad to meet you. I like Americans. I like America. There's a feeling about it. I once worked in a New York drug store and that opened my eyes. Three months in a drug store does a lot to explain America's present position in the world. Your drug stores have lost all the old romanticism of our apothecaries with their stuffed crocodiles, coloured water and herbs. You wiped out all the legend and love potion nonsense, and you've done the same in everything. Sir, you should be proud to belong to a nation that would laugh at the idea of wearing a piece of cheese on a string round the neck to cure neuralgia. The English would do this, but you sanely, coldly practical Americans do the right thing and eat the cheese. You must come home and have some tea with me."

"I say, that's kind of you, but I'm afraid I ..."

"Don't make futile protestations. You're walking, aren't you?"

"Something like that. Sort of vacation."

"All the better. I haven't had anyone to talk to and tell lies to for a month. You must come with me. I expect I can find you a bed. Let's take our hats off to Taurus, he always brings me luck."

Without allowing Paul to object, the young man, who introduced himself as Michael Stormry, began to lead the way across the moor and Paul followed obediently, glad for once that he was to submit to someone else's initiative.

During that walk to the little cottage in which Michael Stormry lived, Paul learnt quite a lot about the man. Michael had, as he said, seen a great deal of the world, though he had not seen so much of it as he would have had people believe.

At the age of eighteen he had run away from school and a stepfather, and shipped as a deck hand on a tramp steamer from Cardiff to Rio de Janeiro. At the end of seven years' absence he had more than shattered the puerile illusion of romance which a life of wandering and vagabondage had once possessed for him, and he had grown considerably wiser than on that hot July day when, the rest of the school being at the river, he had motor-cycled to Cardiff.

Not to many people would Michael have admitted his wisdom—since he was not consciously aware of it—or his disillusion—since he was secretly ashamed of that. Instead, he tried to recreate in reminiscence the romance of his youthful escapades and presented to the world a gay, slightly garrulous front, which was generally successful in disguising his real character and personality. For the last three years he had been earning his living as a hack writer of boys' adventure stories, under an assumed name, and writing serious novels, mostly of a morbid, psycho-analytic theme, of whose existence the public—if sales can be taken as any indication of their real feelings—were hardly conscious. Had it not been for the insatiable juvenile hunger for lurid stories of men from Mars, war in the world of A.D. 3000, adventures of cockney messenger lads and the exploits of master gangsters or criminals, Michael would have been forced to take once more to his wandering life or settle down to the torpid monotony of some office occupation.

By the time they had reached his small cottage on the fringe of a little spruce plantation that swept down to a small stream, Paul had been treated to a kaleidoscopic review of his life and imaginings, his lies and his desires, and if Paul did not believe all he was told he was very definitely attracted by this pleasantly-mannered young man, and felt that he had met someone who could—did he but know the circumstances— understand and sympathise with his own peculiar troubles.

The cottage was an indescribable muddle of books, furniture and oddities which Michael had acquired on his travels. As they entered the living room a large bull-terrier woke from its sleep on the rickety refectory table and, yawning indolently, jumped to the floor.

"Meet Necropolis," said Michael, as the dog stood on its hind legs against Paul and sniffed at him.

"Necropolis?"

"Yes—he eats anything that's dead, from rabbits to beetles." Necropolis, satisfied with his examination of Paul, was frustrated from taking up his position on the table as Michael began to set a meal, and consoled himself by lying on the cool bricks of the fireplace.

Paul washed himself and then the two sat down to a meal, during which Michael kept up a running conversation that his mastication in no way impeded. While they were eating a brown hen came in from the garden, moving in the jerky mechanical way of hens, and pecked the crumbs that fell from the table.

"That's Mother Ceres. She's just suffered a severe blow to her philoprogenitiveness. I set her on a dozen partridge eggs and when they were hatched I kept intending to clip their wings, but I put it off from day to day until it was too late and they flew away. She's not properly recovered from their lack of feeling for their foster-mother. See the wan look in her eve?"

The hen, pecking at the crumbs, ignored the attention which was for a moment focused on her.

"You certainly seem to have an interesting collection of animals," observed Paul, smiling, and surreptitiously removing a slug from the lettuce leaf which he was about to eat.

"Yes, I love animals, and it's a great disappointment to me that they so seldom have any discrimination. They regard all men as their enemies, yet nothing would give me greater pleasure than to be on calling terms with the creatures about here. When I was in New Guinea I had a pet tapir that used to follow me about like a dog. It was, I believe, though naturally I wouldn't like to say definitely, the only recorded instance of a tame tapir."

"Is that so?" Paul nodded with sufficient wonder. "That reminds me of a fellow I met in Mexico. He had a tame firefly that used to hover over the page of the book he read on the veranda at night. It's a fact," Paul affirmed solemnly. "I've never seen a man more upset than he was when a nightjar caught it. He gave up reading after that. Said the sight of a book made him want to weep."

Even this gentle irony did not daunt Michael.

"How interesting. That reminds me of an incident which occurred to me in the Andaman Islands. Do you know the Andaman Islands?"

"No—only that they're somewhere in the South Pacific Ocean."

Michael laughed. "You're mixing them with the Falkland Islands. The Andamans are in the Arabian Sea." He proceeded, having ascertained Paul's ignorance of the Andaman Islands, to reveal his own in a picturesque fiction which would not have discredited the Arabian Nights Entertainment or been unworthy of Baron Munchausen.

"Well, you've surely got enough experience in your life to give you plenty of material for writing. It's always been a mystery to me how you writer chaps can sit down and reel off the pages and pages of stuff," said Paul, as Michael came to the end of his story and finished the tea in his cup.

"Oh, it isn't so easy as that, you know. 'Tisn't only having the experience, it's turning it into decent fiction. That's the job. And you can't always use your experiences—they'd sound too improbable. Truth is stranger than fiction, you know. You've got to be observant to be an author. You mustn't miss anything. One might almost describe it as being a detective. A laugh from a man in the street, a car whizzing by in the night … they all suggest ideas to me. I don't like to boast, of course, that's foreign to my nature, but I suppose I'm about as observant as anyone. There's not much gets by me. Look, for instance, how I spotted right away that you were an American, even though your accent is not well marked—"

"Yes, you were pretty quick, I must agree."

"Yes—but that isn't everything. Observation—and then leading an exciting life. That's what I lack now. Abroad there was always plenty of action and strange things happening, but you forget those days and now in England nothing exciting ever happens. You just go on from day to day. Nothing ever happens, at least not to most men, and especially me. Sometimes I feel like chucking things up and going abroad again, but I've got to think of my public now. They'd be disappointed if I stopped writing."

Whether the few dozen people who constituted the most consistent part of Michael's public would have been disappointed is debatable. Probably they would have taken some other book from the free library shelf and forgotten Michael Stormry the author of *Lunatic*, the story of a deranged mind from infancy to death, and *Nymphomania*, the odyssey of an actress.

Paul wished he could tell Michael his story to see whether that would change his conviction of the monotony of life in England.

The dance music, which had been coming softly from a radio while they were having tea, stopped and Michael looked at his watch.

"Six o'clock," he said. "We'll listen to the news and then, if you feel like it, we'll stroll down to the village and buy ourselves a pint of beer."

"That sounds good to me." Paul settled himself with a cigarette to listen to the news, while Michael, the observant and avid seeker after adventure, dropped on to a comfortable, shabby settee and began to stroke Necropolis's ears. The radio announcer began to speak.

"Before the news bulletin tonight there is one special announcement. We have been asked by the Commissioner of Police to broadcast the following. The police are anxious to ascertain the whereabouts of Peter Angel, the American crooner, who is wanted on a charge of fraud. The crooner disappeared from his London hotel last Tuesday, and has, since then, evaded the police. It is thought that he is somewhere in the Midlands and may have adopted a disguise ..."

The announcement came so unexpectedly that Paul had no time to be surprised or alarmed. He sat, his face impassive and his hands tapping the table-top, as though the announcement had no interest for him.

"... keepers of boarding and lodging houses are asked to keep a sharp lookout for anyone answering this description ..."

Michael was still pulling the dog's ears and Paul was glad that he was lying in such a position that he could not see his face.

"... information to the Chief of Police, Scotland Yard, telephone number Whitehall 1212."

As the announcement came to an end Michael rolled over, pushed the dog from the settee and sat up.

"There's a lad for you, if you like," was his comment. "Gets away with a bag of money and the police have to enlist the aid of the public to find him. I should like to know what I pay income tax and rates for, if I have to do the work of public officials and servants? If I were Chief of Police I'd have had that fellow in no time."

"How—perhaps he's very good at disguising himself and covering his tracks?" suggested Paul, glad to see that Michael obviously did not connect him with the crooner.

"How? Gosh! Do you think an American could be at large in England for long without being spotted? I'd get him within a day. I'd have police make a search of every beauty spot, every birthplace of famous men and all cathedrals. Why, I'll bet that fellow's at this moment standing outside Anne Hathaway's cottage, gaping like a fish out of water and chuckling at the absurdity of the police. I remember once in Lagunal, that's a one-eyed town in Ecuador, I was instrumental in bringing about the capture of a brigand. He was a murderous fellow, but if it hadn't been for me he'd have got away. And it was only a small thing that gave him away. I told you you've got to be observant, and I—though I don't ask for any credit, since it's a sort of second nature with me—spotted him. Merely the peculiar way he had of tapping his teeth with the end of a spoon as he ate ..."

Michael, ignoring the voice of the announcer, who was concerned with the activities of a League of Nations committee, went off into an account of his adventures with the brigand, and Paul let him ramble on, glad that he was not lingering over the possibility of Peter Angel's capture.

Michael's disparagement of the police was far from justified. They had, indeed, been watching all the popular resorts of American tourists in England and also trying to sift from the hundreds of rumours and false alarms which came to them about Peter Angel, those which had a semblance of veracity. Now, at this moment while the two talked, Paul would have been surprised to know that his movements had been checked so far as the Leicester episode and that the police had taken, but given no publicity to, statements from a taxicab driver and a small boy who, even in the face of the law, could not abate his avarice for picture-cards of English kings and queens.

Michael's attitude was a common one. He blamed the police for calling in public aid when there was little necessity for it beyond the incessant demands of the national press. The difficulty was not, as Michael imagined, to find where Peter Angel was, or was likely to be, but to eliminate from four hundred reports of the presence of Peter Angel, in localities so divergent as Yarmouth and Paisley, the three hundred and ninety-nine which were myths and fictions of overwrought local constables and hysterical old ladies who still cherished flaming memories of the spy-hunts of the Great War days.

There is a popular saying that everyone has a double. If the reports that people recognised Peter Angel in twenty different places at the same time were true, then it must be acknowledged that everyone has some two dozen counterparts. The police, very wisely, refused to credit this plurality of persons and the delay, if there had been much appreciable delay, in their investigations other than that insisted upon by the press, had been occasioned by the thoroughness with which they examined each report they received.

Paul had no great opinion of English police methods, chiefly because he cherished a fable, which is dear to most Americans, that they could not compete with the efficiency of the American police, and largely because they had so far given him very little trouble. Yet had he known just how closely the police were on his trail it is doubtful whether he would have set out with Michael for the village with so much confidence and well-being.

XV
Margaret again persists

Paul, as they approached the village, discovered, what so many travellers have discovered before him, that when he had left the Fleckington Arms to escape from Margaret, he had travelled in a circle. They were well down the main village street before the sight of the signboard hanging over the pavement before the Fleckington Arms informed Paul that he was back at his starting point. Whereas he and Margaret had entered it from the east, he now with Michael entering it from the west. Momentarily a panic seized him and he made up his mind to turn about and leave Michael. At any instant Margaret might appear and that would lead to explanations and recriminations which Paul had not the slightest wish to meet or give.

Before Paul could do anything Michael had taken him by the arm with a friendly motion and hauled him into a public house, the Lonely Carter, which lay across the road from the, by comparison, lordly Fleckington Arms.

Paul sat down on the hard settle and grasped his pint tankard like a mariner clutching at a lifebelt. He was safe while he remained in the bar. If Paul's conversation was dulled by the prospect of Margaret's discovering him Michael did not seem to notice it. He talked incessantly all the time, to Paul, to the barman, a nodose individual with a ginger moustache which paled by the side of Michael's red hair, and to everyone in the bar. He involved himself in arguments where neither party had any knowledge of the subject they were discussing. He stood drinks all round and borrowed the money from Paul to pay for them. He lectured the publican on the right way to keep and tap beer. He horrified a horse breeder with a tale of the Siberian pampas and Mongolian ponies, and at nine o'clock while Paul was still sober from a dull apprehension which would not leave him, Michael strode into the street aflame with the intoxication of his liquor and more garrulous than ever, but now with his verbal flow there was mixed a belligerent animation. It was, so he carefully explained to Paul, the maternal Irish strain in him which only appeared after five pints and three arguments and then, to use his own phrase, "Not even the Colossus of Rhodes could keep me down!"

Paul would have been glad if they had directly left the village and gone home. Michael was far from ready for bed.

"Going back?" he answered Paul's question. "Not on your life. Why, the night's still young. Look—" an. unsteady finger wavered into the sky—"Mars has hardly started her eastward journey."

"What are you going to do?"

"Do—anything. Whatever the gods send. I'm a great believer in the gods."

As Michael finished speaking, a doorway some paces up the road opened and a bright shaft of light cut an oblique diamond on the pavement and there came into the warmness of the evening the sound of music, turbulent, jaunty, lilting, irresistible music.

"Terpsichore, here I come," Paul heard Michael murmur and he was being dragged off to the dance hall where was in progress a flannel dance in aid of the local cricket club. Not daring to protest, since he had no more reasonable ground for objection than a desire to leave the village, Paul obediently paid their entrance money and they entered the hall.

They were greeted by a blast of hot air and music and the jumble of hundreds of voices.

"We're in luck," exclaimed Michael and with unerring instinct headed towards a little bar which had been rigged up in a cloakroom of what, during the daytime, was a village school.

Paul followed him and as the gaiety and unconcern of the dance hall closed around him he felt easier in his mind. It was unlikely that Margaret, if she had remained in the village, would come to such a place and here, at least, he was safe until the late hours, by which time she would be in bed, and he could walk back to the cottage with Michael.

His mind freed from the thought of detection Paul decided to enjoy himself. It seemed a long time since he had been able to forget himself and enjoy life, and now the opportunity had come he did not intend to let it pass him. With commendable, but unwise, emulation, Paul set out to reclaim the lost ground which lay between himself and Michael. Within an hour there was little—if Michael's unquenchable fund of fantastic stories were excepted—to choose between them.

The hall lost its dimensions, gave up all claim to angular respectability and became for Paul a whirling cosmos of bright dresses, loud music and laughing couples. He danced for a while and then, exhausted and bruised by the provincial interpretation of his own steps, sat down by the wall to recover.

Everywhere was noise and movement and colour. Girls went by him, their healthy red faces masked with powder and their bodies, strong as young heifers, clad in home-made frocks of voile and silk, frocks whose chief claim to festive symbolism seemed to be huge bows and large sprays of artificial flowers which ran in red and white splashes from their breasts to their shoulders. Their faces shone through their powder with the strain of their dancing, and their hair, at first so neat and waved, grew wilder, more intractable and determined to spread to their shoulders which rose and fell as they swooped, swirled, turned and swept about the room.

Paul, who had an instinctive love of colour and motion, half closed his eyes and let the atmosphere of the scene soak into him. The band blared away in a popular number which recounted the indiscretions and final downfall of a country girl called Little Mary. The story of Little Mary is too long to tell here, but for a country girl she must have been a phenomenal mixture of ignorance and simplicity, her chief fault being a complete lack of biological knowledge, which is rare in the country. A butcher's son, a member of the band, suffering from the delusion that he could sing, stood and moaned into a megaphone so that the king beams and corbels of the hall flung the husky echoes of his voice from rafter to rafter where they beat at the roof in a frenzy of despair to be let into the freedom of the night. The piano tinkled and followed hard after the wailing trail of the two violins which seemed to be at a perpetual disagreement one with the other, due no doubt to the divergence of opinions and class of the players, since they were the local poacher's son and the head gamekeeper of a nearby estate. An insurance collector, who greatly influenced the mortality rates and expectations of life of his neighbours during his leisure hours by practising the saxophone, continued his practice with a fine, autocratic disregard for everyone in the hall. He started a number half a minute before the band and finished it half a minute behind it. The drummer beat his inoffensive instrument and nodded, half dazed with the magic of music, as it responded in booms of contented rapture as though it were some cat purring at the stroking of a caressing hand.

The song came to an end. The band forgot Little Mary and, hurrying after the saxophonist, started away on the saga of a gentleman from Uppsala. The dancers, rested in the short pause, grabbed partners and the floor was a pattern of couples again. As they moved about the hall, Paul watched them, their forms making constantly changing patterns, swerving and turning into momentary constellations of laughter, of love and daring.

And outside, high over the hall of the dancers, the heavens looked down on the bright spot of noise and movement and conducted their own dance with a greater solemnity and a finer pattern. Away into the vast darkness, beyond the flying bats, above the tips of the gently murmuring poplars, beyond the peak of the coldest hills, danced the constellations of the night. But Cassiopeia meant nothing to the saxophonist, and Andromeda would have had to be a fruit juice before the butcher would recognise her.

Not one of the dancers cared fcr the stars. But there were two people who looked at them, though in their minds there was no contemplation of the glory of the starlit night. Margaret, standing outside the hotel, heard the sound of the dance music and, as she debated whether she should go to bed and forget Paul, her eyes were fixed on the lizard-like form of the Archer where he sprawled above the crest of a hill; and lower down the street, where a motor-car had drawn up outside the dance hall, Cableton, the *Daily Globe* reporter, as he left the steering wheel of his car, looked up to the sky and winked at the bright, confident gleam from Altair, before turning to his companion. Altair, so an astrologer had once told him, was his star and he had found its position in the sky and invoked it whenever he felt himself to be on the verge of a scoop, and at that moment he felt he was very close to a scoop. Not even Cableton could have guessed just what kind of a scoop lay waiting for him.

"Come on," said his companion. "But remember, you must keep in the background all the time. You shouldn't be here by rights."

"Forget it, Sherlock. You know me and you don't have to worry. I wouldn't interfere with Scotland Yard. I suppose that local bobby wasn't making any mistake?"

"Well, you've just heard what he said. I'm going to see for myself."

"The old bobby was a bit peeved because you didn't want him to come along."

"I know." His companion, a short man with a slouch hat pulled down over his forehead, laughed. "The sight of him would have scared the bird—if it is the bird—at once. And I can't afford to have that happen. Come on!" He snapped his fingers impatiently and walked towards the door of the hall with Cableton following him …

The first intimation Paul had of the presence of the detective, whose name was Jones, was in the little bar. Paul was trying to suppress, tactfully, Michael's application for an additional loan to further his already advanced state of intoxication. Into the middle of this argument came Mr. Jones, Detective-Inspector Jones of Scotland Yard and a well-known cultivator of sweet peas in the districts adjacent to Belsize Park. Jones had watched Paul for a few moments, compared him with the descriptions which he had photographed upon his mind and had come to very definite conclusions. But the last thing he wanted was any attention from the rest of the dancers.

"Excuse me," Mr. Jones touched Paul on the arm.

Paul looked round.

"What is it?" Michael turned round, too.

"I'd like a word with this gentleman if you'll be kind enough to excuse me for a moment," said Mr. Jones.

"What do you want me for?" asked Paul suspiciously, though without apprehension.

"It's rather private," intimated Mr. Jones.

"Private!" Michael laughed loudly. "Listen, he's my friend and I bet there's nothing private about him I don't know."

"That may be," agreed Mr. Jones, noting Michael's state. "Still, I'd like to speak to him in private."

Paul resented the man's repeated request for privacy. "If you've got anything to say to me, you can say it here," he said firmly. "I don't mind my friend hearing it, so why should you?"

"Hear, hear!" called Michael. "Let's all have a drink on it. Lend me five shillings, will you?"

"Shut up, Michael," said Paul. "Now, what is it?" He faced the man again where they stood in one corner of the bar.

"All right," Mr. Jones declared resignedly; "if you want it that way. You may regret it."

"Here, what the devil is this?" questioned Paul, a sudden tremor of nervous excitement creeping over him.

"Just this, that I have a warrant in my pocket for the arrest of—"

Mr. Jones never got any further. Michael pushed forward at the words. "What, arrest my friend? So that's what you are, a dirty little policeman coming round here and spoiling the fun, just when I was going to borrow five shillings and make the evening a real one. Why ..." The words poured from him in a torrent which overwhelmed Mr. Jones and gave Paul a brief space to consider the position. "Why ... I remember once in Buenos Ayres a gendarme coming up to a pal of mine with the same yarn and what do you think I said? I said, 'Friendship is the sweetest thing in life and for it a man should be prepared to sacrifice everything, yes, everything, even his reputation,' so I swiped the gendarme, or was it a carbinattorio, on the nose and settled the matter, just as I am going to settle you for insulting my friend." And as Michael finished speaking he put a characteristic full stop to his torrential speech by hitting the detective on the nose with such force that it toppled him backwards to the ground, where he lay quietly among the sawdust and cigarette butts, unconscious and uncaring.

"Michael ..." Paul was horrified.

"Shouldn't insult my friends ... Whoa!" cried Michael, as a crowd began to form. "Whoa! This is a rough house!" His eyes lit with a devilish fire as he picked up a small beer bottle and with a loud cry swung it at the solitary electric light in the bar. The sound of crashing glass broke through the dance music and the bar was in darkness. As Paul stood hesitantly in the gloom he heard a woman scream in the hall. The next instant he was alive to his situation and moving. He could hear Michael roaring with tipsy laughter and the confused murmur and cries of the dancers as they crowded towards the darkened bar.

Something like panic had possessed Paul for a while and then his head cleared and the effects of his drink were dissipated by the shock of the incident.

"Come on, Michael," he urged, "Let's get out of here."

But Michael was too happy to worry. "The fun's just beginning," he said. "Why this reminds me of a time in Nigeria, when—"

Paul did not stop to listen. He could see that there was no hope of persuading Michael to leave. He moved quickly to the back of the bar where he had noticed a small door which probably gave on to the street.

He found the door. When he opened it he discovered that it gave on to a small passage-way that ran parallel with the hall and finally debouched through a main doorway into the road.

He slipped into the passage-way, which was lit by a single electric globe and hurried forward. He was halfway down the passage when a door opened on his left. As it swung out and then shut he obtained a glimpse of the lighted dance hall and various groups of eager dancers, all looking towards the bar. Then the door was shut and Paul felt a hand on his arm. He halted and found himself confronted by a short, fat man who wore a golfing cap pushed back on to his head.

"How are you, Mr. Angel? You seem to be in a hurry?"

Paul recognised Cableton at once, and he was surprised to find that there was no anxiety in his mind. Within the last few days he had been forced into so many awkward and compromising situations that now his mental machinery was beginning to refuse to be thrown out of gear by the intrusion of the unexpected. He experienced a confident, almost overwhelming feeling of superiority.

"It's you, is it?" he said in a level voice.

"It's me all right," Cableton assured Paul, "and you know what I want."

Paul put his hands into his pocket and regarded the reporter with a steady look. "Have you got a car here?" he asked.

Cableton was surprised at the question. His ridiculous eyebrows stretched themselves like scanty roofs round his gibbous eyes.

"I have—but what of it?"

"Nothing for the moment," said Paul, wondering at his own composure, and then asked, "Have you ever been shot at—with a revolver, I mean?"

Cableton's face now assumed a lunar wonder. His eyes were wide and staring, his cheeks rosy and puffed and his mouth fell open loosely. "Shot at?" he queried.

"Yes, you're getting the idea. Shot at."

"No—not that I remember. You see," he added, not quite knowing why, "I'm a reporter."

"Well," said Paul firmly. "Unless you do exactly as I tell you within the next few minutes you're going to be shot. I can promise you that a bullet through the chest is nothing to trifle with."

"What—what?" Cableton for once found himself unequal to a situation. If there had been a bottle of whisky within reach he could perhaps, after prolonged assimilation, have dealt with Paul, but now he was helpless, and to add to his demoralisation Paul poked the stem of his pipe against the stuff of his pocket. The bluff had helped him once before, there was no reason why it should not serve again.

"Get going, mister, get going," said Paul, inducing a harsh note into his voice. "And if you try to pull anything on me you'll get enough lead inside you to make a guttering round your own homestead. Lead me to your car and don't forget I'm desperate."

Cableton, with commendable resignation, accepted his own impotency and Paul's order with an alacrity that surprised Paul.

"All right, all right, but go easy with that automatic," he pleaded as he led the way out of the hall. Behind them the noise was subsiding and Paul wondered whether the detective had recovered consciousness.

"This is it," said Cableton, pointing to the car which stood by the kerb.

"Good, get in!" ordered Paul, and then, thinking the dramatic gesture was required from his renegade role, he spat inartistically yet lustily over his shoulder.

"Get in?" Cableton looked at Paul as he spoke.

"Yes, get in—you're going to drive me—and don't argue about it or I'll settle with you right away."

By now, however, Cableton was gradually reclaiming his lost confidence, and his surprise was occasioned less by Paul's demand than by his own good luck. He had imagined that Paul would merely commandeer his car and leave him with half a story; but here was this young man taking him off to drive the car and putting into his hands the greatest story of the year. Cableton's eyes filled with tears of gratitude. He could see the story … "At the point of a revolver, which I knew this young desperado would not scruple to use, I was forced into the car. The subsequent ride through the night was a revelation to me and an experience which I would not wish to have again in my lifetime …"

Curtailing his half-formed story, Cableton entered the car and Paul still covering him with his pipe slipped into the seat beside him.

"Now then, we'll go north as fast as you can go, and don't try any funny business. Get going."

Cableton nodded and started the engine. As he did so a shadow fell across him and he looked up. Standing by the kerb, her slim figure silhouetted against the open doorway of the hall, was a young woman. She bent down and looked into the car, and smiling at Paul said:

"Why, there you are, darling, and I thought I'd lost you. Are you in trouble again?"

Even this interposition did not upset Paul so much as it might. He returned Margaret's smile with a stern look.

"Get going!" he barked at Cableton; "And you—" he addressed Margaret with strained politeness, "I'm afraid are not wanted. I am sorry to have to say this."

165

Cableton, undecided as to what he should do, or who the girl might be, bowed down before the omnipotence of the gun and forgot his native curiosity. He let out the clutch and the car shot forward. As it did so, both he and Paul were horrified to observe that Margaret had jumped on to the running board. The car moved down the street. Paul shouted warningly to her, but she took no notice and, as it turned the corner and left the dance hall behind, she managed to open the door and let herself fall in on to the back seat.

"Say—who is she?" Cableton could not control his curiosity. He had the two million readers of his paper to consider. They would be avid for this sudden romance.

Margaret, sitting upright and tidying herself, supplied the answer to his question. "I'm his fiancée," she replied, "and where he goes I go."

Cableton was delighted. His fear was now entirely evaporated.

"What a story. So you're his gun-moll—"

"His what?"

"Gun-moll. By heck, what a yarn!"

"Enough chatter," commanded Paul. "I'm in charge of this outfit, and as she's come I suppose she must stay, but both of you'd better understand that what I say goes, otherwise there'll be trouble." He tapped his pocket significantly, not displeased with his authority.

Margaret watched and listened in amazement. This incisive, curt Paul was a new character. For a second she wanted to laugh at his absurd, dignified criminality and then she realised that she was his accomplice. Cableton's description filled her with delight. Never in her life had she been mistaken for a tough, hard-boiled, quick-shooting gun-moll, the companion of a gangster, and the part appealed to the errant unorthodoxy which was so large a feature of her personality. She decided to accept the role in the spirit in which it had been assigned to her.

"Yeah," she said. "I'm his dame and for all he says I'm going to stick to him. He's gotta have someone to look after him. He's a babe when it comes to stunts like this. Ain't you, honey?"

She leaned forward and patted the shoulder of the amazed Paul. He made no reply, but inwardly he was consoling himself with the only logical solution to her behaviour. She must have been touched by the sun during the day's walk. Nothing else could account for her sudden metamorphosis from the daughter of a respectable shipowner into a gum-chewing female of criminal tendencies.

"And who are you?" Margaret asked Cableton, since Paul did not appear to relish her conversation.

Cableton chuckled. "Shall I tell her or will you?" he asked Paul, and Paul resented the growing informal atmosphere. It was beginning to sound more like a picnic than an abduction.

"If you want to talk you can, but remember what I told you."

"All right, Mr. Angel. I promise I won't try any tricks. I don't want to spoil a good story." And Cableton, his red face beaming in the darkness, his pudgy hands holding the wheel and itching to get to a typewriter, began to outline to Margaret what had happened.

When he had told the immediate story he went on to explain how he and Jones had trailed Paul. And now Paul found himself listening with interest. He heard how from Leicester he had been traced to Bert Clements and from there to Matlock, where Margaret's car had been found. After Matlock the next information had come from Fleckington, where the village constable had reported early in the afternoon the arrival of a man and woman, the man corresponding to the circulated description of Peter Angel.

"We were at Matlock and came over to investigate and that's how we came to find you," finished Cableton. "I'm friendly with Jones, done him some good turns in my time, and he always lets me in on a thing if he can. But it seems I'm going one better than him this time."

"You are," agreed Paul. "I left him unconscious, but I may have to leave you dead. You're going to be a nuisance."

"Sure," said Margaret, twisting her mouth, "it was a mistake to bring him. What'll we do with him, Peter? Bump him off somewheres?"

"Will you please keep quiet?" requested Paul.

"Say, you can't keep me down!" retorted Margaret. "I'm in this as deep as you. Listen, Mister Cableton, what kind of death would you prefer? Shooting, drowning, or asphyxiation?"

"You couldn't manage to wangle it so I died of over-drinking, could you?" asked Cableton, and Paul felt that the gust of laughter which emanated from the two was indecent.

"It's a pity we've got to fix you," went on Margaret as the part grew on her. "I always think it's so hard for the widder and kids. We haven't bumped off any married men before, not unless you can count that guy in Cincinnati—and he weren't properly married, I guess."

"Cincinnati?" Cableton inquired.

"Yeah, a tough guy, he was." Margaret, to Paul's horror, began to detail a fabulous story which would have done credit to Michael. While she delighted Cableton's news sense with her story the car rocked through the night, driving northwards as fast as Cableton could make it, and with every mile that passed Paul felt happier, though he could not suppress a quiet feeling of despair that he should be going farther and farther from the one place in England which he really wanted to visit. He sat back in his seat and wondered if he would ever get to Wisbech. And from wondering he developed a determination to reach Wisbech in spite of everything; not the police, Margaret, Cableton or the whole of the British Army and Navy should prevent him. He would get there in the end.

He must have dozed as he mused, for a jolt of the car woke him in time to hear Margaret saying: "Yeah, we buried him in a lime-works. Lime's good stuff for bodies."

XVI
The Press is taken for a ride

Paul, though he did not know it, had been acting in his few days in England as an animated question mark, a living question which had been hurled at various people, and according to their natures, eliciting entirely unrelated reactions. He had passed from one person to another and annoyed or delighted or worried or exasperated them in turn.

All of them remembered him for different reasons. From Mr. Partingale he had brought forth a vein of pride and curiosity, piqued pride and growing curiosity. Mr. Partingale had been, and still was, resentful of Paul's disclaimer of the power of money and anxious to prove to him the foolishness of this, Mr. Partingale considered, heretical theory. And as he sought to justify his pride Mr. Partingale found himself immersed in a growing curiosity about Peter Angel. With characteristic directness he had set about his task as soon as he had left the coach at Leicester, for he was convinced that the young man who had escaped from the coach was Peter Angel. At the time when Michael was hitting Detective Inspector Jones on the nose, Mr. Partingale, through the medium of private investigation and his own influence in certain circles, was wondering just what Margaret Sinclair, the daughter of his great friend Mr. Sinclair of the Oceanic Transport Company, had in common with Peter Angel that she should be shielding him from the police. His consolation, since his curiosity could not be satisfied until Mr. Sinclair returned to London, was that despite Peter Angel's contempt for money he had not been unwilling to accept the assistance of a wealthy young lady for whom Mr. Partingale had an almost avuncular affection. Mr. Partingale's assumption that Margaret was helping Peter Angel was founded chiefly on the evidence of her car left at Matlock. He determined that he would see Mr. Sinclair as soon as he could, and until then he contented himself with the philosophic beatitude which is the peculiar asset of philanthropists who are also millionaires, and assiduously added to his observations of bird life.

Mr. Wimpole's reaction to the impetus of Paul's contact with him had been swift and revolutionary. Within the space of a few hours it had induced within him a daring which all his life he had never until then known. After losing Paul on his trip to Wisbech, Mr. Wimpole had been disappointed, not merely because the possibility of a reward had slipped by him, but also by the anticlimax of his adventure. He resented its tailing off into a fiasco which was chiefly notable for his wife's ire when he returned. He had nothing to offer her in explanation and he could only submit with his usual meekness to her termagant railings against his crazy extravagance and indiscretion. Yet, within himself, he had discovered a new Mr. Wimpole, a Wimpole who was ready for high adventure and danger, a Wimpole who could face the swift turn of dramatic events, unshaken and fearless, and a Wimpole who was mildly scornful of the poor cattle who went contentedly about their daily tasks and had never been able to indulge in the exhilarating risks of criminal hunting. This new spirit gave him a confidence which he had lacked before and, though he dared not exhibit his enriched personality at home, he gladly indulged his alter ego in the bar of the Hare and Grouse.

Men who had ignored him for years now listened to him and, which was entirely to his credit, did not ask themselves afterwards why they had wasted time with him, and the barmaid, who for years had snubbed him, now submitted to his orders and listened enthralled to the hitherto unsuspected fund of his incredible stories of personal experiences. What Mr. Wimpole had missed by losing the trail of Peter Angel he made up for by the invention of a dozen fabulous adventures in the past, and while he talked and forgot his home life, he told himself that as long as Peter Angel was still wanted by the police there might come another opportunity for him to display his talents; meanwhile he talked more than ever, and spent more money than his wife knew on newspapers as he followed the press accounts of the chase of Peter Angel.

Michael's reaction had been swift and imperative. From the grey coldness of the next morning he had reviewed the fiery succession of events which had terminated in the prostration of Mr. Jones. Under the aegis of the proverb about drunkards, his homeward journey had been safe, if somewhat tortuous, and marked by the inconsequent, though persistent, conversation of a well-meaning labourer who had taken upon himself the task of piloting Michael to his cottage. The conversation had been remarkable for its harping on the two phrases, "They say 'twas that there crooner chap, Peter Angel," and "What did 'ee do it for, Mr. Stormry? He was a police chap."

As he ate his cereal Michael sorted his recollections and marshalled them in order and very soon he had satisfied himself that not only had he entertained Peter Angel, but had also aided him very considerably in evading the police. He had unwittingly, yet joyously, interfered with the duties of a police officer and his knowledge of the law was sufficient to convince him that he had done enough to secure for himself a considerable sentence. He did not regret what he had done, but he had no intention of accepting a punishment for his actions which, he argued, had been carried out in all innocence. He decided that the best way to avoid the consequences was by flight, not explanation, so he hastily finished his breakfast, made arrangements with a neighbour for the care of his animals and, while Mr. Jones from his head-quarters at the Fleckington Arms, was making inquiries concerning his assailant, Michael was beginning a journey which should put a lot of ground between himself and Mr. Jones.

His thoughts centred with a certain tenderness and gratitude round Peter Angel for introducing into his humdrum life an element of danger and excitement which had been missing so long, and already he was indebted to the crooner for several suggestions for future stories of the more lurid type.

Of these three, Mr. Partingale, Mr. Wimpole and Michael, none of them knew of the existence of the others, and while they pursued their courses in accordance with the dictates of their respective natures, the other three were driving steadily northwards. They drove all night. Paul would grant no respite to Cableton's tiring body and even Margaret, indefatigable as she had been in her new part, found the monotony of the dark drive wearying her. She longed for the dawn. But Paul did not share their feelings. After his one period of sleepiness he had awakened to a vivid consciousness of the night, and he was glad that the conversation in the car had wilted to monosyllabic brevity.

He sat and stared along the glaring path of the headlights and watched the spectres of the road leap into being for a second and then fade into the murk behind. The lights were like wide sweeping skirts and, as Paul looked, he found that it was possible to deceive himself that the car was not moving forward but rushing backwards and trailing behind it wide folds of misty white cloth that swerved and trembled in the motion of their passage. Sometimes from the black maw that confronted them, there was spewed forth the chimeric shape of a house, the side of a wall with dead windows that threw back the light in a quick quiver of reflection, as though for a moment an eye had opened and surveyed them and then dropped back to slumber.

For the rest of the night they went north, along the wide roads that lead from the soft south into a land of bleak uplands and wide moors, where the wind meets no obstacle but the low parapets of thorn bushes and the craggy sweep of headlands. They went through sleeping towns and their tyres made protesting murmurs on the cobble stones and fantastic patterns across the tramway lines. Nothing seemed to care for their progress. There was no sign from country or town that anyone evinced any interest in them. Everything slept, the towns wrapped in dreams of the morrow and the country heavy with the somnolence of men and women who know that toil is their lot. Only the moon, that showed itself occasionally from behind the high banks of cloud that had now crept into the sky, seemed to notice them and even then its attention was no more than perfunctory, as though it resented the sudden obfuscation of events by the clouds which a west wind rolled rudely across its face.

Paul was glad of the silence during this part of the drive. The gentle hum of the engine, and the ceaseless song of the tyres over the road surface created a little world about him which was loaded with a curious, satisfying peace. He felt all his worry and anxiety, all his doubts and fears for the future, drained from him by the encroaching darkness. He was an autocrat of a tiny community and his power gave him solace for the irksome knowledge that, outside of this little world which he mastered, there existed a larger, wilder, crueller world that regarded him with the same intolerance that was accorded to escaped menagerie animals.

Once Cableton turned to him, his face sleepy and smiling, and asked for a cigarette.

As Paul, without protest, handed him one and helped him to light it, he heard Margaret's deep breathing from the back seat and they both smiled as they turned and momentarily eyed the sleeping figure.

"Poor kid, she's had a hectic time of it lately, I expect," said Cableton compassionately. His face was almost paternal.

"She brought it on herself," replied Paul tersely.

"Maybe," Cableton allowed, and then, shaking from him his desire to sleep, he turned to Paul. "You know, Mr. Angel, for a talented man you're about the biggest fool I've ever met."

Paul met this discourtesy with the blandness which such a misstatement merited. "Don't forget that I've got the gun in my pocket," he reminded the reporter.

Cableton laughed, a mild laugh that meant many things, but chiefly that now his common sense had enabled him to conquer his fear.

"You can't frighten me any longer with that"

"What do you mean?" demanded Paul quickly.

"Just what I say, Mr. Angel. You may have a gun, but you know as well as I do that you'd be afraid to use it in England. This is England, you know, not Cincinnati. As I said just now, you must be a fool to get yourself into this mess, and you'll be a damn sight bigger fool than I think you are if you bump me off."

"You're getting very confident?"

"I am. I've just remembered that all this is happening and not coming from Alice in Wonderland, and I'm kicking myself for being taken in by it so long. What do you think you're going to do with me?" Cableton did not wait for Paul to reply. "Some time or other you've got to drop me and—no matter where it is—it'll only be a matter of hours before I get in touch with my paper and the police and in that time you won't have had a chance to get any distance. Don't you realise, you silly young fool, that you're bound to be caught?"

"Is that a bet?" asked Paul airily, refusing to be depressed by Cableton's verities.

"No, it isn't a bet. I don't bet on certainties; I feel sorry for you, I reckon."

"I should have thought that in your present position you would have needed all your sorrow for yourself," retorted Paul with a touch of hardness in his voice, as though Cableton's life was no more to him than the last pea on a plate waiting for the fork or forgetfulness.

"I never pity myself, but I've got a feeling for you—perhaps it's because you had the decency to swipe old Jones across the nose and make a good beginning to my story. You know, of course, that you're giving me the best story any paper has had since the outbreak of the Great War?"

Paul ignored the comparison between his own news value and that of the war. "It wasn't me who hit the detective on the nose," he countered.

"It will be, whatever you say, when I write my story," said Cableton confidently.

"That'll be a lie," said Paul.

"It'll be a good story," Cableton replied, and at this impasse, this cross-roads where fiction and fact met, the two stopped and their conversation died a very common death.

The night passed and daybreak came with no fine burst of sun over the distant ridges of the hills. It caught them as they worked through the narrow streets of a town whose chief characteristics seemed to be copies of evening editions in the gutters and a dirty white dove that preened its bedraggled feathers on top of a statue of Queen Victoria. They entered the southerly side of the town in a dim, tenebrous haze of night, and left the northerly side with an unfriendly grey light suffusing itself over the face of the land. The day crept, like an unwilling dog, back to its accustomed haunts, crept regretfully westwards still thinking of the sprawling Urals and the wide steppe vistas which it had left behind, dreaming of the wide rivers and dark lines of firs, the shining cupolas and minarets and the dusty humour of bazaars and ragged splendour of fiestas. Yet after a time, when the dew was half dried from the tall spikes of sorrel and gone from the tips of the mulleins and scabious, it seemed more at home and greeted the familiar places with a more cheerful air, an air of duty that was not incompatible with pleasure. The drifts of cloud that had outstayed the night began to fade and shred themselves in the wind and the sun catechised the landscape with a warm, if belated, geniality.

At eight o'clock they stopped at a small village and Paul directed Margaret to purchase rolls and breakfast sausage while he superintended the refuelling of the car. They ate their breakfast sitting under the wall of a little churchyard. Cableton sat between them and when the last of the food was gone, there arose a discussion as to what was to be done to the reporter. The discussion was complicated by the unwillingness of the victim to submit to any fate. As a member of the press, Cableton, with an impish glee that sprang from his conviction that nothing serious could possibly be done to him, was determined to object to any theory which infringed his liberty more than was concurrent with decency.

"It was a mistake to bring him," insisted Margaret, exploring the epidermis of the sausage for any overlooked fragment of food.

"I wish," said Paul with warmth, "that you wouldn't keep saying that. We're not discussing what was or was not right. The question is what do we do with him?"

"If I may make a suggestion," put in Cableton, "I think it would be wise if you all adjourned with me to the nearest pub and while we have

174

a drink I could write my story and call the police. It is easily the wisest thing."

"I think," said Margaret seriously, since she knew that the suggestion would not find favour, "we ought to shoot him and dump the body somewhere safe."

"But you can't do that—" objected Cableton. "I've got to write my story yet."

"We are not interested in your story," said Paul. "But I agree with you, we can't do it. It's too drastic. I'm not a murderer."

"Most people," interposed Cableton, unable to resist the temptation, "would put crooners and murderers in the same category."

"Quit the foolin', and keep quiet!" ordered Margaret, throwing the sausage skin away so that it hung untidily, like a great red blossom on the breast of a clump of toad-flax.

"I wish I'd never seen this country. I've had nothing but trouble since I landed," Paul broke out with a sudden burst of impatience and annoyance.

Neither of the two could find any sympathy for him; Margaret because she was too engrossed in her part and Cableton because there was creeping into his mind the idea that all this was too fantastic to be real and therefore none of the participators was entitled to emotional considerations. He found it almost impossible to entertain any fears for his own safety and he was still less able to pity Peter Angel.

"And you're going to have a lot more unless you listen to me," he added.

"Now," Margaret patted her knees with a commanding gesture, "let's be sensible about this. We must review all the possibilities and settle upon the only wise course. If we can't shoot Mr. Cableton then we can't kill him in any other way because the same objection holds good—"

"That's true," commented Cableton, much in the manner of a committee member supporting a speaker.

"So if we can't kill him—which is a pity in many ways—we must get rid of him in some other way."

"Why," questioned Cableton. "The longer I stay with you the better my story, the greater the news value."

"Why? Because we want to get out of this country quickly and your presence would be a hindrance. If you were a gentleman instead of a reporter I'd release you now and extract a promise from you to keep quiet. But that's impossible."

"Quite."

Paul listened to the two and unexpectedly found himself choking back an almost overwhelming desire to laugh outright at the absurdity of affairs. Here they sat, a couple of executioners debating the fate of their victim. It was medieval, it was so antique that it was unreal, distorted like the truths that live on as folk-tales. He determined that it was time he put an end to the nonsense.

"We can't kill him—that's obvious, but we must get rid of him. And the only way to do that is to leave him stranded somewhere. If it only gives us a few hours start we shall have to risk that."

"And where do you propose to leave me?"

Paul turned to Margaret. "You probably know this part of the world. Where can we leave him?"

It was the first time Paul had directly solicited her help and Margaret felt that it marked a very definite step forward. She stood up and frowned, looking very pretty as she did so. She was conscious that her frown became her and she continued it for a few seconds after she had made her decision.

"I know," she said, and led the way to the car while Paul followed with his pipe making an ominous bulge inside his pocket for Cableton's benefit, though this bellicose gesture was entirely unnecessary now since Cableton would not have left Paul willingly. They entered the car and, with Cableton driving under Margaret's direction, set off. Paul was as ignorant as Cableton of their destination, but he relied upon Margaret to bring them to some isolated spot where Cableton could be safely jettisoned while they made good their escape. He did not dare to contemplate how long they might escape detection after this. He only knew that he still wanted to reach Wisbech and that if the chase grew too hot for him the wisest plan would be to go to the police and make a clean breast of everything.

XVII
Margaret arranges things

For the rest of that morning, the car, under Margaret's direction, went steadily northwards and Paul saw towns which for years had only been names to him. And for the first part of the journey the road seemed to take a delight in sending them through the ugliest sections of the towns and the dullest part of the country. Along its dusty length were situated tall pit-heads and mean houses, where washing hung in pathetic lines from one window to another, and children played in the gutters and gathered round the unsavoury windows of sweet shops and the fronts of cinemas, where the commissionaires, in their Saturday morning undress, were washing the steps and pinning new photographs to the gaudy frames that advertised the coming films.

It was a real Saturday morning world. Everyone was busy with the frantic, hurry-scurry scamper of a morning in which a day's work had to be completed in order that the afternoon might be free.

As the three passed through the towns in the car they could catch the spirit of that Saturday morning. The lolling barbers who trimmed the polls of schoolboys and waited for the hairy influx of men in the afternoon, the pot-men cleaning their bars and tankards, the drivers oiling their coaches and eyeing the weather ... everywhere men and women were preparing for the afternoon, and only the shop-assistants seemed a little mournful as they viewed the approaching freedom of their fellows, and wondered if this Saturday afternoon and evening would be as busy as the last and marvelled that their midweek half-day seemed so far behind and the one to come so far away. In the towns the tempo of life beat higher and quicker with the approach of the weekend; there were more smiles on faces, more cheery remarks, more fun and joking.

But in the country that lay between the towns Saturday was unheralded. The cows stood beneath the elms, placid, round-eyed, gazing gently at the traffic on the road and swishing their tails at the flies that swarmed like clouds of locusts about their flanks. Labourers weeded methodically between the rows of potatoes and mangoldwurzels and a scarecrow flourished its mildewed arms over a field of oats that rustled and swayed daintily in the wind. Saturday was nothing to the scarecrow, Saturday was nothing to the flowers that struggled for life between the oats, and to the field-mice and partridges that walked the green corridors of the fields there was no other distinction between the days than the change of weather.

Paul could sense the difference of spirit between town and country. In one was a turmoil of labour and anticipation of pleasure, and in the other, a deeper, stronger, more permanent spirit that flowed strongly and silently, a spirit that was derived from the hedgerows and fields, that rested in the pale lilac of the milkmaid blossoms and lived in the white patches of campion and stitchwort. Here there was no end or beginning, only a great circle that held everything within its periphery and relinquished nothing.

And to Margaret and Cableton Saturday meant nothing. To Margaret time had ceased to have any but a nominal meaning, she was scarcely aware that it was Saturday. Since she had committed herself to this chase after Peter Angel, or Peter Angel's double, she had forgotten the days, and now in her new part she had time for nothing but contemplation of the future. She did not see the great glory of a magnolia tree that drooped in heavy beauty over the wall of a garden or the dying wonder of cowslips in the corner of a meadow, where a river laved the grass and rivalled its greenness with an array of soft rushes and spiked reeds. She was wondering how long this farce would last, what its end would be and whether she was being wise in helping to continue it.

And Cableton, too, was wondering how long it would last and hoping that he could continue it. He was full of questions, of curiosity and theories. There was a lot he wanted to know, yet despaired of getting. Who was this girl? Her acting, spasmodic enough, had not convinced him that she was other than an English girl, and what sort of madman was this Peter Angel, who airily supposed that he could escape capture? As a representative of the *Daily Globe* and millions of readers, Cableton felt that he had a very clear duty. All England would want to know what he wanted to know and he was saddened by the thought that all England would not know just yet. Cableton felt that life was unfair to withhold from him the proper counsel for his case. Life, he felt, should be as compact and accessible as the bibles in commercial hotels, where there were indices to help a man in trouble. *If trade is poor, read Psalm 37. If out of sorts, read Isaiah 1, 5 and 6 ...*

They began to leave the region of industrial towns and to climb. The car swerved to the left more and mounted the great mass of upland which thickens the Pennines and sprawls away towards the Lakes. Houses became scarcer. They passed wide reservoirs circled by lines of dark firs and watered by streams that leaped down narrow valleys, and from the slopes sheep straggled on to the roadway with suicidal casualness that demanded all Cableton's attention. The road wound over the slopes and between the dips, always avoiding the skyline and never going lower than it could help. Away from the road stretched the wide moors of coarse grass and heath, broken here and there by a crouching gorse bush that showered its yellow petals over the earth as though they were bribes given to ensure peace against the wind that blew almost incessantly. There was little life beyond the scurry of rabbits and the flight of birds and it was here that Margaret had decided to maroon Cableton. The road forked before them and a green cart track ran way to the right. She directed the car along it and after a lurching, swaying ride of a mile they stopped on the peak of the moor.

As Cableton switched off the engine a curious silence settled over everything. So far the purr of the engine had kept at bay the silence of the moors, but now it seemed that the hills and long vistas were gathering themselves together for an assault upon the intruders. The silence was almost uncanny. As far as they could see rose hill after hill, carpeted by browning grass and green tips of bracken and broken by occasional clumps of larch and the black mark of water-courses, but there was no house, no inn, no hut, no shelter at all. The only signs of civilisation were the road they had come by and the giant, straddling limbs of a set of pylons that faded in diminishing perspective across the hills, as though they were frightened by the loneliness and anxious to have done with it.

"And this, I presume," said Paul, "is where we get rid of our friend?"

"This is where we drop the pilot," said Margaret, and then added maliciously, "and, if it helps or consoles you, Mr. Cableton, I happen to know that the nearest house is about five miles away and the village a good ten. Also the road we came along is very little used so your chance of getting a lift is negligible."

"Is that all?" queried Cableton, unperturbed.

"Not quite. The rainfall in this part of the world is considerable and it looks like rain—and you haven't a coat, so I should say you might get wet."

"Perhaps we'd better leave him a rug from the car?" suggested Paul. "It's a bit …"

"A bit what?" demanded Margaret. Then, seeing Paul hesitate, she went on, "Don't be silly, darling. We've got to be harsh with him. He won't have any mercy on us. You mustn't be soft-hearted. He's only a reporter."

Paul would have liked to point out that even reporters must presumably be subject to pneumonia, but he decided not to waste time by provoking an argument and he consoled himself for their uncharitableness by the hope that it would not rain.

"All right! … We'll leave him here."

"That's kind of you," said Cableton. "Suppose I refuse to leave the car, since I feel you intend to drive it away."

"You certainly won't do anything so silly," ordered Paul. "You'll get your car back in time, and if you make a nuisance of yourself by refusing to get out I shall have to employ force. I guess I could pull you out."

Cableton looked at Paul, noted his fine physique and particularly his strong arms, and decided that Paul spoke the truth and made a note to use the adjectives "strong and handsome" in his story.

"All right—you win. But you're a couple of mugs."

"We don't want you to inform us of our intellectual capacities," said Margaret curtly, enjoying herself. "We've got business to do, so scram!"

"Very well, I'll go," said Cableton resignedly, getting out of the car. "Before you drive off there's one thing. Won't you give me some statement for the press? That can't hurt you. Just a few words?"

Margaret looked at Paul and he shook his head.

"We've got nothing to say. Why should we?"

"Oh, come on—only a few words," pleaded Cableton.

"Not a word!" said Paul firmly and Cableton's protest was lost as Margaret, taking his place at the wheel, started the engine and began to back the car round.

Cableton refused to give up hope.

"Only a sentence—think what it means to me …" he cried and to enforce his plea jumped on to the running board of the car as it moved off.

180

"Go away!" cried Margaret.

Paul, realising the impotency of words, put out his hand and gave Cableton a push in the face that dislodged him from his perch. The rotund reporter stumbled backwards and the last the two saw of him was as he picked himself up from the ground and shook a half angry fist at the retreating car.

"Well, that's got rid of him," said Paul, as they reached the main road. "Now what do we do?"

"Are you asking me, Peter?" inquired Margaret sweetly.

Paul recovered himself. "No, I'm not. I was just thinking aloud. And now that we've got rid of him, perhaps you'll explain just why you came along. Haven't I told you often enough that it's dangerous for you? Haven't I explained the difficulties? Haven't you any sense at all? If you're going to marry me you'd better learn to obey me."

"Oh, Peter, don't speak like that to me," said Margaret with easy tearfulness. "I shall think you don't love me any more. You do love me, don't you?"

Paul was helpless. "Please, Margaret ... don't be like that. I don't mean it ... but this is hardly the time for love—" Paul hastily placated her.

"Not the time for love? Peter, you don't love me? 'Some future day, perhaps, he may be moved, to call his blue-eyed maid his best beloved!'" Margaret laughed and accelerated quickly, so that Paul was shot backwards in his seat.

"I don't know what you're talking about!" he snapped angrily, rubbing his neck.

"Not understand, darling? What, the bit about blue-eyed maids? That's Homer. You remember Homer?"

Margaret's eyes were wide with simple astonishment. She knew that it was wrong of her to tease this young man, but the temptation was irresistible. She was repaid for her dereliction.

"There have been times, Margaret Sinclair," Paul declared almost rudely, "when I have been prompted to spank you! If you were a man I would not have tolerated you for more than half an hour. Please try and remember my position. This is no joke for me!"

Against this onslaught Margaret was wisely silent. The car moved on and after a while dipped to a plain where they came to the fresh green of meadows and the shade of tall sycamores and oaks.

"How long," said Paul, "do you think it will be before Cableton gets in touch with the police?" He spoke with some reluctance, for by now he had regretted his rudeness and was wondering whether Margaret's silence represented sulkiness or indignation.

"I should give him about two hours," replied Margaret in a tone which implied that she had quite forgotten the incident.

Paul could not understand her attitude. Sometimes she was mocking, sometimes pathetic in her demand for his avowals of love, and sometimes incredibly matter-of-fact in the face of startling developments. Once or twice he had caught himself wondering whether she had discovered that he was only an impostor, but he had dismissed these suspicions. Why should she be following him and showing such evident interest in his predicament?

"Two hours—then we must do something quickly. We can't go much farther in this car."

"That's true, Peter dear. But do what?"

Paul looked at her and then confessed, "I don't know. I'm getting just about played out."

At once Margaret was sympathetic. "Now, you mustn't feel like that. Things aren't really so bad, you know. We must face these difficulties bravely."

"But how?" Paul felt curiously weak and helpless.

"I'm almost afraid to advise you—you seem to resent it so much." This air of contrition suited Margaret very well and the sight of her pretty face turned towards him, the faint draught from the windscreen flicking up the collar of her dress, filled Paul with a queer tenderness. At heart she was a nice girl, he thought; a girl a man could like. It was a pity he had had to meet her in circumstances such as his were.

"Please, Margaret, don't feel like that. If you've got a plan let's hear it. You must"—he was suddenly aware that the real Peter Angel was still alive somewhere and probably waiting to get into touch with Margaret—"not think I'm so difficult. I still love you, but I have had a trying time and it makes me kind of jumpy."

"Of course, I understand. Forget about it, dear. It's all a horrible nightmare. There ..." With a grand defiance of road laws and caution Margaret put one arm on Paul's shoulder and patted his cheek, and Paul, for once, found the movement restful and soothing. "The thing you have to do is to get out of this country as quick as you can. That's your only hope. I'm not going into the ethics of what you've done. We'll leave that until we have time to discuss it sensibly and without hurry. Until then,

I think I can manage to get you out of the country. That is, if you can evade the police for another couple of days—"

"It's nice of you to say that, it certainly is; but how can you do it? Remember, I'm pretty low in cash. It can't be done."

Margaret took up the challenge eagerly. For the first time she felt that she was being of genuine assistance to this strange young man. "Yes, it can. Listen, this is what we'll do. I'll drive on for another twenty miles and land you on the fringe of the Lake District and you can hide yourself there for a couple of days. That should be just possible, because Cableton won't know which way we've gone. Then I'll drive back as far as I can in this car towards London. I shall have to take a risk—"

"But why London?"

"Silly—because father's in London."

"What has he got to do with it?" Paul was unenlightened.

"Have you forgotten that he's a shipowner, and he's sure to have a timber boat going across to Europe, you know, the Baltic or Russia. You could go on that."

"What?" Paul was hard put to overcome his astonishment. The Baltic, grey seas and foreign capitals where everyone wore strange clothes and spoke a stranger language; Russia with phlegmatic workers trudging the streets. Everything he had read in the papers of bread queues, internment camps, hunger strikes, free love and paganism came back to him in a horrific wave.

Margaret did not notice his reaction. Her eyes were bright as she planned for him.

"Yes, that's it. I'll fix up a boat going from Newcastle. That's the nearest port for us, and I know dad has boats working from there. And I'll get some money for you, about fifty pounds, which you can repay later."

"But, I don't want to go to Russia," Paul almost wailed.

"But you must—or somewhere over there. It's your one chance of safety. You'll be all right. Besides, I must go back to London to get a change of clothes—these feel as though I've worn them for months." Margaret indicated her dress, which was crumpled and dirty with the rigours of the last few days.

"But Russia ... I ..."

"Now, Peter, be sensible. You want me to help you, don't you?"

"Yes, of course, but it seems rather unnecessary to go there."

"Nonsense, no one would recognise you in Russia or Denmark."

Why no one would recognise him Paul was not told. He pondered this enigmatic statement while Margaret went on.

"It's now Saturday. I could get back to London late tonight. See father tomorrow and be back by Monday evening at the latest. Do you think you could hang out until then? We could meet at Keswick, say outside the Blue Moon Hotel, which is the largest hotel and in the main street ..."

While Margaret was speaking a scheme had suggested itself to Paul. From where it came he had no idea, unless it was born of his own resentment of the batterings which he had experienced since landing in England. He told himself that very frankly he was tired of England. He had come to see Wisbech. In an impulsive moment he had let himself in for much more than he had anticipated in order to escape the penalty of an innocent joke. He was weary of the constant evasion and longed, if he were to be denied Wisbech, for the comforts of America and the sanity of his correct character. He had a job and a reputation to consider.

That this reasoning was belated did not affect his scheme. Without money he could do nothing. The question of money had not arisen before. He had had enough for his wants in England from Simpkins. Normally he would have cabled for money after winning his bet by reaching England as a stowaway, but circumstances had now made that course impossible. But if he let Margaret get him some money he could—and would, for he decided that he had played the part of Peter Angel long enough to merit a pardon—give her the slip and go down to Southampton and there approach the shipping company and offer to pay for his passage across and back, apologise for his bad behaviour and tell them that he had swum ashore from the liner. It would mean swallowing his pride, but common sense indicated it as the only sensible course. The shipping company, knowing him for a stowaway and accepting him as John Denver, would not connect him with Peter Angel and would probably give the event no, or at the most, little publicity. And he would be free to return to America. The idea of taking Margaret's money and using it for his own purposes worried him. It was a mean act which he found very difficult to countenance. His chief argument for such a course was that by duping Margaret he was really helping her. As long as she was with him she was in danger. Once he reached America he could write her a letter of explanation and apology. He dared not risk telling her the truth now. Even with his altruistic reason it was some time before Paul could bring himself to accept the measure. Then, as he realised that it was the wisest and easiest plan, he began to feel happier and even wondered

184

whether he might digress to Wisbech on his way back. He turned and smiled at Margaret.

"I think it's a grand idea, Margaret. Of course, I shall pay it back. I shan't forget this." Overcome by a wave of shame as he thought of the advantage he was to take, had to take, of her good nature, he leaned across and planted a chaste kiss on her cheek. Some day, perhaps, he would return to England and meet her in happier circumstances.

Margaret looked back at him and he was surprised to notice that she was blushing.

"Oh, Peter, I'm so glad you're being sensible. Now I do love you more than I ever have done. And we'll soon put an end to all this horrid business and square things up."

"Sure, we shan't be long now. You know, Margaret, this is the first time for some days that I've felt so happy." Paul drew a deep breath and surveyed the country as though he were a Hannibal cresting the Alps, his objective gained. He suddenly felt full of confidence and tried to express his assuredness.

"You know, this reminds me of our New York days, driving together and planning things. Remember them?" asked Margaret, and then went on, "Those were happy days. Guilty days, but I was happy even though we kept everything so secret from father and the rest of the people. I love secrets and excitement, don't you? Life's nothing to me unless it has danger and secrets that you daren't whisper. I often try to explain that to daddy, but he just doesn't understand. He's more concerned with tonnage and freights, but you're different, darling ..."

Paul was content to leave the conversation at this point. just how different he was he did not wish to discuss.

So, while Mr. Cableton, stirred into more than eloquence by his enforced walk, plodded towards the nearest telephone and composed his story as he walked, Paul and Margaret hurried farther away from him towards the Lake District, and it was on the fringe of this strange region of hills and lakes that Margaret left Paul.

They had made all their arrangements and it was time she began to head for London. She left Paul at Kendal, where he caught a motor-coach for Ambleside, and then she drove away southwards to Lancaster and there, judging that it was dangerous to drive a car which would shortly be, if it was not already, listed by the police, she left Cableton's car in a side street and with the last money in her purse bought a third-class ticket for London.

185

That night Paul retired early to sleep in an Ambleside boarding house after a very frugal evening meal. Yet, though his interior had been denied its wants, his mind was at rest, for he knew that the next few days would see the end of his quest and discomforts. He slept happily, his dreams a chaotic mixture of blue lakes and long lines of firs, of dark woods and quiet quaysides, of boats tilting on the mud at low tide and jerseyed sailors spitting on cobbles as they eyed the gulls searching for lob worms in the mud. And as he dreamt, the London newsboys were shouting a special edition of the *Evening Saturn* and Cableton was travelling towards the capital like an emperor in triumph. His story had been delivered over the telephone. He had done his work well—the newsboys testified to that—and flushed with success and whisky he regretted that he had not made a better story than he had done. Already several new items had suggested themselves to him. He consoled himself from the bottle he had in his hand and then went to sleep in the corner of his compartment from which, some hours later, he was lifted reverently by a welcoming committee from the *Daily Globe*, and borne solemnly to the editorial offices, where a group of colleagues waited for his revival with something like the interest which must have enlivened the faces of onlookers when Daniel walked out of the lions' den.

XVIII
Paul gets a wetting

Cableton's story was a good one. The account in the *Evening Saturn* was a colourless paragraph compared with what graced the front page of the *Sunday Globe*, the devout disguise of the *Daily Globe* on Sundays.

Margaret had not read the evening edition. She had been dismayed at the absence of her father from home and had not heard the newsboys. But as she waited on Sunday morning for him to return, as he was expected, she read the *Sunday Globe*. For all her sophistication she was amazed at the plausibility and exaggeration which Cableton had worked into his story. *Amazing interview with Peter Angel! Journalist Taken for Ride with Wanted Crooner! Who was the woman?* These and other headlines were only the prelude to greater disclosures and sensations. As Margaret read she chuckled. Cableton described how, at the point of a revolver he had been forced to drive Peter Angel away from the dance hall ... "I knew there was no hope of escaping from this strong, handsome villain. If I had made the slightest move I would have been shot down without hesitation. I could see from the cruel curve of his lips that he was desperate and ready for anything and the woman behind, that mysterious figure in his life, she too was regarding me with baleful eyes, eyes that seemed to look right through me and dare me to do anything else but what I was told. And as I drove they openly discussed their crime, for the woman seems to have played an important part in it, and laughed at their wickedness. From time to time Peter Angel helped himself to courage from a hip flask and when the night was growing old he began to sing in his beautiful voice all the songs which had made him famous. There was something pathetic in that singing, and something horrible that chilled me to the marrow … On the whole I was treated with respect, but I am convinced that their only reason for allowing me to go free by marooning me in an isolated part of the Yorkshire moors was their vanity. They knew I was a reporter and they wanted the story of their daring to appear in the papers. But their vanity will be their undoing. The police are closing in upon them and, perhaps even now, they have been apprehended wherever in the north they have taken refuge.

"As they left me stranded I asked if they had any message for the public. Peter Angel answered, with mock courtesy, 'Convey my deep regrets to the Scotland Yard Head of Police for having given him so much trouble, and tell him that his police are so slow that most of them are still celebrating last Christmas.' And the woman, that strange half-English, half-American figure with her cultured accent and vulgar phrases, said, 'Tell the big public, honey, that when the dollars get low we'll be putting another hand in the pocket of their pants!' With this, they were gone and I was lucky to be left with my life."

Margaret had to admit that Cableton had not spared himself. To the bare bones of fact he had brought all the coloured dress and fine appendages of fiction. His description of the debate as to what should be done with him, before the solution of marooning him on the moors had arisen, read like a catalogue of tortures used by the Inquisition and represented a fairly complete inventory of homicidal crimes.

The account occasioned Margaret no alarm. From his description of her, she knew that she need not fear detection, and she hoped that the bogus Peter Angel would have enough sense to make himself as inconspicuous as possible for the next two days. Everything then, she told herself, would be all right. And her interview with her father tended to confirm this opinion.

He was a tall, grey-haired, rather distinguished-looking man whose one affectation was a monocle, which kept dropping from his eye leaving him with a look of astonishment on his face at this ungracious desertion.

"Yes, there is a timber boat sailing from Newcastle on Tuesday evening. I could write to the master tonight and ask him to take this young man you're interested in. But what is it all about, Margaret? Who is this fellow?"

"Please, daddy, it's quite all right. He's a young friend of mine who's rather interested in the low side of life. You know, writing and all that, and he wants to travel as a seaman to get material. At least, that's what I think he intends—"

Margaret excused her lie by her last sentence and justified her evasion by the urgency and seriousness of her position.

"Sounds very peculiar to me, my dear. Still, you know. Where d'you say this fellow is now? Keswick?"

"That's where I'm meeting him tomorrow. I'll take him across and introduce him to the master if you'll give me the details."

"Very well—" his face assumed a wary, startled look as the monocle defaulted. "I suppose, my dear, you're not on the verge of doing anything silly again?"

"I resent that again," replied Margaret, smiling and taking him by the arm. "It's unnecessary!"

"Well, my dear, you know how I feel about the liberty of the child and the duties of parents, but sometimes you have been rather indiscreet. You are inclined," his face resumed its natural cast as he replaced the monocle, "to let your sympathies overrule your common sense."

"Nonsense, daddy. But don't forget to write to that master for me, and now I must fly as soon as you've given me those details. I'm sure you must be busy after being away so long. Did you have a nice time?"

"Fairly, but it was marred because I had no letters forwarded. There was some mistake in the house here. Apparently no one knew exactly where I was and I've been wanted by quite a lot of people while I was away. Most annoying."

"It must have been, daddy." Margaret took the slip of paper with the details of the Newcastle boat and, after kissing her father, left the room.

At first she had thought she would return to Keswick by train to meet Paul, but on second thoughts she had decided against the railway. She would go by car and then they could travel across to Newcastle quietly and without subjecting themselves to any suspicion from railway officials who would be on the watch. Her own car was still at Matlock and she decided that it would be unsafe at this juncture to reclaim it. Instead, she had made arrangements with her father to borrow his for a few days.

As she left the house to return to her own flat to make arrangements for her journey, she noticed a huge Daimler car come down the roadway, and it was not until she was almost at her destination that she remembered why the car seemed so familiar. It belonged, she recollected, to Mr. Partingale, who was a very great friend of the family. But she very soon forgot Mr. Partingale as she made ready to leave London for Keswick. Although she had to meet Paul there on the following evening, she had a long drive before her and preferred to do it in two stages.

Mr. Partingale's first remark after greeting Mr. Sinclair might have startled a normal parent. Its only effect on Mr. Sinclair was a mild look of inquiry which facilitated the escape of his monocle and changed the expression to astonishment which he did not feel.

"Is your daughter a criminal?" asked Mr. Partingale, smoothing his crisp black hair and smiling.

"That sounds like the title to a Sunday paper article, Partingale. What do you mean?"

"Just what I say, Sinclair. Is your daughter a criminal, or does she mix with criminals?"

"I haven't the faintest idea, Partingale, not the faintest. She seems to move in a very mixed society; her friends include—so she tells me—people in every class from tram conductors to privy councillors, and I expect there must be a few criminals among them. It's inevitable."

"Then you are entirely without suspicion of her movements and associates?"

"Good Lord, Partingale, you're talking like an inquisitor. I'm more than that. I'm entirely ignorant of her movements and associates and I prefer to remain so. You know my views about young people. Let them have their head. Margaret's far from being a fool, and I trust her—that's all, and that's enough for any sensible parent."

"I know, Sinclair. I feel the same way about her. But—forgive me if I seemed a little rude just now—I'm rather worried about Margaret."

"But why worried?"

Mr. Partingale did not answer the question. He stood up and looked out of the window, at the dusty plane trees and the line of traffic moving slowly up and down the street.

"Have you heard about this Peter Angel fellow?"

Mr. Sinclair laughed and joined him by the window. "Is this another joke about him? Has anybody not heard about him? What with the press and the wireless and talk in clubs ..."

"Did Margaret ever know him?"

"She may have done. She was in America recently with me, but I never heard about it if she did."

"Well, believe it or not, Sinclair, I happen to know that this Peter Angel has been helped by a woman once or twice and that it has been established that he actually used Margaret's car at one period—"

"What are you talking about?"

"Peter Angel. I think that Margaret's helping him. In fact, I'm pretty sure, and so are the police."

"Then why haven't the police said anything to me?"

"For various reasons. You've been away, address unknown, and also I have been able to satisfy them in your absence on certain points. I put them off about the car by suggesting that it had probably been stolen from Miss Margaret. I happen to have some influence in the right quarter. But I'm sure that at this moment Margaret is with Peter Angel. Have you read the *Sunday Globe*?"

Mr. Sinclair nodded and drew his hands over his chin thoughtfully.

"You may be right, Partingale. She's capable of any mad thing, that girl of mine, but she's not bad—far from it. And I'm certain she's not with this fellow now, because she only left me half an hour ago."

"Left you?" Mr. Partingale swung round, his thin face alive with interest.

"Yes, she came to make arrangements about a passage for a friend from Newcastle." Mr. Sinclair explained to Mr. Partingale what Margaret's errand had been.

The motor-car manufacturer spread out his hands and examined the veins in them as he spoke.

"And don't you see what she was doing? She was getting a passage for this crooner."

Mr. Sinclair nodded. Even now it was all very clear to him he was far from worried. He shared with Margaret a grand imperturbability that was incompatible with anxiety. Margaret was all right. There was an explanation somewhere waiting for him.

"What do you suggest that we do?" he asked after a pause.

Mr. Partingale was gratified at this attitude. It made things much easier for him.

"Nothing. You leave everything to me and I promise you that Margaret will not be allowed to do anything stupid or criminal. I'll go up to Keswick and keep an eye on her—"

"That's very good of you, Partingale. Do you think I ought to come?"

"Not at all—I'll see this through. There's no need for you to worry, and I think it would be better if you preserved a discreet ignorance of everything if the police call on you. But I don't think they will, somehow."

Ten minutes later Mr. Partingale, too, was making all arrangements for a journey to Keswick.

And while all this was happening in London, Paul equipped with a map of the district, was setting out to lose himself amongst the lakes.

By the afternoon he was truly lost. He had set out early from Ambleside to avoid the townsfolk before they rose, and with some sandwiches in his pocket had worked his way up the steep side of Loughrigg Fell which hung above the town like a giant for ever guarding it, and then coming down into Grasmere had walked along a tree-shaded road by the side of the lake. At Grasmere, unheeding its poetic associations, forgetful of the shades of Wordsworth and De Quincey, he had eaten his sandwiches and bought a glass of beer from a public house. Then, confident with food and refreshed by his drink, Paul had struck away north-east along a valley which slowly rose to distant crags and sharp lines of hill.

The day was very hot and a slight mist hung over the tips of the distant fells and a heat haze set the ground shivering before him. He walked at an easy pace and let his mind wander where it would. He had thrown aside his guise of Peter Angel and to himself he was just Paul Linney Morison, enjoying himself in the English Lake District as many another American tourist had done before him, and he was far from insensible to the beauty arounct him. He was astonished that so much beauty could be packed into so little space.

Here he walked, like a Lilliputian through a setting of magnificent jewels that hung closely to the rugged frame in which they were set. From the top of Loughrigg that morning he had been granted a wonderful vista. Around him was the sweet smell of browning grass and heather. On top of a cairn of weathered stones a wheatear perched and dipped its tail to him and tiny hover-flies hung in the strong breeze, like humming-birds. And at his feet, dipping down the steep hillside and reaching away until distance and the haze wrapped them in friendly obscurity, were hills and fells and lakes until the eye was confused by their profusion and sought security and ease on the farthest point. The whole landscape was the handwork of a fastidious master. The rounded slopes, the sharp crag-tips and the shining lakes were scattered and disposed with a liberality and feeling that captivated the mind by its beauty and bewildered the eye by its variety. Here, in epitome, was all that England could offer: steep pikes where the buzzard still nested in safety, valleys where the grey slates of houses and the stubs of church towers pushed through the thick foliage of sycamores and limes, long straths alive with moving sheep and powdered by drifts of fallen stone from the heights, sharp clefts in the hillsides where the white fury of waterfalls made a quick contrast with the fresh green of rockbrake and unfurling bracken that bent towards the spray, lakes of ever-changing colours where trout moved on agile fins and gudgeon nosed about the pebbly strand, fields that rivalled the changing greens and silver of the lakes where cloud masses threw their moving shadows across them with passing caresses, and swelling mountains that did their best to intimidate by grandeur the peace and contentment that dwelt in the valleys.

Paul loved the open spaces of the hills. There was a freedom in the wind that swept across the upland slopes, a royalty in their ruggedness and a charm in their hidden dips and hollows that cradled black-water tarns and patches of mossy swamp where the streams had their birth.

It was one of these streams which Paul was now following. The path ran along by its side, sometimes crossing it by rough stepping stones that slipped and swayed as he trod on them, sometimes curling away from it for a while to avoid wastes of marsh that came down to its edge and waved white banners of cotton grass about its banks. At times Paul sat and rested himself on the bank. He could see the stream, widening and twisting to the valley and lake, and before him tumbling down from the head of the valley. And as it ran, it sang softly to itself and whispered the secrets which it had gleaned from the hills to the spongy mosses and tall thistles that flanked its bank. Higher up, in the morass of quaking sods and gurgling mosses where the stream had its beginning from the rain, there had been little company and it had talked occasionally to itself or grumbled at its solitude, but once free from the confines of the marsh and started on its journey to the lakes it found company.

First had come the rough grasses that dropped their white seeds into its turmoil. Ravens had croaked to it from the tops of rounded slate boulders, sparrow-hawks and kestrels had torn their victims by its side and wide-eyed rabbits had jumped across its puny width. For two miles of ragged hill it had travelled with only sheep and the birds of the uplands to talk to it, but now it swirled in deep pools, gushed over dams of fallen rock, wetted the points of felspar and festooned the pebbly reaches with a tiny detritus of dead grasses and twigs from the thorns and juniper that clung close to its bank for shelter. In places, the wrecks of holly leaves were jammed together, stranded on their way to the lakes and rotting under the fierceness of sun and wind.

Lower down, the stream was to find stone bridges in the place of stepping stones and to receive on its bosom the leaves of oak and elm and provide a mirror for the pale faces of rock-roses and the boldness of the yellow worts and centauries.

Paul was loath to leave his resting-place. On his left the dipping sun marked a golden line along the ridge of the valley and showed the corrugated line of peaks as black masses where the shadows were marshalled. He looked up the valley and had his path set out for him, until a knoll hid it, by the succession of tiny cairns which served as guides in mist and darkness.

As he rested, a pair of walkers caught up with him. There was a thin, almost undersized man who struggled under the burden of a knapsack and thick heavy-nailed boots, and with him a woman who wore green velvet shorts and held a map in her hand like a talisman. Her body was of Amazon proportions, to the lower part of which her shorts gave strictured emphasis.

Paul greeted them and, although it was obvious that the woman was anxious to be on their way, the man seemed grateful for the excuse to halt.

"Going far?" asked Paul, offering the man a cigarette, which he refused, murmuring something about preserving his wind.

The woman replied by opening her map and proudly indicating their route. Already that day they had covered what to Paul seemed a prodigious, even fantastic, mileage, and the remainder of their journey was equally ambitious.

There was something avid, almost indecent, in the way in which she indicated the pikes they had climbed and were going to climb and the crags which had yet to fall beneath their iron-shod boots.

"You certainly are going to see everything," he remarked with suitable awe. "I am afraid I must seem lazy compared with you. I just go as I please and rest when I want to."

"That's all wrong," replied the woman. "We organise our rests. So many to the hour. Yes, we are going to see everything. We shan't be content until we have stood on top of everything. Come on, love."

The man was forced to his feet and with a wan smile he followed her. Paul felt sorry for him. It was obvious that he would rather have sat and talked. For a time Paul listened to the clank of their monstrous boots over the stones of the path and the sound seemed an appropriate comment to his thought that a man who married such a woman deserved to be dragged about the Lake District for his foolishness. And women, anyway, looked horrible in shorts. He thought of Margaret and knew instinctively that she would never wear shorts. She had too much good sense and taste. He lay back on a soft bed of blaeberries and thought about Margaret. Paul's ideas about women were romantic, for he had not had enough contacts to destroy his chivalrous conceptions. He was impressed by the high quality of her fidelity to him. If he had been the real Peter Angel he knew that nothing could have been more welcome. It was a revelation and a disappointment to him that this strong loyalty should be lavished on one who was so obviously unworthy of it. He could not account for the illogicality of women who can love the unworthy with a sincerity and attachment that are seemingly unlimited. At the thought of Margaret's unswerving loyalty to the other Peter Angel, an unaccountable feeling of sadness possessed him.

A fly with high metallic iridescence on its wings settled on his hand and a grasshopper close by fiddled violently. He sat up, and as he did so a huge bank of cloud passed before the sun and plunged the valley into a cold gloom. The coldness took the sparkle from the water and turned the sweeping hills to grey shapes that crouched around him, like jackals waiting patiently for what might come to them.

Paul got up and went on his way. He had a fair distance to go before he stopped that night and the afternoon was passing. Already the two walkers were out of sight.

For an hour he struggled up the valley. It grew steeper at every step as it ascended towards the neck of the pass, and the muscles of his legs began to tire until he longed for the welcome relief of going downhill again. It seemed that there never had been a time when he had not been climbing, his back bent and his breath coming in strained periods. At last he reached the end of the valley and by a boundary fence threw himself down to rest. He quite expected to find the thin man prostrate there, but there was no sign of the two anywhere and Paul could only assume, when he had recovered enough to allow himself the luxury of thought, that the thin fellow possessed abundant stores of reserve energy in his body.

He did not rest for long. The cloud which had obscured the sun in the valley was the forerunner of others and, as he rose to continue his journey, a splash of rain fell upon his face. Already filmy mists were sweeping down the sides of the crags and covering the dips with banks of grey haze that crept lower with every second.

From the boundary line the land swept away in a wide basin that ended in a circle of green hills. Paul judged from his map that he would have to cross the basin and climb the last ridge of hills before he could begin to work downwards towards human habitations and a place to spend the night.

The raindrops thickened to a chill mist which coagulated into a drizzle, not yet heavy enough to obscure the outlines of the land. Paul pinned his coat collar close to his neck, wished that he had bought a raincoat in Ambleside, wondered if it were a peculiarity of this district that a fine day could suddenly turn to a wet one, and started off for the hills.

Half an hour later he was still plodding across the basin and the hills seemed very little nearer. He could catch glimpses of them as the wind twisted the rain veils aside at times. He was wet, but not miserable. As he walked his feet slipped and squelched over the rough turf and sank into the boggy patches and his suit, which had once belonged to the Leicester actor, began to exude a queer smell, as of protest against the onslaught of the rain. When at last he reached the first slope of the ridge he found that he had lost the path. For a time he had followed the cairns, but the thickening rain had bemused him and now he was breaking across rough ground and not sure that he was going in the right direction. He knew that he had to climb the hills.

Catching at boulders, his feet slipping on wet grass, his hands muddied where he had to hold to the ground for support, Paul climbed the side of the basin and gradually his struggle began to assume titanic proportions in his mind. It seemed that he was fighting the hills. They wanted to keep him trapped in that sodgy, boggy basin, and he wanted to escape. From the mist and rain came weird sounds like the calling of women's voices, and the mist, harried by the wind, contorted itself into strange shapes, phantasmal and mocking. Before him danced grotesque imps that changed, as he panted onwards, into lumbering prehistoric monsters and then scurried into nothingness when a sheep jumped from the lee of a boulder and sent chills of alarm rocketing along Paul's spine. He stopped to regain his breath and the chorus of the murmuring rain and fluting wind seemed to press more closely about him, until their mutter deadened the sound of his own heart beating, and he was glad to begin walking again for the company of the sound of his own progress.

When at last he reached the top of the ridge and was free of the basin he found no relief. Before him stretched a murk that offered no familiar pike as a guide. He might have been standing on the brink of some smoky cauldron, for his view was now restricted to a few yards before him. Had he been suddenly transported there Paul might have felt some despair, but the struggle to reach the ridge-top had wakened in him an obstinate courage and whipped his mind to exhilarating determination. He chose a direction which he thought might lead him to his objective and started off. He even attempted to whistle as he walked, and the sound of his piping shredding into the wind and rain might have been a challenge to the hills to do their worst.

And for the next two hours the hills took up the challenge and did their best to crush and beat Paul into subservience and dejection. He was flung down slippery slopes. Crevices caught at his ankles and tried to twist them. Apparently firm ground developed boggy propensities as he stepped on it. Little bushes parted from the earth as he clutched them, stones rocked beneath his feet and the rain gathered on his eyelids, trickling from his hair, and confused his vision with changing rainbow patterns whose beauty be was too occupied to appreciate. The obstacles that confronted him made him desperate with reckless courage. He climbed over loose screes at a pace which would have alarmed any mountaineer, scrambled down the sides of rocky shelves and jumped from boulder to boulder with a suicidal disregard for the wet surface and his rubber soles. But he did not care. There was something grand and primitive in the conflict with the land and the weather. His suit was stained with mud, he was wet, and his cigarettes and matches useless, and despite all this, he was happy and his face was smiling when a treacherous slope robbed him of his balance and sent him rolling downwards to finish with a spray of raindrops in a bed of bracken and bramble.

The bramble heartened Paul, for he guessed that he must be reaching the lower slopes of the hills. After a time he reached a stream, and taking it for a guide he followed it down, only forsaking it when it slid into rocky gorges where he could not follow.

Gradually the nature of the country altered. He met trees. The stream grew wider, less turbulent, and a plantation of spruce trees rose from the mist and greeted him. Paul entered their damp and gloomy shade and found a path. The path was a symbol of success. It must lead somewhere. As though the hills acknowledged their defeat and were calling off their forces the rain slowly dwindled and the mist, lightening in a freshening wind, was blown away to reveal the landscape once more bathed in the subdued greys and browns of evening.

Paul stopped at the first house that the path encountered. It was a white farm house with a sign outside showing that there was accommodation for tourists.

The farmwife was horrified at Paul's condition and before he fully realised it he was divested of his clothes in an expeditious, yet essentially decent, fashion and was sitting before a fire in a blanket having his supper. He slept in a night-shirt of the farmer which enveloped him like the deflated fabric of a balloon. He lay in bed for a while listening to the wind in a tall birch outside his window and then dropped into a deep sleep from which he did not stir until the farmer's wife knocked at his door in the morning with his dry clothes.

XIX
Once in a blue moon

At half-past six on Monday evening three men were sitting, talking together, in the saloon bar of the Blue Moon Hotel, Keswick. It was not unusual that there should have been only three men in the saloon at that moment, for the popular bar was the public one at the other side of a passage which was hung with eighteenth century sporting prints, and also on this day the town was celebrating a carnival and most of the citizens were in the streets, or on the shores of the lake, making merry. The saloon would be busier later in the evening, though the public bar was already filling with a noisy, good-humoured crowd.

One of the three men was Mr. Partingale. He sat in the window and occasionally looked into the street, which was bedecked with flags, as though he were expecting somebody. Sitting opposite him was a tall, red-headed young man whose face showed considerable excitement, which might have been derived either from the beer he had taken or the enlivening effect of the conversation.

"I don't know who you are," he was saying, "but I won't be rude enough to say I don't care. Yet all you say is wrong. You've got an entirely wrong set of values. Your outlook is warped, inhuman and unchristian. You're a pagan of the worst order for you have no mysticism in your paganism. Money—" He spat with fine direction at the spittoon. "It's of no use at all! Courage is the only currency which this world can't ignore. Now, I remember once I was lost in the Matto Grosso. Absolutely lost and with only a small hatchet to defend myself against the terrors of the jungle. Terrors! Anacondas, man-eating Indians and fish in the streams that will devour a man before he can cross from one bank to another!

Money didn't help me that time—but courage did. It's a long story and begins with a grey December day on Brooklyn Bridge—"

"Perhaps we'd better skip that and stick to the argument," came the suggestion from the third member of the party, who was a thin-framed man with a very large head from which a pair of bright eyes glowed in startling contrast to the pallor of his skin. He cracked the joints of his fingers as he spoke and went on, "I agree with the gentleman that money is practically a universal force. It can obtain most things, and what it can't buy nothing else can. I was once mixed up—on the police side, of course—with the case of a famous financier. A man who dealt in millions and held interests all over the world. When he was arrested I was just in time to stop him from poisoning himself. Now there was a man for whom money had lost its power. It couldn't help him, nothing could. I met him years afterwards while he was serving in Brixton Prison. He said, 'Wimpole, you would have been kinder to have let me kill myself.' I answered that as a man perhaps I would, but I was first of all an agent of the law. You've got to sink your sympathies and be ruthless if you enter our service. I remember once a famous painter, a drug addict, murdered his wife and then—"

"Perhaps we'd better not digress into a discussion of murders," put in Mr. Partingale. "It's too fine a day for such talk. But I still maintain my principle. Money is the strongest thing in the world. It means happiness."

"There's very little happiness in this world," declared Mr. Wimpole. "Very little. We pay so much for our experience that we've got little left over to buy happiness with."

"You talk like a wayside pulpit!" exclaimed the red-headed young man.

"I talk," said Mr. Wimpole with mysterious emphasis, emphasis which seemed to suggest that if he liked to speak fully he could horrify them with information which even the yellowest press would have to reject as absurd, "from experience. I've seen, I have heard and I have drawn my own conclusions from life. It's an unhappy affair for most people."

"It's an unhappy affair for most working people!" said Michael, draining his tankard and accepting Mr. Partingale's invitation to another. "Nowadays there's little generosity left in the world. There are too many bloodsuckers. Look at most of the people who run industries. Squeezing poor, muddleheaded workmen and making fat profits from their sweating. I'd like to take one or two of the bloated plutocrats that the penny press is so fond of talking about and plonk them down in the middle of the Turkestan desert and see how they'd get on out there.

They'd sweat for a change then. Why, I remember once, just south of Khotan, being overtaken by a host of locusts, not the ordinary kind, but a rare species. They settled over everything and covered the sky until it was like looking through a dirty dishcloth. In two minutes I didn't have a stitch of clothing left on me, except a few buttons and the metal parts of my suspenders, and I was a good two hundred miles from the nearest water. How do you think I managed?"

"You seem," said Mr. Partingale quietly, and evincing no interest in the solution of Michael's dilemma in the desert, "to share the common delusions of the mass—"

"Are you trying to insult me?" inquired Michael with a wild flourish of his hand.

"Of course not. I'm trying to correct your wrong opinions. Capitalists, bloated plutocrats, are not what you think they are. Most of them are as helpless to redress the evils of the economic system as the workmen they employ, and all of them are forced by law or trade unions to pay their employees a living wage. The people who are dissatisfied are the agitators, the square pegs in round holes, and they never will be anything else because they're paid to be dissatisfied."

"That's true," commented Mr. Wimpole sagely. "I was once on a case of sabotage; a big steel foundry in Sheffield was blown up just as the firm were about to start a large order for Bolivia. The Ogpu were mixed up in that and I was sent across to Moscow to make inquiries. Tact is what counts with the Russians, specially the Bolshies. Use tact. They're like children and I treated them like that and brought things to a satisfactory end. Lenin gave me an autographed samovar when I left—"

"That's your sixth glass of beer, isn't it?" said Michael pointedly.

"Fifth," Mr. Wimpole corrected him. "I presented it to the British Museum, but they refused it as propaganda likely to controvert the public from allegiance to the commonwealth. It's in the apple loft at home now. I shall try again when we get a Labour Government—"

"Which we never shall while the owners of industry are what they are," declared Michael.

"Which means," suggested Mr. Partingale with a smile, "that's it money that counts in politics, just as in every other thing you can think of—"

"You and your money!" scoffed Michael, carefully counting the change from his beer. "What's money? It's courage that counts!"

"No, it's tact and a steady hand when it comes to shooting," affirmed Mr Wimpole, spilling his beer as he raised it to his lips.

"Don't think I'm pleased at the part money plays. I only want people to be sensible and recognise its omnipotence. You can deplore it, as I do, but you can't ignore it," insisted Mr. Partingale.

"Anyway, there's no need to keep on about it, is there?" asked Michael. "What's the matter with you? Anyone would think you're a bloated capitalist yourself, the way you stick up for them!"

"Perhaps I am," suggested Mr. Partingale, sipping his beer like a woman and rolling his cigarette butt between his firm fingers.

Mr. Wimpole laughed hollowly into his empty glass.

"Not you. I don't want to be personal, but I take a professional interest in everyone I meet and I've been looking at you since we met—"

"Well?". queried Michael. "What about him—does he remind you of a woodcut by Dürer or a Hogarth caricature?"

Mr. Wimpole ignored him. "I should say you're the fifth or sixth son of a fairly good county family and at the moment you are trying to supplement a small allowance by free-lance journalism."

"By the tail of the Holy Wombat, we've got the shade of Sherlock Holmes with us!" cried Michael.

Mr. Partingale laughed and, not denying Mr. Wimpole's deductions, said, "And how do you arrive at that conclusion?"

"It's easy to the trained mind," confessed Mr. Wimpole. "You drink your beer as though it were wine—that denotes good family. You were looking at that painting over there of the Cumberland Handicap, 1759, and I noticed a frown on your features as you observed the traditional error of eighteenth-century painters who always portray a galloping horse as having both hind and forelegs extended in running—that shows a knowledge, intimate, of horses and marks your station in life; and at the same time there was mixed with your frown a peculiar tenderness and longing—"

"And what was that?" inquired Michael.

"Obvious—he was thinking of the times he had ridden at point-to-points and wishing he could afford it now—"

"And my comparative poverty and free-lance writing?"

"Again obvious. You are wearing a fifty-shilling suit and from time to time during this conversation you have made notes in a pocket-book and kept looking out of the window at the carnival crowd for local colour."

"You're a marvel!" breathed Michael, and felt a grand, absurdly illogical desire to kiss Mr. Wimpole on his bald pate.

"And why a fifth or sixth son?" probed Mr. Partingale. But Mr. Wimpole was immersed in the now exacting procedure of ordering another round of drinks. When the drinks came he held his aloft and smiled at the two men.

"Gentlemen, here's to us, and particularly myself. If I may say so, we all seem to be a pretty experienced, widely travelled lot. The Three Musketeers, eh?"

They drank and Mr. Wimpole settled back into his chair to fill a pipe, and as he did so his mind was a pleasant furnace of roaring thoughts. He was thinking mostly of his wife; that shrill, shrewd, despot whose reign of terror he had ended on Sunday morning.

"Why," she had demanded, her arms floury with cooking and her face red with the heat from a cooker; "do you think you can suddenly walk into my kitchen and announce that you are going off to the Lake District for a holiday?"

Mr. Wimpole had not answered with strict accuracy. His condition would not allow it, for he had spent the best part of that morning sitting in the Hare and Grouse, detailing to three visitors a colourful account of a chase of his after a demented press lord, who had escaped from a lunatic asylum—where he had, because of his previous good behaviour, been allowed to conduct his newspaper—with the avowed intention of putting a stiletto through the heart of the Prime Minister and poisoning the Cabinet. The visitors had been liberal in their treating and, after they had left, Mr. Wimpole, surrounded with a glow of self created vigilance to which the shades of Sherlock Holmes, Pinkerton, and Sexton Blake ministered, had read Cableton's account in the *Sunday Globe*.

The story wakened new visions in him and he decided, after some debate with himself, that it might be wise for him to go north for a holiday. He might get another opportunity of catching Peter Angel. There was little indication of the whereabouts of the crooner, but Mr. Wimpole decided that if he were in Peter Angel's place he would most certainly make for the Lake District to hide. Anyhow, he thought, once in the Lake District it would be an easy matter to move anywhere in the north where the crooner might be reported.

He walked home, his resolution steadying his feet, and made his intentions clear to his wife, though he said nothing of the possibility of a thousand pounds reward. That, indeed, had sunk into a secondary place before the thrill, the joy of chasing, detecting and cornering a wanted man.

"I should like to know who you think you are?" his wife had demanded angrily, banging the oven door and spoiling a cake.

Mr. Wimpole, filled with an immense self-confidence, had smiled enigmatically, as though his identity was something he alone could ever know.

"I repeat," he said, "that I am leaving for the Lake District this afternoon in the car. I'm going to have a week's holiday."

"And what do you imagine I shall do?"

"Imagination plays no part there, my dear. I know what you will do. You will stay here, do your cooking and housework, play bridge in the afternoons and address the Women's League on Thursday on 'The Secret of a Good Sponge Cake.' You will remember that I typed your speech last week and I found you a good quotation from Robert Bridges, 'I, too, will something make, and joy in the making,'" he quoted.

"Edward Wimpole!" she declared firmly, "I forbid you to go. How many glasses of beer have you had this morning?"

This curt and unconnubial attitude had its effect on Mr. Wimpole. It was inconceivable that he should be spoken to like this. He, who had held the fates of financiers, actresses, press lords, prime ministers and red rioters in the hollow of his hand, was being browbeaten by a woman. All that was masculine crowded to the fore in him and he felt his lineal connections stretching right back into that primordial community where an ancestor of his had once, with sanguinary unconcern, flogged an unruly wife into lovingness.

He walked up to his wife with a daring that did not come solely from drink, and he snapped his fingers under her nose with a vicious gesture.

"That for you, my dear. I am going. I have always been a kind husband to you and I always shall be, but when I want a holiday I shall take one, and I'm taking one now. If I have time I will send you a picture-card."

"Edward Wimpole"

Mr. Wimpole cut short her remonstrance. "Have you ever been beaten, my dear? Then be sensible, otherwise I shall have to chastise you!"

His alcoholic determination and firmness won him the day. With a suddenness which surprised him for a moment, she plumped into a kitchen chair and began to sob, and after she had sobbed for a while, he came and kissed her tear-inflamed eyes and apologised.

Then, when she had tried to take advantage, unsuccessfully, of this contrition, by ordering him to stay at home, she accepted the inevitable and Mr. Wimpole, feeling free in his own house for the first time, sat down to a slightly burnt lunch before setting out for the Lake District.

On Monday, hearing of the carnival in Keswick, he had gone there in the faint hope that he might spot Paul in the crowds and after three hours walking about had retired to the Blue Moon to refresh his tissues and slake a thirst which the hot sun had engendered. He had soon realised the hopelessness of looking for the crooner in such a crowd.

And in the saloon he had met Mr. Partingale, who, following Margaret, had arrived a few hours before to take up his position as unofficial watchdog. As these two had been engaged in desultory conversation, there had come into them a dusty, thirsty, vociferous and happy Michael who, since punching Mr. Jones on the nose, had been wisely incarcerating himself in the silence of the hills. The silence, and solitude had lasted him for a few days and then had palled. In Keswick there was offered him the company he longed for.

He came to the table and joined the company.

"I come from the hills, from the solitude of lakes and tarns and the barren company of the winds," he said, reverently lifting his glass and drinking. "Ah," he breathed freely and went on,

> *He that commends me to mine own content,*
> *Commends me to the thing I cannot get.*
> *I to the world am like a drop of water,*
> *That in the ocean seeks another drop.*

I don't know any more, but I'm tired of talking to myself. Have you ever, sir," he addressed Mr. Partingale, "been alone for a long time, alone and slightly afraid? Then you can appreciate the blessedness of good company. I remember once in the Andes, I broke my ankle trying to reach a sea-eagle's nest ..."

And from reminiscence the conversation had gone, like a dog working a rough field, from point to point, and not one of the three ever thought for an instant that they were linked together by other bond than that which makes men chary of drinking alone.

And while they drank and talked, Margaret, who had passed Sunday night in Preston, was sitting on the roadside by the edge of Thirlmere, hoping that soon an obliging motorist or pedestrian would come along and save her the trouble of changing a punctured tyre. She sat, reconciled to the fate of being late at Keswick for her meeting with Paul. Behind her the sun cast great shadows over the length of that stretch of water which receives all the streams that pour down from the lofty Helvellyn screes and the fells which hide it from Borrowdale and Derwentwater; water which eventually gushes through miles of pipeline, through town and forest, over moor and main road and meets a splashing death in the sinks and baths of Manchester, a death that is only the gateway to another existence, darker, subterranean and viscid, another life whose tragedy, odyssey and end has no need to be sung. Margaret was of the school which held as its chief tenet that a girl who possesses a pretty face and a car need never perform any mechanical act so long as she could produce a smile. Margaret primed her smile and waited for the note of an approaching engine.

And while Margaret sat and waited, so Paul sat and waited some ten miles away on the shore of Derwentwater. He sat on the edge of a low wooden jetty which sprang out from the foot of the woods around the lake's side and to which, so an obliging native had informed him, a motorboat came at intervals to ferry people over to Keswick.

That morning he had dressed in his dried clothes and, clean-shaved and well fed, for the good wife believed that a man could look after his own intellect and morals as long as a woman took care of his stomach, he had left the farm and started for Keswick. The day, as though it repented of its boorish yesterday, was fine and pleasant. The sun ruled in an arena of blue, across which marched a procession of white chariots and wild animals and amorphous carriages, and from every living thing the sun evoked a song of thanksgiving. The pigeons cooed to the tips of the spruce and birches and occasionally rose from their perches with a sudden clap of wings and then glided down to the fields to search among the high wheat and grasses for food, and a woodpecker ran round the white skeleton of a beech, pecking and listening as though it were the incarnation of a railway wheel-tapper.

Paul found a path that ran along the river and began to work towards the end of the valley where the lake received the water from the hills. The path was fringed with tall thistles and fragrant from the pads of marjoram which studded the fields. On either side of him the hills came down through bare rock to grass and found the river in a mass of trees. Here and there great angles of fellside jutted over the valley, covered in a growth of ivy and twisted trees, and reached over the river like dogs guarding a bone, and the whole place was a mass of colour; colour that ran and twisted, gathered in great crowds and loitered in the solitary glory of tall mulleins and nipple-worts. Cinquefoils rivalled the sheen of the grass with their yellow, and blue vetches poured their beauty over the hedges, and above the tips of yarrow and mignonette drifted erratic squadrons of cinnamon butterflies and bright-banded flies and bees.

Everything moved or shone with the brightness of the day. The clumsy bees buzzed and struggled into the necks of the yellow toadflax. Dragonflies moved swiftly over the surface of the river, their reflections startling the little trout that lay, nose upstream, on the gravelly bottom waiting for the grubs and refuse that came to them on the current.

Paul tossed a stone into the water, causing a disturbance amongst the water fleas, and then went on his way with the busy, fussing sound of a family of tits accompanying him until he had left the trees and was walking along a winding piece of lane that led away from the river and curved up the hill slightly before coming down to the lake. He did not see the lake until he left the road and, taking a small footpath through a belt of spruce and birches, came out on to its edge and met the cool rush of the wind and the slap of breaking waves over the grey rocks.

Derwentwater lay before him, stretching away until its farther end was lost in the haze that sank down from Skiddaw and touched the grey towers of Keswick.

He wandered about the edge of the lake for a while, the scent of gorse bushes strong in the air and the waves making a tiny, leaping sound as they played along the gravelly beach and tossed the detritus of straws and driftwood over the stones. Away across the water floated tiny green islets, little worlds that swam in the universe of water with a strange air of complacency and detachment, while round them circled and moved minute planets and stars where rowing boats, bright splashes of colour upon the sapphire lake, sent the glimmer of oar-drips sparkling towards the pale clouds. A seagull came wailing out of the sky and passed close to Paul with a faint *swish, swish* of wings that reminded him of the S.S. *Pandaric* and his first meeting with Simpkins.

Although that had been only a few days ago, it seemed far back in the past. He sat on the edge of the wooden jetty with his reflection waving beneath him in the water, which turned from sapphire to turquoise and then to bright emerald streaked with layers of waving brown, and he wondered what had happened to the real Peter Angel, and from Peter Angel his mind wandered to the days of his own enthusiasm in New York when England had seemed so very far away. It was with something of a start that he realised acutely that he actually was in England. Here he was in the Lake District, and America, New York, was thousands of miles away. Away to the back of him across the tramp-smudged and cargo-blackened industry of the Irish Sea, beyond Ireland, and the waste of water that was the Atlantic, lay America, the America which he had left upon a sudden impulse to see the place of his mother's birth. As yet he had not seen it, but before long he might be there. The moment of completion of his quest seemed too paradisaical to allow of fulfilment. It was incredible that at that moment as he sat on the jetty and watched the flutter of flags about Keswick, there were men and women walking unconcernedly about the streets of Wisbech, shopping in its market, licking icecream in Woolworth's and working about the wharves …

The noise of a motorboat approaching disturbed his reverie. The boat came alongside and Paul dropped into it. Half an hour later he was standing in the main street of Keswick, the dome of Skiddaw hidden by the houses about him. He had walked through the crowded streets without any qualms. He was conscious that in his present dishevelled state he stood little chance of being mistaken for Peter Angel, and what risk there was he decided to accept in a spirit of fatalism.

Paul had arranged to meet Margaret at half-past seven outside the Blue Moon Hotel. He had no difficulty in finding the hotel. Its sign, a crescent moon, hung out into the street, cradling a tiny star in the concave gesture which it made to the windows of a restaurant on the opposite side of the road. It was seven o'clock and Paul decided to go inside to while away the half-hour before Margaret's arrival.

Mr. Partingale did not see Paul enter the Blue Moon, although he had been very vigilant in his scrutiny of the patrons as they entered. His dereliction was due to Mr. Wimpole and Michael. Mr. Wimpole, made bold by beer, had ventured to doubt the veracity of one of Michael's anecdotes, though why he should have decided to doubt the truth of this one, when he would have been equally justified in doubting any other of the twelve which had preceded it, only Mr. Wimpole knew. Michael, resentful of this implication of prevarication, had raised his fist and thumped the table to emphasise his own probity of reminiscence. The result was that both his and Mr. Wimpole's beer were knocked over and flooded across the table upon Mr. Partingale's knees. As Mr. Partingale sprang to his feet and pulled his handkerchief from his pocket, Paul came along the street. He entered the public bar of the Blue Moon while Mr. Partingale, awkwardly assisted by the two others, was trying to relieve with his handkerchief the clammy wetness of his trousers.

XX
Anybody's quarrel

The Keswick Carnival was no worse and certainly not any better than any other English carnival, but it had attracted to the town a large crowd of people intent upon enjoying themselves.

Paul found the public bar almost full of men who had taken refuge from the spirit of carnival in its cool atmosphere, though the atmosphere was steadily being vitiated as they spat on the slate floor, blew great gusts of smoke from pipe and cigarette into the air and talked with a persistent monotony. The chief subject of discussion was the possibility or impossibility of the firework display on the lake to be held late that evening.

Paul bought a glass of beer and sat down on a side bench to listen to the debate on pyrotechnics.

The man sitting next to him raised his face from his beer and Paul was confronted by the biggest nose he had ever seen in his life. It rose from the brown depths of a tankard like a pale, weary sun rising over the flood waters of the Mississippi after a night of torrential rain and storm. It was pink, a horrible, diseased pink, with white leprous spots like mildew sprinkled over its rugged contours.

"Hallo!" A mouth moved beneath the nose and the man nodded towards Paul.

Paul did not reply. He was staring fascinated at the enormous appendage. For a moment it obscured everything in the room.

"Hallo!" said the man again, and then seeing Paul's wonder, he laughed, rather uneasily, like a boy caught in the middle of a doubtful prank.

"Don't take any notice of this," he said, and then bashfully unhooked the elastic which held the artificial nose to his face. Paul was relieved to see a normal nose.

"I certainly imagined it was a real one for the moment," he said, smiling. "I was wondering how you'd managed to escape the museums with a nose like that."

"It's these carnivals. Some girl, dressed up in her best frock, made me buy it to help something or the other. You up here on business or for the carnival?"

"I'm holidaying, on vacation, you know," replied Paul.

"Lucky you! I'm working. I'm a traveller." The man seemed to be in a communicative mood and Paul did not try to stop him. "Tobacco," he added cryptically, and Paul noticed that for all his apparent sobriety he had taken plenty of liquor.

"Travelling in tobacco—that's an easy job, I should say, always plenty of custom."

"Easy!" the man snorted. "Not so easy as that. We have to work like anyone else, though I'll admit it's not quite so hard to get orders. I've seen a bit of the world, I have."

"Have you?"

"I have. I come from Bristol. Know Bristol at all?"

Paul's negative reply wakened a stream of words and he found himself listening to an eulogy of a town which he knew only by its historical association with Cabot. He was well contented to sit back and let the man talk. Here in the bar he felt safe and secure from the world. The men were all too busy with their drinking and talking to bother about Peter Angel, and soon Margaret would have arrived and he would be on the way to Wisbech and finally to America.

"Yes, I'm proud of Bristol." He clasped his hand together and Paul noticed his nicotine-bannered thumbs.

"You're lucky, then." Paul tried to stem the flow of words. "Not many men would say as much as that today. They all seem to have some complaint. I suppose you travel about a good amount?"

"I do—don't suppose there's a town in England that I haven't been in at some time or other. But there's not one to touch Bristol. If ever you go there you'll say the same. Durdham Downs on a Saturday afternoon with all the local lads playing football." He breathed an alcoholic sigh of satisfaction.

"Have you ever," inquired Paul, after buying him a drink, "been to Wisbech?"

"Wisbech—let's see that's in …"

"By the Wash," prompted Paul.

"Oh, I know it. Yes. I've been there."

"What did you think of it?" Paul was delighted at the opportunity of getting an opinion of the town from a stranger. He felt a curious tenderness for this man who had seen Wisbech. His tenderness was destroyed very quickly.

"Think of it?" The traveller paused, refreshed himself from his glass, and then went on. "I think it's the rottenest town in England. The beer's bad, the girls ugly, the men mean, the trade lousy, the hotels crummy and the country around as uninteresting as last night's paper."

Paul could scarcely believe that he was hearing aright. The attack had been so sudden, so devastating and, to him, so unwarranted that he was left speechless for a second or two.

"And that's what I think of Wisbech," finished the traveller, well satisfied with himself. Actually he had no definite views about Wisbech. When people asked him his opinion of a place he either said it was good or bad, and, today, because of his mood, he had decided that Wisbech was bad and expressed just how bad in the fullest and completest manner which his vocabulary would allow.

"Say, surely you're wrong? It can't be like that?" Paul began to recover himself.

"I'm not wrong. It's worse than that. Ever seen it?"

Paul had to admit that he had not.

"Then how can you say I'm wrong?"

"Well, my mother was born there and she used to tell me about the place."

"Mothers! Listen, never believe all your mother tells you. Wisbech is the last place on earth!"

"I can't believe it!" Paul was growing indignant at this violation of his ideal.

"Can't believe it? Do you mean to say that you think I'm lying? Perhaps you'll say in a minute that I've never been there?"

"Say, I don't mean it like that. But—"

"Go on—say it!" encouraged the traveller with drunken vigour. "Go on, say I'm a damned liar and that I've never been to Wisbech." His voice began to rise.

"Ssssh!" Paul tried to calm him.

"I won't sssh for you or anyone!" cried the man. "No one can say I'm a liar and get away with it—"

"Please, please," said Paul, "I'm not calling you a liar. I merely think that you've made an overstatement about Wisbech. I happen to know that it can't be so bad as you say—"

"Overstatement! A pretty name for a lie! Why, you young whippersnapper, for two pins I'd take you outside and beat the dust from the seat of your trousers. If you think you can insult an honest traveller because he tells the truth you're very much mistaken!" The man was shouting now, his face as blotched and spotted with ugly colour as his false nose had been. The men in the bar turned to see what this irruption meant.

Paul lost his patience with the traveller.

"Sit down and don't make a fool of yourself before all these people!" he commanded curtly. "Who do you think you are—Mussolini?"

"Mussolini!" shrieked the man. "He's insulting me again. I'm an Englishman and damned well proud of it! I'll show you …" He swayed forward and struck at Paul with his left hand.

Paul caught his wrist and gave him a push. The traveller swayed upon his unready legs and then collapsed with a heavy sighing sound on the floor, his head striking the side of a table. The blow was not a hard one, but it roused him from drunken indignation to fury. He struggled to his feet, shouting and waving his arms, and before anyone in the bar could stop him had flung himself upon Paul.

His arms closed round Paul's neck and the next moment the two were struggling on the floor.

"Let go, you fool, and behave yourself," cried Paul, trying to disengage himself. "Let go!"

The man hung on to him like a leech and the men in the bar, forgetting their beer, crowded round and with laughs and shouts encouraged the two, while from the back of the bar the bar-tender hurried away to fetch the landlord.

On the floor the two wriggled and lurched as Paul tried to free himself and the traveller did his utmost to prevent him from escaping.

"Called me Mussolini—called me a liar!" shouted the traveller, and he drove his free hand into Paul's stomach. Paul bellowed with surprise and anger at the blow and, losing his temper, hit the man with the flat of his hand on the ear. The blow resounded and echoed about the bar, making more noise than it caused the traveller pain. There was a disapproving murmur from the crowd and a protesting shout from two men, who were as drunk as the traveller, as they shot forward to reprove Paul.

211

What happened after that Paul never really understood. The whole barful of men seemed to converge upon the struggling pair and in an instant the room was a writhing mass of men, some trying to rescue Paul, for whom they had definite sympathies—this was the more sober element—and some, the less sober, hurrying to the support of the traveller who had received such a resounding thwack.

Feet scraped on the floor, elbows pressed into sides and fists met flesh with luscious sound as men panted and swore and breathed beery breath into one another's faces. The copper jugs and bright glasses reflected a scrimmage of legs and arms, and the pictures and advertisements on the walls danced in time with the thud of moving feet. In half a minute no one cared about Paul or the traveller or who was fighting whom, but the spirit of carnival was abroad and each man buffeted his neighbour with hearty and eloquent impartiality.

The landlord arrived back with the barman, took one glance at the mass of belligerent humanity and decided that it was beyond his control or jurisdiction.

"Fetch a policeman, Bill," he ordered and with superb husbandry began to collect all the glasses which he could reach in the bar. In the course of this duty he received a stray kick in the shins, and, forgetting his glasses, plunged with commendable fervour into the morass of panting, hugging, shouting, singing, swearing, tearing bodies to search for his assailant. The traveller, like a straw in a whirlpool, was thrown to the outer edges of the scrum and, coming to rest against the side of a chair, surveyed the mêlée for a moment and then, slipping to his feet, left the bar and hotel as quickly as he could. As he passed along the corridor he had to step aside to allow the forward rush of three men.

Mr. Partingale, Michael and Mr. Wimpole had heard the noise, ignored it for a while and then, impelled by curiosity, had decided to investigate.

They stood in the doorway surveying the many-legged phenomenon before them and, as they watched with surprise and wonder filling their faces, the heavier constituents of the human mixture began to sink to the bottom and the lighter elements come to the top. There was a burst of groans from some unfortunate, a flurry of arms and from the living yeast there was evicted the head and shoulders of Paul Morison. For a few seconds he was at the tip of the pyramid of struggle, then he sank again into the labyrinths and dark ways of the massed men. But those few seconds had been enough to allow the three to recognise him. They forgot each other and knew only that in the middle of the scrimmage lay the one person in the world they would have expected to be there, and in their hearts sprang different emotions.

"It's him!" yelled Mr. Wimpole with fine disregard of grammar, and leaped towards the struggle which enveloped and received him as gratefully as minestrone a carrot.

"Incredible!" cried Mr. Partingale and he moved forward with a nicety and caution of movement which availed him nothing, for a hand shot from the scrum, caught him by the ankle and he disappeared, fists flailing, into the morass.

"*En avant les Stormrys!*" bellowed Michael and, with a grand refutation of cause and an eye solely to effect, he jumped forward and hit the nearest man under the ear in his efforts to rescue Paul.

The addition of this trinity to the fight livened it considerably. As he fought Michael sang a ditty of uncertain length which was concerned with the exploits of a one-legged horse-thief who lived and died in the Grand Chaco, and every now and then the rollicking chorus of the song came stealing and twisting from the fight:

> *Oh, I can't keep from stealing,*
> *When I hear the ponies squealing*
> *In the land that lies between the Rio and the sea*
> *I forget about my leggio*
> *And steal until I'm deadio*
> *In the land that lies between the Rio and seeeaaa!*

And Mr. Partingale, stung into a fine fury by a chance blow on the forehead, ploughed his way into the fight, reciting in tune with the rhythm of his arms the details of the new model which his factory was producing that year.

"Fluid flywheel!" His fist cushioned into a stomach. "Syncromesh!" His lowered head rattled against the breastbone of an honest but intoxicated plasterer. "Oil and petrol filter units, permanent jacking system, fog lamps, two folding tables, cocktail cabinet, central ashtray …" And to each detail someone provided the required emphasis as he worked towards the centre.

Only Mr. Wimpole was silent. His was a devilish silence. For the first time in his life he had licence to indulge all his most savage atavisms. He fought in the same awkward fashion as a girl throws stones, but he enjoyed himself and at the cost of bruised hands and bleeding knuckles he left behind him a trail of rapidly swelling eyes and flushed faces. Somewhere in the muddle of men was Peter Angel, were one thousand pounds and the possibility of a liberty he had been almost too timid even to dream about. Nothing could stop him, so he thought. But something did stop him from reaching Peter Angel. As the crowd swung and panted round the room, the centre of the vortex passed over the spot where Paul lay and the fight raged on the far side of the room.

Paul found himself lying, lonely, on the floor and two feet away he could see and hear the scrimmage which still continued. He sat up and rubbed his head where a flying foot had caught him, knocking him slightly dizzy. He smiled foolishly at the fight and, in his bemused condition, being vaguely aware that it had something to do with him was about to attempt to re-enter the argument when a firm hand caught him by the arm and he felt himself pulled to his feet.

"There you go again! I can't leave you by yourself for any length of time before you're in trouble. Come on!"

He looked up to find himself staring into the worried face of Margaret, and without giving him an opportunity to protest, she pulled him along after her. A few seconds later Paul subsided without remonstrance into her car and she started the engine.

"I should like to know where you would be without me?" she questioned severely.

Paul, who was now recovering, smiled wanly. "Still fighting, I expect."

"What," said Margaret, relaxing her severity a little, "was it all about?"

"About?" Paul, now recovered, laughed. "It's rather difficult to say what it was about. It just seemed to happen. But I assure you," he said hastily, "I didn't begin it."

"It's a curious thing," remarked Margaret sceptically, "that all fights just seem to happen without anyone starting them!"

XXI
It's Peter Angel

The fight at the Blue Moon was ended by the interposition of a curt, official voice above the noise of strife and respiration.

"Here—what the hell does all this mean?" boomed the voice. The effect was of the sound of the bell at a boxing match. The fighting ceased at once. The turmoil sorted itself out into something akin to respectability. Men sat up, brushed the dust from their clothes and rescued their ties from the back of their necks and vainly tried to button shirts which had lost their buttons.

"Now then—what's all this about?" boomed the voice, and the policeman thrust out his chest and moved forward into the bar.

The landlord sat up and, helping himself by the wooden counter, reached a vertical position. His face twisted with the pain of a kick on the shins.

"These men, officer, started fighting in my bar. I've kept this place respectable for the last fifteen years, and you know it, and now for no reason at all they start a brawl. I'm a respectable citizen and pay my rates and taxes regular and I'm a churchwarden and I don't see why—"

"What men?" the officer cut his autobiography short.

"These men—" the landlord's arm indicated everyone in the bar.

This accusation brought forth a volume of protest from the innocent parties.

"It ain't the truth!"

"The dirty liar!"

"We didn't start it!"

For a moment there was considerable danger of a fresh outbreak of bellicosity.

"Now then, now then—one at a time!" bellowed the policeman and there was a little murmur of apprehension as he took out a notebook and pencil.

He wetted the tip of the pencil, wrote the date at the top of the page and then the name of the hotel.

"Now then—who started all this?" he questioned.

"It was him!" piped Mr. Wimpole, his excitement getting the better of his good sense.

"It was who?" Everyone in the bar swung round and eyed Mr. Wimpole, and there was a threat in every glance.

"It was him!" persisted Mr. Wimpole, not so loudly or firmly.

"Who?" asked the policeman.

Mr. Wimpole looked round the room, but the figure he sought was not there.

"He's gone," he said lamely. The men nodded agreement and relief.

"Yes, he's gone—the man what started it's gone!" put in the barman.

"There was two of 'em—they started arguing."

"That ain't no excuse for everyone joining in!" reprimanded the officer severely. "You ain't a lot of ten-year-olds. I'm ashamed of you. And on a day like this, too, when Councillor Jones 'as just been talking about brotherly love at the opening of the fête! It's scandalous—"

Mr. Partingale, who had been keeping quiet in the background, came forward.

"I think I can explain, officer," he said and his tones, quiet and authoritative, had their effect. "Two men began to quarrel in here and then started to fight. These other gentlemen," his arm embraced all present with a fine movement which brought out a murmur of gentle applause, "these other gentlemen tried to part them and naturally there was a bit of a scrimmage. Unfortunately, they slipped away during the struggle. I don't think there is really anything to bother about now. We were all acting for the best and, if the landlord will allow me, I shall be quite willing to pay for any breakages as long as this affair goes no further. We can't afford to have an affair like this in Keswick on such a day."

"Hear, hear," chimed the landlord, and he came over and shook Mr. Partingale by the hand. "You're a gentleman, sir."

The rest of the men endorsed this statement.

"All right—I'll make no report this time," said the policeman indulgently. "But see that it don't happen again." And he licked the point of his lead and laboriously scratched out the date and the name of the hotel from his page.

As he turned away a shrill voice piped up.

"But it was Peter Angel—you can't let him get away like this. It was Peter Angel, I tell you!"

The officer turned and stared at Mr. Wimpole as a thrush eyes a snail-shell before cracking it. Before he could say anything Michael took Mr. Wimpole by the arm.

"It's all right, officer. This is my friend. He's a bit—" He touched the side of his head significantly. "Quite harmless, but he gets delusions like this when excited. He was blown up in Arras during the war, poor fellow …"

"But it was Peter Angel," insisted Mr. Wimpole, almost in tears.

"Of course, it was, sir," said the officer gently. "Of course, it was, and he had Queen Elizabeth with him, too. I know, 'cos we've just run 'em both in for vagrancy. Now, you go along with your friend and have a sleep, you'll feel better."

Mr. Wimpole was not allowed to say any more as Mr. Partingale—having handed the landlord a note to cover the damages—closed in on the other side of him. Between Michael and Mr. Partingale he was led gently from the room and into the street.

Michael looked at Mr. Partingale knowingly. "What do we do?"

Mr. Partingale frowned for a moment. "My car's round the corner. We'll go and sit in that and talk things over."

So they walked to the large limousine and Mr. Wimpole was forced to accompany them, wondering what was going to happen to him.

"I tell you," said Mr. Wimpole with great decision, when they were in the car, "that it was Peter Angel. I couldn't have been mistaken."

To his surprise neither of them attempted to deny him. "I know it was Peter Angel," said Michael. "But what of it?"

"And I knew it was Peter Angel," said Mr. Partingale.

"You both knew?" Mr. Wimpole stared at them, his round eyes dancing. "Then why didn't you grab him? There's a thousand pounds reward!"

Mr. Partingale laughed. "Because I don't want a thousand pounds—I happen to be a millionaire—not the sixth son of a fairly good county family!" he added maliciously.

"And I take an interest in Peter Angel. He's by way of being a friend of mine," said Michael. "Now, what do we do?"

"Then we are all three interested in him!" Mr. Wimpole was finding it hard to assimilate these new facts.

"That's right. But I fancy our interests are very different."

"What do you mean?" Mr. Wimpole looked at Mr. Partingale.

"I mean that you are interested because you want the reward. I am interested because of a personal matter. He once laughed at my theory of the power of money. You have just had a demonstration of its power in the hotel, but I want to prove to him its power. And this gentleman—I don't know his interest?"

Michael lit a cigarette. "Purely professional. I'm an author and he seems a very good subject. I once helped him out of a scrape and got myself into one. That reminds me of a time in New York when Bernard Shaw's play—"

"Forget that for the moment, please. We've got to come to a decision about Peter Angel," insisted Mr. Partingale.

"I suggest that the wisest thing to do," said Michael, "is to be perfectly frank with one another and confess all we know about this man and then decide upon a plan of action."

"But what about the reward?" cried Mr. Wimpole. "We're wasting time."

"Forget the reward." Mr. Partingale snapped his fingers hastily. "I can afford to give you a thousand if necessary. Another instance of the power of money. Now then, I'll begin and tell my tale."

And so the three sat in the car and told each other what they knew and their motives for following Paul, but not one of them guessed that the man they were following was not the real Peter Angel.

And while they talked Paul and Margaret were travelling northwards towards Carlisle where they were to strike the main road across to Newcastle. About them as they travelled the soft dusk of the summer evening began to close and in the brown haze behind them, where the dwindling mountains receded like disappointed ghosts, there shone the flare of rockets and catherine wheels from the firework display at Keswick. Occasionally long streamers of sparks seared into the velvety sky to fill the country with ghoulish green and purple lights that lasted for a few moments and then subsided before the growing darkness of the evening. An owl cried in the darkness and the hawthorn hedges were powdered with light as the car moved swiftly along the road. Pinpoints of green fire marked the passage of rats and hares across the roadway and against the windscreen came the tap of luckless moths attracted by the brilliance of their lights.

Paul discovered with surprise that the thought of his approaching separation from Margaret was saddening. She had helped him very considerably and he felt that there was a certain homage due to her. A strange feeling of gratitude and affection for this adamant girl stole over him, and his thoughts grew in tenderness until he apostrophised himself for a fool and concentrated his mind on the shifting picture which danced before them as they swept round corners, illuminating the sides of houses and the white limbs of signposts.

It was dark when they reached Carlisle and found the road which runs in a slight north-westerly direction across to Newcastle. Although Paul did not know it, the road ran parallel with, and in some places actually coincident with, the wall which Hadrian had built to enable his garrisons to stop the raids of the Picts into Northumbria.

Today parts of the wall still stand, the Roman mortar between the stones green with moss and the holes in the masonry making nesting sites for thrushes and wrens. Where the Dalmatian cohorts kept their vigil in the cold breeze and remembered the soft zephyrs of the Adriatic, the sheep now crop and call monotonously to their black-coated lambs, and hawks share with the foxes the duty of quartering the wide, rolling country to the north of the wall over which the soldiers of the Twentieth Legion once watched, and the bustling garrisons of Borcovicus and Cilurnum are now museum pieces to draw gapes from tourists ... Paul had no thought for the Roman exiles in this wintry land. He was thinking of the approaching end of his own exile from America. He felt the crisp notes which Margaret had given him move inside his pocket as he lit a cigarette, and a little smile of relief played round his lips. The smile died away as he thought of the shock it would occasion to Margaret when he gave her the slip, and he was chastened by the knowledge of the interpretation which she would have to put upon his action.

Some way from Carlisle, Margaret stopped the car and they had a consultation. They decided that it might be unwise to go to Newcastle that night and risk the possibility of detection in such a large town. It would be better to stop the night on the road and arrive at Newcastle in such time that it would be possible for Paul to go straight aboard the ship.

Paul made no objection. He welcomed the proposal, for it would enable him to escape more easily. They stopped at the next hotel, which lay in a little hamlet where the road dipped to a valley through which ran a stream and a railway. The stream they discovered as they entered the hamlet over a small bridge. The railway remained an unknown factor until they had retired to their rooms and then a succession of trains passed, whistling, every ten minutes, or so it seemed to Paul as he lay trying to formulate some scheme for evading Margaret before they reached Newcastle.

And in her bed Margaret lay wondering, too; wondering just how far this young man who was posing as Peter Angel would go with his subterfuge, and trying to rationalise the curiosity which was gradually beginning to get the better of her. She decided that unless events made his identity clear to her very shortly, before she let him go aboard the boat at Newcastle, she would confront him with an accusation and demand an explanation.

The trains whistled by the hotel, shaking the building to its foundations and causing Paul to curse. As he dropped off to sleep it was almost midnight and in Carlisle three men were just entering another hotel.

After a long debate the three, Mr. Partingale, Mr. Wimpole and Michael, had come to a common agreement, and as Mr. Partingale knew that Peter Angel and Margaret would be making for Newcastle they had decided to follow them. Their debate had lasted so long, due to the interjection of anecdotes from Michael and Mr. Wimpole, who had fast recovered his composure, that they had agreed to spend the night at Carlisle and go on to Newcastle in the early morning, when they hoped to catch the two at the boat, details of whose sailing Mr. Sinclair had given Mr. Partingale.

Mr. Wimpole slept that night in luxury such as he had never known, for Mr. Partingale insisted upon leading the expedition and financing it, and he never used any but the most expensive hotels, for he was a man who treated his body and appetite with the utmost consideration.

So they slept, the pursuers at Carlisle, contented after a late but sumptuous supper, and the pursued, tormented by the howling of goods trains and the hardness of bad beds, and while they slept, unknown to them all, the police net was slowly closing round Peter Angel.

XXII
Fly away Margaret

The next morning there came an opportunity for Paul to escape. They had breakfasted and the car was waiting outside the hotel for them to move off, when Margaret discovered that she had left her handbag in the bedroom.

Paul smiled as she excused herself and re-entered the hotel to fetch it. He could have wished that she might have given him an opportunity to explain his behaviour, for he did not want her to have too bad an impression of him. But there was no way of telling her. Here was an opportunity for him to escape and he had to take it. He might not get another. He knew she had enough money to see her safely home. For a moment he thought of leaving her a note, then he decided against this. He would have to leave his excuses until a more propitious time.

He got into the car and, while Margaret was still climbing the stairs, he had driven away and was mounting the low hill which wound up the opposite side of the valley. It was early morning with a fresh wind coming across from the sea to the west and the air was warm with the promise of a fine day.

When Margaret reappeared with her handbag outside the hotel she was greeted laconically by the landlord, who was seated on a bench in his shirt sleeves filling a pipe.

"He's gone, miss."

"Gone?" Margaret stared at him, and then was conscious that her car had disappeared.

"Yes, he's gone. Must be a joke."

Margaret was dismayed for the moment. He had gone, given her the slip when an explanation of the mystery surrounding him seemed so imminent. She was vexed, and controlled with difficulty an inclination to burst into angry tears. The landlord saved her.

"What are you going to do, miss?"

"Do!" Margaret stamped her foot impatiently. "I'm going to follow him. Which way did he go?"

"Up the hill—it's a joke, I suppose?" he asked anxiously.

"Yes, it's a joke," Margaret assured him, but her mouth was set in a tight line which was no indication of humour and her cheeks were coloured with annoyance. She looked around her and found, perhaps not the ideal means of pursuit, but at least a swift method. Leaning against the side of the hotel was an old motor-cycle. Although the owner of the cycle, a farm-hand who was at the back of the hotel delivering a message to his sister who was one of the maids, cherished the antiquated machine dearly, it had long outlived its period and should have been finishing the last of its days in the South Kensington Museum.

"Whose is that machine?" asked Margaret, going over to it.

The landlord explained.

"I'm going to borrow it for an hour or so—here, give this to the owner and make my apologies to him." She handed the landlord a note from her bag.

The man lost his air of mild curiosity and was alive. This was the most startling thing which had happened since a traction engine had run away down the hill and crashed through the wall of the school and interrupted a geography lesson. He felt that it would be sacrilegious to put any hindrance in the way of this new event.

"I don't suppose he'll mind. But it's difficult to start."

Margaret inspected the machine. To her mechanical mind it seemed as though it had been designed with the sole view of baffling any attempt to start it.

"What do you do?" she asked impatiently.

"You pushes it until it goes, miss."

"Well then, come and push me!" commanded Margaret imperiously. She was in no mood for courtesies. She straddled across the saddle, tucked her handbag inside her belt, then pressed her hat unbecomingly down upon her head and gripped the handlebars. The landlord took hold of the carrier and began to push. The machine wobbled and then started down the slight slope with the landlord panting behind.

"All right," shouted Margaret when she felt the machine had sufficient momentum. She let the clutch in sharply. The motor-cycle, perhaps flattered by the compliment of so charming a rider, responded nobly. The engine fired with a succession of loud bangs, the machine jerked forward, shaking itself clear of the landlord and snaked violently in a series of zigzags across the road as Margaret fumbled with controls and handlebars. Then its direction steadied and Margaret was ascending the opposite hillside with the engine firing rhythmically beneath her.

Her speed increased and she glanced behind to see the landlord interrupted in the middle of an excited salute by the farm labourer. She opened the throttle more and forgot the farm labourer as she crested the hilltop and was greeted by the sight of the road winding away before her.

Paul did not drive very quickly. He did not anticipate that Margaret would follow him owing to the difficulty of obtaining a conveyance. With the speedometer flickering about the thirty-five mark he occupied himself with the prospect of his liberty. From his map he knew that he had every hope of reaching Wisbech, which he had definitely decided to visit that day, and he determined as soon as he could to swing off to the right and make southwards.

The sun swung higher from the North Sea and flocks of cropping sheep moved up the hillsides or gathered in the shade of boulders that rose from the moor. Over the whole countryside lay the deep calm of morning peace, a moving, working calm where cattle grazed and labourers plodded in lonely dignity behind their horses. To the north, in the blue and brown haze of distance, rose the Cheviots, long green slopes cut by ridges of trees and scarred with stone walls and farm buildings.

Everywhere was a heavy contentment, in the measured tread of the horses, the steady progress of the sheep, in the quick movement of birds foraging for their nestlings, and the buzz of flies about the toadflax on the walls, a contentment which seemed deeper because it was founded upon years of hatred and warfare, upon internecine quarrels that exterminated whole families and devasted crops and herds, and bloody raids that left smoking homesteads, outraged women, slaughtered children and wasted lands. For this was the border country, a land used to warfare and enmity, a land where once all men were armed and distrusted their neighbours, and the barons of the castles and the robbers of the marches held the country in their cruel sway. It was here that the mighty Roman empire held its farthest outpost and guarded the wall built of freestone from quarries which still exist as mutilated history. Here after the defeat of

Caractacus and the death of Boadicea came the conquering legions, the bawdy soldiers and the purple-togaed commanders, the dicing captains and the rapacious camp-followers, and here they lived and died and erected their milestones and gravestones, and made libations to the gods and burnt incense to deities who were upstarts when their antiquity was compared with the original druid worship of the land.

Paul, with a complacence which was typically modern, lit a cigarette and wondered at the scarcity of petrol stations along the road. As he did so his eye caught something in the driving mirror.

Behind him a motor-cycle was travelling along the road. As he watched he saw the driver wave and the movement was familiar. He saw that it was a woman driving and then he recognised Margaret.

He lost no time in wonder or amusement at the strange sight which she presented, sitting in an uncomfortable position holding the handlebars as though she were reading. He pressed the accelerator and shot forward at an increased speed. In two minutes he had out-distanced her and his mirror showed a clear road behind him. He dared not slacken speed.

"What a woman!" he murmured. "She's like a leech!"

The road curved down from the high land which it had been following, passed through an avenue of trees and by the entrance to a park and then began to climb through a narrow, high-hedged lane to the top of a hill. Paul had a glimpse of a wide river, of a white boat and a man fishing and then he was out on to the moors again.

For some minutes he kept the car travelling at a steady sixty miles an hour and found time to congratulate himself upon his ability to speed with safety. He swerved round corners, the wheels making protesting noises on the tarred road surface. He passed other cars, going over on to the grass verge and slashing the tall nettles and wound-worts into untidy swathes with his mudguards, and the air, raped by his progress, whined and howled around the car and fretted in little draughts through the windscreen and ruffled his hair. In half an hour he would have left Margaret so far behind that she could never hope to catch him.

Margaret, as she followed, debated whether it was worth while to continue the chase. Some streak of obstinacy compelled her to carry on and her decision was a wise one, for Paul had a puncture.

In these days punctures are comparatively rare occurrences. The good state of the roads and the efficiency of tyres all militate against them. Yet there are few tyres capable of withstanding pieces of bottle glass with knife-edges. The piece of glass which Paul ran over was part of a beer bottle, carelessly thrown overboard from a charabanc by a Newcastle clerk on the day before.

It penetrated his off side back wheel. The air escaped from the gash in a loud report, the car seemed to sag and then, before Paul could control it, began to skid. The road appeared to leap in the air; the car shook itself like a wet dog and then, with decreasing speed, it slid backwards across the road, toppled into a ditch, rolled over once like a horse on grass and came to rest on its side.

Paul, more surprised than scared, pushed open the door by the driving seat and clambered out. The car lay on its side, wheels still rotating gently, with the air of a puppy waiting to be scratched. Paul did not scratch it. He cursed it with a fluency which was entirely American.

From the road behind him there came a distant *chug-chug* and he knew that it was Margaret. He did the only wise thing. He left the car where it was, since he could not move it, and jumping the low stone wall set off across the fields. He had not acted swiftly enough for he was no more than two fields from the road when Margaret came up to the car. She stopped the motor-cycle, let it fall on its side in the grass and began to inspect the car.

She saw at once from the skid marks what had happened and, as she registered the thought that her father would probably have something to say about the wrecking of his car, she saw Paul. She forgot her father in her relief at Paul's safety and then forgot her relief in the prospect of catching him. She climbed the wall and started in pursuit, determined that as soon as she caught him she would extract a very comprehensive explanation from him.

The wall of the second field marked the boundary of a lane. Paul, with one glance behind to confirm that Margaret was following, dropped into the lane and, taking cover behind a row of hawthorns, hurried away. The lane debouched into a road and the road came to a dead end at a pair of white gates. Paul could not go back, so he went through the gates into a wide open space which he saw was a flying field. Quite close to him was a hangar and there were three aeroplanes on the field, one with its propeller ticking over.

He stood hesitantly inside the gates, not sure what to do, until he heard a cry behind him and knew that Margaret had sighted him. He ran across the ground and entered the hangar through a small doorway in the rear.

Inside, the gloom and shade proved a startling contrast to the bright sunshine outside. There was a smell of oil and petrol and in the dusk he saw the dim shape of an aeroplane. He moved over to the machine and saw that it was a two-seater with the rear cockpit covered by a piece of canvas.

A sound from the front of the hangar and the scrape of the big doors as they began to swing open, startled him. Without stopping to think he unfastened the canvas cover and climbed into the rear seat of the aeroplane. As he dropped to safety two things happened, Margaret entered the hangar by the rear door and saw his head disappear and three men came in through the front of the hangar and saw Margaret.

"Hi! You!" shouted the taller of the men; he was dressed in flying kit and had a package strapped to his back. Margaret halted in her rush towards the aeroplane.

"What are you doing in here?" questioned the pilot, altering his tones as he realised that he was facing a young and not unpretty woman.

"I ... I ..." Margaret stammered and blushed for a moment. She knew where Paul was but she was not at all sure that she wanted to discover him before these men. It might be dangerous for him. "I was interested and ..." she began her lie unconvincingly.

"Well, I'm sorry, miss, but no matter how interested you are you shouldn't come in here," said the pilot. "If you want to watch I suggest you go outside and watch from the field."

"What are you going to do?" Margaret could see that the other two men were mechanics and appeared anxious to roll the aeroplane out of the hangar.

"Just going for a flight. But don't get anxious for me, miss, I shall be back soon!" The pilot laughed and gently propelled Margaret towards the door.

"You're coming back here, soon?" she asked.

He nodded. "That's right. You watch outside. It'll be interesting."

Margaret, not knowing what else to do, allowed herself to be taken outside and then the pilot left her. In front of the hangar was a group of men, corpulent, prosperous individuals armed with field-glasses. They accepted her presence with a cold tolerance which was almost disdain, and said nothing to her. Knowing that the aeroplane was going to return and that then she could get to Paul, Margaret composed herself to wait until the flight was over. From the cryptical and monosyllabic utterances of the men she could not understand why they were taking such an interest in the flight.

The aeroplane appeared from the hangar and, as the motor was started, Margaret noticed that the canvas cover was still over the back seat. Once she thought she observed it move, but she could not be sure, though she was sure that the man she wanted must be in the seat.

The pilot waved perfunctorily to the men and there was a little murmur from them in response. The machine roared along the level stretch of ground and swung into the air. For a time it travelled away from the aerodrome. Then, turning, it began to climb in spirals until it was hardly more than a speck against the blue which it hurt the eyes to follow.

The noise of the aeroplane spread about the sky until there was no other sound except its dull roar. Margaret was reminded of the monotonous rattle of a reaping machine. A movement among the watchers attracted her attention.

"He's beginning," one of them said.

"Now we shall see," added another and the field-glasses were raised.

Margaret looked up and saw that the aeroplane was diving in a long slant earthwards. As she watched, a puff of white smoke appeared below the aeroplane and began to drift across the sky.

"He's left it," said one of the men.

"It won't be long now, then," said another.

With a quick spasm of horror Margaret realised that the puff of white smoke was a parachute. She could make out a black spot beneath it which was the pilot. She understood why he had laughed so crookedly when he said he would soon be back. With a little cry, as she remembered that Peter Angel's impostor was in the plane, Margaret put her hand to her throat.

"Oh, it's going to crash!" she cried in alarm and looked wildly round.

"Of course it is!" The excitement seemed to have broken up the frigidity of the men, and one of the more corpulent turned to her. There was no doubt of the aeroplane's direction. It was diving earthwards towards a lonely expanse of moor.

"Oh, it's horrible!" Margaret felt an impulse to wave her arms and scream. "Why don't you do something?" she cried to the man, her heart bounding and her fear robbing her of action.

The man laughed. "Nothing we can do. It'll hit the ground soon and then we shall see whether it works. If those cases are still intact and the fuselage stands up to the smash as the designer reckons it will—then we shall have a winner and it'll go into production right away. Don't forget to tell your paper that. It's a good story—"

"But I'm not a reporter and there's a man—"

227

"That's all right, miss. I know you aren't a reporter. You're a representative. It's a much better word. Whew! Look at it."

And Margaret, to her own horror, found that she could do nothing else but look at the aeroplane as it rushed madly towards the earth. The whole group forgot the pilot, who was floating gently to safety, and concentrated on the aeroplane. Necks and glasses moved slowly as they followed the falling aeroplane.

Margaret shut her eyes with an effort and blamed herself for letting Paul stay in the machine. Inside her, swift emotions tumbled after one another like salmon going up a run, and from the welter of feeling she began to understand something which she had been trying to ignore for several days.

"Well, I'll be damned well damned!"

This unpardonable exclamation in the presence of a lady brought Margaret from the depth of her misery. She looked up.

"What the hell's happening up there?"

The whole bunch of men started forward, murmuring and puzzled, for up in the sky a strange thing had happened. The aeroplane which had been dipping swiftly to its experimental end had suddenly flattened out of its dive and started to climb into the air again.

Mute, astonished, uncomprehending, the watchers saw the unmanned aeroplane rise higher and higher and then dwindle away into the north-west. They watched like frightened cattle, their minds unable to fathom the phenomena. They forgot the pilot, who was cursing from the top of a thorn tree where he had landed. They forgot each other and only saw against the blue the fading spot which they had hoped to see crash.

They were interrupted in their amazement by the shouts of the pilot, who had struggled down from the tree, and was running towards them, having freed himself from his parachute.

His yells drew their attention at last and they turned round to see him gesticulating towards the aeroplane, which had been drawn up outside the hangar with its propeller ticking over ready to take the party to the scene of the wreck, if it occurred farther away than was planned.

The men followed his gestures and were rewarded with the sight of an elegant pair of legs disappearing into the cockpit. Forgetting the mystery of the vanished aeroplane they let forth a concerted bellow of indignation and dropping their glasses rushed towards the aeroplane.

They were too late. With a mighty burst of noise the propellers whirled until they were no more than a steely blue haze that beat lusty gusts of air over the ground. The aeroplane moved over the ground, rocked unsteadily for a second and took to the air with Margaret waving a derisive hand to the crowd. Her relief at the extraordinary behaviour of the first aeroplane had stimulated her into action as she guessed what Paul had done and remembered his telling her that he knew how to fly a machine.

She had to follow him and she took the only course, which was through the air.

The directors of the company halted as the plane left the ground and, with a common instinct, they turned to the pilot, determined to blame him for the chapter of accidents. He stood before them, absentmindedly picking thorns from his hands, and waited for the blow. His composure almost suggested that he was used to being blamed and accepted it as another of the risks and dangers of his profession. He even went so far as to prompt the directors.

"I guess there must have been someone in that rear seat when I took off. They've gone off with the plane, that's clear. It couldn't fly itself— could it?"

This suggestion had not occurred to the directors and they considered it for a moment.

"But what about that reporter woman in the other plane? What the devil does she think she's doing?"

The pilot shrugged his shoulders.

"You can't ever tell what a woman may be doing," he said finally. "I fly aeroplanes—I don't pretend to be able to read the minds of women reporters. The men are bad enough," he added unnecessarily.

"But who is she—what's her game?" One of the directors waved his arms excitedly. They were all at a loss as to what action to take and sublimated their lack of decision in a profusion of exclamations.

In the middle of their confusion there came a curt, authoritative voice.

"I can explain who she is and what it's all about, gentlemen."

They all turned to find that during their debate three men had entered the flying field and were standing close behind them. The wreck of a familiar car on the main Newcastle road had brought Mr. Partingale looking for Paul and Margaret.

The directors and pilot regarded the trio with faint hostility. Then the pudgy man who had spoken to Margaret addressed Mr. Partingale.

"Who are you, sir, and what does all this mean?"

Mr. Partingale smiled. "I can answer all your questions satisfactorily. I am Mr. Felix Partingale of the Partingale Motors, with which you are probably familiar. I thought so." He nodded encouragingly as the atmosphere of hostility melted before the mention of his name; "And the lady in the plane is the daughter of a great friend of mine."

"But what about the other machine. Is she anything to do with whoever's run off with that?"

"She most certainly is. He is her lover, but because of her father's refusal to allow them to marry he wants to forget her, but she persists in following him. I imagine that she chased him here and he took refuge, in the other machine and she decided to follow him. They are both very irresponsible, but I undertake to act as their guarantor if any of your property's damaged. Here is my card—"

"That's all very well," said the pudgy director, "but something ought to be done about this. I mean … we can't let these two people fly away with our planes as though they were free olives to be taken from a counter. What are the police doing, I should like to know, to let this kind of thing happen? I'll telephone . ."

Mr Partingale stepped forward.

"I suggest you do nothing of the sort. My guarantee does not hold if the police are told of this."

"That's right," interposed Michael. "You don't want the police hanging about; I remember once in Macedonia when the peasants were in revolt against the administration of a new marriage law—"

"I'm not interested in Macedonia or marriage!" snapped the director.

"Happy Macedonia! Happy marriage," breathed Michael to Mr. Wimpole.

"I have a suggestion," said Mr. Partingale urbanely, and he proceeded to outline his suggestion, which at first alarmed the directors as much as the abduction of their two aeroplanes.

XXIII
Come back Paul

The directors were astounded at Mr. Partingale's suggestion. "But ... we can't do that. It's ... it's . . ." the fat director tried to express in words the horror and consternation which he and his fellows felt.

Michael came forward." Why not? It's the only sensible thing—"

"And Mr. Partingale will stand all the expense," Mr. Wimpole reminded them.

"You must do it!" insisted Mr. Partingale. "I've made a promise to this girl's father. He's an influential business man and if anything happens to her he'll not be satisfied with the lame excuse that you didn't feel you were doing the right thing."

"Well, if it is so important ..." the director began to weaken, though his whole sense of the orthodox had been shaken.

"Good, then let's hurry or they will have got too much of a start."

Five minutes later the directors were watching another of their machines bump across the flying ground and take into the air in pursuit of Margaret and Paul. In the machine were Mr. Partingale, Michael, Mr. Wimpole and the pilot. As the directors watched it disappear into the haze their only consolation for this unholy plethora of pursuers and aeroplanes, this unbelievable fact that so many people should want to chase after one another in aeroplanes, was the knowledge that Mr. Partingale had more money than their combined wealth and was easily able to foot any bill; and this fact, after all, was powerful enough to persuade anyone to the acceptance of the irrational.

Mr. Partingale, as they flew, did not miss the opportunity of drawing attention to this demonstration of the power of money. Both Michael and Mr. Wimpole accepted it without comment, and Mr. Wimpole tried to turn the conversation by making deductions about the pilot's character and past life, though all he could see of him was the back of his neck and the ragged edge of his hair, which needed cutting.

Meanwhile Paul, in the foremost aeroplane, was recovering from the shock of his experience. How he had managed to retain sufficient self-control when he became aware that the pilot was no longer in the machine and that he was dipping earthwards at a speed which he estimated at anything between one and two hundred miles an hour, he never knew. At such moments the individual becomes a cipher moving to the dictates of a higher and nobler, more resolute and prepared consciousness. The scramble from one seat to another and the moment of faltering, bowel-quaking alarm as he surveyed the strange controls ... they had all flashed by him and he was left master of an aeroplane with the whole periphery of the sky to explore and, at least so he thought, freedom from Margaret. The peculiarity of his position meant less to him than the escape he had effected. Up here he was at least free from the fear of capture; it was only when he landed that the chase would commence and he dared not think of that moment.

Why Paul headed the machine towards the north-west is not difficult to explain. When he took control it was dipping to the earth in that direction and, after he had corrected the dive, he allowed it to continue in that direction because he was not at all sure of his ability to pilot it in any other. Later, when he was more at home with the controls, he had become so accustomed to the direction that it did not occur to him to change it.

For the rest of his journey Paul was never at any time aware that he was being followed. He never once looked behind him, but kept his eyes to the front and watched the changing masses of clouds and the slow formation of the land beneath him.

The wind rocked the machine gently and drove scuds of vapour across the sky in long, ragged streamers until the heavens looked like a flooded meadow with tufts of shadowed cloud marooned in pools and moving spates of light. In the flood drifted broken hencoops, upturned barges, derelict trees, distended cattle and gnomes whose cloudy beards wagged and eddied in the current which was for ever changing its direction. Paul watched the detritus of the sky changing shape with an unapparent swiftness, and when he tired of the clouds he turned his attention to the land below, a country of rounded hills, wide valleys, shallow streams and lonely clumps of trees sentinelling the heights. Although he did not know it, he was over Scotland and soon he passed over a flat, sandy coast, spotted with the ugly cultures of bungalows and holiday camps. Now he was watching coasters and tramp steamers, timber boats and cattle-carriers and once—like a reminder of the coloured charabancs which had crawled below him over the land—he caught the white splutter of foam where a paddle steamer hugged the shore as it hurried from the security of one pier to another.

He brought the head of the aeroplane round towards the north and gradually the nature of the coast and land changed. He was passing over a sea which was set with islands, some small, some inhabited, that splattered the water like a partially completed jigsaw puzzle. Paul flew lower to view the islands. They all seemed to have the same characteristics, a flat plateau of grass, a tiny rift in the plateau leading down to a beach, a ring of white foam and wheeling seabirds that rose into the air like plumes of smoke as he passed. Some of the larger islands were graced with a mountain peak, and hardy bushes and trees dwarfed before the wind and spray.

It was at the moment when Paul decided that it would be unwise for him to depart from the mainland and was about to turn towards the coast that a misfortune occurred. The petrol, with which the experimental aeroplane had not been liberally endowed, gave out. The engine gave a prolonged and unexpected titter and then was silent.

Paul realised at once what had happened. His fear passed, he cursed himself for a careless fool, consigned Margaret, the cause of his trouble, to perdition, and set about landing.

He had to choose between the sea and a small island. The green plateau of the island invited his confidence, and he brought the aeroplane towards it in a low dive. The machine behaved with politeness and a due regard for aeronautics until it was within twenty feet of the plateau, and then it stalled violently. The propeller hit the sward, broke off, and the nose of the machine ploughed a deep furrow for some yards until the tail came curling over the fuselage and the aeroplane came to an abrupt rest against an outcropping boulder.

Paul was flung fifteen feet through the air, landing in a sitting position on a furze bush. The bush, unaccustomed to such incursions upon its prickly serenity, collapsed and deposited Paul upon the ground with more speed than courtesy.

Paul sat up, looked at the bush, then at the machine which, apart from a crumpled wing, broken propeller and undercarriage, had survived remarkably well, and then at the thorns which studded his palms.

"If ever," he said aloud, "I get safely out of all these tangles I'll stick to engineering for the rest of my life and by honest, sober work expiate the folly which led me from New York to this benighted country. It's lousy, it's unhealthy, it's tiring, it's insane, it's backward and it's getting too much for me." And then with patriotic but untuneful fervour he began to whistle the Star Spangled Banner. He stopped whistling, because it reminded him of the incident in the motor-coach, and fell to the more important task of picking the thorns from his person.

For a time he gave a very realistic caricature of a monkey in the zoo. It was while he was in the midst of his simian activities that Margaret arrived.

She had had no difficulty in keeping a safe distance behind Paul. Her machine circled the island once, sent the seabirds flying in alarm again and then she swooped towards the plateau.

Her landing was considerably better than Paul's had been. She touched the turf lightly and ran easily forward, but she had not allowed for the shortness of the plateau. As she tried to swing round in a circle to avoid running over the edge of the cliff, her wheels hit another boulder and the machine tipped gravely on to one side, breaking a wing.

Unaffected by her bad luck, Margaret descended from the cockpit and walked over to Paul.

Paul stood up and stared at her.

"Dr. Livingstone, I presume?" Margaret held out her hand with mock dignity.

"What," said Paul sternly, "are you doing here?"

"Looking for great auk's eggs!" replied Margaret, and as she confronted him, Paul, even in his anger, could not help but think that he had never seen her look so lovely. Her brown hair was blown about her head in rippling waves, as though the wind were experimenting in an informal medium of art, and the green and yellow of the sward and furze bushes conspired to make an effective background for the prim smartness of her navy-blue dress with its white buttons, and cuffs which were stained in places by the grease from motor-cycle and aeroplane. She looked, Paul thought, like a girl on a Christmas calendar, good enough to be framed when the year was out.

"I'm beginning to despair of you," said Paul, forgetting her beauty.

"Really!" Her eyes widened. "That's what daddy said some years ago, but he didn't let it interfere with his affection for me."

"Affection! I've got about as much affection for you as a snake for a mongoose—"

234

"What a clever metaphor, darling. There are times when you remind me of a snake. You have a habit of sliding away—"

"I didn't know you counted rudeness among your many charms," countered Paul.

What Margaret would have answered might have indicated that she included more than rudeness amongst her charms, but at that moment the clouds, which had been marshalling while the two talked, burst into a low growl and a splatter of heavy raindrops fell upon them.

They both looked up at the sky and then around at the bare plateau. Then Paul began to run towards the easterly side of the island.

"Where are you going?" shouted Margaret.

Paul paused and smiled. "I'm going to look for great auk's eggs," he cried, and started running again. Margaret followed him.

Neither of them noticed an aeroplane which circled high above the island, its noise swamped by the roll of thunder. The areoplane turned and flew back towards the mainland.

On the east side of the island the plateau dipped through a small gully to a pebbly beach and on the beach, above the high-water mark, Paul found what he had hoped would be there, a cave.

He paused, ignoring the rain, to gather an armful of driftwood and then, as the storm burst in a frenzy over the sea and island, blotting everything from sight but a few yards of churning sea and wet rocks, the two sat down, panting, on the dry sand of the cave.

"We were just in time," said Margaret.

Paul did not reply. He glanced at her wet shoulders and then began to build a fire. Within five minutes the flames from the salt wood were throwing warm shadows about the cave and little blue jets hissed and spurted with a comforting noise.

"You'd better take that dress off and dry it," Paul said suddenly. "I'm going back to the machines to bring anything that may be useful down here. This storm may last some time."

Without waiting for her to reply, he turned up his coat collar and went out into the fury of wind and rain. Margaret watched him go, wrinkled her brows for a moment, and then slipped off her dress.

Outside the thunderstorm had settled down into a long driving flurry of wind and rain. The waves rolled up the beach, rearing their creamy heads like angry cattle and crashed upon the loose stones with a sound like the fall of a quarry-side, and the rain whipped the hollows of the rollers into a squirming, furious rage. Paul struggled up the gully, the wind beating at his body and the rain stinging his exposed flesh. He could feel the salt on his lips where the rising storm flung the spray clean over the island. On the plateau the aeroplanes and furze bushes flapped in the wind, the strumming of struts and creak of branches lost in the major fury of the storm.

Everything he could find which might be useful Paul gathered into a bundle, wrapped it round with a waterproof sheet and was about to hoist the bundle upon his back when he noticed the rabbit. It was dead and the manner of its death very obvious. It had been lying out in a tuft of grass when the areoplane landed and, paralysed with fright, had remained crouched in the grass until a flying propeller blade had neatly decapitated it.

Paul picked it up by the hindlegs and then, holding the bundle on his back with one hand, began his journey to the cave. He was blown over three times, tripped over twice and once hit in the face by the rabbit when he fell and had to throw up his hand for support.

When he reached the mouth of the cave, Margaret gave one look at him, uttered a tiny scream and rushed towards him. "Oh, darling, you're hurt. You're covered in blood. What have you done?"

Paul pushed her away with a magisterial gesture, though he could not repress a feeling of pleasure at her concern. "Don't be hysterical. It's only rabbit blood." He held up the bedraggled corpse.

"Oh! . . ." Margaret retired to the other side of the fire and watched Paul as he unpacked the bundle.

"You'd better put this round your shoulders," he said and passed her a rug. She took it without comment and watched him as he wiped the blood and mud from his face.

"And now," said Paul, when they were both seated comfortably before the fire and the rabbit was laid away on a shelf of rock for future use if necessary, "what do you mean by following me here?"

Margaret welcomed this return to hostilities. At least it gave him no excuse for silence.

"What do you mean by running away from me when I'd arranged everything so nicely for you?" she countered. "I've never heard of such ungrateful conduct."

"I didn't want to be arranged for!"

"Nonsense—how did you think you could get out of the country by yourself? What is the matter with you, Peter? Are you out of your senses?"

Paul hesitated a moment and then looked at Margaret across the fire. The driftwood sparkled and crackled and the storm fretted across the mouth of the cave, as though it were anxious to get at them, and the sea roared up the beach, reaching towards them.

It was time, Paul decided, that this young woman learned the truth. He had no desire to disillusion her and destroy her idea that he was her fiancé, but it had to be done. There was no alternative for him now.

"My name is not Peter Angel," he said quietly. Margaret concealed her pleasure at this announcement, and feigned surprise.

"What are you talking about?"

"I'm telling you that I'm not Peter Angel. My name is Paul Morison."

Margaret tossed a piece of dried bladder-wrack upon the flames and as it flared up said: "Just exactly what do you mean?"

"That I'm not Peter Angel, that I'm not your fiancé, and that I'm not entitled to the attentions which you have been forcing upon me for so many days ..." Paul was a little disconcerted by her calmness. He had expected her to be indignant at the deception which had been played.

"Then who are you and how do you explain the fact that the police and many other people in England have been chasing you for Peter Angel?"

"The reasons are not so obscure as you might imagine. If you promise to listen quietly I'll tell you the story—"

"It sounds like the beginning of a fairy tale, darling—I mean, Mr. Morison."

Paul ignored this and began his story, feeling something of the emotion which might have been part of Scheherazade's feelings as she entertained Sultan Shariyah.

He explained the incidents and reasons which had lead up to his impersonation of Peter Angel. He made no excuses for himself but gave Margaret the facts as they were, for he felt that he had no right to justify himself in her eyes. Margaret listened attentively and she knew that Paul was telling the truth. She obtained a very definite satisfaction from the story, which she had been longing to hear ever since she had caught Paul after the chase across the fields at Leicester. She was torn between admiration for this young American and wonder at the consummate cleverness of Peter Angel, and as Paul talked she knew, with a clarity which surprised her by its belatedness, that she had never loved the crooner. Her affection had been roused and ensnared by the hard brilliance and overwhelming charm of his manner. Then her admiration for Paul changed as she detected the quixotic streak of sentimentality and chivalry in him which kept him from making a clean breast of everything to her and the police for so long. Was it possible that he really could experience this absurd emotion for a little town like Wisbech, and preserve a loyalty towards an agreement which had nullified itself by the defeasance of the principal party? The essence of the part he had played was so comic that Margaret found herself smiling. When Paul saw her smile he took it for doubt of his story and was more earnest in his affirmations. Margaret was inclined to laughter.

Paul finished speaking and looked at her expectantly. Margaret controlled herself.

"So that's why you've been playing the part of Peter Angel?"

"Yes, that's the reason, and now you can see how difficult it has been for me with you hanging around. I couldn't explain to you your mistake. I had to let you go on believing that I was Peter Angel"

"But I knew you weren't Peter Angel!"

Paul looked up sharply.

"You what?"

"I knew you weren't Peter Angel. You didn't play your part very well, and the moment I caught you on that bridge near Leicester I knew you weren't him. You look something like him, but not enough to deceive me, and besides you called me Margaret and he always called me Retta ..."

Margaret began to laugh as Paul stared at her, wide-eyed and astonished. He presented rather a ludicrous picture, his hair tangled with the rain and his suit crumpled and out of shape and his face streaked with blood and mud.

"You mean you knew all the time?"

Margaret nodded. "But I was anxious to get to the bottom of things. I was curious to know what it all meant—so I stuck to you and played my part."

"But you let me ..." Paul hesitated with embarrassment.

"Kiss me? Of course I did. It was fun and occasionally you did it quite well."

"Fun—" Paul snorted angrily. He was amazed at her confession. "You call it fun, but it wasn't fun for me. Do you know what I think of your conduct?"

"No?"

"I think you acted in a particularly deplorable manner. Not only were you cruel but you were deliberately protracting my discomfort. You knew that I was playing my part of a contract with your fiancé, because I did not want to hurt you—no, you couldn't know ..."

"He isn't my fiancé any longer, and don't keep using that horribly old-fashioned and slightly indecent word fiancé and don't act like a sixth-form schoolboy. You know perfectly well that I did exactly what any other girl would have done, and you know that you wouldn't have wanted me to do anything different. If I'd told the police where would you have been now?"

"At least I shouldn't be on this unpleasant island talking to you and trying to forget that I've landed myself in the most awkward mess that anyone could imagine. And ..." Paul was warming to the subject, "don't imagine that I cherish any grateful emotions towards you, because I don't. You may have imagined that you were helping me, but you weren't. All you've been doing is enjoying yourself at my expense. If you were a man I should know exactly how to treat you—"

Paul got up and stalked angrily about the cave. He was too excited to keep still. Margaret made no answer. Instead she leaned back against the rocky side of the cave and, stretching her feet to the blaze, began to chuckle in a way which infuriated Paul until he was almost ready to forget his chivalrous feelings about women and throw her out into the rain.

"I'm glad it amuses you," he snapped bitterly. "I'm beginning to find it amusing myself. I'm wanted by the police, I've smashed up somebody's aeroplane, I've probably lost my job in America if this gets into the news, and by the look of this storm we're here for the night—"

"Darling," said Margaret soothingly, "don't be so pessimistic—"

"Don't call me darling!" cried Paul. "I'm not Peter Angel—I'm an engineer, not an effeminate crooner who can twist any moony-eyed girl round his finger by the sound of his voice"

"I think you're mixing your metaphors," said Margaret sweetly.

"Nuts!" said Paul, lapsing into a language which American films have sponsored.

"I make allowances for your obvious American breeding," Margaret replied with simple dignity.

"And it's impossible to make enough allowances to cover your obvious lack of decency!" retorted Paul, and after that they maintained a strained silence for the rest of the evening.

The storm continued and night came mixed up with the howling of wind and the thunder of the waves, so that neither of them noticed its advent until the fire began to sink low and burned like a red eye in the blackness of the cave.

Paul roused himself and went out into the windy turmoil of the beach to collect wood. He came back wet and bad-tempered, and the consequent smoke from the damp wood on the fire finally drove them to bed.

There were three rugs which Paul had taken from the wrecked aeroplanes. He gave Margaret two and rolled himself up in the other by the fire.

"Thank you, Paul," Margaret said, as she began to roll herself in the blankets. "I'm not really angry with you, of course."

"Your feelings are a matter of complete indifference to me," Paul replied, and then, because he was tired, he went to sleep and dreamt of Wisbech and Margaret. Margaret, on the other side of the fire, tried to find rest in blankets which persisted in slipping and exposing her to the cold. She slept fitfully the whole night and the next morning was as tired as though she had never slept at all. Paul's heavy, contented breathing during the night had awakened a sense of resentment in her which the morning did not alleviate.

XXIV
Island scene

The morning was an appropriate offspring of the stormy night. The rain had abated, save for occasional showers of ice-cold drops that scudded across the sea, enveloped the island and then were gone, racing toward the distant mainland. The sea itself was still in a fine rage and the wind stayed in the north and kept the rollers swinging against the island and surging up the beach with a fury which plainly indicated that, even if anyone had observed the landing of the two on the island, no boat could hope to make the beach with safety.

Paul slipped out of the cave while Margaret was dozing and went up on to the plateau to fetch wood. He forgot his errand in the magnificence of the sight which the storm made as it swept across the sea.

He stood, the wind flattening his clothes against his body, and watched the grey and purple formations of clouds tower into gigantic fortresses, throwing out bastions and ramparts against the wind and being devasted and flung up into fresh shapes as the gale tore across the sky. The waves tossed with green and white crests over which seagulls hovered. From the shore beneath him came the ceaseless groan and grind of rocks as the water spouted through channels, choked itself in narrow gullies and was flung skywards by the impact of each roller against the grey boulders at the foot of the cliff. Ten yards from the shore was a heaving ring of scum, corks, loose seaweed and pieces of wood. This ring, formed by the backlash of the waves, extended the whole way round the island in a dirty, ragged halo.

Paul tried to see the mainland, but the clouds and sea-spray confined his vision until the island stood alone in waste of turbulent, frothing water.

He collected some wood and went back to the cave. Margaret was awake and watched him as he built the fire up into a blaze.

While Paul had been collecting the wood, he had been reviewing in his mind the events of the preceding day and found that he was, though he considered that he had some justification for his actions, rather ashamed of the way he had behaved. In the grey light of the morning it seemed unreal that he should have spoken to Margaret as he had done.

As he fanned the fire with a flat piece of wood he tried to express his regret.

"I'm sorry I lost my temper yesterday," he muttered. "I hope you will forgive me?"

Margaret, who was peevish from want of sleep and far from feeling forgiving, regarded this overture with suspicion.

"I have already forgotten yesterday," she told him in a tone of voice which clearly indicated that it would be some time before she forgot it, and perhaps years before she forgave. After she had spoken, she regretted her words, but she was too late, for Paul accepted her attitude in a chastened spirit. He felt that he deserved no other treatment.

When the fire was well ablaze he reached for the rabbit. "I don't know about you," he said, "but I'm hungry, and until this storm dies down we can't do anything about getting off the island. I'm going to cook this rabbit."

"At the moment it looks a particularly disgusting object," remarked Margaret. "I don't think I should care for it."

"As you please," answered Paul, "though you are welcome to some of it."

He took out his penknife and selecting a flat rock began to skin the rabbit. It had not been gutted when he brought it into the cave and as he skinned it he found it necessary to tie his handkerchief round his nose and mouth.

Margaret, who hated the sight of blood and could never understand how people could regard heart as a delicacy, shuddered as she saw Paul pulling off the skin. With its skin off the rabbit reminded her so much of the corpse of a very small baby that she could not bear to remain in the cave.

"I'll go for a walk until you've finished your butchery," she said, and left Paul still wielding a penknife.

When she returned Paul was squatted in front of the fire roasting the rabbit's legs on two long sticks and there was a savoury smell of cooking meat mingling with the acrid smoke.

When the legs were roasted Paul shifted his position from the fire and held out one of the sticks towards her.

"Have one?"

Margaret found herself accepting with an eagerness that surprised her. They ate and Paul made no attempt to regain her favour, for he felt that he deserved her censure.

Margaret enjoyed the rabbit. Until she began to eat she did not realise how hungry she was. She finished it, licked the bone and her fingers shamelessly and then, lulled by the warmth of the fire, went to sleep.

Paul watched her from the other side of the fire and when she was asleep he left the cave and walked round the island. He returned to find Margaret still asleep. Her head had slipped from the blanket she was using as a pillow and hung in an uncomfortable position. Very gently Paul moved her head back on to the pillow and arranged it so that she could not slip. His movements were not gentle enough to prevent her from waking. She opened her eyes and stared at him questioningly. For a moment she wondered where she was, and in that moment she eyed Paul with an alarm and resentment which she did not feel towards him.

"I ... I'm sorry," Paul murmured apologetically, seeing her look;" but you seemed so uncomfortable."

Before she could assure him that she did not resent his ministrations he had gone, like a beaten dog, out of the cave to wander about the island again. Margaret debated whether she should follow him and then decided that she had better remain in the cave and finish her sleep. She could not help feeling gratified at his concern for her.

For the rest of the day Paul preserved an anxious silence, and his actions somehow seemed to indicate that Margaret might at any moment strike him.

He tried to tell himself that he had no reason for feeling as he did, that Margaret had deserved the treatment he had given her and that it was she and not he who should be contrite. But nothing put forward in his favour could pardon his rudeness towards her. This was not the first time, he told himself, that he had been rude to Margaret. He recalled other times and, although he had seemed then to have reasons for his actions, he felt them now to be no more than barbarous contraventions of decency and politeness. He wandered about the island in an agony of mind which the day before he would not have believed possible.

He was nearing the gully that ran down to the beach on his sixth circuit of the island when he noticed that Margaret had left the cave and was climbing up towards the plateau. He stood on the turf, braced against the wind, and watched her climb.

She was half-way up the gully and about to jump from the top of one boulder to another when Paul saw her stumble and fall. He stood shocked into immobility by the sight. Upon the wind came a faint cry.

With a start he roused himself and hurried down the gully, jumping from rock to rock and heedless of the narrow crannies and slippery turf. Margaret was lying on her side between the boulders, groaning and rubbing her left ankle with one hand.

"Margaret! Margaret!" Paul exclaimed excitedly. "What have you done?"

Margaret twisted round and smiled with a face that was contorted with pain. "It's my ankle—I've hurt it. What an awful nuisance! I'm sorry to give you all this trouble but do you think you could help me back to the cave?"

"Of course I can. This is all my fault. If it hadn't been for me you wouldn't have come to this island ..."

Margaret smiled at him gratefully and said, "Shall we postpone the debate until we get back to the cave?"

With Paul's help she managed to stand upright. When she tried to put her foot to the ground Paul saw her face wince with sudden pain and, without the slightest warning, she fell back into his arms in a dead faint. Margaret made no claim to be an actress; but her simulation of pain and her fainting deceived Paul completely. As she fell backwards Margaret prayed that he might act in the true conventional manner and catch her, otherwise she was going to be bruised. Paul caught her very neatly. He held her, bewildered, for a second, as though she had been a wailing infant suddenly popped in to his arms by a stranger on a railway station. Then he picked her up firmly and began to work his way down the gully.

At first he was so concerned with picking his way carefully and safely over the wet rocks and turf that he had no thought to spare for the bundle in his arms, but when he reached more level ground he found himself glowing with reasonable masculine pride, and his feelings towards the girl in his arms were full of mingled compassion and tenderness. Then as the wind raged up the beach and flung salt-spray over them he tightened his arms about her protectively. The sensation was more than pleasurable and he wished that the cave was farther away so that he might go on carrying her.

He came to the cave and taking her inside laid her down on the blankets. Margaret lay perfectly still and Paul noticed that even in a faint she retained a delightful colour. He pushed the hair from her eyes and arranged the blankets about her, and as he did so his face came very close to her. A stray tendril of her hair tickled his eyelashes and he caught the odour of her perfume and could see the fine down that mantled her upper lip and cheeks.

Paul was human and could not resist the temptation. Most men placed in a similar position would have done the same as he and with less inner debate. He lowered his head and kissed Margaret lightly.

Paul was trapped like Laocoon. Margaret came from her faint with a rapidity that was astounding. Two strong arms whipped from the blankets and caught Paul in a firm embrace round the neck and he felt her lips pressed against his. Margaret held him in her embrace for a moment, despite his struggles, and then released him.

Paul floundered backwards across the sand and came to rest against the far side of the cave.

Margaret sat up and a peal of laughter echoed about the cave.

"Oh, Paul—you've got the reddest face I've ever seen!"

Paul went hot and cold and fidgeted like a schoolboy. Not for a fortune would he have allowed himself to be caught in such a forward act.

"I … I . . ." he began, but Margaret cut him short. "Don't be silly, Paul. You don't have to apologise for kissing me. I should have been annoyed if you hadn't. It was the right thing to do. What do you think I fainted for? Look how quickly it revived me!"

By now Paul's countenance was assuming its rightful appearance and he had some control over himself.

"Please, I want you to understand that I'm very sorry for my actions. I must have been mad to do it—"

"But you weren't mad, and you aren't really sorry, you know. If you like, you can kiss me again," Margaret added, enjoying his embarrassment.

Paul started nervously. "Don't joke about it, please. I certainly acted like a country hick, but I ask you to forgive me."

"I thought you did it because you loved me," said Margaret ingenuously.

"Love you!" Paul ran his hands through his damp hair.

"You do, don't you?"

"I … I don't know," Paul confessed.

Margaret frowned and her grey eyes were serious as she sat up and addressed him sternly.

"What do you mean, you don't know? Do you hate me?"

"No … no … certainly not, that is …"

"Then if you don't hate me, you must either love me or be entirely indifferent towards me. If you were indifferent you wouldn't have kissed me so …" Margaret paused.

"So—what?" Paul found himself asking the question in return to Margaret's specious logic.

"So you must love me—what other explanation could there be?"

Before this challenge Paul found himself strangely confident and assured. He had half an idea that this young lady was playing with him, possible making fun of him in order to while away the time on the island. One minute she was angry with him, another feigning a faint to tempt him, and then making him admit tacitly that he loved her. He decided to carry the warfare into her camp.

"And what about you?" he asked boldly. "Do you love me?"

"Of course I do. I thought you knew that?"

"You love me?"

"My dear, silly Paul—what else? You surely don't expect me to be all modest and maidenly about it. Remember we have slept together—"

"Please, please …" Paul was horrified.

"Not in the same bed," Margaret pacified him. "There are many other things which point to the affection I owe you. Didn't you realise all the time I was following you that I must love you to take such risks? At first, I just wanted to help you. You seemed so helpless; but later when I realised that you weren't so helpless I began to love you. Isn't it peculiar? I've been making love to you all this time, instead of you making love to me … but I didn't mind. You can make up for that now."

Paul did not answer. He gave one wild look at Margaret and then left the cave hurriedly as she made a move towards him.

Margaret did not follow him and as he struggled up the gully he thought he heard her laughing.

For the rest of that day he avoided her, trying to work things out in his mind. He sat in the lee of a furze bush on the other side of the island, watching the storm and trying to solve his difficulties. But the only solution was the one he could not take, for Paul knew that everything that Margaret said was perfectly correct. In some unaccountable way he had come to love this girl—and she loved him it seemed. Yet his whole nature rebelled against the matter-of-fact declaration which had been made. It was wrong. It was somehow slightly indecent. And even if he acknowledged her love and his for her it was still wrong.

He could not possibly allow her to have anything to do with him. He was in trouble, wanted by the police, if not as Peter Angel, as a stowaway, and he had smashed up a valuable aeroplane. The chronicle of his misdeeds and misfortunes filled him with such gloom that he could find no joy in the knowledge that Margaret loved him. She did love him. Underneath her banter and laughter he recognised, now that he could review things in peace, the essential and fundamental fact that she spoke the truth about him.

No, he decided, he could have nothing to do with her. He would have to renounce her for her own sake. He was a dangerous man for any woman to love at this time. Later, perhaps ... He shook his head sadly. Later ... she would have forgotten him and be in love with someone else.

When he arrived back at the cave it was dark and several things had happened. Margaret had gone to sleep waiting for him and Paul had made his decision.

During the night the storm dropped and when Paul woke at five o'clock the sea was as still as a mirror and the water gurgled contentedly round the shore rocks as the tide ebbed.

Taking care not to wake Margaret, who was in a deep sleep, Paul made his preparations. He wrote her a note, explaining that although he did love her he could not allow her to love him as it was unwise in his present position. He apologised for his rudeness in leaving her and promised to repay her money as soon as he reached New York. Then he made his clothes up into a packet and wrapped them round with a piece of waterproofing from the aeroplane. Then, with a large pocket handkerchief wrapped about his middle and the bundle tied to his back, he stole down the beach and entered the sea.

Paul enjoyed that swim. He was happy because he felt that he was doing the right thing. The mainland was not more than three miles away and he was confident that he could reach it. When he got there he would send someone out for Margaret.

The water lapped round his shoulders and bathed his body in gentle caresses. A knot of seagulls kept pace with him, but after a time they left him and flew back towards the island. The sunlight glittered on the water and far below him he could make out the fresh green of waving weeds and the white blur of rocks and sand. He swam on and on and was surprised when he realised that he had almost forgotten about Wisbech. He began to wonder whether he would get there after all, but his mind refused to entertain that subject for long and he slipped away into thoughts of Margaret. Once he looked back towards the island, which was dipping into the sea. He could not make out anything in detail. Very soon he was occupied with a steady current which was doing its best to sweep him miles down coast.

XXV
All's well

"This reminds me of the time when I sailed with a friend from Vancouver to Wellington in a converted Nantucket whaleboat," said Michael. "The sea was as calm as this all the way. It's rightly named the Pacific."

"I wonder if I shall be seasick?" Mr. Wimpole addressed the company aloud.

"You will if you keep thinking about it," answered Mr. Partingale. "Seasickness is more a mental than physical complaint—"

"Every illness begins in the mind," said Michael. "I once knew a man who cured himself of impetigo by—"

"I don't know how you people can talk so lightheartedly at such a time," said a tall, worried-looking man who was sitting in the bows of the motorboat which Michael was piloting.

Mr. Partingale turned to Margaret's father.

"There's nothing to worry about, Sinclair. I've told you that we saw them both on the island walking about, and if it had not been for the storm we should have been out there before now. Their only trouble may be food, and they can't have starved in so short a time—"

"I hope not," said Mr. Sinclair. "It's a confounded nuisance all this business. You know, Partingale—" His eyeglass fell into his lap as he looked up. "I'm terribly grateful to you for the trouble you've taken."

"Don't mention it. I've enjoyed it, and I'm sure the others have."

"It has had its moments of compensation," admitted Michael, one hand on the wheel. "Yes, distinctly had its moments. Indeed it compares favourably with the time when I was left stranded—"

"There seems to be something coming towards us!" Mr. Wimpole interrupted excitedly. "What is it?" The four men looked in the direction which Mr. Wimpole indicated.

"Dolphin," said Michael authoritatively, and sat down. "They get a good few off this coast."

"It can't be a dolphin," denied Mr. Wimpole. "It's got arms."

"It's a mermaid, then," said Michael. "Probably escaped from Blackpool Zoo!" He began to steer the motorboat towards the object.

"It's a man," Mr. Sinclair declared. "A man with a bundle on his back."

"Then it's probably Father Neptune coming to pay a social call," suggested Mr. Partingale.

The motorboat curved to the left and gradually came up with the swimmer. Three minutes later Paul was sitting in the boat.

"What are you doing?" Mr. Partingale asked.

"I was swimming," answered Paul.

"But where?"

"To the mainland. What are you doing here, and these other gentlemen?" He nodded to Mr. Wimpole and Michael as he recognised them.

"We were coming out to look for you," Michael explained.

"To look for me—I don't understand?"

"I don't expect you do," began Mr. Wimpole. "It's a long story."

"Young man—is my daughter all right?" Mr. Sinclair regarded Paul anxiously through his eye-glass.

Paul nodded. "Yes, she's all right. But would someone mind explaining things to me. Why are you all together? Where are the police?"

"Police?" The exclamation came from Mr. Sinclair.

"Yes, if you knew I was on the island, surely you told the police?"

"What for?"

"Well, I'm Peter Angel, aren't I?"

Mr. Partingale laughed and shook his head. "I think I'd better begin from the beginning and put you right." He told Paul how the four of them came to be in the boat, how they had followed and had to wait for the storm, and as he finished he pulled a paper from his pocket. "And as for Peter Angel, he was caught by the police yesterday in London. I fancy they forgot all about you after that fight in the village hall in which our friend here played a prominent part. Mr. Jones, although he was hit on the nose, was smart enough to recognise that you weren't the real Peter Angel, but they let the newspapers think that you were so that they could get on the trail of the real Peter Angel without interference. By now they have forgotten about you—"

"You mean they don't want me?" Paul took the paper and glanced at the account of the capture of Peter Angel. Everything was as Mr. Partingale had said. He sighed and shook his head.

Mr. Partingale guessed his thoughts.

"And I don't think you need worry about that aeroplane. In fact you need not worry about anything. I've taken all that in hand and— regardless of your opinion that money is powerless to do anything, you remember our meeting in the coach?—I've put everything in order."

Paul did not know what to say. He dropped the paper and looked at them. Then he realised that he was still wearing only a handkerchief.

"If you're going over to the island to fetch Margaret, I'd better put my trousers on," he said, and he began to unpack his bundle.

"You know," said Michael, "this reminds me of the time I spent four days on a raft in the Indian Ocean. When the moment of rescue came I was too overcome to talk intelligently—"

"I doubt," said Mr. Wimpole softly, "whether you have ever fully recovered."

Michael swung the wheel and began to whistle, while Mr. Wimpole watched the white wake of the boat and thought of the reward which had slipped from him, and found that he was less regretful than he should have been. He had discovered other things, greater things than rewards and money.

The island grew larger until it had dwarfed their horizon. The seabirds flew up in a squawking cloud and, as the keel grounded on the pebbles and Mr. Sinclair sprang eagerly over the bows, Margaret came from the cave and ran down the beach to greet them.

With a happy light-headedness which coloured the whole world, Paul did not even wonder how a girl with a supposedly strained ankle could run. Margaret disengaged herself from her father's embrace and tidied her hair.

Mr. Partingale smiled at her paternally.

"I'll bet anything that you're at the bottom of all this," accused Margaret.

Mr. Partingale pulled his chin.

"In a way, I suppose, I am. You see, it's like this: this young man is not Peter Angel. The police have found the right one and he's now quite free—"

"You're not telling the truth, Party," she cried affectionately. "I know he's not Peter Angel, and I'm glad to hear the police have got the right one, but," she turned to Paul, "you're not free—are you, darling?"

Paul shuffled uneasily. "I ... I don't ..."

"He's bashful, aren't you?" She turned to her father.

"Mr. Sinclair," she said with mock dignity, "may I introduce you to your future son-in-law? He proposed to me last night. It was lovely—one of those old-fashioned romantic proposals—"

"Margaret!" Mr. Sinclair dropped his eye-glass so that it hit the hard pebbles and shivered into a hundred tiny pieces. Then he recovered himself. He even chided himself for displaying surprise at anything his daughter said or did. He smiled." I'm happy to hear it, my dear. I wish you both every happiness."

Paul fidgeted and tried to speak, but he could not command any words.

"Well?" Michael began to light a pipe. "What are we all waiting for?"

"I think it is usual at such moments for the engaged couple to kiss," suggested Mr. Wimpole, enjoying Paul's confusion.

It was not till Margaret had her arms about him that Paul recovered himself, and then he returned her kiss with a commendable vigour. Then he faced the group.

"That's right, sir," he addressed Mr. Sinclair, holding Margaret in one arm. "I want to marry your daughter, but on one condition?"

"What's that?" asked Margaret before her father could reply.

"That part of the honeymoon is spent at Wisbech!" As he finished speaking the newspaper, which Mr. Partingale had dropped on the beach, fluttered into the water and the saturated paper sank slowly to the bottom so that the photograph of Peter Angel on the front page was covered by a thick trail of brown seaweed.

Preview

When George, the eldest son of Matthew Silverman, announces he won't follow his father's footsteps as editor of the family-owned local newspaper, the family finds itself on a course for change. The newspaper has been going for nearly 100 years.

With younger brother Alexander and sisters Loraine and Alison growing up fast too, and gradual progress in the world around them, can Matthew do what's best for them all?

The Uncertain Future of the Silvermans, by Victor Canning

Also Available

Mr Edgar Finchley, unmarried clerk, aged 45, is told to take a holiday for the first time in his life. He decides to go to the seaside. But Fate has other plans in store...

From his abduction by a cheerful crook, to his smuggling escapade off the south coast, the timid but plucky Mr Finchley is plunged into a series of the most astonishing and extraordinary adventures.

His rural adventure takes him gradually westward through the English countryside and back, via a smuggling yacht, to London.

Mr Finchley, Book 1

OUT NOW

About the early works of
Victor Canning

Victor Canning had a runaway success with his first book, *Mr Finchley Discovers his England*, published in 1934, and lost no time in writing more. Up to the start of the Second World War he wrote seven such life-affirming novels.

Following the war, Canning went on to write over fifty more novels along with an abundance of short stories, plays and TV and radio scripts, gaining sophistication and later a darker note – but perhaps losing the exuberance that is the hallmark of his early work.

Early novels by Victor Canning –

Mr Finchley Discovers His England

Mr Finchley Goes to Paris

Mr Finchley Takes the Road

Polycarp's Progress

Fly Away Paul

Matthew Silverman

Fountain Inn

About the Author

Victor Canning was a prolific writer throughout his career, which began young: he had sold several short stories by the age of nineteen and his first novel, *Mr Finchley Discovers His England* (1934) was published when he was twenty-three. It proved to be a runaway bestseller. Canning also wrote for children: his trilogy The Runaways was adapted for US children's television. Canning's later thrillers were darker and more complex than his earlier work and received further critical acclaim.

Note from the Publisher

To receive background material and updates on
further titles by Victor Canning, sign up at
farragobooks.com/canning-signup

CPSIA information can be obtained
at www.ICGtesting.com
Printed in the USA
BVHW070308281222
655043BV00006B/404